This Sweet and Bitter Earth

Alexander Cordell

This Sweet and Bitter Earth

ST. MARTIN'S PRESS,
NEW YORK

First published in the U.S.A. by St. Martin's Press in 1978
Copyright © 1977 by Alexander Cordell
All rights reserved. For information, write:
St. Martin's Press, Inc., 175 Fifth Ave.,
New York, N.Y. 10010.
Manufactured in the United States of America

Library of Congress Cataloging in Publication Data

Cordell, Alexander.
  This sweet and bitter earth.

  I. Title.
PZ4.C794Th 1978 [PR6053.067] 823'.9'14 78-4009
ISBN 0-312-80067-3

*For Ernest Roberts of Bangor,
in the North, and Don Griffiths
of Tonypandy, in the South, and
the men who got the slate and
coal, from Bethesda to the
Rhondda.*

I am grateful to many librarians, also to the old gentlemen of Industry — sought out in homes for the aged, their little front rooms, in the street and on park benches; in their way they compare with the respected historians — people like Mr. R. Page Arnot, to whom all miners are indebted.

Without the aid of such men this book could not have been written.

One

1900

I

Six days ago, when the workhouse cart left Wrexham, there had been eight of us, but the Crowther lads had hopped off at Denbigh and the Rhubarb Twins left us in Conway. And so, when we came to Bethesda, there was only me and Ma Bron left. With my legs swinging on the footboard I was watching the stars above the Glyders when she asked:

"Where you off to, then?"

Bluenose, our workhouse driver, was hunched black against the moon, and his old mare, knowing he was drunk, clip-clopped along the summer road as if she knew the place like the back of her hoof.

"You deaf, or something?"

"I'm going to Padarn," I replied, wanting to be rid of her.

"You got people there?"

"Sort of." I shrugged her off.

"What you mean — sort of? Either you got people, mate, or not."

"Got a grandpa, if he's people."

"You'm lucky," said she. "I only got aunts."

"Do they live in Bethesda?"

"Pesda, they say."

"Same place."

She spoke again but I let her ride, for she was a fancy piece, this one, and she'd got a six inch nose on her since leaving Wrexham workhouse, and my mam always said you shouldn't let too many into your pantry, which applied to sixteen-year-old Welsh bits. It was a gorgeous April night, I remember, with the moon as big as a

9

Dutch cheese, sitting on the top of the Flights of Penrhyn, and the Ogwen River was strangling the fields with a quicksilver flood.

"You raised in these parts, Toby Davies?"

Down to Christian names now. "Sort of," I said again, pretty civil.

She fluffed up her bright hair, looking like a great fair dove on the footboard and peered at me, her eyes dark smudges in the pallor of her cheeks. "You know," said she, "you're a stitched up fella, ain't you? — down south in Porth they'd open you up with a razor."

For all her talk, I've never seen a woman at sixteen as pretty as this Taff from the south; there were some flighty bits turned up all the years I was in the workhouse, and some of them had babies, but I never did see a girl there to hold a candle to her, with her bright, laughing eyes and tumbling gold hair. She was a warm piece, even for the Rhondda, I heard the Master say; sure as fate someone will turn her into two, and some folks reckoned he did.

There was no sound but the wind and the clopping of the hooves, and Ma Bron sighed like the well of life going dry, took a deep breath and opened the buttons of her bodice; the baby in her arms hammered and sucked.

"How old are you, Toby Davies?"

"Sixteen, same as you."

"You Welsh speaking?"

"Aye."

"I'm not." She smoothed her baby's face. "I was raised down south, but we only talked English — I suppose I'm half and half." She smiled at me. "Will you be my friend when we get to Pesda?"

"Ay ay," I said, making a note to cut and run for it, for I once had an aunt in the back pews of Pesda's Jerusalem, and I know what she'd have done to people arriving with black sin babies. We looked at each other, Ma Bron and me, and then at the baby, and she said, raising her face:

"You like my little Bibbs?"

"She's all right."

"She's mine proper, ye know — she ain't just a foundling."

"Who's her father?"

We glared at each other.

"You've a dirty mind on ye, Toby Davies," said she, "just like the rest of 'em." She fondled her baby's face. "Hasn't he, Bibbs? He's a dirty old bugger, ain't he?"

The cart left Nant Ffrancon Pass behind us; the chimneys of Bethesda began to steeple the moon. The baby slept. Ma Bron and me swayed and juddered together on the footboard; she said:

"I liked your ma before she died."

I bowed my head and salt was on my lips.

"She were helpful to me when my baby came."

I did not reply.

She said, "You only stayed on, really, 'cause your mam was ill, didn't you?"

I nodded.

"Best for you to be out and about, now your mam's gone."

Aye, best, I thought, when once your mam's away in the box.

Bron sighed at the moon. "Mind, you're a big boy, ye know — soon you'll be gettin' across the women. And your grandad's going to have fits with his legs up when he sees you in the nose-bag." She stared about her at the cottages of Caerberllan. "Is this Bethesda?"

"Coming up now," I said.

"You know these parts?"

I nodded.

"You heard of Pentir, where my aunts live?"

I didn't tell her that this was my land in childhood; that this big country was my history. All my memories were of Bethesda, Deiniolen and Tregarth, when my parents brought me up from the south on visits that lasted months: now I remembered the Sunday teas, the day of rest from the quarry, with people sitting around in starched black, waiting for chapel. Welsh cakes were on my tongue; in my head was the thunder of the sea at Port Penrhyn where the great ships came in, and the sound of the quarry hooter echoing in the valleys. It was slate country, hard and daunting, yet I loved it, and the mountains rearing up about me brought again the old, unfathomable excitement.

"How d'ye say that again?" asked Ma Bron, staring back at the cottages.

"*Caer-ber-llan*," I said.

Once, when young, my mother lived in Twelve Caerberllan.

"Pity about your mam dyin' so sudden," said Ma Bron at the moon. "She were a nice little thing. Had a hard time at the end, didn't she?"

I stared at the road.

Bluenose took us up into Capel Bethesda, along the town's night-deserted road; the taverns and cottages of the quarrymen squatted like bull-frogs in the moonlight, awaiting a spring. "Where does your grandpa work, you say?"

"Black Hill Quarry," I replied.

"A labouring fella, is he?"

It stirred me. I said, "He drives the engines *Rough Pup* and *King of the Scarlets*. He takes the trains out of Gilfach and along the lake to Bethel, and the sea."

"Is he an owner?"

"*Diawch*, no!" I warmed to the subject. "But he's Number Two driver to Assheton-Smith, and . . ."

"Who the hell's Assheton-Smith?" She made large eyes above her baby's face.

"And . . . and he says that if I settle with him, he'll get me down to Port Dinorwic on the incline-loading, or even work me as a *rybelwr*."

"What's that?"

"Special trade — slate labourer — you're a girl, you wouldn't understand."

"Is there money in it?"

"Aye, woman. And if I cart the rubbish clean I can split all sizes — for money on me own!"

She didn't reply to this. I made a fist of my hand and struck my knee. "Aye, damn!" I said fiercely.

Suddenly, the dawn was uncertain in a red fleece of a day, and amid moon-darkness the sun was driving the world before him, shepherding the night clouds like sheep over the rim of the mountains. I stood up, turning on the footboard, crying: "You see that big hole?"

Standing, too, Ma Bron nodded; the caverns of the biggest man-made hole in the world had made shape. I cried, as the cart slowed, "If you buried all the people in the world in that hole, and all the people dead already, and all the people going to die, you'd never fill it, Ma Bron, you hear me?"

"They can hear you over in blutty Wrexham."

"That hole's so big it would never fill with people, missus! You could just go on piling the bodies in, an' you'd never get to the top — you realise?"

"It's an interesting thought."

"And this is the biggest slate town in the world! Welsh slate's the best, you know."

"Well, I never did," said she.

Sitting down on the footboard I screwed my fingers, hating her.

But all would happen as I had planned it, I thought. Already I could feel the bite of the rope around my thigh and the rock face danced in wetness above a hundred foot drop. In the eye of my mind I saw the stone splitting its face to a gunpowder flash, and white smoke pouring from the riven mountain. I heard the shouts of men as the drills stuck fast in the greystone vein, which my mother had said was richer than gold: I was aboard the *Cackler* and the old *George B* again, rumbling and swaying along the line to Lake Padarn, as I had done with my grandfather in childhood, up from Tonypandy on a visit. *Velinheli* and *Cloister*, Bethesda and Llanberis — these were the magic names! I would work the two and four foot gauges to the giant L.N.W.R., for my grandpa had driven them all. And I could see him now in that coming dawn, a giant in strength and purpose, his big hands on the engine brass as we clattered down to Bethel for the port-incline, and the song of it danced in my brain.

We had stopped outside the Waterloo public now: the only one watching us was an urchin with his finger up his nose.

"Where's Pentir, then?" asked Bron, easing herself down off the boards, and rubbing her rear. "*Diawch*, mun — eight hours up by there, it's a wonder I ain't split me difference."

The urchin bawled, in Welsh, "*Y ffordd orau i Bentir ydy drwy'r caeau!*" and Ma Bron said, staring at him:

"Chinese, is he?"

I answered, "He says it's over the fields to Pentir — I'll take ye, shall I?" and I picked up her bundle.

"Oh, no you don't," said she, "you put it down."

The dawn sea-wind whispered and was cold on our faces.

"Don't trust you," said she, and pulled the shawl higher about her baby's face. "Don't trust anybody, do we Bibbs? — you bugger off, Toby Davies."

The cart had gone. Uncertain, we stood looking at Bethesda, then she hoisted her bundle higher and strode off down the road to Bangor.

"Might see you some time, yeh?" I called after her.

"Not if I see you first," cried Bron.

2

THE COCKERELS WERE knocking their heads off by the time I reached Deiniolen, and there was a smell of bacon on the wind as I trudged up to Black Hill Quarry, where somebody told me Grandpa was working.

Here thick wedges of quarrymen were pouring out of the cottages, and I joined them: silently they marched in the thin sunlight like men raked from dreams and few gave me more than a glance. Behind and below us, as we marched upwards, the sun spread disclosing patterns of gold over the fields of the upland farmers.

All about me in that upward climb there grew a black desecration. The fields began to tremble to concussive shot-firing and quarry bugles sang. Rounding a bend in the road I came upon whining mill machinery, wagons and locomotives: trucks, harnessed in threes, were climbing and descending slate inclines. The men about me tramped with a quickened pace, as if the quarry working had injected them with a new fervour. Here, the mountain seemed to have exploded, and from the gaping mouths of caverns, relays of clanking wagons emerged. At the quarry gate a foreman said to me:

"You after rubbishing, son?" This in Welsh, and in Welsh I answered:

"I seek Ezra Davies, sir."

"There's half a hundred Ezra Davieses."

"Grandpa of Tabernacle Street — he's expecting a grandson," said a man in passing.

North or south, the Welsh don't miss a lot.

The foreman pointed. "Down the incline to the barracks." He asked, "You wanting work in slate?"

"Aye, sir." I stood decent for him.

"God alive, you're madder than Grandpa."

As I began the descent to the barracks I saw the Anglesey men coming out of them for the shift; these, like Grandpa, apparently, lived in the little cabins that dotted the mountainside: they greeted me as I approached them; tough men, cast in the same womb-mould, mainly clean in the mouth. One said, nodding at my bundle, "Just starting, lad?"

I looked him over for trouble but his eyes were kind.

"What's your name, boy?" he asked.

"Toby Davies."

"Where from?" His ears, I noticed, were thin and bloodless; criss-crossed with tiny, broken blood-vessels; the hallmark of the quarryman, bought with cold.

"Tonypandy — my dad was in coal."

"O, aye!" He spat slate dust. "I was Rhondda once, God knows how I landed here — a woman's eyes, perhaps." He grinned wide. "But I'm back there first opportunity, it's best down south."

I said, "D'ye know where I can find Ezra Davies's cabin?"

He smiled at the sun. I said, "The driver of *The King of the Scarlets* — Grandpa Davies."

"We got a Grandpa Ez as an orderly in *Caban* Two, but he don't drive."

Just then I saw my grandfather open the door of this cabin and come out with a broom.

So much for dreams.

Through ten years I remembered him, seeing him then — right back to when we visited him from Tonypandy, down south. He was a fine, fierce old grandpa then, northern Welsh to the marrow, but he had a thick ear on him from mountain fighting I'd have sold my soul to possess, and he'd given me a course of boxing lessons, I recall. But that was years ago. Now the Clock of Time had got its hands on Grandpa; change, constant and enduring, was upon his face as he patted his chest for dust, leaned on the broom and peered at me in the sunlight.

"Well, well," said he, "if it isn't my little Toby!"

Taking off my hat I screwed it before him, and I saw one who had earlier towered above me; in the lined parchment of his face I glimpsed the jumping footplate as we went through Bethel with slate, and I heard again the clicking of the valves and the *shee-shaa, shee-shaa* of the *Cackler*'s pistons come alive in wounds of spurting steam. Grandpa said, as if reading me:

"Don't drive no more, Toby boy — you come for engines?"

"It don't matter, *Taid*, I come to be with you."

The slate labour beat about us and there was nobody in the world for us then, save ghosts. But I still always remember that fine April morning when all Nature was painting up for a beautiful summer, and the face of my grandfather as he leaned on the broom, gasping, for slate-smoke had got him proper. Seeing him was like being with my mother again, for she was of his features.

On those visits years back we would start out together, my mam and me, for the wayside halts, to meet my grandpa bringing trains down to the port. Hand in hand with her, stretching my legs to match the stride of her laced-up boots, we went together, and her head was high, her skirt billowing, bonnet-streamers flying.

"How did she go, Toby? I never got word of it," Grandpa asked.

"The heart took her."

"Wrexham workhouse, was it?"

"Aye, I stayed on working there, to see her through."

"Dear me," he said at his fingers.

Men were coming out of the *caban* and they shouldered Grandpa aside; it filled me with a sudden anger, and I pushed one back.

"Hey — easy!" I said.

The men glared, their humour changed. Behind my grandfather's thin shoulders I saw the cabin bright and clean.

He said, wearily, "Now you come for a job?"

I took him inside and sat him on his bed. Some off-shift quarry-men called in earthy banter.

He said to me, staring up. "It's . . . it's me chest, ye see — I got dust."

I looked around the cabin that soon would be my home; for a time, anyway, I thought, until I could get money enough to take

Grandpa south and get into coal, my father's trade. Coal was all right, the Coal Owners said — being vegetation, it did no damage to the lungs; in fact, to breathe a bit of coal-dust was healthy for a man, they reckoned . . . though later I learned the truth of this. But this slate dust, the smoke of granite, had changed my grandfather into a walking wheeze; since he had been on engines when I left him, I wondered how it had happened.

"When they took me off the locos, they had me in the mill," he explained.

I sat beside him on the bed, wondering if slate-masters found it difficult to breathe.

"We got to get south, Grandpa!"

"First you get the fare," answered a man nearby, and wandered towards me; his Welsh was pure and he had a set of bull shoulders on him.

"Tom Inspector," said Grandpa. "This is Tobias, me grandson."

"You the foreman?" I asked.

The men in the cabin laughed with boisterous humour. One cried, "That's his ambition — he's a rubbisher."

"Got the wrong politics, eh, Tom?" said Grandpa.

The man said, "And religion denomination. What are you, boy?"

"Congregational."

"You'll change; the foreman's a Calvinistic Methodist, but jobs come ten a penny, if you've got a pound."

"You got to bribe 'em, see," said Grandpa.

I thought, desperately, I've got to get south, *south* . . .

The men gathered about us. One nudged me, nodding at Grandpa. "His lungs are gone; it's harsh up here for the old 'uns."

I gripped the few pence in my pocket, and looked slowly around the rough cabin walls.

These cabins — built mainly for single men working away from home — were dotted all over the quarries of Caernarfonshire; they were halls of richness when it came to oratory, with a Lloyd George under every bed, said Grandpa.

The men in this one were mainly large: enjoying a surly strength, their speech was the high sing-song of the Lleyn peninsula; their wit sparkled under the low, slate roof: politics, unionism and theology flourished; the need for a Workers' Combination against the twin masters, Lord Penrhyn and Assheton-Smith, dominated all discussion.

There was Dick Patagonia, who was always going to emigrate; Yorri Jones, who had bad feet. Sam Demolition was a shot-firer; Dico Bargoed, an old southern mountain-fighter come north to die, was the cook in this *caban*; my grandpa was its cleaner. But the man I remembered best of all arrived after the others, while I was settling me down in a bed beside Grandpa: the twenty men in the *caban* stared up in expectation as Ben O'Hara opened the door.

I think I knew, in the moment he set eyes on me, that his destiny was linked with mine.

"Somebody signed on?" He was tall, handsome, and with a brogue on him like the bogs of Connemara.

"Grandpa's kid," said Tom Inspector.

"One thing's sure, he's got Grandpa's chin." O'Hara beat his hat against his thigh for dust. "What's ye name, wee fella?"

If I was wee it was only in the shoulders, for I nearly matched his height. Getting up, I faced him, and smelled the drink from yards.

He strolled closer with arrogant grace, shouting, "What ails ye, Grandpa? Must you feed him to the dust? Isn't one enough in the family?"

"I got no option," said Grandpa, moodily, "the lad insisted."

In the middle of the room O'Hara pulled out a flask, swigging it deep. "And if he had any sense he'd up and go. Thought you was too old a cat to be messed about wi' kittens."

"Mind your business, Ben, and I'll mind mine."

"How old is he?"

"Sixteen," I said.

"And didn't we say in the Combination that we'd keep down the rate of lads? The rubbishers are starving to death under Assheton already — what's he going on?"

"Port Dinorwic, if I can get him," said Grandpa, coughing.

"You'll do him a good turn there on his bollocks."

"I aren't having him in the dust!"

"Damned old fool — can't you talk him into the farms?"

"No," I said, getting up.

It turned him, flask in hand; his great, dark eyes switched over me. "*Arrah!*" he said, softly, "the mite speaks for itself."

"And Grandpa now," I replied.

He smiled. "That's fair and decent. What's your name?"

"Tobias," and he retorted:

"I'm talking to men, lad; when I talk to boys they get the back o' me hand." He swung away from me, facing my grandfather. "They're yellin' for farm hands down in Peris, why cough him up on dust in this forsaken place?"

"He won't get dust at the port, that's the idea," said Tom Inspector.

"The foreman down there's a bastard, an' he'll work his tabs off — now come on, Granfer, come on!"

Grandpa hunched his shoulders, saying at his hands, "He's a Davies boy, and them's coal or slate; I'm not havin' him on the land." He raised his face defiantly. "You're always on the talk about Combinations, aren't you? Now you sign him on! When I come up here first I tasted the earth and the water, and it was good. I cleared the scrub up here in my time, when Penrhyn stole Llandegai; we dug and ploughed and sowed, and all we growed was loneliness."

Ben O'Hara said, with a fine Irish lilt, "Are you speakin' to me or to God, fella?"

A silence fell on the room; the men shifted with uneasy application, their hands untidy, stitching and lacing; mending boots and holes. Ben O'Hara dropped his coat behind him and stripped off his shirt: there was a rough-hewn strength about him that the ill-fitting quarryman's clothes hadn't concealed; black hair was on his chest and forearms as he wandered to the cook-stove where the old Rhondda mountain-fighter was bending, half asleep.

"What's eating, Dico, me son — lobscows?"

The old man didn't reply, but rose, wandering away from the simmering pot with the catlike grace of the athlete in age; in his burned out brain, contused with blood, were the spattered memories of three hundred fights, they said. Ben O'Hara grinned after him, then spooned the broth to his lips and whistled at the steam.

"Dico'll have you, tasting the supper," said a man.

"He couldn't hit a hole in a wet echo."

"Go easy, Big Ben," said Tom Inspector, "this was his trade."

And Grandpa roared, "Are you taking him or not, ye bloody Irish yob?"

Over his shoulder, O'Hara said, "He's on the farms, me old son; I'll not be recommending him, neither for the quarry nor the port." He flung down the spoon.

Grandpa said, holding his chest, "And this is why we drop our pennies to Parry's blutty Combination!"

O'Hara replied, "Come off it, Grandpa. If you'd had Parry's Combination thirty years back, ye wouldn't be eatin' dust today."

I cried, "You can count me out of the Combination, whatever you call it, Mr. O'Hara — I'll get a job on me own."

"It's a free country, son, you can try, but you'd be happier on the land, d'ye see?" Hands on hips, he surveyed me, grinning wide, the handsome bugger. "If ye insist, then, here's the bribe — you can pay it back at a shilling a week." He offered me a sovereign.

"I'll do it on me own," but I took it later, to please Grandpa, who said with moody discontent, "One never knows where they are with you, Ben O'Hara. I wonder how Nanwen puts up with it."

Vaguely, I wondered who Nanwen was.

3

MY GRANDPA MIGHT not have been driving the trains any more, but he had a pull with the drivers, and next morning we went down to the loco sheds for a puffer that would get me to the port. The shunt moved on a string-chain and we lay together with our boots cocked up and slid down on a slate-haul into the station of the valley.

Lying there beside my old grandpa, with the cold kiss of slate under my head, I listened to the singing of larks above the grinding wheels, and through narrowed eyes watched gulls soaring in the enamelled blue of the sky like handfuls of feathers flung to the wind.

How wonderful, I thought, is the gift of sight; God must have pondered the treasure long before breathing eyes into the heads of people. The whole world was a song of sight on that bright summer morning: the sparkle of the diamond dew of the mountain, the creeping legions of sheep; the contrasting colours of lane, field and hedgerow glowing in the sun; the waving poplars, oaks and elms. Momentarily, I closed my eyes, and in the suffused lightness of blood and sun, the blindness that came in dreams shouted from redness. But, when I opened them again, the country smiled, bringing me to peace.

All about me on that downward slide was the song of summer; framed between my hobnails were the twin lakes of Padarn and Peris; rearing up to my left was the 'Lady of Snowdon'. And in that swaying, bucking run on the wagon there was a sense of freedom greater than I had known: it spelt release from the bondage of

Wrexham workhouse, it cleansed the loss of my mother. I felt a new, wild hope for the future, and this hope grew into a stuttering excitement when the slide ended in the valley and I helped Grandpa out. Slapping ourselves for dust we went together down the platform where a little engine was puffing and farting, impatient to be off to Port Dinorwic, and Grandpa shouted up to the driver:

"You take my grandson to the Incline, Will'um?"

Beefy red was the driver. "This herring in boots? *Diawch*, man, it'll be a disaster on his crutch. Lifting and stacking, is he?"

"Ay," I said. "Are ye taking me, or not?"

"If ye shovel," said the driver, and I was up and behind him, with the fire-box open and the coal going in. He added:

"Don't make it the biggest thing in your life, lad — just steam her," and he dropped a handle and we were away, with his gold hunter watch out and two hoots on the whistle, and I never saw Grandpa go.

Out of the station we went, rattling and bonking in a hissing of steam and soot explosions, with twelve wagons behind us bucking to come off in the sun-struck, verdant country.

"You got a good old grandpa, mind," yelled the driver.

To hell with Grandpa, it was the engine I was after.

On, on, whistling and hooting, stuttering along in a clanking thunder, with Lake Padarn flashing silver at us one side and the mountains lying on their shoulders winking at the sun: sheep fled in panic, cows scampered, for here comes that little black bugger again, good God — thumping over the level crossings, with the peasants standing obediently, faces lowered to *The King of the Scarlets* all black and gold and red, and I wouldn't have changed places with the King of France. Before us stretched the rolling hills of Wales; behind us, curtseying, the parasite wagons carried the black gold of the earth, and all in a *click-clack, woosha-woosha*, thundering through Penllyn where the horse was killed, to Bethel, Pensarn, and the sea. Open with the fire-box door again and heat and flame struck out in search of me as dust whoofed up, and I slammed it shut with my foot.

Approaching Dinorwic, he slowed us and the brakes screamed in pain.

In a thunder of silence we stood while steam wisped up.
Harsh commands now at the top of the incline, the drop to the port.
"Turn-table! Where the hell are ye?"
"Come on — come on!"
Men running; shackles clanked; disengaged, the little engine swung.
Marvellous is the ingenuity of Man, using the pull of the earth to Man's advantage. Fascinated, I watched. Four wagons on the parasite slid down the incline; full to the brim with slates for the world, they crept down the rails into the maws of Port Dinorwic. The beefy driver said:
"Right you — off, me son. Off! This isn't an annual outing."
I walked down the track-incline into the port.
I'd have given my soul to have stayed on that engine.

Here, either side of the great sea-locks, was a vast storehouse of slate; enough to cover the thatched roofs of Europe. Along a network of narrow gauge railways half a dozen little engines were fussing and fuming and wagons clanking from one pile to another; down the tunnel incline, through which I had come, the wealth of Llanberis was pouring; the finished slate from the bowels of the mountain, undisturbed, until now, since the world was made; split, fashioned and squared by the craftsmen of ages.

The dock itself was a network of spars, sails and steaming funnels — the new era of steam, the great eighty and a hundred tonners: sloops and ketches, square-rigged schooners; little barges from the Thames estuary, Holland and Spain had thronged through the gates of Port Dinorwic; even bigger ships were standing off nearby Port Penrhyn, awaiting their turn for loading. Whistles were blowing, mule-whips cracking, commands bellowed by bully overseers; cranes were swinging in belching steam, ghosts of grey dust were labouring in hundreds, heaving the slate cargo aboard the decks in hundred pound stacks — the Mottles and Greens, the Wrinkles and Reds, they told me later — slates of different size and colour; the imperishable roofing that neither laminates nor cracks in Arctic snow nor Sahara sun.

I took a deep breath and strode into the yard and the first ominous thing I saw was the port foreman: very powerful on his knees, this one, according to Grandpa; doing the breast stroke along the back pews of Calfaria, with fornication punishable by stoning, and what the hell do you want?

"Come for work, Foreman," I said.

"South, are you?"

"Me mam was Bethesda."

"Ye look a string-bean to me. Where do you lodge?"

"Black Hill Quarry."

"Then why not vote for Assheton-Smith by there?"

"My grandpa's got dust," I said.

He saw the sense of it, which surprised me, for most Welsh foremen were only half human: dumpy and fat was this one, and a watch-chain across his belly like the chains round Pentonville. Through puffy cheeks he regarded me.

"Name?"

"Tobias Davies."

"Age?"

"Sixteen."

I dropped the sovereign Ben O'Hara had lent me, and he picked it up and bit it in his teeth. "Where you from, you say?"

"Wrexham workhouse."

"When did ye get in?"

"Yesterday."

"What you wanting?"

"Loading and stacking, Foreman — give us a start?"

"Shilling in the pound for me — first twelve weeks?"

I sighed. "Aye, God willing."

He watched me, his little eyes switching. "Are you a religious boy?"

I shone with anticipation. "Oh, yes!"

"Denomination?"

"Congregational."

"Bugger off," said the foreman, and gave me back my sovereign.

I mooched back over the fields to the cabin in Black Hill Quarry.

Grandpa said at the door, "Mind, they're always changing the blutty foreman at Dinorwic. A week last Sunday he was a Church of England."

"You made a right cock o' that between ye," said Ben O'Hara.

25

"Mind you," said Ben later, "I could get him over to Blaenau."

I ate that night in the *caban* at Black Hill quarry amid the banter of their horse-play, one victim after another selected for their bawdy humour. In the company of men, with Grandpa eating beside me, I spooned up the delicious lobscows, which seemed a standard fare, and packed in thick wedges of black bread behind it, gasping at the steam. Everybody talked at once, it appeared, and none took offence, despite the difficulty of language, for there were men of the southern Welsh counties there, and the Welsh was different: a man from Lancashire, thin and wiry from the pits, was arguing with another from Tyneside; Ben O'Hara feeding them to a quarrel with Gaelic interjections which nobody understood. A few were silent; tongue-tied men, cabin-riven, who had never known a home; others, like Joe Dispute, were engaged in fierce verbal combat upon the benefits and disadvantages of the new workers' Combination everybody was talking about. Dai Half-Soak was giving a sermon up in a corner in his night-shirt. Dick Patagonia was explaining the merits of mass emigration, and Sam Demolition, at the end of the table, was tying up explosive charges. Ben O'Hara ate with untidy relish, his dark eyes shining at me over the table. He said:

"Hard luck, Tobias, but your luck might change over in Llechwedd."

"Llechwedd?" I asked.

"Llechwedd is an underground slate quarry in Blaenau Ffestiniog, owned by the Greaves," explained Grandpa. He munched his white whiskers on the food; I could tell by his switching eyes that he didn't like Ben O'Hara. He added, "If the lad works away he lodges away, an' that costs money."

"Nanwen might have him," said Ben.

The men went silent at her name.

"Your missus?"

"Why not?"

"Because people will talk," said Grandpa.

"Ach, come off it, Grandpa," said Tom Inspector, "he's only a kid."

"I could ask her," said Ben.

"He'd keep his tabs that way, mind," said a man. "Those loads at Port Dinorwic are for men, not boys."

There was little sound but the whisper of the wind in the eaves and the metallic tinkle of spoons. Grandpa said, "What trade?"

Ben said, "Rubbisher, for a start — they're always shouting for *rybelwrs* over in Llechwedd — they get big waste."

"He can ruin his tabs just as easy on rubbishing," grumbled Grandpa. He patted me with benevolent understanding. "Ye got to watch ye tabs, ye see, Toby lad. It don't sound decent to talk of it, but you got to keep your tabs right in slate, or you're in trouble."

I looked at him. "Rupture, son," said Tom Inspector. "Slate's queer on the lift, for your feet are loose. If your boot slips on a hundredweight load, ye tab comes down, and you get no wages. And if the slate slides on the lift, you've got no blutty feet."

"What about your missus, then?" asked Grandpa, and Ben lit his pipe.

"He could try her. I'm not promising her — nobody promises for Nan."

"Would she take him?"

I said, "I'd rather stay here with you . . ."

"I asked if she'd take him," said Grandpa. "He's my grandson, you know."

"She'd show the cobbles to the Prince of Wales, if she didn't fancy him," said Ben. "I'll give him a letter for her — leave it at that."

Tom Inspector said, "The pay's good, son, and the Greaves are better masters than the Asshetons and Penrhyns."

"The lad's got brain, ain't he?" called another. "Finish up in the office, perhaps."

"He'll have to get on the right side of Jesus."

"You take Llechwedd, lad," said Ben O'Hara. "Here, you'll not make enough money to fill a virgin's lamp."

Grandpa said, "That's fixed, then — you go in the morning. And you treat Mrs. O'Hara with respect, remember."

"I take that for granted, or I wouldn't be sending him," said Ben O'Hara, and his searching, dark eyes were steady on my face.

4

THE HEDGEROWS WERE swiping about and the trees waving me goodbye as I took the road to Blaenau next morning. Though sad at leaving Grandpa, there was a large excitement in me at the thought of going to work in Llechwedd, which men said were the biggest slate caverns in the world! So big were they that the candles of the quarrymen were like glow-worms in the dark, and men lived and died in them without ever knowing their size.

Through Nant Peris pass I went and struck over the mountain to Roman Halt while the pale moon was thinking of breakfast. In the Land of the Eagles I walked with the summit of Snowdon piercing the clouds to the west and Moel Penamnen to the east was spearing at the sky like a hunter.

Things were happening fast, I reflected; within two days I was out of Wrexham workhouse, in and out of Port Dinorwic and on my way to Blaenau with sixpence in my pocket, a letter to Ben's wife, and a tin of Grannie Ointment in my bundle, which was a cure for chilblains, breast ulcers and sore feet.

God, I was in love with the world that morning!

The curlews were shouting to me from the marshes, the larks going demented, and the late April blossoms were streaming wind-alive around me. Striding out for the Crimea Pass now and through the Lledr Valley, I was helloing right and left to strangers in passing carts. For people were up and doing, and I gave the eye to a couple of young ones — (maidservants in Elen's Castle) putting years on themselves as they milked the doorsteps. All that day I walked, taking short cuts along the river to watch the otters at play: at dusk I slept, to awake ravenous, and bathe naked in the shallows, splashing around with the morning trout, and picking my shirt free of quarrymen's fleas. With the old sun soaring overhead, I reached the top of the mountain and stood there, gasping, looking down on Blaenau Ffestiniog.

It was Bethesda all over again; a slate town sprawling and slicing itself to death: mountain after mountain of slate slag gleamed dawn wetness in the morning sunlight; the ravaged land festooned with tramways and ropeways.

I took a deep breath and went down into the valley, shouting in Welsh to a passing man, "You know Lord Street, Bodafon, mate?"

"Near Uncorn — look for Tabernacle." He limped past me, gasping, broken by slate.

Coming to One Bodafon, which was Ben O'Hara's house, I opened the little gate and clanked up the path.

Awkward I feel when meeting strangers: stand on the slate step, sideways in your jacket and with your trews on backwards; knock like a mouse: half the curtains in the street go back and women rush out with arms full of washing.

The door comes open; Nan O'Hara stands there, smiling.

How am I supposed to tell of her, with only words to use?

The sack apron she wore enhanced her beauty; there played on her mouth the smile a woman uses to a boy, but if she made seventeen I doubt it, a year older than me. And Ben O'Hara nigh twice her age was the truth of it.

My fingers shook as I gave her his letter; tearing the envelope, she read swiftly, and her eyes danced at me: black was her hair, I remember; her lips were red.

"Well now," she cried, "come in, Tobias Davies!"

I tiptoed in my bulls-blooded boots over the slate flags and there was daylight under me and the hall floor: now a shining, black grate and a red-toothed fire. On the doorstep she'd been my height; in the kitchen I leaned above her.

"You're a valley Welsh, Ben says — that right?" She was cracking herself to put me at my ease.

"Aye, missus," I replied, rolling my cap. "Rhondda, really."

Her voice had the sing of the north in it. "But you speak Welsh?"

"A bit — me mam was Gerlan, so she said."

"Bethesda way? I might have known her."

"Not now. She's dead."

A silence stole between us and she fussed up and patted herself to see if she was still there, saying, "Ah, well — you think you'll be staying here for a bit — working Llechwedd, like Ben says?"

"If it's all right with you," I said, falsetto, which was happening from time to time; one moment soprano, next a double bass; she didn't appear to notice.

"I got good neighbours, remember," said she, severe. "Decent chapel people — no drinkers. We don't like drinkers."

"Nor me," I said, dying for a pint, for it was thirsty work coming over Roman Halt.

"You don't drink, Tobias?"

"*Dammo di*, no, the filthy stuff."

Nanwen put the kettle on the hob, smiling at its tears, looking demure and beautiful perched on a chair, and I sat, too, fidgety. I raised my eyes to hers when she said, "You . . . you prefer to work for the Greaves instead of old Penrhyn over in Bethesda?"

"O, aye! The Greaves pay over the odds; Penrhyn skins it and bottles his water."

She did some coughing at this; something gone down the wrong way.

"Didn't . . . didn't your grandpa work in Bethesda once?"

"Christ, aye — years back. But then he was Assheton's driver — he got no truck with Pharo Penrhyn now."

"You're lucky to be able to choose. Ben and I are off to Bethesda soon."

"Off to Bethesda?" I rose. "He's leaving Deiniolen area? He didn't say!"

"It's the Combination, you see."

"But I've only just come!"

"The moment he gets a cottage we'll go — Ben's a Parry man, the quarryman's champion, and he's in Bethesda — that's where the Combination's needed."

"Nobody mentioned it," I said, dully.

Rising, she swept the kettle off the hob and the tea died in hisses and scalds. "Ben's not a man to splash his business over Town."

Beyond her smooth profile, as she sipped her tea, I saw through the window the slate tip, dark and threatening; one day, I thought, it would do the slide and come down with its razors: it appeared obscene that she should be here, I thought, instead of walking in a sunlit field. Also, it seemed impossible that she belonged to Irish Ben O'Hara, he of the muscled, hairy body. Outside in the street a herring woman was shouting her wares, and Nanwen glanced up, sadly smiling; there was about her a submissive calm mingling with a young, capricious mischief; she said:

"Such a stare, Tobias . . . why such a stare?"

"You call me Toby, missus?"

Rising, she put her cup on the table and took mine from my hands.

"Will five shillings a week kill you? I can keep you on that."

"For sure!"

"Ben comes home some weekends, you know. Will you give me a hand to shift the boxes out of the back bedroom?"

It stilled me. I had forgotten about Ben coming home.

We stared uncertainly at each other. Then:

"A good breakfast before you go to Llechwedd, morning shift — you think Mr. Morgan will take you on?" she asked brightly.

"Mr. Morgan?"

"The overseer — he's a good man — Ben knows him; many of our friends like him are moving to Bethesda soon, so make a friend of him."

"That's the man I've got a letter for, I think," and I took it out of my pocket.

We stood looking at each other. "Two letters! Ben's done you well, Toby — a place to live, a job. . . ."

"Aye, he's all right."

Up in the back bedroom, shifting the boxes, I said, "If you call me Toby, shall I call you Nanwen, then?"

"Oh no," said she, going to the door. "You call me Mrs. O'Hara."

And down the stairs she went with her sack pinny held out before her like the Queen of Sheba. She didn't part with a lot, this one, by the look of things.

"A good dinner when you get back from shift — you making off for Mr. Morgan now?" she called up the stairs.

"Yes," I said, sober, for she was slipping away from me.

At the door later, I said, "I just call ye missus — that suit ye?"

"Of course."

And the moment I was out in the street she shut the door.

Dull as ditchwater, in love with Nan O'Hara, who didn't give a damn for me, I lounged along to Llechwedd.

5

AFTER CHECKING IN at the entrance to the galleries I walked the tram-road looking for Mr. Morgan, the overseer, and the first one I came across was Sam Jones: he was standing near the Mill with a ring of other apprentices around him and I could tell by their faces that they were looking for trouble.

"Well, well!" said Sam, expansively. "Is this one a pansy?"

"Drop your coat and you'll know," I said.

"Dear me," said he, sad. "A valley man? Shall I do him now, or after?"

They ringed me in a giggle of girls, but they had no real wickedness. Most were *rybelwrs*, the labourers of the teams; some, like Sam Jones, were apprentices working with the grizzlers, the old slate craftsmen who could split a razor. Now real men were shoving past us, crunching up the road to the caverns of darkness and Sam and his mates followed on, hawking and spitting in the swirling dust, and a few rubbishers were pushing some wagons before them.

In the candle-light where the galleries yawned either side of us, men were already forming into teams; horses were snorting in the dust-laden air: winches shrieked here, wire ropes whined in stiffening bars down the inclines; rank on rank, below and above us, were formed the slate pillars that supported the mountain. The air was freezing, a subterranean arctic; I was shivering by the time I reached the big Victoria by the passing loop.

"In there," said Sam Jones.

"Gang overseer I'm after, remember."

"And got him — Mr. Morgan — in there, I say."

"What's his religion?" I asked.

"Got none, he's a Christian."

In the cavern three candles burned in the blackness like the jaundiced eyes of disembodied ghosts, each in a radiance of swirling dust, the lung silica. One swaying candle approached me, grotesquely hewing out the face of a devil; the lowering shadows of brow and mouth I saw first, then teeth; the caverned sockets of his eyes; the devil spoke, and its voice was kind.

"New apprentice, lad?" The candle went higher.

"His name's Toby Davies, Mr. Morgan," said Sam Jones, still at my elbow.

"I got a letter," I said, fishing it out.

The foreman read it in squints, his weak eyes puckered up. "Ben O'Hara, eh? Sober for once? There's a sample of a Combination secretary!" He smiled at me. "I'll take you, but you got to work, son."

"He'll work," said Sam, "or he'll have my boot up his jack."

He didn't look much in the dark, this Sam Jones; I decided to try him in the light. "Stay here with us," said Mr. Morgan, "we're a rubbisher down on the team; we'll see how you get on. Here's your candle-tack and matches." He pointed into blackness. "Over there's a wagon — fill it, push it out through the loop, empty it and bring it back. When the whistle goes up there, Harri Ogmore's blasting, so duck — understand?"

"You duck into the blast shelters," added Sam. "You'll learn, after a couple on your nut."

"You'd best get along, Sam Jones," said Mr. Morgan.

I took my saucer with the candle on it and walked into darkness.

All the time I worked in Victoria cavern at Llechwedd, and I never saw it. Some said it were just a little hole in Blaenau; others reckoned it was like the dome of St. Paul's. For my world, from the time I entered it, was the world of the individual miner — the five foot radius of my own guttering candle, the candle of Mr. Morgan, the team foreman, Harri Ogmore's candle eighty feet up in the roof (he was our rockman) and that of the splitter, a man called Tom

34

Booker. On that first shift the rock waste boulders seemed screwed to the floor as I heaved them up; the wagon was ice-cold to my bruised fingers: I moved by commands of sound and sense and the iron wheels grating before me on the push in blackness, with the patter of little feet running before me, the rats.

"Mind our little friends," said Harri Ogmore once, come down from the roof, and he flung a piece of bread into the darkness.

"Our dear little four-footed comrades, what would we do without them?"

Nobody killed a rat in Llechwedd. With no other place to do it, except on the floor . . . somebody had to clean it up.

"No lavatories, see?" Sam Jones explained. "We tried big tins once, but people fell over 'em in the dark."

The shift hours, they told me, were six to six: after five hours of collecting slate rubbish I wondered if I'd last it.

At midday a bugle sang, and the foreman cleared us out of the cavern while Harri Ogmore, high up in the roof, having drilled a hole in the rock with his *jumper* and tamped in gunpowder wads, lit the fuse: the mountain shuddered. Crouching in the blast shelter, my world of darkness was riven by bright, orange flashes as the rocks cascaded down. Candles waved in the suffused light amid choking dust; men stumbled about, tripping over the fall: from the loop came the clip-clopping hooves of the great farm horses who toiled along the inclines, hauling wagons from the seven floors to the turn-out and the downward runs to Porthmadog, and the sea.

The splitter and I returned to the Victoria to find Harri Ogmore staring up into the darkness.

"I split her on the whole face of the bargain," said he, and he did not cough: neither he, the splitter, nor Mr. Morgan: only I was coughing, retching my heart up beside them.

"A bit or two o' silica don't hurt nobody," said Harri, his hand on my back, patting. "Cough on, me son, you'll get used to it."

"It's new lungs, you see," explained Mr. Morgan. "Wait till you start breathing on one, like me."

"Then you only cough in winter sunlight," said Harri Ogmore.

But there were consolations to exchange for dust, and one of them

35

was Nan O'Hara. After the first week working in Llechwedd I couldn't believe my luck.

The old larks were at it again when I finished that first week's work, the air out of the cavern was sweet and clean and the sun caressed my aching body as I walked sprightly down the High, knocking up my cap to people left and right, especially women between nine and ninety, for you never know what's cooking. And there, waiting for me in One Bodafon, was Nan O'Hara, polishing a plate for my dinner and a smell of lobscows halfway up Lord Street to greet me, and here I bumped into Mr. Dan Morgan, who had taken me on.

"You all right, young 'un?" In daylight he was a happy, fat little man with a cherubic, jovial face.

I assented, standing respectable.

"Are you warm for chapel come Sunday?"

"Aye, sir!"

"Denomination?" His eyes wrinkled with kindness.

"Same as you," I replied, carefully.

"Congregational, eh?"

There's a bit of luck. I'd have been a Passover Methodist to be allowed to stay on with Nan O'Hara.

Sam Jones, whom I saw a few days later in Lord Street, lived a few yards short of Bethania Chapel, but this didn't have a holy effect on him: his hobby being to get the Blaenau girls into positions where their parents couldn't assist.

A year older than me, he was a big-shouldered lad; fierce dark with hair on his chest and quick to quarrel. We walked together down High Street, Sam and me, and I sensed the strength in him.

"Where you lodging, then?" This he asked in Welsh.

"One Bodafon."

It stopped him, mouth open. "Ben O'Hara's missus?"

"Aye, what's wrong wi' that?"

"You're a lucky old bugger, mind."

He said no more then, but I knew what he was thinking, and there

36

descended upon us an awed silence broken only by our boots, then he said:

"Big Ben Irish send you?"

I nodded, eyeing him.

He joined the gangs down the line.

"She's a pretty little piece, man, but you watch old Ben; he's got her signed for, sealed, and ready to be delivered."

"What's wrong with that?"

"She's not much older'n you."

The men off shift caught us up in banter, and suddenly, above their clamorous voices there grew a wild, discordant sound, the accident bugle. I heard Dan Morgan shout:

"Right — everybody off the line — *everybody*! Accidents are coming up from Five."

A man near me yelled:

"Back, lad — back to the mill turnout. They'll be needing the likes of you."

I joined the groups of running men in the race back to the mill; as we neared it the accident bugle changed its single, clarion note to a gasping, broken calling. From below ground there came concussive blasting, the shot-firing of the new shift but I also felt on the soles of my feet the strident panic of uncontrolled explosions. Sirens began faintly to whine from the cavern entrances as the crush of workers pushed up to the turnout; here was a sea of waving candles and the breathless bawling of frightened men: above them all, ringing out, was the voice of Mr. Morgan.

"All right, all right — it's Number Five road; six accidents on the wagons, watch your feet."

I stood with the quarrymen on the edge of the line and peered into the darkness of the tunnel; the ranks of waiting rescuers were coughing in the dust-filled air after the exertion of the run: in the flickering light I saw their taut limbs; red-eyed men, their faces wavering like ghosts as the wagons began the outward clatter from Lefal tunnel. And, as the accident train crawled nearer in its metallic thunder, the candle-tacks went up one by one; men leaned over the line.

"Aye, it's Number Five, all right, like Morgan said."

"A rockman ran out of rope?"

"Don't be stupid, man, it must be an explosive pack gone up — there's six wagons comin'."

"My mate's on Two, and he just said . . ."

"Sod your mate — it's a premature — must be — a team and a half are hit."

"Is Oakeley hospital told?"

"Aye, Tom Evans went down."

"They got the beds?"

A man said, with deep authority, "Ned O'Leary's one — the Irish. He lit the fuse before the bugle and collected his mates in the fall."

"Where?"

"In Clough, they say."

"End of the line?"

"The end of the line for some, lad."

I noticed, with growing surprise, that apprentices were pushing through the crush to the entrance down at the Mill. A man called, "Hold it, lads, don't panic — wait, you!"

"Here comes the Apprentice Stakes!"

"One bang and they're off — I told you to *wait*!"

"Grab those boys," cried Mr. Morgan, and men scuffled and tried to hold them, but the boys ducked down and ran in head swerves for the light. I said to Sam beside me:

"Where're they off to?"

"You'll soon find out." He pulled himself clear of me and we stood momentarily, checked in silence; there was no sound in the tunnel now but the heavy breathing of men. Then, above the grating advance of wagon wheels, I heard a faint, unholy sighing.

"What's that?"

"That's the halt and lame," said Sam, and he was off: I watched the men about me staggering for balance as he shoved his way down the line. Mr. Morgan said, close by:

"You stay, Tobias — it's decent to stay. You may be needed."

The wagons slid into the lights of the candles. Pushed by volunteers, they stopped before us and from their boxes came the sighing of pain.

In the trolley box before me was a mess of blood; I saw a face, stark white, a smashed arm and leg where the splintered bones pushed up through soaked red rags of clothing; amazingly, the face smiled at me.

"Who is it?" asked somebody.

"Ned O'Leary."

"The other five?"

"Happy Travers, the English — his team, and Bill Williams's men. But poor old Ned's worst hit."

"What happened?" asked Mr. Morgan. Men kneeling now, their rough hands spreading into the trucks, easing limbs, finding new positions, their voices consoling. A man said:

"It were a premature; two rockmen came down, and the rest were caught in the slides."

"God Almighty. Get them over to hospital, this one's bleeding to death."

"Ned don't need the Oakeley, mister, he needs a priest."

"He's a good Catholic, mind."

"You going to shift him?"

"If I can get an apprentice."

"There's one by 'ere," said a voice beside me, pulling me forward.

"Lift him, then."

The maimed quarryman rose miraculously out of the wagon; willing hands momentarily held him above the boards.

"Right you." A man elbowed me. "Get you in."

I stared at their wet faces. Mr. Morgan said, "He got some chance if he don't get pneumonia, young 'un. Your young body will keep him warm for the run to Oakeley — just get in and lie, and we'll lower him into your arms."

I stared at Ned O'Leary's now unconscious face. Eyes wide open in his dying pallor, he stared back, snoring defiantly. A man commanded, "Go on, get goin'. We can't hold 'im up all night!"

I saw the ring of their shadowed faces, the humped cheeks, the sparkle of their eyes in the candlelight. Shivering, I slid over the rim of the wagon and laid down in the warmth of Ned O'Leary's blood. I heard a man say:

"Ye wasn't sharp enough by half, Tobias. Your mate, Sam Jones, be halfway up Bethania now."

Another said, "When the accident bugles go ye don't see apprentices for dust."

They laughed in a sort of doomed banter: somebody pulled a blanket over us both. One thing about Ned O'Leary, I thought — he had to come to Wales to die, but he did it snug. With him in my arms I lay in blackness, listening to the trickling of his blood.

Ten minutes later, in the forecourt of Oakeley Hospital, they lifted him off me.

"He's dead," said a nurse.

I could have told her that half a mile back.

Nanwen was waiting at the door as if expecting me; the accident bugle had its own particular message; I left a trail of blood over her hall; in the kitchen by the fire she had a bath filled with steaming water.

"They told you?" I asked.

"Get your clothes off."

I said, "It . . . it isn't decent, Mrs. O'Hara; nobody but you and me in by here."

"Don't be daft," said she.

So I took them off and there was a shyness in me and a great business of covering the front of me, since nobody but my mam had seen it before, but to my surprise she wasn't the least bit interested.

But I soon forgot about Ned O'Leary. I'd got my hands full with Nan O'Hara now, to say nothing of my new mate, Sam Jones. And I could think of worse people than Sam to get drunk with on a Saturday night in Blaenau, which had twenty publics for ale and more chapels for confessing sins next day. I found Sam in the spit and sawdust of the Queen's, and I was just about to kill a pint when the door opened and Bando Jeremiah Williams came in; this, apparently, was the local beer bully and pew polisher, with God sitting on his shoulder, in search of harlots; a crush on Nanwen had he, and God bless Queen Victoria. Seeing me now, his hands spread on his stomach, he said expansively:

"Damme, boys, what have we here, eh? Nan O'Hara's lodger?"

The Gospel according to St. Sam, apparently, was to hit them as they lifted their glass, but this one topped six feet.

In the slant of my ale I saw Nanwen's eyes . . .

"A good cook, is she, Toby? Down to Christian names, aren't we?" said Bando, putting his stomach against the teak bar.

"He's a man, remember!" whispered Sam, lifting his pewter.

The room went silent; men with their heads together, whispering about Nan O'Hara: Bando Jeremiah, all seventeen stones of him, weighed me for size.

"Leave it Tobe, let it slide," said Sam quiet, which was pretty good advice with Bando Jeremiah the terror of the neighbourhood. "We'll 'ave him presently, not to disappoint him," and pure and sweet he smiled his widest smile at Bando and elbowed us both to the room next door.

After our third pint, coming past the gold clock on our way out of the Queens, Sam said, "You got a shine for Nan O'Hara, have ye?"

"My business."

"Ye know," said he at the moon, "if I got a shine for a woman I'd be telling you about it, but that's the difference between us, I expect, you comin' from the south."

"North or south makes no difference."

"Like my gran used to say before she kicked it — Welsh brain, Welsh tongue, Welsh heart — north or south, all the same — we both come from caves."

I nodded, seeing him with affection in the heady swim of the hops. "Aye, that's true, boyo."

"Though up here in the north, mind, we 'ad carpets in ours."

6

Come Sunday week I was there beside Nan in Chapel, all spit and polished up, with my new hobnailed boots sparking and my Emporium collar under my chops, and I walked her into the back pews with pride; Nanwen O'Hara and her new lodger. All about us, as the harmonium got going, were thronged the quarrymen in their Sunday best with their virgin daughters and comely wives, for people fed pretty well under the Greaves, give them credit. And there was beating in my ears a glorious harmony of tenors and contraltos, basses and sopranos, the Quarryman's Hymn:

> '*O ! Arglwydd Dduw rhagluniaeth*
> *Ac iachawdwriaeth dyn,*
> *Tydi sy'n llywodraethu*
> *Y byd a'r nef dy hun ;*
> *Yn wyneb pob caledi . . . pob caledi . . .*
> *Y sydd, neu eto ddaw,*
> *Dod gadarn gymorth imi*
> *I lechu yn dy law.*'

I sang hesitantly, watching Nan's mouth for the words, for while I was rapidly getting back into the northern lilt, I was remembering it from my mother's knee. And I could not fathom that this was a part of Nan O'Hara I could not comprehend: this, a secret language locked within herself, she shared with nobody but her country. She was instantly the very breath of Wales, singing joyfully, leaving me empty and bereft of friendship, but with an undying consolation: Irish Ben O'Hara wouldn't have understood a word of it.

The great hymn, *The Eternal Refuge*, rolled on, and I felt a sudden sense of pride that though my father was of the south, I was becoming a part of these northern people, who were ancient when the world was young. And Nanwen, as if guessing the emotion within me, bent towards me, mouthing the Welsh, making me her pupil.

People around us were watching, I noticed — Bando Jeremiah Williams the rent-collector, for one. Sam Jones, captured by his mam and dad, gave me a silent groan across the aisle.

Next weekend it wasn't the same; no longer did I have her to myself.

Ben came home.

Sit chewing with your elbows on the cloth in Number One Bodafon, and watch them at it.

Eat with your eyes cast down in their presence; pretend that you are not there, for they do not really want you: nothing is real in the presence of lovers, and you are alone.

He was a handsome beggar, give him that: at Black Hill Quarry, with the immensity of everything about me, I hadn't realised the size of him. She, so small and slender beside him. . . . I feared that he might crush her if he moved. Her dark eyes moved swiftly in her flushed cheeks as she served the meal — a rabbit that had committed suicide as I walked over the mountain; even the way she cooked rabbit made me fall in love with Nanwen.

"You all right, Toby?" Her eyes flashed up, concerned; which was reasonable, the way I was behaving. Ben said, bassly:

"Nan tells me you're settling in at Llechwedd, lad."

I nodded. His arms, bare to the elbows, were crawling with black hair; his chest, with his white shirt open to the waist, was matted with it: Nanwen's arms were smooth and white. Compared with her sensitivity, he was drunk with strength. More, his age and the bottle were touching his face; the skin taut and tanned by the quarrying wind; stubbled with the beard of a man who should shave twice a day, a class of ape. He said:

43

"I met Dan Morgan coming in tonight."

"Dan Morgan?" My voice went falsetto, and he smiled tolerantly, as men do with boys.

"Your foreman. He reckons you're working good on the bargain, so he does."

The bread was dry on my throat. He spooned up the rabbit broth, "Got you on the Cathedral, he says."

"Ay ay."

"Don't you look at people when you talk to them?"

I raised my face to his. Nanwen said, instantly, "Oh, come, Ben — you hardly know each other — shy, aren't you, Toby?"

I wanted to die, I was so ashamed. I thought, let him talk, he won't get much; why the hell couldn't he have stayed in Black Hill, with Grandpa? Nanwen cried, coming from the grate, "We went to Chapel together last Sunday, didn't we, Toby?"

"So I heard." Ben broke the bread with large hands; his nails were dirty, I noticed: it was sickening to have to eat with people who didn't wash their hands before eating: vaguely, I wondered if Nanwen noticed it.

"Who preached?" he asked.

"Mr. John Trevelyn from Pentir — remember, Toby?"

Distantly, my mind asked me where Ma Bron was: I wondered if she was having as bad a time as me, with her aunts in Pentir; straight-laced and pure, most of these aunts, especially the maiden variety.

"A few caught it at Llechwedd recent, they tell me," Ben observed.

I nodded.

"And they had you for a mattress?"

"Under Ned O'Leary, but he died."

His hand scurred on his stubbled chin. "Dan Morgan said you did right by him; ach, I knew the fella — as Irish as a bog: if you had him on your belly, you did the Micks a turn."

Nanwen beamed, saying, "Mrs. O'Leary wrote you a letter, didn't she, Toby?"

I was thinking of Ned O'Leary. Up in the cemetery they kept an open grave planked and strutted, ready for the next one down, and poor old Ned filled it, for he bled to death in my arms. The Oakeley

44

hospital was a good run away from Llechwedd; this meant that injured men had to be trucked or stretchered down the roads and over rough country. Dan Morgan reckoned that you could trace the route by the bloodstains, so Ned and I must have followed the trail like bloodhounds.

"I'm glad she wrote to you," said Ben.

It was becoming a stupid conversation: steamed dry of things to say, we were sitting like upright mummies in wraps of self-consciousness, talking nonsense, while in my mind Ned O'Leary bled to death. And we ate in fits and starts in a white tablecloth silence of colly-wobbles, the nerves of unspoken questions — Ben challenging, me on the defensive. I'd have liked him stronger still: why the devil couldn't he say "I want to be alone with my wife, so lodgers must get to hell out of it"? Instead:

"Grandpa had a turn, day before yesterday."

"What happened?" asked Nanwen, concerned.

"The dust took him coughing; I thought he'd never stop." Ben drank the beer Nanwen had given him (she didn't give me any) and said:

"You know he wants to get back to Bethesda?"

"No," I replied.

"Aye, it seems he worked for Penrhyn once and left him for Assheton-Smith on an exchange."

I nodded. "To get the locos — he wanted the driving, see?"

Ben said, "Well, it appears he sub-let a cottage in Bethesda in those days — one of the Caerberllan Row — to a fella moving in, and it's still in Grandpa's name."

"Yes," I said. "Number Twelve. My mother lived there when she was a girl; years back she used to take me there for holidays."

Nanwen said eagerly, "And he wants Toby to go back there to live with him?"

"If I can fix him a job in Bethesda — Mr. Parry may manage it, he's still got a pull."

Her eyes shone and she momentarily gripped my hand. "My, that would be fine, wouldn't it, Toby?"

Yes, I thought, and you would be rid of me.

"But there's more to it than that," said Ben. "Grandpa wants us to live there with him, too."

"All four of us in Bethesda?"

"Why not? The Combination wants me over there — we'd have to find a place, anyway, and I can't see Lord Penrhyn's agent handing over cottages to Union men like me. Grandpa's different — he was once on the Penrhyn books."

"When's the tenant moving out?"

"Next week. Grandpa said he don't want it standing vacant — if it's empty, questions'll be asked." He added, "Dan Morgan is moving over, too."

I said, "To Bethesda? Why the rush?"

His eyes gleamed and he rose, thumping his fist into his palm. "Because this is where we're having the fight — God alive, this place is bad enough, but it's a bitch to nothing compared to Bethesda. Besides, once Pharo's pulled down, people like the Greaves and Asshetons will naturally fall, it's in the law of things."

Nanwen said, "You think they'll agree to a Union man in occupation?"

"I'm not in occupation, am I? — Grandpa'll pay the rent. That's the idea."

"And if Grandpa goes, what then?"

"We'll meet that when we come to it," said Ben. "Penrhyn's already agreed to the exchange."

"The exchange?"

"Of the bargain teams — a switch of men between Black Hill and Bethesda — according to the slate-masters' Union that meets in Caernarfon . . ." he narrowed his eyes at me ". . . they disperse the troublemakers by switching us around." He drained his glass and gasped. "This time they've done it in the right direction. Not so intelligent, are they?"

I gave him a grin. "And Pharo don't know what he's getting in Bethesda!"

"Ach, now you're talking!" He laughed, pointing at Nanwen. "Did ye hear that, woman? The babies are from long clothes at last. Aye, we'll give 'em lock-outs and reductions in wages!"

Something hit the door to have it off its hinges and Sam Jones

46

stood there polished and quiffed, with creases to cut his throat and a posy in his buttonhole big enough for a wake; it was Saturday; he was after lowering ale and lifting the birth-rate.

"No drinking now, remember!" said Nanwen, her finger up. She tightened my coat and smoothed my hair with her fingers.

"*Diawl!*" exclaimed Sam, "d'ye think we're heathens, Mrs. O'Hara?"

"Near enough," said Ben.

"Have a good time and keep off the women," said Nanwen.

"Don't hurry back," said Ben.

The house was silent when I got back with quarts aboard; back teeth awash, I took off my boots at the bottom of the stairs and crept within the cosy smell of the kitchen. All about me were signs of Ben O'Hara: yesterday, it was only in magic that he even existed; now he was here in the bed upstairs, his hat and coat on the kitchen door; his clay pipe, in the hearth, was still warm to my fingers. In a fug of ale I stared at the cracked face of the alarm clock ticking on the mantel.

Up the stairs in my socks now like a wraith out of the churchyard: slipping into my room, I began to undress. Naked, the blankets gave me rough kisses. With my hands behind my head I watched the moon rolling tipsy over the slate mountain; echoing footsteps died into silence outside Tabernacle where the dead were whispering with dusty lips; down in Lord Street a baby was strangling its cries.

Blaenau slept, mostly: but lovers were awake.

Ben O'Hara and Nanwen O'Hara, for a start.

I heard his bass whispers and Nan's replies. And she laughed softly once, a high breath of a laugh that ended in a sigh: after this the house talked to itself, as houses do at night; the careless bed, ever betraying, complained.

On my wedding night, I thought, I shall have mountain grass beneath me and the sky for a blanket: I shall take my woman to some quiet place and make no sounds to pester another's loneliness.

To be needed is the heart of yearning: the love sounds of two, the intimacy of the pair, brings to the hearer a most solitary sadness, yet, because I loved her, I was happy for her joy: I could even sanctify her pleasure and cherish her relief . . . but I could have killed the one who was bringing her this unity.

To insist that Ben was her husband, that my thoughts were adulterous, brought no consolation. Lying there, it seemed to me that every man in Blaenau was loving his woman; that only I was lying alone.

The bed told the rhythm of their love-making and I turned my face into the pillows and pressed my fingers into my ears, seeing in the portals of my mind the smile of Nanwen's face.

"Oh, Ben, *Ben* . . . !"

This is what makes for the hollowness.

Next morning she was up and doing, dashing about with secret smiles, fetching tea, making ready for Chapel; pink, flushed and gorgeous — never have I seen her more beautiful. And, by the innocence of her face, she hadn't been up to anything.

Her lips were red, still blooming under his mouth.

I preferred her husband; he was dazed, grumpy and normal.

From the red-barred grate, as she fried the bacon, she shot glances of affection at me over her shoulder, and her hair was black and tumbling about her face. I saw in her shining eyes her love of her man. He had again possessed her; it was the water on her throat, this certainty of his love.

"You all right, Toby?"

I stared at my plate.

"Sleep well, did you?"

I could not meet her eyes.

"Oh, come, *bach*!" she cried, dancing up to me. "There's another one outside like you — all grumps. With such bears around, how do you think I feel?"

Soft, I thought.

Leave her to her chap. Away out of this, me.

Find Sam Jones again: you want decency, you've got to seek men.

"Oh, Toby, what's *wrong*?" She begged with her hands, her face full of concern.

Away!

7

TROUBLE WAS COMING, said Sam Jones, who wasn't overloaded with intelligence; but even he could see it.

"If we move to Bethesda we'll walk right into it," said Nanwen.

"Then why go?"

She looked at me. "Because my husband says so."

Earlier, I'd caught a big spit-gob spider for her, knocked him off and ground him into a bowl of onions; the idea of this was to make a hot poultice to put on the chest of one of the Emma Hoppy sisters next door but three. The delicate one was Emma, and twice a week Nanwen rubbed her in oils. The other Hoppy was called Angharad, and I'd have rubbed her chest any time she'd liked. I never did discover why they were called the Hoppys.

"You agree with the Combination business, then?" I asked, and Nanwen said, "Will you tell me when women's advice is asked on anything?" and her eyes, like saucers, threatened to drop from her face.

"Ben's right," I said, "that Penrhyn's an old bugger."

"Do you have to swear?"

But he was, and the rest of the owners weren't much better. The Slate-Masters' Union was meeting every month to sink champagne and sing God Bless The English Prince of Wales, while their agents were busy dismissing quarrymen who even breathed about a Union: the Bethesda agents were employing tale-bearers and scabs to work among the teams, according to Ben, and they informed on the workers: son against father, brother against brother — a pound a

tale they called it in Tregarth. Get across Mr. Young, Lord
Penrhyn's agent, and he would telephone Black Hill Quarry, in case
you thought of slipping over there; back-chat Assheton's agent and
you'd have to crawl on your belly to the Oakeleys of Blaenau.

"But I give it to the Greaves, though," said Mr. Morgan, our
team foreman, "we do get a good eisteddfod."

"Another twopence on the bargain and they can keep their
eisteddfod," answered Tom Booker, lighting his candle. "Eighteen
shilling a week? Give it to me hat and coat, I told the agent — they
don't have to eat. The sod, he whistles me up, you know, like I
wasn't human."

"Go flat on your belly again when that agent whistles, mun, and
ye'll be right down the road, remember," said Mr. Morgan.

Tom said, "If he whistles me like a dog I'm behaving like a dog."
He hawked and spat. "Same as that bugger over at Oakeley — 'Ye
can afford to smoke, eh, Booker?' said he. 'Ay ay,' said I, 'at
threepence a week,' and the psalm-singing yob, d'ye know what he
said? — 'If God had intended ye to smoke, Booker, he'd 'ave put a
chimney on your head.' 'Is that right?' I asked him. 'And now I'm
pulling this blutty truck — why didn't he put a hook on me arse?' "

"God'll 'ave you one day, talking like that, Tom Booker," said
Harri Ogmore.

"Meanwhile I keep me independence," said Tom, and cupped
his hands to his mouth, shouting up to me, "What the hell you doing
up there, young Tobias?"

"Trying out the chain," I yelled down from twenty feet up the
rock.

"Then bloody come down, laddo — I'm rockman on this bargain,"
and Harri Ogmore spat on his hands for the climb.

"Are you climbing today, lad?" asked Dan Morgan, our foreman,
and I took him by the sound of his voice in the dark, for his candle
was out.

"Aye, sir."

"And you watch it, yeh? Or I'll be answering to Nan O'Hara."

This he spoke into my face, in blackness; I didn't see Mr.
Morgan's face, but he saw me. Like a cat for the dark was he, said
his missus, who was a Scot. 'An' this come from bathin' his eyes

wi' water — his piss-water, d'ye see son, an' it has to be his own, ye understand, not mine, not his feyther's. Every night that man bathes his eyes wi' his water straight from the pot.' Now the eyes of Dan Morgan, unseen in the darkness, burned into my face.

"Harri Ogmore's mad — be careful, yeh?"

"Yes, Mr. Morgan." I liked my foreman. Jesus sat on his shoulder. Standing near to him, waiting for Harri, I listened to his dust-filled lungs going like harmonium bellows.

"I'll take up," said Harri, and I heard his boots scrabbling. Mr. Morgan said:

"How do you like that for a musical chest, lad?"

"Is it bad with you, sir?"

"It anna as good as me eyes, though I'm near blind in daylight."

"Will you get a pension, Mr. Morgan?" and Tom Booker heard it.

"A pension?" cried he. Skinny as a lathe was Tom, with a face on him like Lazarus before revival. Now he cackled, "A pension? A quarter of a million that Penrhyn paid for his slate castle at Llandegai, and they think him benevolent when he lays out for pauper's coffins."

"Leave it, Tom," said Mr. Morgan. "Toby's going up," and he gazed at the darkness above us.

"He'll break his blutty neck."

"He'll have to risk it some time."

Faintly the voice of Harri, our rockman, floating down; tiny gleamed his candle-tack from the caverned sky above us, sixty feet up.

"Climb careful," said Mr. Morgan.

Our team in Victoria was much like any other.

Dan Morgan was our foreman, and he argued the 'bargain' with the agent, which was the amount of yardage we had to cover at a time: Tom Booker was the splitter — he cut the slate to handable sizes after Harri, the best rockman in Llechwedd, dropped them down from the bargain. And he had an eye like an eagle, did Harri, hanging on by his eyebrows up in the roof. In the guttering light of his candle you could see his 'jumper' tool gleaming as he bored for the explosive charges, chug-chug-chug, *bump, bump, bump,* then in with the gunpowder, and he'd take that rock down the vein as neat

51

as a curlew's whistle. Once down, Tom would get at it, driving holes for his plugs and feathers, hitting them in to the metallic ringing of his hammer; and he'd run them apart with the accuracy of a knife — just small enough for a block and tackle lift on to the wagon. Down the line to the turn-out I'd push the wagon then, with my arms as stiff as black bars; on to the turn-out for the mill, where our two dressers were waiting: known as countess and duchess, ladies and standards, all sizes would come out, cut as clean as box-wood and ready for the roofs of Europe: half the Continent would have died of pneumonia long since, said Dan Morgan, if it hadn't been for us. And the best reward in the world was in the mill shed with the engines going: the very best brand of silicosis for the very best slates: ten years in the mill shed is where Dan Morgan caught it. 'Give me Bethesda and the Great Hole any time,' he used to say. 'You dangle in fresh air, summer sun and winter cold. But rockmen don't get the dust so bad, and a hundred foot drop to the lower galleries is a decent death compared wi' the choking. For slate is razors: clean amputations, a decent way to die!'

"Remember what the old fella said," Harri had said. "Get on the face — you be a rockman."

"Ay ay!" I cried, delighted.

"Right, you, come up and show me your guts. You scared of heights?"

"Don't know."

"You climb, *bach*, you'll soon find out."

He was queer, was Harri, for he was never happier than with his feet off the ground and nothing below him, in darkness. I've seen him with the rope half-hitched around one thigh — the standard rockman hold — and the rest of him in space, eating his dinner. But Mrs. Ogmore said, "There ain't no sense to it, Toby Davies." (She was a London cockney.) "The man's just a flower. Two years now I needed my chimney pointing, and the fella's too frit to climb the roof, ain't you, Ogmore?"

"But I'll do it after dark, missus," cried Harri. "I could break me neck from ten feet up, in daylight."

"Ye daft ha'porth — how can ye point a chimney in the dark?" and she had emptied her hands at me.

52

"But that's the trick of it," explained Dan Morgan, "anything goes in the dark — no head for heights, see?"

I stared up at Harri's candle swinging like a glow-worm in the roof of the Big Victoria. "You goin', son?" asked the foreman.

"Aye," I said.

It is eerie to be rising from the ground, in darkness. It is as if the night is enveloping you in prayer-book arms: before you your candle-tack on your hat flickers blood on the rocks, the slate is cold and wet-slippery to your fingers. Up, up, hobnails scraping for a hold, don't look down for God's sake, says Mr. Morgan, lest you see a candle; fingers slither for loose places, rubble falls in little avalanches: and Harri Ogmore, swinging in space with his candle, the show-off, comes nearer, nearer: the dust is in your eyes, your mouth, your blood; sweat trickles its ice down the middle of your back.

"Come on, come on, what's bloody holdin' ye?" yells Harri in the dome of roof.

In the pity of Jesus . . .

"Don't look down, Toby!" This from Mr. Morgan, the unseen pygmy on the ground.

This, they tell, is when the man is made: he either rises or falls. All men look the same when they fall on slate: I sensed the terrifying desire to let go with my hands, to enjoy a brief sensation of hissing space, the impacting smash of flesh and bones. Already I had seen a man fall from forty feet in Lefal; I saw again the shapeless limbs grotesquely akimbo, the live, red bones thrusting up through the rags. I paused, flattened against the face, gasping.

"Come on, lad, don't make a meal of it."

Whimpering with fear, I climbed higher, hands seeking a hold.

Now, within reach of him, I tore away one hand and reached up for Harri's boot. "Oh, God, I'm going to fall!" I yelled.

"Bugger me, I wouldn't do that," said Harri, cool, and pulled his boot away. "You climb and like it, son."

The air was cleaner here, fifty feet up, for the dust had lain; and I heard an elemental song of freedom that diminished my terror. I looked down for the first time, seeing below me two pin-points of flickering redness, and these were the candles of Tom Booker and

53

Dan Morgan: above me, swinging on a chain from the domed roof of the Victoria was the spider body of Harri Ogmore, and he was rodding out a bore-hole with his auger and whistling.

"There's me lad," he cried, grinning down in the light of my candle. "Come up 'ere and be a rockman."

There was a ledge in the rock; on to this a short length of steel rail had been laid, buried under stones; around this rail Harri had linked his thigh-chain; from this he swung, making his web; I got my hand around it like a drowning man.

"Now, *come off it*!" protested Harri, "that's my blutty chain."

Through the sweat of my eyes I saw his face square and strong above me, floating disembodied against the roof of the cavern; nothing but that candle-lit face moved in my world of fear; below me was the echoing voices of the team in blackness. I gasped, "*Arglwydd!* Give us a hand mate."

"Balls to you," said he. "We got to think o' the bargain — we haven't got all day. Look," and he swung on his chain towards me. "Here's your rail and here's your rope, and don't you drop 'em or you'll crown the blutty foreman."

I flattened myself against the rock face in horror.

I don't know how I took it and I don't remember burying that rail on the ledge.

Harri said, swinging away to his borehole. "Right, you — now tie your rope to the rail and half hitch the running end around your thigh."

This I managed to do, clawing with bleeding fingers.

"Right," said he, "now swing out into space — go on, let go of that rock and swing out."

Shivering, with the rope around my thigh, I clung to the face of the drop, and he cried, "Swing out, or I'll give ye one," and he struck out at me.

Eyes clenched, I clung there as if stitched to it.

"Let go, what's stopping ye?" Grabbing me, he braced his feet against the roof and hauled me off the rock by sheer force. Drifting out we swung like twin pendulums in the darkness while velvet voices thudded in my ears: legs thrust out, Harri pushed again, and

54

we swung out again in wide arcs, clasped together in the hissing blackness. Round and round we went, dangling from the Victoria roof, as generations of rockmen had done before us.

"So you want to be a rockman, yeh?" cried Harri

Fear convulsed my throat; I clung to him.

"Then get off my chain and swing on your rope."

He prised me away from him, levering off my clutching hands. I was slipping down the front of him to the length of my rope; it was the first sensation of the total drop. I yelled; no sound came forth; I fought him, but he had the greater strength.

"Go on, get *off*!" and he thrust me away.

Isolated, held by my own rope for the first time, I began the circular, pendulum swing from the roof. The very action of the swinging I interpreted as dropping, and awaited, my nerves clutched tight within me, for the smashing blow of the floor. But, when I dared to open my eyes, there was nothing of violence; there was no sensation save that of absolute freedom; weightless, I was swinging like a star in an arc of darkness, with Harri's candle circling above me, the moon of my night. The pendulum slowed; gravity brought us together in a succession of gentle bumps.

"Good, man — now climb."

With him beside me, I did this, and reached the ledge upon which he was working. "Now this," said Harri instructively, "is the bore-hole. Get the right charge in here and we've got half the bargain down, yeh? You drill just the same as for splitting, understand?" His grimed face went up and he grinned at me, a handsome devil in that eerie light.

"Just you, me and two candles — sixty foot up — yeh?"

"Aye!"

There was growing within me a large sense of pride.

"You like it up here?"

"Ach, indeed!"

He laughed bassly and bawled down between his feet:

"Got another rockman, Mr. Morgan!"

Three happy months I spent with Nanwen in Blaenau: looking back, I reckon they were just about the best of my life to date, for it was fair working with Dan Morgan's team under the Greaves — barring some weekends, that was, when Ben came home and messed things up. May smiled at June, and she was a right one that year — setting the old currant bun ablaze over the mountains, filling our world of showering blossom with a new radiance. Sometimes, on the weekends when Ben didn't come, I'd give Sam Jones the shove and spend the day in the country with Nanwen: she'd even bring a little picnic out — real plum cake which I loved, and bottled tea. And we would walk clear of slate country to places like the Roman Halt and sit together on the short mountain grass, listening to the curlews; seeing the kingfishers flashing their colours over the brooks. On times like this I'd sit windward of her, so as to get her perfume, for sweet as a nut she smelled to me when the wind was right; but with queer glances in my direction at times, as if she suspected I was weak in the head.

If ever a chap nearly set alight with passion — this was me that following July. Mad, mad in love was I: got her on my mind all day in Llechwedd; had her on my pillow half the night.

It is the very devil, mind, to be living with the one you love, yet dare not lift a finger. So perhaps it was for the best — for my sanity, anyway, when a letter came from Ben towards the end of that month, saying that he and Grandpa had moved into Twelve Caerberllan, and asking me to help Nanwen pack for the journey over.

"A letter from Ben!" cried she.

I groaned deep in my soul.

She lowered the note-paper and smiled at me, her eyes alive. "Oh, Toby, we're going! They've actually moved in! And they want us to join them just as soon as we can arrange it — isn't it wonderful?"

Marvellous, I thought.

The letter had built a little gravestone over all my sweetest dreams.

8

AND SO, AFTER three months together, Nanwen and I left Number One Bodafon, and I was sad.

She was a feast of the mind that July day, in her pink Sunday Outing dress down to her ankles (with real grandmother lace at throat and sleeves) and her white poke-bonnet with streamers.

Very proud was I, taking her between the lines of neighbours; all down Lord Street the people were out watching the furniture cart, the quarrymen hiding their pints behind their backs, the Blaenau urchins skipping along beside the rumbling wheels, and Sam Jones sweating like a dray in the shafts.

There were others going to Bethesda on the 'exchange of workers' but none as grand as we. People took note of it as we entered the station terrace; with porters and suchlike hitting their caps off, I reckon they thought we were some of the high class Greaves. People were taking note of the furniture, too, elbowing and nudging each other, for I'd got all the privates like chambers and chinas well underneath and all the teak and marble conspicuous on top, there being an art in carting in public.

"And where might you be going?" asked the ticket man in the booking office.

"Why, the damn cheek of it!" whispered Sam, shocked.

"Oh, no you don't," I answered, for half Lord Street was in the office and most of Llechwedd breaking their necks for news. And I was just writing it down when Nanwen came up.

"Two singles to Bethesda," said she, and paid four shillings.

Four shillings for two singles and a load of furniture to Bethesda!

"Bloody highway robbery," breathed Sam.

"Husband and wife tickets do count cheaper, Mrs. O'Hara, remember," said a voice, and from the crowd came Bando Jeremiah Williams, and he leered at me from a crimson, whiskered mouth, and swept his hat low at Nanwen's feet.

"My husband is not travelling, sir," said she. "He is meeting me at Bethesda."

"Happy am I to hear it," said Bando, straightening his stomach. "And relieved I am to know that you will enter your new home out of the company of drunkards and lechers," and he gave me a look to kill.

Crowds of people now, pushing and shoving in gay humour, for everybody off shift came to see the trains come and go, but a few tears, too, for young husbands and old lovers travelling south for the coalfields of the Rhondda, to get out of slate. Sam and I were like labouring blacks getting Nan's furniture on to the railway flat when the train gave a whistle and people scrambled aboard.

Bando Jeremiah Williams I saw again then, and his eyebrows shot up in mute surprise when I tapped his shoulder, turning him to me.

My first man; I was in the service of Nanwen.

"Here's one to remember from the drunkards and lechers," I said, and hooked him square and his shoulders went back and his boots shot up.

"Oh, what a dreadful thing to do," I heard Sam say as he helped Bando to his feet and began to brush him down. And he straightened him with a left and hit him flat again with the right.

"See you over in Bethesda, mate!" I yelled as the train puffed away, but he didn't see the going of me, since he was top speeding in the opposite direction.

It's good to be knocking around with people like Sam Jones — drink together, fight together — and we don't understand each other, really — he being from the north and me from the south.

But we make rugs out of gorillas when it comes to slandering Nanwen.

9

IT WAS A few weeks before the Big Strike that we all moved into Number Twelve Caerberllan — Nanwen, Ben, Grandpa and me, and it was two up and two down, with Grandpa in the next best bedroom and me downstairs in the kitchen under the table. Going under the table in these times made it easy for the others doing shifts, but it weren't so good when they came down to breakfast, with people's boots on your chest.

Bethesda wasn't much of a place about now. With some three thousand quarrymen employed by Lord Sholto Douglas, and mostly at his throat; the town had gone to the dogs, according to Grandpa. The old generation was beating its breast and thanking God for being poor, the new generation of slate-workers were meeting in secret up on the mountains or sitting on the ten-holer latrine in Port Penrhyn (where foremen were forbidden to enter) trying to form a Union.

Time was when the Penrhyns were honoured in the land, and no real need for a Combination of Workers, the old ones told us. I used to lie under the table in those early days in Twelve Caerberllan: off-shift, weary as a lame dog, I'd listen to Grandpa and Ben going at it hammer and tongs; it gave us a life of it, Nan and me, wondering who was right.

Said Grandpa, "You got to be fair, son — the Penrhyns built a school for education over at Llandegai, for instance. . . ."

"Aye — be fair, then," retorted Ben, always spoiling for a fight.

"To be a scholar there you've got to be Church of England!"

"And they got a real accident trolley now — never had one in my time." Grandpa munched contentedly on his bread and cheese.

"An accident trolley! Is that what your generation calls progress? You accept the dust, the typhoid, the black list?"

"Got to be reasonable," said Grandpa, calmly, and munched on. "We're workers, they're gentry."

I never saw a chap eat as good as my grandpa with no teeth; I couldn't take my eyes off him, with his pruney old chin slapping up and his shaggy white eyebrows coming down: God knows what was going on inside those chops, but on purple gums Grandpa could shift more lobscows in fifteen minutes than a squad of Welsh Guards.

"Reasonable?" shouted Ben, taking the bait. "Would ye be mythering about a man like Pharo, and giving him the credit, when he's maiming more good men than the Crimean war? The first hospital they had here, man, was in Bangor, and they'd carry a man wi'out legs for three miles on a litter, ye daft old faggot!"

"Enough of it, show some respect!" cried Nanwen.

"Respect? The old bugger's soaked in it — three times to chapel and God bless the owners for starving us?"

"You got to have God, son," said Grandpa, vacant. "That's the trouble with you and your Combinations — you'm forgetting about God."

And Grandpa chewed on, oblivious to anything. I lifted my eyes from my plate and caught Nanwen's glance as she soothed Ben.

Sixteen stones, and weak — I'd met others like him. Hair on their chests, tears in their eyes; Grandpa had his measure, and Grandpa knew it.

But, of the two of them, Ben was right; this young Lord Penrhyn, with his pay stoppages for the smallest offence, was bringing his workers to the point of mutiny. Indiscipline brought instant discharge; the quarrymen's families were cutting the bread thin and scraping on butter, while he was turning over a hundred thousand a year; he was taking all and giving nothing, except to chosen favourites.

Lovely places like Tregarth were being turned into hotbeds of

6c

men who could be bribed. Chapel congregations were being split apart; enmity existed where once was harmony.

As the Old Lord was loved by Bethesda people, so his son was hated.

Fifty years ago the Old Lord was feted when he married Lady Fitzroy; the people of the town decorated it with flags and pennants; bonfires had been lit at Garth Point, guns discharged by loyal subjects.

But now, with the son, whom the quarrymen named Pharo, in Penrhyn Castle, the people of Bethesda had the ashes of a despot in their mouths. The slave-owners who had taken Government compensation for the emancipation of the plantation slaves, were back, the quarrymen said; and making new profits from slavery in Bethesda.

But I wasn't much interested in the Pharos that fine, hot summer evening; there was a rising sap in me for a bit of a romp around and a cock at anything spare, and there wasn't much doing round Caerberllan, it appeared.

The summer moon was riding on a thousand sheep of gold as I went out to find Sam Jones, recently come from Blaenau, I'd heard. All over Pesda were posters asking good men to come and die for Queen Victoria, because there was a war going on somewhere, apparently, and I thought it might be a good idea to go and die if I couldn't get a job next day. And, damn me, the very first person I came across down High Street was Ma Bron, and I don't know who was the more delighted of the pair of us.

She being the quickest death Bethesda offered at the moment.

"Good heavens," said she, looking glorious, "fancy seeing you so soon — Sam Jones said you'd come over to Bethesda."

"You know Sam Jones?" I asked, astonished, for the beggar hadn't been here more than a day or so.

"O, aye," said Bron, fluffing up her bright, fair hair. "I know Sam Jones all right," and she made no eyes to speak of. "What you doing here, then — milking old Pharo?"

"Been doing errands and things round Town," I replied. "Trying Pharo for a permanent job tomorrow morning, Ma Bron," I said, denting my bowler. Luckily, I was dressed pretty decent that night for woman-killing; in my new double-breasted jacket and my home-spun trews washed out pale and creased and ironed by Nanwen.

I don't know why, but I was shy of her now; so fair and beautiful and got up was she as the people scurried about us: bonnet on her bright curls, peacock feathers, purple cape and high-buttoned boots; with her skirt on the ground she looked like something out of a Paris salon like Nanwen talked of, never mind Wrexham workhouse.

Stepping back, she glowed at me. "My, ain't you growed big, Toby Davies! In three months I say you've growed blutty feet. Me baby died, ye know."

"Your Bibbs? Sorry about that, Ma Bron."

"Got the Penrhyn fever — they can't do much on the fever. What time is it?"

"Pretty late," I said.

"I got to go," said she.

She was a woman: in weeks, she had grown older than Nanwen, and the sight of her sent me palpitating, for she was a well set-up figure with the carriage of a queen and splendid breasts, unusual for Bethesda, where schoolgirls used a quart pot to shape a pair of thimbles. And the wind was taking her hair, blowing it about her shoulders in gold abandon, yet there was little gaiety in Ma Bron. Indeed, there was about her face a pale, famished beauty; as if the artist of youth had stripped her cheeks of flesh and blood and laid upon them the sheen of white jade: no life was in her, although she was young.

Her red lips moved against the whiteness of her teeth, saying:

"I be kept, ye know — terrible, ain't it?" And the old Bron momentarily came back, and winked. "I got a posh gent in Bangor — I'm back there now just, but I'm coming home soon to Bethesda." She sighed, looking sad of a sudden. "I ain't been any too good, neither — I had the fever, too — you had the fever, Toby Davies?"

I shook my head, watching her sad beauty. "You coming back here, you say?"

The chance that she might walk a lane or two with me filled me with an inner, expectant hope, drying my throat. Indeed, there was growing in me a curious wish for her that was beyond desire; it was a strange and inexplicable movement of love, something protecting: she was usually so gay; I could have wept for her sadness.

"Aye," said she. "Besides," and she suddenly clapped her hands together with a little delight, "I met Sam Jones!"

It seemed to explain everything. "But best be kept, meanwhile," said she, "with the strike comin', and all that — best to have a roof." She looked wistful. "Besides, he's such a lonely old soul, an' I wanted to make him happy — good to keep people happy ain't it?"

She was lost to me.

It was as if she had loosened my kiss on her mouth and moved out of my arms.

Perhaps I was staring at her, for she said, smiling, her head on one side:

"You all right, matey?"

"Never been better."

Her eyes were suddenly alive. "If you come across Sam Jones, will you do something for me?"

I nodded, and she said, "Tell him I'm comin' back, eh? Tell him I'll turn up that gent in Bangor if he'll take me on, eh?" She fluffed up and patted her hair. "Barmaid at the Waterloo, if I'm lucky — may be next week!"

"Sam'll like that."

She gripped my arm. "He's a queer cuss, though — never knows where you are wi' him. Ask him to pop over and see Bron again soon, is it?"

"You got better equipment than me, mind."

"Tell him?" Her eyes begged.

Never in my life have I known a chap like Sam Jones for getting on the right side of a woman's particulars.

"I promise, Bron," I said.

Bethesda leered at us. She said, as if agitated by his very name, "Now he knows I'm a loose, he don't come to me, understand . . .?"

"You're all right," I said.

Reaching out, she smiled and touched my face. "Goodbye, my lovely."

There was an emptiness in me after she had gone.

The first chap I saw in the Waterloo after that was Sam Jones.

"Ma Bron's looking for you," I said, getting an elbow in among the quarrymen of the bar.

They were off shift from the Big Hole and the talk was mainly of Pharo and Young, his English agent; over in a corner a man was preaching the benefits of W. J. Parry's workers' Combination. Sam didn't reply to me, so I said:

"I come here with her first, you know."

"Have her if you like, mun."

The landlord slid my glass towards me. I drank, watching Sam. "Don't want her, but she's had it bad — keep it decent, eh? She's gone on you."

"The way they all fall for me, sometimes it frightens me," said Sam. He drank and wiped his mouth: fine and handsome he looked, his shoulders filling out for a man. "What's she to you, then?"

"Nothing. Just treat her good or I'll float you out of Bethesda."

It pleased him; his dark eyes shone. The noise of the quarrymen beat about us. He said, "You got your hands full in Caerberllan they say."

"Watch your mouth."

"No offence. Just that there's talk."

"About who?"

"You at the moment — they're scared of Ben O'Hara. But he can't hit his way out of a paper bag . . . you'd be safer with Ma Bron."

"Let them bloody talk," I said, and gripped my glass, staring at the ale. A few men were looking my way, I noticed. Sam said, "They got to talk about somebody, mind. You signing on tomorrow?"

I nodded.

"Got your sovereign for the foreman?"

"See you down there," I said, and turned for the door.

"That was quick."

The men were staring at me. Sam said, "Sod 'em all, Toby — you stay." He grinned. "Next they'll be talking about Grandpa."

The moon was shining over the slate mountains as I took back home to Caerberllan.

64

Quite a few people I saw that night on my way home — little Eddie Jones, for one, aged six, and he shouted through the grime of his urchin face:

"*Gwell Bantu na hwntwr!* Toby Davies? *Gwell Bantu na hwntwr!*" (Better be a Bantu than a South Walian) so I yelled back the standard Welsh reply:

"*Gwell wog na gog*, Eddie Jones!" (Better be a wog than a North Walian).

He shrieked with delight and ran off into the dark. Some said he lived in the workhouse at Bangor, but he was always around Bethesda quarries.

Mrs. Pru Natal, the midwife I saw next, hurrying along to Bodforris where somebody was confined. Responsible for the next generation of quarrymen was she, with her threatening bedside manner and box of ground pepper for difficult cases, and I knew a surge of joyous expectancy; I sometimes worried about this, wondering if I was normal, for the very sight of a midwife always switched me on, while I could pass a pair of lace-trimmed spacers on a wash-line without the bat of an eye.

Nanwen was standing outside Number Twelve like a goddess in white with an apron, looking at the moon; her face was pale, the shadows deep in her cheeks.

She leaned towards me, smelling my breath and she was warm from the fire and comforting to the senses. Had there been any justice in the world I would have swept her into my arms and away to a place of loving a hundred miles from Bethesda, for a wedding in white.

"You been drinking, Toby Davies?"

"Damn me," I said, "what do you expect?"

There was in her an impression of expectancy, even anxiety in her moments of waiting, and I drew closer.

"I love you," I said, but nobody heard; she was gazing towards the road now, her hand to her mouth; never had she looked so beautiful.

"Ben's late," she said.

10

In the middle of a hot July, I signed on at the Big Hole to work for Pharo Penrhyn.

Everybody in Twelve was up at dawn, Nanwen cutting the tommy boxes and filling tea-bottles, patting and smoothing Grandpa, as if sending him off with Ben and me was the most normal thing in the world, but I knew she was worrying in case he wouldn't get a shift.

"Pharo gave ye the cottage, didn't he?" said Ben at breakfast.

"Aye, but I got me doubts about Young, his works agent," said Grandpa. "When we gets to the quarry things may come different."

"Don't be daft, man. If you're on the Penrhyn books you're on the books."

"The left hand don't know what the right hand's doin'," said Grandpa.

"The land agent who ticked us for this cottage isn't the works agent, mind. They give me the cottage but there was no talk of a job."

"Meet it when we get up there," I said.

We chewed away in silence amid Nanwen's bustling smiles of encouragement; I watched her slim fingers sweeping the kettle off the hob; she filled the cups with nervous, anxious hands; then:

"There . . . there's always a place for a good craftsman, isn't there, Ben! From splitting and dressing to locos, Grandpa knows it all — got to have instructors, haven't we?"

"Not over seventy, with bad dust," said Grandpa.

"You're special," I said. "That's why you got this place."

"Aye, well, I was sweeping the cabins for Assheton and I can sweep again; we'll see, won't we? — 'cause I say the rent man's made a mistake. We shouldn't be here in Caerberllan."

"Cheer up, cheer up!" cried Nanwen. "First day working at Bethesda, and you're as miserable as black coffins."

Ben chewed on, ignoring her, tearing at the bread with his huge, hairy hands.

Now along the Row we went; doors were coming open, brass being polished, slate steps being milked. Out on the road to Betws-y-Coed the quarrymen were flooding out of Bethesda: they were coming from Gerlan and Rachub, Sling and Tregarth — some from as far afield as Bangor and Pentir — a six mile walk for many; men and boys, the rockmen and setters, rubbishers, dressers, loaders; a few, mainly foremen and agents, wending a path through the marching army on penny-farthing bikes, the latest craze. And the drumming of hobnails on the flinted tracks grew to a thunder.

And the Penrhyn hooter, the call to work, shouted over the mountains.

"Here's a fighting force, if ever the Combination wants it," growled Ben.

Mr. Morgan, my old foreman (just arrived over from Llechwedd on the exchange), was walking in front of Ben, Grandpa and me with Guto Livingstone who wasn't quite a full pound up top (being a dreamer of distant places ever since he stopped a boulder on the nut, according to Sam). 'My cross,' his poor old missus used to say, but he was still the best rubbisher in Bethesda, being great in the shoulders, if brainless. Also there was Mr. Albert Arse, a neighbour of ours in Caerberllan, mainly thus called because folks will insist on dropping their blutty haitches, said his missus, Annie, who was a London cockney. Very partial to the Arses, I was, he being one of the finest rockmen Penrhyn had, according to reports, and Annie the best mother in Bethesda according to Nanwen, cockney English or not. And what went for Nanwen was always right with me.

"Give old Penrhyn hell, Toby, lad!" yelled a voice in Welsh, and down the ranks I saw Sam, bright-faced and quiffed, with his trews as white as a cricketer's flannels, despite his mam being ill, folks said.

"Ay ay!" I shouted back, seeing beside Sam his dada for the very first time: a cock-sure little five-foot preener, this one, with a face like a hen's arse.

"Sam's father," I said, elbowing Ben, and he growled bassly:

"Aye," he grumbled, "small and evil — in God's humour he sired that big fine lad — Sam takes after his ma, sure enough. A fine woman she is — dying slow of an illness, folks say, but she labours herself to the bone for them."

"Is Mr. Jones in the Combination?"

"Would a fussy apology like him be in the Combination — talk sense!"

"Combination or not," said Grandpa, wheezing at the pace. "Don't you trust him — he ain't Congregational, ye know — they reckon she 'as to chloroform him to get her weekly wages, poor soul, and her with a cough like death's trumpet."

"We've got 'em, mind," said Ben, dourly. "Christ, we've got 'em."

The army swelled to a thousand tramping boots up the pitch to the Big Hole.

They came from the cottages that once their forebears owned, these quarrymen — nearly a thousand of such cottages existed on the Penrhyn estate alone, each with its tidy little patch of vegetables. They marched from the scores of tiny smallholdings that dotted Llandegai mountain; from the inns, taverns and the *cabans* where they lodged (earning about six pounds a month) — men born in the language of slate, mostly, but also English and Scots, and Irishmen who had taken Welsh wives. Isolated by language, the foreigners kept to their own sects. Yet they lived and worked together in mutual respect and harmony, bound by the same ideals — the Combination of Workers they were trying to forge, and their fierce dislike of the young Lord Penrhyn.

In the surly countenances of the men going to work on that first morning I sensed a sullen anger: none spoke, after initial greetings, to others joining the ranks: apart from the thundering boots, the breathless lungs, the silence was as great as the temple of Solomon.

Trouble was coming: it stank on the wind.

As we neared the Head I saw a cluster of men waiting by the check-in: those already employed went to the right; we, applying for jobs, marched left. I remarked, "I hope Sam Jones, my mate, gets in," and Ben grumbled reply:

"Don't bother yourself — they'll love Sam Jones with that sort of a father."

"Because Mr. Jones is against the Combination?"

"Aye, and because he's known for a blackleg."

"Then what hope have you got?"

"I got recommendations of a different sort, me boy."

"And Grandpa."

"See to yourself, young 'un — never mind about Grandpa."

I had come across a few agents and foremen since I'd been in slate, but never one like this. Rolling fat was he, Irish born and Irish temper, and sure to God don't you come from the same fair county as me? asked Ben, grinning wide.

"Name?" asked the man.

"Ben O'Hara — ye can count me in for a special recommendation, sir? — me name's on the books already."

"Benjamin O'Hara of Limerick? This the one?" He examined his list.

"Ay ay, man, and strong for the Roman Catholic."

"Save it for Black Hill, it don't count here." Out with a notebook, very official and thumbing it with grubby fingers. "Have you got the letter of recommendation, then?"

"Mark, Mary and Joseph, I nigh forgot!" and Ben passed him an envelope: the man took it, crinkling it for money.

"Also me young friend here, Tobias Davies — Welsh speaking, remember."

"That won't help him."

New men pressed about us, faces stretched out, yearning for work. I watched. The agent put the envelope into his pocket.

"Are we in, then?" asked Ben.

The man nodded heavily, eyes switching around the questioning faces.

"Splitters, dressers and rockmen I want particular," said he. "Rubbishers are ten a penny."

"Then here's the best slate-dresser in the business — me grandfather," said Ben, and pushed Grandpa up in front of him. The old man braced back his thin shoulders. The agent peered.

"Do I know you, Grandad?"

"Should do, Mr. Agent," replied Grandpa brightly. "The Old Lord and Mr. Assheton-Smith — fifty years I served 'em, man and boy."

"Age?"

"Sixty-five."

"Dust?" He listened on Grandpa's waistcoat.

"The bellows aren't what they used to be, but they don't affect me," answered Grandpa, and his chest was howling.

The agent said to Ben, "Grandads I can't do — not with that chest — he goes home."

We stared at each other; the men shifted like nervous sheep, dying for their turn.

"You and the lad," said the agent to Ben, "take it or leave it."

"Don't Pharo get old too, then?" asked Grandpa.

"Now, now, none o' that!"

Bully State of Maine, the pugilist, shouted nearby, "He be a bloody expert, Mr. Agent. I know'd him good — he tells the trades to boys. Perhaps he don't have to breathe, but the poor old sod's got to eat, ye know."

"Come on, move along, move along!" Big men behind the agent began to threaten. We moved aside, Grandpa with us: empty, we stood, with the crag winds blustering about us at the height: I heard the commands of the team foremen as the rockmen lowered themselves down the faces of the galleries.

Grandpa said, "I done it all — rock face, splitting, dressing — I even done *rybelwr* at the start, and drove the engines: then I'm sweeping cabins, now I'm off." He stared about him. "Yeh?"

"Lose yourself, old man," said the agent.

I said, "You was here in case you was wanted, *Taid*."

The Welshness pleased him. Grandpa smiled.

Standing with Ben I watched him going down the pitch back to Caerberllan, and Nanwen.

Every night when we got home, Ben and me, we'd find Grandpa sitting humped in his chair by the grate while Nanwen prepared the evening meal. I can see him now, staring at nothing; remembering the days when he was young, perhaps, though he never said much about it. And up and down the little Caerberllan Row of cottages came the sounds of men returning home from work.

Say what you like, there's nothing like living in a community — one big family, with all the family's fights and loves and grief and happiness. Children yelling, plates clattering as daughters laid the tables, cups of tea being poured, and come on off the settee, you lot — make room for your da. Steam from a dozen kettles spurting up, grates being poked, babies crying at being put to bed in daylight, chairs scraping flags as people sat up to table; the bass voice replies to wifely questions, shrieked threats to chirping children. And smells better than the spices of India are wafting down that Row: lobscows and steak and kidney, the basted corpses of suicide hares and rabbits, fried trout out of the Ogwen, tickled out by experts on the way back from the Great Hole.

I've lived in a few places since then, but nothing ever came up to those autumn days in Caerberllan, before the Big Strike and the following Big Hunger.

"Toby, stop dreaming," said Nanwen. "Sit up at table."

"Lest Grandpa eats off your plate," added Ben, and put his fist under Grandpa's chin to lighten him, poor old dab.

But still I listened to the song of Caerberllan.

Once, all these cottages were built and owned by the men who arrived there seeking work. Deciding to mine for slate, each immigrant selected a little bit of common ground; together they built this row, for instance, and named it Caerberllan. All over Llandegai mountain this happened, and scores of tiny slate caverns were opened by the peasant investors. But then Lord Penrhyn arrived. Under the Land Enclosure Act he seized the whole of Llandegai mountain for a start, laid out roads and fenced it in.

"He stole it," said Ben now. "It was common land, and on this

71

common land the people built their homes; but since the cottages belonged to the land he enclosed, Penrhyn stole those, too."

"And what are you doing about it?" asked Grandpa.

Ben said, "He owned the whole community. If an employee argued about wages, he was sacked and blacklisted with other slate employers: once sacked, he could be evicted from the very cottage he built, because it was now a tithe dwelling."

Nanwen said, "It's a scandal. In their time the owners of these places starved and were then evicted. And they could no more rent out their cottages than eat them."

"That's one in the eye for the Old Lord," said I. "The way you've been talking, you've made him out a saint."

"He is, compared with young Pharo, his son," said Ben. "But don't you worry, me son, the Combination will see to him."

"O, aye?" asked Grandpa, innocent. "Your fine Mr. Parry's got a deal of things to see to before he gets down to halting tithe rent — fifty years from now these cottages will still belong to the Penrhyns — and take it from me, ye Irish mare, young Pharo will take care of your blutty Combination."

Bedlam then, with me and Nanwen jumping in to act as referees.

Mind, I reckon old Grandpa only did it to bait Ben, the old criminal.

"THE FACT REMAINS," said Nanwen, "now Grandpa's laid off we shouldn't really be here. Now he's stopped work, the bailiffs will evict us."

"The land agent can shift us from under this roof whenever he pleases," I said.

"Meet it when we come to it," growled Ben, "we have trouble enough for now."

The autumn faded: the country grew into a deeper gold.

The 'bargains' were getting tighter, the hours shorter, the pay thinner.

"Three shillings a yard suit you, Mr. Morgan?" asked the overseer.

Ferrety thin and crippled was this Penrhyn agent; a blue, peaked dewdrop of a nose in the late autumn cold and a face as lined as Crewe Junction.

"How many yards?" asked our Mr. Morgan, smooth.

"Eight yards opening over nine days." He tipped back his hat. "Yeh?"

Our foreman pondered it. "It's thin."

"Thinner where there's none — take it or leave it."

"What about roofing?"

"I'll gift ye a pound for the roofing," said the agent.

"And drilling by 'jumper'? God, man, you'll kill us."

The agent sighed deep. "Look — you can poke holes in it with your fingers."

"Then you bloody try," said our Mr. Morgan.

"Enough of that, Mr. Morgan," said the agent.

Ben stood silently, watching, his eyes brooding with a cold violence.

He said, taking a chance, "Before you came, we had old Dan Shenkins on the bargains, and he were fair with us. If he saw you figure out a bargain like that he'd turn in his grave, he would."

"He'd do more," said Grandpa, coming up, "he'd do a blutty handspring."

Strange about Grandpa these days. He came to work with us, he came back home off shift with us; sitting around all day on the tumps, pretending he was needed. Many old men did this in Bethesda.

"You're not dealing with Softy Shenkins now," said the agent, "this is me." And he limped off, leaving us with slavery. Mr. Morgan said:

"Reckon I'd do better to find a widow with a bad cough." He scowled.

"When he goes for burial I'll dance on his grave," added Ben.

"They should bury buggers like him when they're alive," said Albert Arse.

This was unusual for Mr. Arse; for a quiet man with an aristocratic name, he was sometimes very revolutionary.

For my part I wasn't very interested in the bargains our foreman got, so long as I drew my pay — eight shillings a week now, five to Nanwen, three to me. And, now that the nights were drawing even colder, I was away by moonlight most Saturdays, coat collar turned up against the wind of the mountains, down to the Waterloo to meet Sam Jones, with Ma Bron, the barmaid, in the offing.

There was a brass band playing along High Street, trying to get the blood warm on martial music, for some people called Boers were playing hell with the Army over in China, or some such place.

"Africa," said Sam.

"How d'ye know?"

"Dai Forceps told me."

"There's a mine of information," said Ben.

It was cold, even for October, as I went up the Row for town and Mr. Roberts, the deacon of the big Ebenezer, was standing in his window looking out on to a frosted world. As I went past I pulled off my bowler to him, he being respected in Caerberllan; a quiet man of God was Mr. Roberts, and keeping a diary of all the Ebenezer events, such as who preached, and when; and on his mantelshelf he kept a picture of Jesus framed in sea-shells.

One day, I thought, I would present myself before such a man as this; with Nanwen beside me, I would stand in the Ebenezer with the congregation putting up a harmony of tenor and soprano, and mud on the boots of the big bass quarrymen. And then home to tea and ham; everybody fussing about with happy congratulations. And I would take her away to a far corner of the earth where she'd forget she had ever set eyes on Ben O'Hara.

I coveted her.

For less love than mine, some men would have put Ben to bed with a shovel. I could not rid my mind of dreams. After all, as Grandpa said, none of us is perfect: take all the sinners away from the saints, and all you've got left is Moses and his Tablets.

Mr. Sudden Death, the Co-op insurance man, was coming round the corner of Bodforris, so I pulled up my collar and coughed myself blue in the face, and went up to town to kill a pint with Sam.

Get mixed up with the Co-op on a Saturday pay night and they'd have a policy on your life and a bottle of your water before you could bat an eye.

The bargain crews were huddled against the cold under the naphtha flares of the stalls, and the cockle and mussel women were shouting their wares. Hugh Fish, a wisp of skin and bone on his cart, was waving his herrings under passing noses, shouting, "Fresh out of the bay, with bellies like gentry. Buy, buy!" and old Marged at her crockery stall was holding up chamber pots and shouting, "Friends for life, remember — not a word of what they see, never mention what they hear." And then I remembered, when I saw the stalls thickening more, that this was also market day. The team foremen were tiptoeing over the holy marble of the bank, drawing

75

the long-pay sovereigns (I'd had mine earlier) and one of the first with a fist-full of silver I came across was Sam Jones:

"Did you hear what happened at the Ffridd Gallery today?"

"No?"

"You remember the teams there ran the contractors out of the quarry a week or so back?"

"Ay ay!"

"They did it again today — and stoned 'em."

"That means trouble — Penrhyn won't stand for that!"

Together we pushed our way into the bar of the Waterloo and there behind it was Ma Bron, her face powdered, her hair curled, and showing enough bosom to kill the Pope.

"Well, well, look who we have here," said she, pouring jugs.

"A couple of pints and a little less tongue," said Sam, and leaned to me. "Young, the agent's dancing mad, and Penrhyn's after the men who did it."

"You can't stone contractors," said a voice, and there stood Deacon Tossle with his pew duster in one hand and a pint in the other — having just slipped in from cleaning out Jerusalem: very popular was Deacon Tossle for liking ale as well as God; even Jesus was not averse to a little nose-varnish, given the right occasion, said he. For months, to my certain knowledge, Deacon Tossle drank in the taps before his mates discovered it, and then he cleared the Big Seat by a foot; most of the drinking being done in the vestries.

"Aye, but we got to cut out this new contracting system," said a rubbisher, leaning over. "A bargain's a bargain — we worked it that way with the Old Lord. Why the hell do we have to put up with Pharo's middlemen?"

"Treat us like pigs they do, mind," said Albert Arse, solemn, and how he got in there at twopence a pint beat us, with his army back home to feed.

The roars and banter beat about us, and a drunk yelled, "Aye, me lovely girls, you should 'ave seen 'em go — like the clappers wi' bricks behind 'em."

"The victory is yours now, perhaps, but you'll rue it in the end, mark me," said Deacon Tossle.

76

The cockle women were coming in with baskets; smooth-faced matrons dressed like nuns, and their soprano cries mingled with the clash of glasses and argument.

"D'you stand for Penrhyn, then?" asked Bully State of Maine, belligerent.

"I stand with you, fighter, because I'm a good quarryman," came the reply. "But violence on the works doesn't serve Mr. Parry, your leader, since he condemns violence."

"Don't we get violence all the year round from Pharo?"

"In violence you are breaking the law," Tossle insisted. "Is there a man here who can justify it to Mr. Parry face to face?"

The second mention of W. J. Parry stilled them; uncertain, they growled about them like bulls at a manger. For Parry was their champion, their hope for justice.

"What we going to do, then?" I asked. "Just sit down under it while the contractors take middleman cuts? It lessens the bargain pay-out, remember."

"Ah, yes." Tossle looked me over. "Toby Davies — Grandpa's lad, isn't it?"

"Aye."

"And how old are you?"

"Knocking seventeen."

"Right — ten years from now you'll see the sense of arbitration, for which Mr. Parry stands. The young are bringing us to violence, and it is the young who will suffer. Bribery, swindling at the face, corruption in the galleries, this is our lot. You will never change it by bricks or gunpowder, but by civilised argument."

I asked soberly, "What d'you reckon will come of it, Deacon?"

Mr. Tossle drained his pint. "Ask Colonel Ruck, the Chief Constable, when Penrhyn calls in the military."

"Right, mun, let 'em come," yelled Dai Forceps, mate to Bully, "we'll give 'em soldiers — this is a peaceful town!"

"It used to be," said One-pint Tossle.

A silence fell upon us after he had gone, and Bully cupped his chin in his hands and smiled at Ma Bron, who was filling the tankards with professional flourishes.

"Ye know," said he, "I'd rather watch her than listen to deacons.

She serves that ale, does our little Bron, like a woman with a divine right."

"She's got a divine left, too," said Sam.

Together, as mates, we pushed our way through the sawdust into the lamp-flaring street.

Bron followed Sam with her eyes, her hands pausing on the jugs. I winked at her, but she ignored me, watching Sam.

Got it bad.

Sam didn't spare her a glance.

Ugly Dic, the police sergeant, was abroad in High Street that market night, and with good reason, for the Romanys were coming in from the mountains at dusk with their gay clothes and banter, followed by their dancing wives: bright were the trinkets and paste diamonds of the stalls.

Mr. Price of Cloth Hall, with his mauve shawl over his shoulders, was measuring cloth; Joe Bec, the Gerlan baker, was throwing up crisp, brown loaves in competition with the English Bakehouse, and people were slicing it off and plastering it with wedges of farmhouse butter.

There were fortune-tellers, a strong man from Caernarfon, and a woman doing a ballet, dressed as a dying swan; sheep were thronging in with neat little cobs, for auctioning. Benny the Brave from Rachub was already in tears as he held up his coloured umbrellas, crying, "If I don't clear this lot, what will Marged say?" Bill Brunt (whose brother died on Snowdon rescuing Pharo's stupid gentry) was in a different sort of tears, wandering the gutter, half-minded, in search of his relation. And the mountain farmers were also coming into market — the men who tore down Penrhyn's fences as fast as his bailiffs put them up — stern-faced and in rags they came. Fiddles, in contrast to their savagery, were shrieking about them, street urchins picking pockets. And then, right in the middle of it, a pony and trap appeared, and in it was sitting Mr. Parry, the quarryman's leader: severe and unforgiving was his square, handsome face.

Sam, excited, was yelling, "Mr. Parry, Mr. Parry — *look*!"

This was the unpaid solicitor who was head and shoulders above

78

all leaders in Caernarfonshire, and that included Lloyd George, men said.

"I bet he's off to give old Pharo hell!" yelled Dai Forceps behind me.

In the event Pharo gave hell to us in Bethesda.

Down the middle of High Street, pushing aside the hawkers and urchins, a little mob of quarrymen were coming, and I recognised men of the Crimea galleries, the Agor Boni and Ffridd; those who had stoned Pharo's contractors. Laughing, cheering, they surrounded Mr. Parry's trap and marched beside it with a military bearing, holding their arms like men carrying guns. Guto Livingstone I saw in the ranks, who didn't know if he was in Bethesda or Bolivia; and there on the flank was Albert Arse holding up old Dick Jones, the miser who bottled his water: nine sheets in the wind, most of them, too; I saw the disgust on Mr. Parry's face. And behind all this lot came the recruiting brass band giving us *Rule Britannia*, and I don't know who was making more noise, the band or the rowdies. But others were thronging in, too — decent quarrymen of sober habits — people like Mr. Roberts, for instance, who never touched a drop. These stood fifteen deep, watching.

"We going in, mate?" asked Sam.

"You bet." And we doubled through the ranks of men and got close to the carriage, giving it a pull, and we didn't stop until we had turned it in the street and come back to the Public Hall.

Silence as Mr. Parry rose to his feet in the trap, smiling around the intent faces; come to beard Pharo in his slate temple; removing his hat, he said:

"All right, men, it's pay night, and market day. It's right that you should celebrate. But your spirits are running as high as the ale — no trouble with the police, remember!"

Clasping his hands before him, he continued, "Aye, not a spot of bother with police, so oblige me, for we've trouble enough on our hands — with the hotheads who ran the contractors off the gallery for the second time in a month."

The men eased their shoulders, staring about them in search of scapegoats. Mr. Parry said:

"Understand this — trouble is coming. Yet you keep tying my hands. You are not dealing with the Old Lord, remember — indeed, you are not answering to anybody: you leave that to me — to face the Honourable Sholto Douglas, not the easiest of men — on your behalf, and for a quarryman's wages: I am scarcely an overpaid solicitor on thirty shillings a week." He lifted a finger and swept it over the silent faces. "So mark me now, if you didn't do so before — in the town, in your homes, on the gallery faces. I am your elected spokesman. Don't take my legs away if you want me to make a stand. Unruly behaviour in Bethesda tonight, and the police will be here in force from Bangor: violence in the galleries will bring in the military from Caernarfon." He waited, watching them; we stood like men hypnotised, and he added, "The first man at fault accounts to me."

It was so quiet that I heard the hissing of the naphtha lamps.

Then ragged cheering began, swelling to thunder, and those still left in the inns and publics came racing out, slopping their tankards. We pressed about the trap, shouting his name, but Mr. Parry didn't appear to hear us.

He stood apart, the loneliest man in Bethesda.

Then he reined up his pony and the trap clattered over the cobbles towards Bangor, and Penrhyn Castle.

Sam and I bought faggots and peas and went on a tour of the Bethesda publics.

12

Nanwen looked prettier still a few weeks later.

Smooth and pale was her face as she sat at her sewing, and her dark hair, shining in the table lamp-light, lay in flowing waves over her shoulders.

I loved her hair. Sometimes she would tie it with coloured ribbons, and this would make her into a girl again; then she would let it hang loose, and this turned her into a woman. Now she lifted her eyes in a whimsical little stare and her hands paused on the needle.

She always did this when I was watching her; her smile greeted, yet her eyes admonished. Sometimes I wondered if she knew of my love for her.

Ben said, grumpy, drunk with strength, "You heard about Penrhyn summoning those twenty-six men of the gallery for stoning his contractors?"

"Here we go," said Grandpa.

"You think this is the start of trouble?"

"You bet your boots."

"I 'aven't got any boots," said Grandpa.

I said, "Mr. Young the agent's up in Great Yarmouth, they say — people reckon Penrhyn's moving too fast."

"Will there be a strike?" asked Nanwen, quietly.

"There's going to be a protest," rumbled Ben, getting up. Fisting his face he wandered the kitchen. "Would we be decent if we sat on our backsides and watched friends go to gaol?"

"Will it come to that?"

"They won't go free, woman — Penrhyn's got the magistrates sewn up neat in a bag."

"It's a scandal. He waters their wages and then summons them for protesting," said Nanwen, and I was a little surprised. The skin of her face was stretched tightly over her highboned cheeks, her voice was strained.

Often I had wondered about her having a baby; the thought brought me to an inner sickness. Up and down the Row and round the corner in Tangadlas, the women were knocking them out; the washing lines waving full of napkins, belly-bands and comforters; it was more like a sprog farm than a slate town, and the hammering and squalling going on turned the mind of a lonely bachelor. I tried to get a peek at what Nanwen was sewing, but I couldn't make a head or tail of it. I didn't want her to have a baby, unless it could be mine.

Bang, bang on the back and I got up and opened it. Mr. Morgan stood there with slate dust on his face. He peered:

" 'Evening, Mrs. O'Hara — you there, Ben, lad?"

"Dear me, come in!" cried Nanwen, delighted, sweeping him in with her skirts.

"Can't stop — the missus is waiting — I haven't been home. Up at the Hole there's talk of the summoning, you heard?"

"I have, and he'll never get away wi' it," observed Ben grimly.

"He's done more, man, he's sacked all twenty-six."

"No!" Ben roamed the room like a tiger caged, but I was looking at Nanwen.

One day, I thought, I will take you from here, away from this worry and his disregard. One day I will build a house on a hill for you where a little river runs, with servants to wait upon you and there will be nothing for you to do all day but walk under a parasol. And there will be an end to the sack apron, the slate dust, the eternal confrontations. A strike was coming, and a fight with Penrhyn would be a fight to the death. Everybody would suffer, most of all the women.

People nearly starved to death in earlier strikes. The dismissal of eighty quarrymen in 1870, because they had tried to form a Combination, had disgraced the name of Penrhyn. Then, four years back, in a fight for fair wages, a lock-out came, and Bethesda went thin for a year.

Ben said, "He's sacked twenty-six men before the court finds 'em guilty? — the fella's ravin' mad, so he is!"

"You're not dealing with an ordinary employer," said Mr. Morgan, and Grandpa raised his hands to the ceiling and cried in a cracked voice:

" 'Go in, go in, speak unto Pharaoh, that he let the children of Egypt go out of his land!' — Exodus 6; 11 — what d'ye think of that, boys — 'And say unto him that if you refuse to let them go, I will smite all thy borders with frogs!' "

"Quiet, Grandpa," I said.

Ben shouted, "Get some sense into this — what does Mr. Parry say?"

"I came in to ask you that," answered Mr. Morgan, "you're the Combination man. It's serious, you know. If the men walk out now they won't go back for years," and he left us.

Nobody realised how right he was.

It was strange, in the light of what happened afterwards, that Sam should bring us the final news.

"Anybody there?" he asked, knocking and opening the door.

It was near midnight, and we were yawning for bed. Sam was a stuttering rush of words:

"Word's just come that Pharo will suspend quarry working if the men march on the Bangor magistrates, Mr. O'Hara!"

"And who says they'll march on Bangor?"

"Mr. Parry, not an hour ago, yeh?"

"Parry said that? — talk sense!"

"Come in, come in!" called Nanwen, and Sam entered, tearing his hat to bits.

"It all just happened — Mr. Parry says to the devil with Pharo — that we're entitled to make a peaceful demonstration. And he will lead the march on Bangor."

"When?" I asked.

"Tomorrow — Parry's sending people round with the news — I'm one. Everybody to be in High Street by eight o'clock in the

83

morning — going to close Port Penrhyn, stop the ships, and march on the magistrates!"

"God help us," whispered Nanwen.

I got up. "Better to starve than live crooked."

"He'll suspend the town for this," said Grandpa, spitting in the fire.

"Let him," said Ben. "He can suspend us, even sack us — he can't eat us alive."

"Damn near, according to my da," said Sam, uneasily.

"Luckily, your father doesn't represent the opinion of this town — will you be there tomorrow, Sam?"

"If me da is, Mr. O'Hara."

Ben nodded, turning away. "That means you won't, because your father's spread on the Penrhyn blanket."

"I'm coming, I tell ye, Mr. O'Hara — I'll be there, won't I, Toby?"

I did not reply.

Already the doubts were starting, and the strike hadn't even begun.

There was fine talk that Lloyd George himself would march at the head of the strikers in the morning.

"A politician?" asked Nanwen, innocent.

"He'll watch which way the wind blows first," said Ben.

He must have done.

Next day he was still tucked up safe in Caernarfon.

In the morning the sky was cold and grey and the town was filled with the clatter of boots; to High Street went the men, summoned by their leaders, to march on Bangor in protest at the summoning.

"You don't go," said Ben.

I stared at him. "Why not?"

"Neither you, nor Grandpa. The house is in his name, and when he is gone it falls to you; we need the roof."

"It's sense," said Grandpa.

"God alive!"

"Please," said Nanwen, begging with her hands. "We daren't risk eviction."

Only that morning I had awoken to the sounds of her stifled retching of sickness, and knew that she was with child.

It had confirmed my inner fears.

So I left them, sick at heart, and mooched up High Street, where the men were assembling; they were a brave sight with their bantering and threats and a Lodge band forming up to march at their head. One of the first people I saw was Ben, up on a barrel, swinging his fist into the faces of a crowd.

"This is a peaceful demonstration of strength, remember!" he cried. "We will surround the court house and await the sentences. If our comrades are gaoled, we'll tear the place down."

They leaped to him, lustily cheering.

"But, sure to God, will any magistrate dare to sentence a single one, with three thousand quarrymen waiting outside? Now we'll know the stronger — the Workers' Combination, or Pharo!"

The town trembled to the cheering. It was the first time I had seen Ben as a Combination man, and I was strangely proud. He cried:

"We are peaceful men seeking justice, but force will be met with force. Even Mr. Parry is behind this official protest — are ye with him now?"

They bawled their assent, and he shouted, "Right then, form up decent and march like soldiers — let Pharo suspend the town if he wills — tonight we will return to Bethesda with our twenty-six comrades!"

"*Cythril!*" ejaculated a man behind me in the crowd, and I turned to see the little wizened face of Sam's father. "The Devil himself is in that Irish pig."

"He speaks for the town," I said, "be fair!"

"He'll have the lot of ye out of Caerberllan in time for Christmas — d'ye realise?"

"Our business."

"It'll be yours in the end — and Grandpa's, mark me. Harbouring that madman, you've less brains between ye than a chocolate mouse. The town's not all for Parry, remember — a lot of us are for Penrhyn. Ye don't shoot all the dogs because a few 'ave fleas."

I tore myself away from him and mingled with the crowd to lose him. I looked for Sam among the marchers, but could not find him.

A sudden desolation gripped me: I was aware of approaching disaster; it was more potent in its threat than anything I had experienced before.

"Come snow, the five of ye will be on the road," said Sam's father, tugging at my sleeve. "With O'Hara loose, man, you'll be beggin' for bread."

I ran, to save myself the sin of murder.

Sickened, I wandered the empty street after the men had gone.

Nanwen was going to have a baby; the least she could have done was to tell me. In the midst of this fear, it was like an adultery. I knew a great and awful emptiness.

So I was glad to find Ma Bron sitting on the steps of the Waterloo, with her arms folded on her chest and her skirt six inches above her ankles.

Enough to send any normal chap raving mad.

" 'Morning, Toby Davies," said she. "Good looking people around town these days, ain't there?"

I knocked up my bowler at her, standing sideways in my trews, which was the effect Bron always had on me: it took a Sam Jones to handle her.

"Seen Sam this morning?" she asked.

"Gone with the marchers, I expect."

"Oh, no he ain't — he's widowing up in Rachub. Never mind, mate, you'll do. Like a cup o' tea?"

The sun was warm on her bright, flowered dress; winter forgot it was November: all about us the deserted balconies frowned their chapel allegations.

Ma Bron jerked her thumb. "Nobody in 'ere, gone on the march, ye see, even the blutty landlord." And she preened and flounced her beauty at the morning. "After all, Toby Davies, we're sort of workhouse mates, ain't we?"

It seemed fair enough in the face of Nanwen's defection.

I followed Ma Bron into the tap-room with its smell of stale beer, my hobnails hammering the saw-dust.

"You like to see my room, son?"

Unaccountably, I was remembering Randy Andy, aged eight in Wrexham workhouse, who, orphaned, fell in love with the tailor's dummy. One day they missed him and found him down in the cellar among the coal; standing with a candle in one hand and his arm around its waist: nothing but a knob for a face, a canvas bust and moulded mahogany where her legs should have been.

People got to love something, said Randy.

Being in love with Nanwen was rather like this, I thought.

They had a hedgehog in the kitchen of the Waterloo to eat the crickets; Ma Bron's room was next door to this, warm and snug from the grate where stew was simmering: the brass-knobbed little bed with black stockings draped over the rail, a hint of perfume, and Ma Bron's white eyes in the darkness of the corner moved like a dance of the senses.

"Has Sam Jones been in here?" I whispered.

"O, aye," said Bron. "Some I favour, Sam especially."

The clouds sank over the window in bleak understanding; the room was in false twilight: I saw Bron only by the whiteness of her face now, and her hands that floated, disembodied.

"You like me, Toby?"

"Ay ay."

I heard the rustling of Ma Bron's skirts, saw the brightly flowered dress mystically rise, and heard her gusty breathing. Parched in the throat and trembling, I watched: it was like an evaporation of the soul.

"Would you like to make love to me, Toby Davies? — I called you in special, ye know — Sam being absent."

"The deacons'll have us," I gasped.

"The deacons never got Sam Jones," said she.

We stood apart; the world died in our breathing. My loins knew the old, stifling sensations; as iron is forged to heat and shape, and my hair was standing on end.

"You ever done this before?" She approached me, a wraith of wickedness in flouncing petticoats. My heart thumped in my throat, as she added, "After we've finished up here I'll take ye downstairs for a bowl of custard an' apricots. You like apricots?"

"*Diawch*," I said, "I go daft over custard and apricots."

"Dear me," said she, "this is going to be a blutty tricky one."

87

There was a place of childhood that I remembered, and here the harvest stooks had been set; on the evening I came to watch the mad hares dancing.

There was a man and a girl, laughing in the wheatfield, and I watched, aged nine, on a day's outing from the workhouse. The bodies of these two matched the gold of the autumn; the man was big, his shoulders naked, muscular from reaping: the girl's arms were round and smooth, her skin as lustrous as ironed satin, as was Ma Bron's under my hands, in that sunlight.

Never before had I touched a woman's breasts; it was a sweet and awful ecstasy.

And so, as my two lovers mated, the girl's hair became entwined about the body of the man in lovely wreaths of shape, even as Bron's hair, fallen about her, became a richness in my hands.

Later, the man and girl rose and walked away. Examining the stubbled wheat where they had lain, I could trace the outline of their bodies; the fulfilment, for me, of all things beautiful. I was spent, almost by the contemplation of such beauty, for the man had made love to his girl with singular respect: and she had been gentle with him, undemanding and quiet. Later I touched the ground, and it was still warm as if vibrant with life.

Ma Bron's loving was not like this; it was tempestuous, like people gasping.

Suddenly she twisted herself out of my arms and flung herself away on the bed; in that light her eyes were green, the shadows deep in her breast.

"Jakes alive, fella!" she gasped, "you don't give much away, do ye?"

Hating myself for my inadequacy, I sat there, head bowed.

"You're tighter than old Dick Jones, mun, and he bottles his water."

If only she would be quiet, I thought desperately, I could imagine, in this dim light, that she was Nanwen.

"You ain't a patch on Sam Jones, ye know — pays his respects to me, do Sam, and proper."

I raised my face. It was sad and vulgar to sit there half dressed and half a man. Bron said softly:

"You'm just a little boy, ain't you, Toby Davies? — you'm damn useless to a girl, so be off!" Rising, she flung my clothes at me. "You ain't grown up yet — go on, blutty hop it!"

And I didn't get my custard and apricots.

The town was deserted of decent people as I went home.

Yet, I thought, I had known her, my first woman: it brought to me a sweet, sad sense of pride.

She might, in dreams, almost have been Nanwen.

Yet, amazingly, for all my first love's failure, I knew a strange and secret contentment — that it had been with Bron . . .

13

The winter sky was jewelled like a crown above Llanberis Pass. Heaped with snow drifts, the galleries of slate howled their desolation. January swept out February 1901 in icy blasts; March came in with her soprano arias.

The town froze. Icicles hung gleaming over the Ogwen river; the trees creaked their scarecrowed branches under frosted moons. Silent was the Big Hole, a refuse heap of ghosts. The little cottages were barred against the cold, but the turrets of Penrhyn Castle glowed with light, its lawns sparkled to the great occasions, now the military were in Town. Elegant were the scarlet uniforms of the Hussar officers; beautiful were the coloured dresses of their ladies.

Despite the dirty old strike, Nanwen was very pretty about now, being peaches and cream and dainty in the front, as women generally are when carrying. Sometimes, when she was stretching up for the washing-line, there was a fullness in her. Not that Ben appeared to notice, since he was busy drawing up Combination meetings and writing his political speeches for the Public Hall. Very simple it was for me to pretend that the baby was mine, so I became careful with her lifting and carrying, and mind you don't fall, *fach*, in case you damage the brain, and more than once Grandpa raised an eye and Nanwen herself looked at me very old-fashioned.

A lot of funny things were happening in Bethesda about now.

Grandpa, for one, was acting queerer than most.

"Ah well," said he, after breakfast, "time I was off." And he smarmed down what was left of his hair in the mirror and put his teeth in.

Off to work, was Grandpa: with the town on strike and the Big Hole deserted, he was off on shift; it had been this way with him for the past fortnight.

Fear was in Nanwen's trembling hands, as she glanced at Ben.

"Leave him," said he, doing his Union books.

"But it isn't sane!"

"Leave him, I say!"

I got up from the table. A cold winter mist was swirling down the Row; most of the strikers were still abed, their doors shut tight against the wind. Above the slate tumps the Glyders were suffocated in cloud; hoar frost from the night sparkled like diadems on the walls. Making a big occasion of polishing my boots, I asked:

"Shall I come, too, *Taid*?"

The old name stilled him as usual; I rarely called him this.

"Ach, no, son — it's an old 'uns parade. The agent wants advice on the Sebastopol gallery, ye see?"

"Are they having trouble there, then?" asked Ben, writing.

"Well, the face has stopped dead," explained Grandpa. "The thirty-five slope changed to forty-eight a month back — more'n ten degrees — the vein ended."

"A lamination fault?"

"Dan Morgan knows about it, for it's been hitting the bargains." He chuckled. "Yeh?"

"And they've called you in to help?" asked Nanwen, her eyes bright.

"Aye, well, we old stagers know, don't us?"

At the door he stared about him. "Anyone seen me other boot?"

"You'd go better with both of them on, old china," called Ben.

For weeks now he'd been boning his new boots with ox-blood paste, making them shine: it had set us back, but he had to have a new pair; the old ones were snapping at the furniture. Nanwen said now, kneeling:

"It must be under the table."

"If it was I'd have seen it," I said, for this was my bedroom.

Ben said, "Now come on, Grandpa, you can't lose something as big as a boot!"

But Grandpa could, and I was the one who found it.

It was on the top shelf of the dresser, hidden behind the photograph of Grandma.

"Poor little man," said Nanwen.

Guto Livingstone, in Seven Caerberllan, due for a belly full of Accumulation Pie (this being Saturday night) finished off his bread and dripping and sat with his little dump of a missus by the grate: warming their hands to a fire not there.

" 'Evenin', Guto," said Ben and I coming in with the Union funds.

Pinched and pale, these two, taking the strike bad, people said, and I'd give him bloody Penrhyn if I could lay me hands on him, said Mrs. Livingstone, whose English name was Bid.

"Now now, my South Sea island beauty," whispered Guto, light in the head, and she sniffed her disgust and heaved up her rags like a nag in a bone-yard.

"Soon I will take you away from here," said Guto, "to a lovely place on the rim of the world."

"Risca would do," she replied, "though it ain't the end of the earth — anywhere away from this bugger up in Penrhyn Castle."

We entered on tiptoe, Ben and I, so as not to fan her wrath. "Things not goin' so good, Mrs. Guto?" asked Ben, and she upped and flounced about.

"Well, it's indecent, ain't it? Once he promised me the earth, but I didn't get farther than blutty Bethesda."

"One day, my lovely," whispered Guto, looking at his maps. "Venezuela don't appear so bad, ye know, my little concubine?"

"Likely he'll land me in Blaenau Ffestiniog, the daft nit," said she. "Dreams, all dreams — what you doin' there, Irish?"

Ben and I were counting out the Union money.

"Three and tenpence, missus," I said.

"Three and tenpence — the Union dues? What the hell can a woman do on three and tenpence?"

"The fare to Boston has dropped to three pounds, mind," said

Guto. "Oh, to see the sun rise on the Allegheny in Pittsburgh!"

"With this idiot here and the children crying upstairs?"

"It's all the Union can afford, woman," said Ben.

Mrs. Guto Livingstone lowered her head and fought her tears, saying, "Down south it were better'n this — God Almighty!"

"Mind, they don't get strikes in Italy, people say," mumbled Guto. "The Pope's in charge of the Union."

I said, touching her, "Perhaps it will end soon, Mrs. Guto."

She raised her tear-stained face. "Life, you mean?"

"Don't cry," said Ben, "it anna fair — not with people here."

She was from the south; talk had it that women didn't cry north of Corris; leastwise, not in company. Now she said:

"All my life I been on strike for something or other. What for now?"

"Guto will explain it," said Ben.

"Guto? Half the time he ain't even here!"

"May our enemies never be as happy as us, I say," said Guto. "You ever been to Spain, Ben O'Hara?"

His wife said, "There's fine slate for the taking and the quarry stands empty. In the Eastern Valley it were the same — business wanting coal an' the seams gone wet."

Said Ben. "Now listen to me, woman — whether ye know why he's out or not, it doesn't matter, sure to God. What matters is that he can't go in. So will you stick it, eh?"

"By God, Irishman, ye ask a lot," said she, hands screwing. "I got two kids upstairs, remember."

"Some women have six. Now answer me — on three and tenpence a week, will ye stand for the Union? A week, a month, a year? I need it for this book."

And Guto said, smiling into her face, "You only got to ask, girl — I got the whole world waiting for ye. Now, wouldn't I look a dandy wi' a fez on me head in Persia? Ach — with you beside me, my little belly dancer, I'd sail on a board to Alaska, or on a catamaran across the China sea. Now then!"

She said, "Do ye hear that? Dear God, I got trouble!"

"But will ye stand, woman? — that's the point. You're sane, so answer me — will you stand if the Union calls?" asked Ben.

Sighing deep, she put the pencil into Guto's hand.

Pity, I was finding, is something you don't expect from God.

"Is this for the tickets?" asked Guto, vague.

"That's right," said she. "We're away on elephants to Africa, and I'm as addled as you — sign your name."

Ben's distribution area of strike money, I discovered, was generally Bethesda South: thus, with fifty or so sub-treasurers doling out the money, nobody could abscond with a fortune. We even had a couple of Union clients in Tregarth — one, of course, just had to be in the cottage next door to Sam, and out came his father and reviled us as loafers and layabouts: I saw Sam's mother grieving her breast by the fire, but no sign of Sam, thank God. Next, it was our privilege to call on the great Mr. Parry — he who could have earned thousands a year in London, shared every humility with his quarrymen, and carefully signed for his few strike shillings. It was then that we remembered our own strike pay, and that of the Arses in Number Two Caerberllan, so we made back home damned frozen.

Bang bang on the door of Number Two and it opened an inch on a chain and there was Albert Arse peeping through the crack as bare as an egg.

"*Diawch!*" said he with his lovely valley accent, "it's the Combination man, get your socks on, Annie."

"Six shillings from the Union," said Ben, and I followed him into their kitchen, and there was the tin bath by a shining grate and Tommy and Rosie Arse, aged six, splashing within it, also the triplets, Miriam, Dan and Agnes, and not a stitch between them; with Mrs. Annie Arse swilling them through the suds as fast as she could catch them, and them playing 'touch me last' in shrieks, and I've never heard such a commotion since the Ladies' Guild got into Handel last Easter.

"You got a penny for me, Uncle Toby?" This from Agnes, climbing up my trews.

"Sherbert dabs, mind — you promised," cried Miriam, and she dripped through my lace-holes.

94

"Ain't they lovely?" shouted Mrs. Arse, hugging Rosie. "A pity, ain't it, that they 'ave to grow up into people?"

"Tom's doin' it in the bath again, Mam," yelled Rosie, and I saw in her child's breasts the woman she was going to be as she splashed and screamed.

"How much did ye say?" asked Annie, belting Tom.

"Six shillings," I replied, and she laughed, her head back.

"Six shillings to feed this lot? Reckon old Pharo spends more on snuff." She pushed back her hair from her shining face and steadied Miriam; whipped the towel off the fire-guard, and hugged her into it, eyeing us. "That right we've got traitors going back to work already, Ben O'Hara?"

Ben raised his great dark eyes at her. "Not true."

She nodded. "Only wondered, see, 'cause when the kids get skinny the *bradwrs* come out, ye know."

We stared at her, and she smiled, adding, "And when the traitors come out you can count on me . . ."

Albert said, appalled, "Annie, you can't mean that! *Break strike?*"

"Aye." Tom fought to be free of her now, and she tucked him under her arm. "I've had nothing but trouble since you landed me up in Bethesda, remember? — and I don't need more." She swung to us on her knees. "My chap here don't drink nor smoke nor chew, yet we don't own a penny piece to bless us, and all I hear about is you and your damned Combination."

"Please don't swear, Annie," said Albert.

Now she rose, hands on hips. "Don't swear, eh? You're dreamers, you men — the bloody lot of ye, so now I'm tellin' you something. Before my kids go on the starve I'm on me knees to Penrhyn or share an agent's bed."

"Annie!" Albert covered his face.

Lifting the strike money she slammed it down on the table. "Pinch and scrape and beg? Not me, mate — I'm a Bow Bells cockney. I don't fight for Wales, Bert — I don't even speak the lingo."

Albert was instantly beside her, patting and smoothing her while the children wallowed and plunged, but she pushed him off and said:

"Sod you for bringing me here, Albert!"

95

As struck in the face, he stared at her: then, uncertain, he stroked her arm, cajoling her:

"It will be all right, Annie, me love. Things'll change, you see. Only yesterday Lloyd George said . . ."

"And sod him, too."

Silence in a dripping of water. The children, bereaved, gaped up.

We waited within the indecision of her troubles, and Ben, shifting uneasily, said, "The point is this, Annie, we need the women: sure as faith, we'll win if the women stand . . . just put your name in this book . . .

"Count us out, O'Hara, I'm signing nothin'!"

We turned to Albert; in the silence of pent breathing, he almost hid his face.

"Well," asked Ben, the pencil towards him.

"It . . . it's what my woman says, really . . ." said Albert.

They were still apart when we left them. The naked children, scared at the rift, stood like white aborigine statues about them.

Outside in the Row, I said to Ben, "That's one family we've lost. You've got two good traitors there when Penrhyn offers bribes."

"Don't you believe it," said he, and ticked Albert's name. "She's a Londoner — she's had all this before. When those kids get hungry she'll give him bloody Penrhyn."

14

PEOPLE SUFFERED A lot during that first winter of the Strike; few realised that there would be two more strike winters to come.

The place was freezing solid now, with ice outside and hunger within; some, like poor old Tam Dickie, the roadsweeper, froze all through. Yet the snow-drops brought to the mountains a tiny hint of spring.

"Is that you, Tobias?" asked Tam, leaning on his broom that dull old day.

"Christ," I whispered, and made to slope off, for I knew he was going to tell me about his missus leaving him again.

"Aye, it's me, Tam," I said, stamping for warmth and steaming.

"My missus 'ave left me, ye know?"

He'd told me eight times already, poor old sod, but I steadied him in the High Street to the blustering shoves of the wind. With his moleskin hat and long black coat he could have put the broom through his knees and gone round chimneys. A vixen shrieked from the hills; I thought it was a witch.

"Sorry in my heart I am, Tam," I said.

He snuffled at me. "Roadsweepers anna good enough for some people."

Nothing to do with road sweeping, I thought: his missus, half his age, got up one morning and put on black stockings: she had a run in the left leg. When she came home that afternoon she had the run in the right leg, and there was at least one randy baker up in Sling.

I waited upon his suffering. "You never see her now, then?"

"Gone three weeks — she entertains gents, ye know."

It was his second wife; rumour had it that she was living in Manchester; that Tam paid her like the others — five shillings a visit.

He turned his grizzled face to the pale stars; they were cold enough that dusk to faint right out of the sky. "She's a good girl, really, ye know — I know her, see — she anna doin' nothing wrong, though she's up in Manchester." He munched his iced whiskers at me. "Just that she married a bit young, eh? It were my fault, really."

"Tam," I said, "I got to go."

"Dear me," he said at the snow. "There's empty I am without my girl."

I was tiring of him. Youth has scant respect for troubled age.

"You've still got your daughter, though."

He brightened, wiping his eyes. "Ay ay, I still got my Elida. She's at Llandegai School now, ye know — one of the Penrhyn's scholars."

"Aye," I said, dull.

Because he was a roadsweeper she used to pass him in High Street on her way home from school.

I took off my hat to him.

The children were singing in the High Street near the police station, baiting Ugly Dic: the broken-teeth urchins of the terraced rows thronging outside the shop of Mr. Clark the Photograph, and in his window I saw the notice:

'The people whose photographs appear below owe me money.'

Distantly, behind me now, the children began to chant:

> *'Mae'r ffordd yn rhydd i ni*
> *Mae'r ffordd yn rhydd i ni*
> *Waeth be ddywedo'r plesmon*
> *Mae'r ffordd yn rhydd i ni.'*

(The way is clear to us. No matter what the policeman says. The way is clear to us.)

It was a funny life, I thought: the Queen's cavalry prancing down empty streets while the people starved behind their battened windows; the Bethesda police threatening us with their batons while the deacons were powerful on their knees in chapels; and Madam Good Thing had a notice over her bed saying *Thy Will Be Done*.

Everything was upside down in Bethesda about now, I reckoned.

With the place still on strike, Nanwen had her baby; even that, being a breech birth, didn't come out right.

"What's wrong with you, then?" asked Ben O'Hara.

"Nanwen's crying," I said.

Never have I heard a woman cry in labour like Nanwen.

Grandpa said, after the third day, "They're a sight longer than most in getting that baby, mind."

Dour and glum, Ben worked on his Union ledgers, and there was no sound but the wind wolf-howling in the eaves of Caerberllan, and Nanwen's crying in the room upstairs.

"It's a first baby — sure to Jesus, it's bound to be difficult, the sweet mite," said Ben.

I was tortured by inner fears; every sound of her wracked me. Once I had looked through the door of the bedroom where the midwife and the neighbours had gathered around the bed like assassins over a bomb, and I heard Nanwen calling for her mother.

"Can't you do something for her, Ben?"

He emptied hands at me. "What? It's women's business."

"It's yours," I said.

"One day you'll have your own woman, then you'll know."

Aye, I thought, and I'll treat her better than this.

Presently Nanwen stopped her crying, and another began to cry, and the house was stilled. I slept, and the crying of this new one did not disturb me; in the morning, when I came out from under the table, they told me it was a girl.

Later, the women brought it down the stairs, billing and cooing and handing the thing around. It had a red face, a behind like a prune, and bags under its eyes like the flesh-pots of Jerusalem; I couldn't bear to look at it, for the pain it had given Nanwen.

At night they took me in to see her, and she was feeding it; I turned away my face; I could not bear to see her breast in that predicament.

"Isn't she lovely, Toby? See now, she's the spit and image of Ben!" and she humped the thing around her shoulder to bring its wind up.

Away out of this: up through Tregarth and away for a walk up the mountain to clean places, me.

The sly contagion of my love could not have touched my face, for Nanwen didn't appear to see it: better things were afoot to please her mind — Ben O'Hara and her baby, Ceinwen.

Spring sped away on skimpy feet; people grew thin. Summer came, fanning live along the hedgerows, bringing June, and it was Traitors' Day.

Like flocks of birds wheeling and cawing over the valley, the people were on the march, to watch the scabs come in. Grandpa, preparing for his shift that never was, rushed out down the Row, and back again.

"Ben, there's hundreds coming!"

Like a bear at feed Ben lurched into the Row.

"So Penrhyn was right, then," said Nanwen, rocking Ceinwen.

"He give us fair warning," said Grandpa, "he pinned it up on the gates. He said he'd break the strike."

"If he pays scabs to work, there'll be a bloody riot," growled Ben.

"Five hundred and fifty starting today," I said.

"You know, and I don't?"

"Sam Jones told me."

"And wouldn't he be the first to know? The fella's a scab like his feyther, ye realise that, I suppose?

"He is not!"

"God Almighty, Toby — do ye want it down in writing? He's a scab, I tell you — only the night before last I saw him in the public, listening to Young, the agent."

"That doesn't mean he's a scab!"

Nanwen said, "Leave it, for God's sake," and she sighed.

"Aw, well," said Grandpa, "I'd better be off."

I followed him down to the gate of the Row, to see the Old Loyals coming in to break the strike.

"Dear me, Toby," said he, patting his chest, "if only people didn't 'ave to breathe."

I restrained him. "With the blacklegs going in, is there need for you today?"

"*Duw Duw*," he wheezed, "your grandad was behind the door when Jesus handed out breath."

"Then stay in today, *Taid*."

"*Diawch*, no! I got to earn me money, man — Penrhyn's paying us over the odds as it is."

I watched him going through the gate and over the river to the quarry.

The road to Betws was clattering to boots.

They were coming from Rachub and Gerlan, from as far afield as Llanberis and Dinorwic, from Llandegai Mountain and Pentir: the Penrhyn quarrymen, as if summoned by a distress rocket — on strike for better wages — all came down to the Big Hole, to watch the scabs go in.

The *Daily News* had it, so did *The Clarion*: Young, the agent we hated, was handing out papers, and it was pinned up on the Works gate — the strike was broken and the men were going back, he claimed. To enforce the lie, Colonel Ruck's special constables were marching three deep along the Bethesda pavements, batons at the ready; a phalanx of blue ready for battle.

The cavalry of the military, straight from the stables of Penrhyn Castle, jingled along High Street; sunlight flashed off the scarlet coats and drawn cutlasses. But the Workers' Combination was out on the streets, too, flourishing their banners of the Benefit Clubs and Lodges, marching in step to the beating of drums: Bethesda was crammed like a netful of shrimps that day; every quarryman for miles had come in, their moleskin and corduroy coats and trousers scrubbed white for the occasion.

By midday they were heading for the bridge of Ty'n-Twr over the Ogwen, yelling the scab song at the top of their lungs, taunting the five hundred who had come to break the strike. Flanked by the prancing Queen's Bays they came, lining the route where the scabs had to pass, with urchin children doing cartwheels in the gutters and wives shrieking encouragement.

"I'm coming, too," said Nanwen. "I'll get Ceinie."

"You're staying here, woman," commanded Ben.

"I'm coming, I say — I'm in this as much as anyone."

At the bottom of the Row the sounds of the men grew louder. Insults were bawled in Welsh and English, as Young, the agent, arrived. Men were chanting, "Pharo, Pharo, *Pharo!*"

Ben said, "I've got to go. Mr. Parry'll be needing me, sure he will — look, will you stay with her, Toby? She's a mad woman in this mood."

Slamming the door behind him he ran down the Row.

Leaning against the door, I faced Nan, barring the way. "It's safer here."

"Pharo's splitting the town into two," she said at nothing.

"That's the way slate-masters work."

"Aye, well, I can forgive him for closing his works because they belong to him, but now he's dividing the town, I'm behind Ben."

"That's how it should be."

She approached me; never had I been so close to her. All I had to do was to reach for her, and she would be in my arms. Faintly, I heard the sounds of the mob, the marching boots, the cheering. With her eyes on my face, Nanwen pressed the latch; the door opened, struck my shoulders and slammed shut again: automatically my arms went about her and my lips were on her face.

It was as if I had struck her. Leaning away, her eyes opened wide.

"*Toby!*" she whispered.

I kissed her lips: gasping, she twisted her face this way and that, fighting to breathe, then pushed me away, to stand staring, in disbelief.

"Toby, for God's sake!"

Beautiful she looked standing there with her hand to her mouth and the redness flying to her cheeks.

"I . . . I am sorry."

"And I should think so!" She was trembling, searching for lost words. "Upon my soul, I'd never have believed it!"

The sounds of the road beat between us.

I said, "Couldn't help it, Nan. I love you."

It was out. Her eyes, wide and beautiful, searched my face.

"It's the truth," I said. "I do . . . I love you."

"Aye, well . . ." she turned away, her fingers twisting together in panic. "Sometimes you don't say things. . . ." Her eyes were hostile now. "Not fair on Ben, is it?"

"I want you," I said.

"And don't say that, either! — d'you hear me? You start talking that way and perhaps you'd better go from here."

Coldness came between us like frost on a rail, yet my craving grew for her: the desire for Ma Bron compared with this had been as nothing.

I replied, "Perhaps I'll go, like you say, but it won't change things. I'll always love you and you'll always know it."

She was trembling. I sensed, within her anguish, something more than an affront; there was in her a growing indecision, and she was knowing its agony. Instantly I wondered if she was suffering the eternal longing that I had grown to live with, and suddenly, without reason, I knew her wish for me: it lay in her eyes, wide open, fixed upon my face.

"Nan!" I caught her hand, but she snatched it away.

"Oh, God, no . . . !" She began to tremble.

Still staring at me, she moved away, leaning against the wall, and she was trembling more. I had scarcely touched her, yet it was as if I had possessed her.

Distantly, a whisper in the room, came the chanting of the mob.

"One day," I said. "You see — one day."

"Toby, go — please go now, eh?"

I turned my back on her, not trusting myself. The shouting of the people beat about me as I leaned against the door, outside in the loneliness.

I was up at the railway line when the scuffling broke out: either side of the line was packed ten deep with quarrymen when the Penrhyn coach came through with Pharo's engine pulling. And Ugly Dic was there with the dragoons in mounted groups, their eyes like needles. The sun burned down on a turbulence of swaying men, threats and cries.

Pushing my way to the line, I saw the end of the coach come open: Lord Penrhyn appeared, resplendent in his morning coat and top hat. Hands on hips, with Young, his agent, beside him, he calmly surveyed the scene about him. A cool bugger this one, give him that. As if in recognition of this, the mob grew quiet.

And in this quiet another group of men, the strike-breakers, marched two abreast up the railway track towards Penrhyn.

The crowd grew to silence; even the trees stooped, listening. The traitors approached; at the steps of the coach, they stopped. And Lord Penrhyn deliberately counted silver and put it into the hand of the first traitor.

And, as the man took it a voice yelled from the crowd:

"*Bradwr!*" — meaning *traitor*.

The name was taken up by the mob. "*Judas!*"

One by one the strike-breakers came up to Pharo to receive the bribe, and, as each one took it, the cry echoed around the valley:

"Judas! *Judas!*"

And then I heard Ben's voice and saw him standing on a crag. With his arms up he shouted, "Repeat their names, men — record their names!"

With bowed faces the *bradwrs* went up to Penrhyn for their bribes, and as each man held out his hand, his name was bawled by the quarrymen:

"John Job Williams!"

"Judas!"

"Will Evans!"

"Judas!"

"George Shenkins!"

"*Judas Iscariot!*"

"Silas Jones and Samuel Jones!"

I pushed men away, peering through the craning heads. Sam Jones and his father took their bribe side by side, and I yelled with the mob, "Judas, Judas Iscariot!"

Other men I knew, respected men, were coming for the money.

The mob was pressing around the little train now, jeering and threatening Penrhyn and his agent: more and more men came up to receive money: he was dividing the town. Over five hundred men took bribes; two thousand more refused them.

Men I respected came up to Pharo, their hands out, their faces low. Dick Patagonia was one (recently come to the Hole). But I didn't expect to see Harri Ogmore. I didn't even know he was here.

Leaning against the Ogwen bridge, I said, "Bloody hell, Harri — *you*, of all people!"

"I got two kids, mind!"

"Albert Arse has five. Christ, you make me sick!"

He slouched away. Others went by in groups to prevent attack, followed by jeering workers: Silas Jones and Sam, my mate, stopped and faced me.

"They paid thirty bob for Jesus, Sam — remember?"

"My mam . . ." The quarrymen pushed and shoved about him, shouting into his face.

"Your mam would rather die first, and you know it," I said.

I saw the hurt in his face. Turning away, Sam followed his father.

By nightfall the quarrymen were painting it on trees, stretching it in banners across the lanes, writing it on walls:

TRAITORS' DAY — 11TH JUNE 1901. *REMEMBER*.

Five hundred and ninety-four workers broke strike that day — among them 242 quarrymen, 82 labourers, 68 mechanics and 117 old men and boys, but Grandpa, although he went to work that day, wasn't among them.

"Time he was back, eh?" said Ben that tea-time. "Any minute now," I said at the clock.

But my grandpa did not come, even with darkness.

The Row was quiet, as if ashamed; the wind played his soprano song in the eaves, like a sobbing child.

"Bethesda will regret this day," said Ben, fist on the table.

"What do you expect of folks?" asked Nan. "Hasn't the strike been on long enough when the children begin to starve?" Drawn and pale was she, her eyes raising in accusation at me over the starched, white cloth.

And then, racing footsteps: a pail went clattering down the Row. A man's cry, and somebody calling my name:

"Toby Davies, *Toby Davies!*"

They brought Grandpa in on a board and I raised the white sheet that covered his face.

"Dead?"

"Aye, dead," said Mr. Morgan, and turned away.

"Bring him in," said Ben.

The men moved, looking from one to the other of us with searching apprehension. One said, "He's in a bad state, man, it was six hundred feet . . ."

I said, "He should have died easy, ripe with years . . ."

Nan began to cry, softly at first, then almost hysterically, her hands over her face.

I asked, clutching Grandpa's hand. "But what happened? How . . . how did it happen?"

"Folks saw him on the edge of the drop," replied a man. "One moment he was there, next moment gone. He isn't the first to jump because he got no wages."

"Bring him in," repeated Ben, but Nanwen cried:

"No, please! Not inside, I couldn't bear it." Lifting Ceinie she turned away horrified. Ben said, his voice rising:

"Would ye lay him out in a field then?"

"Oh, God, this dreadful place!" Nan whispered, and turned to us, her eyes wild. "Take him somewhere else . . . please!"

"Take him where, woman?" Ben stared at her.

"Leave it," I said.

"Indeed I will not!" Ben turned Nan to face him. "Ye'll act like any other woman. The dear man'll come in and you'll lay him out, so ye will." He peered at her. "This is his home. What's wrong with you, in the name of God?"

Nan was sobbing. Annie Arse coming closer, said:

"It isn't given to everyone, Mr. O'Hara, so don't expect it." She stroked Grandpa's face. "I'll lay you posh, won't I, little man?" She nodded, and the men took Grandpa in.

Later, we took him over to Coetmor and laid him in the grave they kept open for the next Big Hole accident, and he don't have to breathe down there, said Albert Arse.

I was a bit suprised about Nanwen.

The women I'd become used to took their share of death.

15

THAT SUMMER MA BRON was prettier still, and to hell with the dirty old strike, said she, I ain't lowering the birth rate for anyone, and she went up High Street past the Public Hall with her skirt billowing and bonnet streamers fluttering, very prominent in the breast, and flourishing in the stomach.

Diawch, I thought, that was a close one. I wonder who got her like that?

Having missed it by inches in one way or another, there was a rising sap in me for anything in skirts about now, and Ma Bron had a wink on her that was more like a promise. And since I was still in love with Nanwen but so far getting nowhere, I'd settle for a smile from her and a romp with Bron, given the chance. Now Bron stopped before me, all dimples and peaches and cream, looking gorgeous, but it was clear, even to one in my need, that she wasn't in the running.

"How gets?" said she, taking off the boys, and I stood my decent act for her, but wary, for ladies in this predicament are usually after husbands.

"Dear me," she added contralto, and patted her stomach, "you're a pretty lad and no mistake, Toby Davies, 'cause I've gone off old Sam Jones now, the blutty *bradwr*."

Her talk was different from Nanwen's. Nan's speech was cultured, like her nature — the close-knit texture of the biblical Welsh, and with the high lilt of the Lleyn Peninsula, said Grandad once. Bron's was rough, tainted with the voices of the valley immigrants of the south — English accent, Irish, too, troubling the true Welshness.

"Do not call Sam that," I said.

"Why not?" The smell of her perfumed the wind and fluttered me down to my lace-holes. "Taking the Pharo bribes, ain't he?"

"His mam's ill," I said.

"Needing an operation, poor soul, they say," and she patted her stomach again. "Dear me, don't we all? Ah well, as long as I can stand near enough to the tap to draw the Waterloo best brew. Sam's the father, ye know — or maybe that gent in Bangor — or even you — I'm not real certain. Got to take it as it comes, don't we?" Head on one side, she smiled prettily.

Does spunk lie in the burly redcoats who had faced the Boers? Or did it lie in Ma Bron, who laughed her way through trouble? I wondered.

"You like to marry me, Toby Davies?"

"*Diawch*, mun, I'm not particular."

"That's what I thought." She sighed deep and addressed the front of her. "Oh, well, me lovely, we'll 'ave to make the best of it, won't we? Goodbye, *bach*."

"Goodbye," I said.

Mooching around, without the price of a drink, I watched the dragoons for a bit, until I saw them watching me; then I walked on, leaning into the wind, and the sunset was playing *paint me up in blood* with the trees; there was in me an emptiness for Sam Jones, and I reckon he was empty for me, now his mam had cancer.

Men were on the streets as I returned from Tregarth, the *Village of Traitors*, and here the little houses had screwed tight their doors and windows, as if in shame: a few loungers were on the walls, dangling their boots and eyeing me, for not many Bethesda folks hit Tregarth these days. Slowing me down outside the cottage where Sam Jones lived, I saw, through a chink in the curtains his mam in her rocking chair and his da at the table getting into his Bible. I hung around for a bit, hoping Sam would come out, but he didn't.

Later, I went back to Caerberllan, for it was rushing in thunder under the Ogwen bridge and I was frit to death of flying vipers:

109

terrible things are these and funny what they get hold of. So I went over the river like something scalded and the first one I saw near the kissing gate of Caerberllan was Ben O'Hara, and he, like me, was going up to Town with the devil behind him. And then I remembered that it was the Long-Pay night (even if nobody got any) and that W. J. Parry, the strike leader, would be addressing us all in the Public Hall, so I leaned into the wind up to High. There, standing on the kerb to make him higher, was Dai Love Jenkins, and Mave, his missus, smarming down his hair with spit, and I'd never yet seen her with her teeth in.

" 'Evening," I said.

No answer: lost were they. The Iron Duke himself couldn't have shifted them, and I heard Mavis say, "There there, my lovely, don't be long now, staying away from Mave. Just do the old Combination and back home to me, is it?"

"Mr. Parry is speaking tonight, mind," I said.

"Got to be presentable, haven't we, *cariad*?" and she smiled her rhubarb smile. "Chest out now, stomach in by 'ere," and she tapped it. "You do know where the fruitful lie, don't you, my precious," and she patted his cheek.

Like a man to the scaffold was Dai, eyes staring.

"Smile, mun," said she, "your Mave 'as got you."

Funny thing about Dai Love Jenkins, he was the best splitter in the trade, especially when vertical, but he seemed lower by an inch every time I saw him.

Outside the Public Hall, Dico Bargoed, the old mountain fighter, now as blind as a bat, felt for my face in his darkness. Sam Demolition, leading him, smiled.

"That you, young Toby?" asked Dico.

"Aye."

Husky and light was his voice; too many throat punches. "You heard I went blind?"

"Yes, Dico Bargoed, and very sorry I am."

The men pushed and barged us and I could have struck their faces. He said, "You heard about my lad as well?"

"*Dammo*, yes — doing good, isn't he?"

His battered old face shone. "Foreman up at Scunthorpe now, you know," said he. "Only rising thirty — rolling mill foreman in a couple of years. Good stuff in him, see?" He leaned, confidential. "You ever got a minute, lad, considering the strike?"

"We've all got spare minutes, sir."

"Then slip down to Pen-y-Wen and read his letters to me, eh? They come Monday mornings regular," and he gripped my shoulder with a fist of iron. "Got to choose who shares ye business, ye see — don't need to be all over Town, do it?"

"Leave it to me, Dico," and behind me Mr. Albert Arse and Guto Livingstone were pushing up my shoulder blades. "You attending Union meetings at last?" I asked them.

"Aye, well, my Annie has sent me," said Albert. "Wants to know what's going on, and Guto wants to book on the Isle of Man ferry, poor old dab."

Thronging into the big hall the air was bee-hum with expectancy. Mr. Morgan, my old team foreman, called over the chairs, "Ben O'Hara speaking, Toby?"

"He didn't say, mister."

His bright blue eyes burned in his cherubic face. "Let's hope he's sober, eh? What's wrong with him these days, Toby?"

"Up to him, Mr. Morgan."

He eyed me. "We don't get a lot out of you, do we, lad?"

One-Pint Tossle was there with his yellow pew duster, as usual; this time thoughtful: rumour had it that one of his sidesmen had defected and become a *bradwr*, because he had a dying child — a dreadful thing to do, with God on the side of the Workers' Combination.

We pushed down the aisle for seats, me guiding Dico Bargoed; I sat down next to an old rubbisher, and he said, as grave as sin:

"Sorry in my stomach I am about Sam Jones."

"His business," I said.

"And Harri Ogmore — God, I'd never have believed it — *traitors!* And I'd 'ave put me last bob on Harri, I would."

"All right, then," I said, "but leave Sam out of it," and Mr. Morgan said, politely:

"Learn the facts before you criticise, man — you call them traitors. I prefer to know them as the men who cannot stand."

"And Penrhyn's turned Tregarth into an armed camp," cried another. "You heard they attacked Agent Young while he was cycling?"

"He'll pedal sharper, the bastard," whispered a third.

"And the blacklegs 'ave got real guns for protection now, you heard?"

"And they'll need them before this strike is over."

The conversation stopped when Mr. Parry mounted the stage; always this silence for the Quarrymen's Champion. I looked around the sea of eager faces; lined faces, many wasted by the dust disease, but all bore in their eyes the nobility of men at peace with themselves.

Reserved men, they were unlike their comrades of the south. Raised in Nonconformity, they lived by the fierce chapel creed bestowed on them by their fathers: few raised their fists to enemies, fewer splayed their boots on Saturday nights. But they were tough men, disciplined; worthy of the Combination.

"Nigh a thousand here, mind," whispered Dan Morgan, beside me, squinting around him, but I didn't really hear him.

They did not bet, these mountain men; they rarely quarrelled, nor did they mountain-fight; they were resentful, though — mainly of the English, whom they didn't understand — and of the Penrhyns in particular. They claimed, and justly, that the getting of coal down south was a Sunday outing compared with the winning of slate; but it was cleaner to die on a quarry face when the rope ran out, than gasp out your life under a fall. They sang with national fervour, and with the same joy as their southern cousins, but their melodies were more in a minor key; they laughed with the same gusty banter: their humour was bitter, tinged with irony.

Everything these men did politically, was governed by the command of W. J. Parry, the man of Bethesda. I straightened in my seat as he came to the front of the stage and raised his hand.

"Can you hear me at the back?" he called, and men bawled assent. "Then let me greet you." He paused. "Eight months we've been out now — time the strike was over, some say? Time Lord Penrhyn saw sense, say I, for people do not elect to starve for nothing. First, the decision, so keep cool heads — does the strike continue?"

Silence. A forest of arms rose all over the hall: there was no sound save the coughing of the slate refuse. Parry cried:

"Time was, you know, when this town was happy under the Penrhyns — aye — believe it, you younger ones. Aristocrat of wealth the Old Lord might have been, but he was a gentleman. Paternalistic, you say? Aye, but approachable." He emptied big hands at us. "True, he was as opposed to organised labour as his son, our New Lord. 'He's an obstinate young man,' said he, when introducing us years ago, 'try not to cross him.' And the reply from Sholto Douglas with whom we are locked in battle now? 'Let him try it, and watch out.' "

He waited for the laughter to subside. "So I think I knew, all those years ago, that we would one day enter the dark valley which engulfs us now. But, could the Old Lord return this evening to his castle, I vouch we'd be back at work tomorrow!"

I looked around the hall. Ben, I saw, his eyes glowing, his fist clenched on his knee, aching for a fight: near him sat Mr. Roberts, the Ebenezer deacon who lived in Caerberllan, his hands clutched together, as if in prayer: sinners and saints sat side by side in the Public Hall at these strike meetings.

In the quiet of starched minds Parry shuffled his papers, smiling down at us; great in strength and purpose he looked then, his fist up. "But we are not without fault, remember! Your honour was diminished when you chased the contractors out of Ffridd Gallery, and injured one with stones. It diminished further when you threatened the magistrates of Bangor. *I tell you this*," and he levelled his finger at us. "Had Edwards died — and he nearly did — men in this hall would have been hanged at Caernarfon. I command you again — no violence! This is just what the agents want; all the police are dying for an excuse to break your heads."

In the following silence came the sound of military cavalry passing on the road.

"And so," cried Parry, "what now? On strike for months, we are becoming experts in the art of the starve. In turn, though, Lord Penrhyn's profits are growing pretty thin. Indeed, it is hoped that the noble lord is going to a shadow — he'll be down, for instance, about a hundred thousand pounds for every strike year. Our children have started to die, but so has Penrhyn's soul. And if the spectre of death is only around Bethesda's corners, the mark of national disdain is on her so-called aristocracy. From all parts of Britain the subscriptions to our cause flow in: the *Daily News* is behind us, and so, now, is the London *Daily Chronicle*. And if the pittance be small when divided up into Union Relief — and I myself am not too proud to receive it — we will not cease this strike until we have gained our just objectives, and here I name them once again — a minimum of 4s. 4d. a day, abolition of the contract system of working, an end to bullying, reduction of Works fines, an annual holiday and democratic Benefit Clubs."

Cheers at this, and he cried fiercely above the roar:

"We must not lower our banner now! It must be a fight to the death with this tyrant, who can congratulate himself on the rise of the death rate here already, so there is no need for him to thin us out with the military, unless, of course, he is dissatisfied with the rise. . . ."

It inflamed them. They leaped to him, waving their fists, and cheering hoarsely; chairs and tables overturned in the rush to reach the stage, and Mr. Morgan shouted above the din:

"Slander now! By God, old Pharo will make him pay for that!"

"But it is the truth," I cried.

"The truth won't save him, lad — not from Pharo!"

Now a harmonium was playing, and the noise died into its chords; we sang again the hymn of old, in full harmony:

> 'O, God our refuge, our salvation,
> Hear this prayer in time of trouble.
> Fold Thy healing wings above us,
> Turn Thy face from our iniquities . . .
> Rise, O rise, Thou God of all creation . . .'

I hadn't seen anything of Sam Jones for weeks; although I had called a couple of times at the Penrala Bakehouse (which belonged to his uncle) I dared not call at his house. The rules had it that you couldn't talk direct to a *bradwr;* this meant finding a go-between who wasn't in the slate trade.

I was sorry for Sam, thinking about his mam.

"They tell me there's a casting out next Sunday over in Tregarth," said One-Pint Tossle, the deacon, just come out of the Ebenezer, dusting pews.

I made a guess. "Ma Bron?" I knew she belonged to the Tregarth Shiloh, because of her aunts.

"The barmaid of the Waterloo," said he.

"Bit late, isn't it? The damage is done." Poor old Bron, I thought.

"Not all is lost," replied he. "Her virtue can be recovered by a public confession; the man responsible for her sinful condition will be publicly denounced as a warning to others." He sighed. "Then, after a week or so they'll be accepted back into the congregation. It is an admonishment, not a punishment, remember."

"They'll still do it, Deacon Tossle."

"That is a lewd remark."

"It may be, but they'll still get up to it — they've been at it for a million years."

He drew himself up in his black alpaca. "I agree with the Shiloh elders!"

"Sam Jones, is it?"

This was usually an official secret; it maintained the virtue of surprise.

"You know?" he asked, affronted.

I looked at the stricken trees and longed for summer. "It'll kill his mam," I said.

"He should have thought of that before."

If animals had souls I'd be interested in their God.

16

THE QUICKEST WAY to empty a Bethesda pub or chapel, these days, was to bring a *bradwr* in; therefore I was surprised that nobody lifted an eye on the night I, a striker, took my seat in Shiloh, the chapel in Tregarth.

It was a big affair in Wales about now, this casting out; the important thing, said Mr. Morgan (now nearly blind), was to fornicate abroad like some town dignitaries, who mainly performed in Manchester or Liverpool: the biggest sin, apparently, was being found out, and, since it is usually the good girls who get into trouble, said Nan, it became a plunder of the innocents.

In the case of this particular casting out — Ma Bron and Sam — neither had cause for complaint: the pair of them should have cleared the Big Pew by inches long since.

For my part I found it astonishing how willingly the rebels comply with the rules. There sat Sam between his mam and dad, stiff-backed and pale before the Big Seat up front, with his hair combed to a quiff, his face polished with soap, and his tall, starched white collar cutting his throat.

Diminutive and furious sat Silas, on his right: on his left his mother was bowed to the agony of her cancer.

Ma Bron, on the other hand, was flourishing; even her dowdy black dress enhanced her loveliness; her comely shape sweetened her beauty. But tears were in her eyes as she turned once, and seeing me there, whispered a smile at me — immediately to be elbowed by the maiden aunts either side of her, a pair of brooms in stays.

The chapel was a box of living mahogany and black, austere stares of conviction; line by line, suffocated by the shame of the event, the people clattered into the pews: in moaning boots and funeral black the deacons entered from left and right, with the head deacon taking the Big Seat. The great room quietened in its emptiness: no sound but the coughing of the Penrhyn tubercular.

Expectant, the congregation awaited its last important member in vain.

Minutes ticked by, to no avail.

Hate, I thought, is the web we spin; nothing saves us from the snares we weave. Dai Significant on the other side of the aisle (the Englishman who felt insignificant without a Welsh nickname) stared at me in sudden realisation — that I shouldn't have been there.

Silence still; the dust-motes danced in yellow lamp-light.

I thought: aye, you are waiting for God, and He hasn't come.

In the winter night of this casting-out chapel, recently built for glory, I thought of lovely things in which to hide myself; things like Nanwen, and Fair Day in the morning.

In this black silence, with people agonised by mock virtue, I lived in a dream of sun, in Pesda's *Ffair Llan.*

I heard the happy cries of the rock vendors whose stalls, where the bright-faced children gathered, were end to end. Here, too, were the crockery salesmen shouting their wares, clanging plates together, juggling with gravy boats and moustache cups, running saucers up and down their arms in a medley of laughter: urchins ran in the lanes of my mind as I sat there, yelling their shrill insults; queueing at Mother Hughes's sweet stalls for gob-stoppers and aniseed balls, spraying the girls spare time with itching-powder and taunting them with squeak feathers and lady-teasers.

There was a merry-go-round with statue horses going up and down chased by gigantic cockerels with feathered plumes and outspread wings; circling madly in blasts of martial music, and a miniature conductor beating time. And, in the middle of the commotion I saw Ma Bron in pink with a farm yokel on one arm and a slate boy on the other, alight with the joy of the fair day.

I love the day of *Ffair Llan*, the twenty-ninth of October, and all its fun and gaiety; running breathless through the crowds with a girl in your hand is better, I think, than being lonely in Shiloh Chapel, among these unhappy people.

The dream was over. The service ended. The head deacon rose, and read:

"Deuteronomy 22, 13, 'If any man take a wife, and go into her, and hate her, and give occasion of speech against her, and bring up an evil name upon her, and say, "I took this woman, and when I came to her, I found her not a maid". Then shall the father of the damsel, and her mother, take and bring forth the tokens of the damsel's virginity unto the elders of the city in the gate.' "

The deacon straightened and gazed about the congregation. Pent and stiffened, they returned his stare.

The head deacon paused, lowering the Book.

"Rise and face me, the girl Bronwen, who is with child."

Ma Bron rose to her feet, with head erect, and the deacon raised the Book, and read:

" 'But if this thing be true, and tokens of virginity be not found for the damsel: then they shall bring out the damsel to the door of her father's house, and the men of her city shall stone her with stones that she die; because she has wrought folly in Israel, to play the whore in her father's house: so shalt thou put away evil from among you.' "

Silence again, save for the crying of the summer wind down the lanes of Tregarth, and the head deacon said:

"For a second time this girl is brought to child; and on this second occasion the man, Samuel Jones, the son of Silas, has admitted to being a partner in her guilt."

The deacon looked about him. "I quote also John, Chapter Four, recalling to you the occasion when Jesus came to the city of Sychar, resting by Jacob's well. There, you will remember, he met a woman of Samaria, and said unto her, 'Go, call thy husband, and come hither,' and the woman answered, saying, 'I have no husband.' And Jesus said, 'Thou hast said well, I have no husband, for thou hast had five husbands; and he whom thou now hast is not thy husband. . . .' "

In pent silence, the congregation held its breath, and the deacon added, "Look well upon this woman whom we are casting out. Is not she also a woman of Samaria, a paramour who will despoil herself with any man? And would not Jesus chide her also, were he present in this chapel tonight?" He looked down at Sam. "Who represents this man who was tempted, and fell?"

Silas, Sam's father, rose.

"And who represents this woman?"

One of the aunts rose, and the deacon said:

"You will escort this man and woman out of our chapel. Only when they are married will they be accepted back into this congregation."

Outside the Penrala Bakehouse (near the grocer's shop of the brothers from Patagonia), the people stood together; in the windows the curtains fidgeted and faces watched: unseen eyes moved in the road to Glasinfryn as Ma Bron and Sam Jones went up to Sling, to the house of his mother's brother. And, following them, I called to Ma Bron.

They waited, standing apart, as strangers.

The wind hit between the three of us in the light of the summer moon.

I said, "I am sorry. Nanwen O'Hara said it could happen to anyone." This I said to Bron, since I could not speak to Sam direct, he being a *bradwr*.

And Sam said, "Tell him to bugger off; we don't need no-one," and Ma Bron said:

"O, Sam, do not pester him. You do good to come, don't you, Toby?" and she leaned towards me and her warmth touched me.

I said to Bron, "Tell him I have money — two shilling saved, if he is going south, to the Rhondda," for this I had heard.

"Toby got two shilling saved, for us — you want it, Sam?"

"Tell him balls," said Sam. "I wouldn't have his two shilling if he were the last one living," and Ma Bron said:

"Oh, my precious, do not be like that."

"Tell him balls," said Sam.

"We got a baby comin', remember?" Pinched and urgent was her face.

"You got a baby coming, not me."

"Say I'm sorry about his mam," I said.

"Toby says he is sorry about our mam," said Bron.

"She's not your mam," said Sam, "she's mine."

"You stop behaving like a bloody kid," said I, "and I'll talk to you direct, Sam Jones."

Bron said, looking at the stars, "D'you know something, lads? My baby moved. Sometimes, she's so sad wi' her that I think her dead, but right then, she moved again," and she held her stomach.

Fishing into my pocket I brought out the florin and offered it to her.

"Cross your baby's palm with silver, Bron. Take it, eh?"

But Sam pushed her aside and brought down his hand and the florin ran in a circle on the road between us. Bron stooped and picked it up.

"I'll have it, Toby. I'll keep it for my Bibbs-Two," said she.

"O, Christ," said Sam, and covered his face. Bron held him.

"I got to go," I said.

"Right, then — you go — don't you stand there watching my Sam, go on, piss off," said Bron.

I took the back road through Tregarth, and I heard her saying while she patted and smoothed him, "All right, mun, he's gone. Now now, Sam . . . there there . . . Don't you cry, my lovely."

Tregarth had something to answer for, I reckon, between the pair of them.

17

MANY OF THE southerners, people born with warm blood, began to drift south again during the spring of 1902 — back to coal, boyo, they were saying, where things are easier. At least it's dry underground, they'd say — no more hanging soaked to the skin down a rock face or hammering slate in the dark with nothing but the light of a candle: no more 'dressing' the stuff in sheds full of swirling dust. Compared with slate-smoke, the killer of the lungs, a little bit of Rhondda coal dust is good for the chest, so say the coal-masters' doctors.

O, aye? I'd heard that one before somewhere, too.

But I will say this — I didn't know it then, but the getting of coal, I discovered later, was a Sunday School outing compared with the getting of slate; given the choice I'd take any pit in the country rather than work in places like Llanberis or the Great Hole. And I'd take any master thrown at me in exchange for the likes of the new Lord Penrhyn.

Summer passed; autumn came; Bethesda and her villages starved down the gold-dusted lanes. The Penrhyn quarries, unworked save for the *bradwrs*, were practically empty of men. Over two thousand quarrymen starved with their families while Penrhyn waited for hunger to beat them. By the beginning of that second winter of the Big Strike the snow was feet deep around the cottages and stamped into ice by the hooves of the patrolling dragoons, ordered into town to keep us behaving. The chapels were crammed to the doors. As with the southern cholera chapels, God, in the midst of the people's misery, was very popular.

"Mind," commented Nanwen that November, "I'll miss the southern people a lot — I've become quite fond of folks from places like Tonypandy," and she gave me a heaven of a smile.

"Don't make too much of it," said Ben, writing on the table, as usual.

"Different people, mind," said I. "Chalk and cheese, north and south, but all good Welsh."

Doing his eternal books, making the figures match, Ben raised his face. "*Arrah!* Here ye go again, you damned foreigner!"

"Is a South Walian a foreigner, then?" I asked.

"No, but it's typical of a foreigner to make a gap where none exists?" His great dark eyes smouldered at us; his white teeth appeared in his unshaven face. The coming of Ceinie had changed Ben O'Hara, for the worse.

Where he gets the money for drinking, I don't know, said Nanwen.

I could have told her: Union funds. It would have needed an accountant to balance Ben O'Hara's books.

Now he cried in his thick bog Irish, "Nationalism is splitting the world — what we want is internationalism."

"I only said that I liked the people from the south," said Nanwen, sewing. Though calm, her face was white.

He swung to me. "Different people, ye say, youngster? How different? Where?"

"North Wales, South Wales. Different blood, different cultures."

"Mark, Mary and Joseph — fancy words now! The lads are out of their drawers!"

"Ben, now mind. . . ." said Nanwen, but, he went on:

"*Ach*, come on, son — we'll mend you in the great debate and shame the illiterate among us, eh?" His black eyes danced and he reached out and thumped me with his fist. "*Culture*, eh? Barriers, d'ye mean?"

"Language, for one," I said.

"O, ay ay — any more?" He was set on trouble.

I added, "Geography and time — even the soil is different: limestone in the south, a softer people. Granite up here."

"*Ach*, be Jesus, geology now, is it? But I'm a beggar for the education, ye know, Toby — give us some more."

I fought to keep cool, saying, "The southern people have the strangers in their blood — French, Spanish, even Italian folks, coming from the east."

"Would it be a sociological question you're raising, perhaps?"

"Leave it," said Nanwen, lowering her sewing.

"I'm not leaving it, woman, I'm just getting started. Sociological?" he peered at me.

"I . . . I don't know what that means," I said.

"Do ye not, now? Isn't that the greatest pity, or I'd be pledged to listen to the wisdom of the street. Couldn't you explain to me — in the simplest of terms, ye understand — what the intellectuals consider the main and basic difference between the Welsh in the north and the Welsh in the south?" He grinned at me over the table.

The room tingled with silence; there was no sound but our breathing and the ticking of the clock. I hated him; I hated his smooth-tongued ability, his arrogance, his cruelty.

Nanwen, as if reading my brain, raised her face to me like a woman baptised, and said:

"In the south a woman will say, 'Come in, love, and have a cup of tea.' Here, we'd say, 'Would you like a cup of tea?' But the tea's the same, and so is the heart. Is that what you mean, Toby?"

I closed my eyes. "Aye."

Ben rose, smiling down at me, but I saw his trembling hands: and he knuckled his fingers as he moved around the table, like I have seen the old Cornish grandfathers do — they who got the tin and China clay, a generation of men who walked on their hands. At the door, Ben said:

"You're lucky to have a woman speak for ye, son. By Jesus, I'd give a lot to have one speak for me."

After Ben had gone, Nanwen said, "Where does he do his drinking, Toby?"

"Drinking?"

She was instantly impatient. "Yes, drinking — he's even been at it earlier tonight. And where's he getting the money for it?"

I got up and went to the window. No woman in the world is having the man out of me. Setting her needlework firm in her lap, she raised her voice. "Now listen, Toby — you men know, so answer me!"

I turned, facing her. "Your chap — you see to him!"

Momentarily, we glared at each other.

Earlier, coming down the Row I'd seen Ben shuffling home, swaying in the wind, and he'd had his Combination accounts under his arm; not my business what he was up to. Then little Ceinie, tottering on the doorstep, had seen me coming, and ran towards me, arms flailing for balance, and I'd knelt, beckoning to her.

"Come to me while I pick you up!"

More like my kid than Ben's, for he scarcely noticed her these days. She was the image of Nanwen with her fine black hair and red lips. Anyway, I'd come to think of her as mine, since Nan and I starved to keep her fed.

The child put her arms up to me again now, and I lifted her against me and wandered around the kitchen. There was a shivering of hunger in me, and I was grateful for the warmth of her. On her knees now, with a great air of independence, Nan said, "He's spending Union money, isn't he?" She furiously poked at the fire.

"You'd best ask him."

She covered her face. "Oh, God, what will happen if he is?"

"If he is they'll near kill him."

"He . . . he must be mad," she said, as if unhearing.

I put Ceinie down. "Ach, he's as weak as piss!"

"*Toby!*"

"Well, he is! Where the hell did you get him from? — couldn't you have waited a bit before lumbering yourself with a big, hairy oaf without the guts of a louse?"

She rose, white-faced. "He's my husband, so mind!"

"And you're bloody entitled to him!"

Ceinie, staring up between us, began to whimper; hail swept the window in a sudden bluster of the wind. As if defeated, Nan turned away, sinking down into the chair. Head bowed, she said, gathering

Ceinie against her, "Oh, God, I . . . I don't know what to do'.

Like a woman in mourning she looked, sitting there; even her hair was lifeless: it took a Ben O'Hara to kindle in Nanwen her youth's vitality. Raising her face, she said, "Are you hungry, Toby?"

All evening there had been a sickness in me for food; we'd all had breakfast, but it was scant enough.

"No," I said.

Heavy-eyed, she stared at the lamp. "Another month or two of this and the town will be six feet under. Old Joe Bec, the Gerlan baker, has had to close down — you heard?"

It was a brave attempt to change the subject; she would do anything, this one, to switch the guilt away from Ben. I shrugged, empty. Joe Bec was only one of dozens. Grocers had been giving away their stocks; bakers baked away their savings, milkmen left milk free for sickly children. When St. Peter tots it all up he'll give good marks to the shopkeepers of Bethesda and the villages round about.

Suddenly, Nan said, "Oh, God . . . I've . . . I've got to tell someone. . . !"

I turned back to her and she raised her eyes above Ceinie's now sleeping face, saying softly, "Do . . . d'you know Mr. Fellows, the Union man?"

"Aye — Assistant Treasurer in the Combination?"

"He came to see us the night before last."

I stiffened. "What did he want?"

"He asked to see Ben's pay books. Ben . . . Ben told him that he had to cast them up, or something."

I nodded. "Did he accept that?"

"Of course — he was very polite. But . . . he wants Ben to bring the books to his house for checking tomorrow night. Toby, what will happen. . . ?"

I said, "You'd best face it, Nan. If he's down on his money they'll sell you up."

In horror, she whispered, "The furniture, you mean?"

"Of course. These are decent men, but they'll have no alternative. It's public money, not theirs, and they're responsible to the Combination — they'll just have to take it back."

She closed her eyes as if in prayer, then whispered, "Oh, Toby, please . . . please help me."

I wandered around, staring down at her. I didn't know what to do. Pity and anger were intermingled with a fierce and growing hatred for Ben O'Hara and everything he stood for. Also, I felt disdain for Nanwen's hopeless, blind loyalty for someone who didn't give a damn either for her or her child.

I said, as evenly as I could, "I'll help all I can, you know that. But you'd best face up to it — all of it. It'll mean eviction too, you know."

She protested, "But . . . but the house is nothing to do with it. Grandpa's name's in the rent book, and when he died it passed to you!"

For a long time I'd been worried about eviction. With Ben ranting on street corners I wondered how we'd lasted as long as this: the land agent was using any excuse these days to shift out strikers and get their traitors in. And the evictions were beginning in earnest now: day after day people were being turned out into the streets. Most families just walked off. Pawning their valuables, they bought train tickets for places like the Rhondda — arriving there like immigrant Irish in the clothes they stood up in: others returned to the farmlands of the Lleyn Peninsula and Anglesey. Slowly, Bethesda was emptying. Heaven help Nanwen and Ceinie, I thought, if they found themselves homeless in the middle of winter. Now Nanwen repeated:

"Surely I'm right, Toby — they can't turn us out!"

"And me harbouring a Union throw-out under the roof?" I sighed. "That's a good situation — we'll see what Penrhyn's land agent makes of that one." Bending, I caught her hands. "I tell you, Nan — face it! The trouble becomes that much smaller if only you'll stop hoping, *and face it*."

She wept.

With Ceinie between us, I held her.

Later, when night came and Ceinie was abed, we sat together, Nan and I, and she said, empty:

"Sometimes I don't know about this place, Toby; all my life I've been in trouble with Bethesda."

Although I could not even see her face in that light, her nearness, the sweet intimacy of her presence was having an electric effect upon me.

She said, "When I was little, I remember my father going off to work at dawn — we lived Port Dinorwic then, for he was of the sea. Then he went into slate — being a ship's rigger he made a good rockman — and Assheton-Smith took him on, but he was soon transferred to Bethesda, on an exchange."

Soon, I thought, I will go from here, and all I will have left will be your voice. These are the precious moments, I thought, yet you talk, talk, when I could be making love to you. She continued:

"So he had a five-mile walk to the Hole in the morning and the same walk home at night; my mam was always at the gate to send him off, or greet him." She laughed softly. "I can see her now — she was a pretty little thing — a girl, really; she married young, like me." Her voice failed.

"Tell me," I said. There was a dryness on my throat; I was hearing her words only as echoes in the mounting intensity of my need for her. Nan said:

"Aye, well cometimes he would go off in the snow, and my mother would kneel on the kitchen floor and pray for the snow to stop; unless it did he'd get no time in, and be sent home; this meant no pay. It was a *smit* day — you heard of this?"

"No," I said. I *had* heard of it of course; *smit*, the essence of a people's misfortune, was a common word in Caernarfonshire.

"They don't use it much today," said she. "He couldn't work the quarry face in snow because of slips, though the men used to beg to do so, because they needed the money. The agents said they'd have to *submit* to the will of God. It changed to *smit*." ·

I thought, desperately; who would know, except us, if we did make love?

The wind was singing his Jenny Jones down the Row, hitting up the doors and windows in fury; in the faint light of the window moon now, I saw Nan's shadowed face and the ragged dress at her throat. She smiled wanly, saying, "It was a bad winter when I was four years old. We starved thin, like now. And when we saw my father coming with the men, we'd shawl our heads and join the other women at the gates, to greet them. They'd be soaked through, and shivering, and always the same old *smit, smit, smit.* . . . The women weren't suppose to cry, but my mother did, because she was young, and my father was ashamed of her, I remember. 'Not in front of the others, Nell,' he used to say. Then one month we hadn't a bite of bread in the house and went on the Parish and Quaker soup — and all it did was snow. Day after day Dada would go off, and come back with nothing. Then, one day, when he'd been to see the workhouse clerk, he came home with the others, and he was crying." She stared at me, wide-eyed. "If you'd known my father you'd have known what that meant. In front of everybody, even his mates, he was crying. My mother took him indoors and got the towel and wiped his face and said it was the rain, but he couldn't stop crying."

I closed my eyes. Nanwen said, "I was hungry. It was a terrible winter, that one — fifty *smits* on the run."

I didn't reply. She added, "Mind, my mother never cried again — not after that."

We sat in silence, listening to the wind. Eventually, she said:

"It's worse this time — a two-year strike. Where would we be without the *Daily News* and the choir subscriptions?"

I thought; one day, I will take you from here, and there will be no more hunger.

"You gone to sleep, Toby?"

"No."

"Terrible about Annie Arse and her little lot, isn't it?" she hugged herself with cold.

"First little Agnes and now Miriam. Do you think I ought to go up and see her again?"

"Leave her for a day or two, she's taking it sore," I said.

I had been in myself when Agnes died — she went the same way as most of the babies we lost — a chill: without decent food they couldn't stand the winters.

Albert had put her white coffin on the kitchen table; very pretty Agnes looked in her little white dress with snowdrops in her hands: like a tiny sacrificial virgin, said Mr. Roberts, the Ebenezer deacon, who came to pay respects.

We all stood around her, I remember, in our black suits and creaking boots, empty of words while the women wept. But Annie, her mother, did not weep: there was no sound but the fury of her eyes; louder than words spoke those eyes.

Now, three weeks later — Miriam, the second of the triplets — was being buried tomorrow. Albert said, empty:

"Maybe it's best that they don't grow up into people, like Annie says."

I had touched Annie's hand. "Sorry in my heart, missus."

No reply. Trembling, Annie stood, staring down at Miriam.

"Don't seem fair really, do it — two in a month?" said Albert.

The sound of Nanwen brought me back to the actuality of the present.

"It's cold down here," she said, rising. "Best go to bed?"

I knew a wild sense of expectancy as I followed her up the narrow stairs.

On the landing, Nan turned to me; astonishingly, I was beset by a strange, heady humour. We were making so much of the pretence of living, yet folks like Sam Jones and Ma Bron just took as they pleased. People like Mrs. Knock-Twice over in Betws, for instance — kept her door unlocked for her man to come back; you only had to tap it and call yourself Fred, yet here we were revering the business of love-making like a biblical text.

"Come in with me, Nan," I said, touching her. "Just for a bit?"

There was in her face, in that dim light, an untroubled innocence.

"Who's to know?" I asked.

"I shall know."

I said, "Do you know something? You're like a little girl with a rag doll. You keep pulling me apart and stitching me up again."

"Not here, Toby." She kissed my face. "Tomorrow? Up on the mountain?"

"In two feet of snow?" We laughed together, softly, for fear of waking Ceinie, and our laughter died into uncertainty.

"Go to bed now, is it?" she said. "*Soon . . . ?*"

I entered my room. The moon, iced to the ears, was rolling drunk over the rickety roofs of Bethesda, shining her frost on the toppling desecration of Penrhyn's refuse. Undressing, I slipped into the icy sheets and lay there, staring at the yellow searchlight of a moon crossing the boards.

18

A FEW DAYS LATER, bored to death with having no work, I took myself over the fields to Bangor in a foot of snow. Strangely, my mind was filled with thoughts of Sam Jones and Bron, especially Bron, and I wondered how they were doing down south. I missed them; their friendship, I thought, was as hopeless as my love for Nanwen.

The night was as black as a raven's squawk as I passed Bodforris on my way home, and I knew something was wrong in Caerberllan when I heard all the commotion. So I broke into a run when I got through the kiss-gate till Mr. Morgan grabbed me in passing and swung me to him, and his face, in the lamplight of his door, was that of a timid nun.

"Don't go down, Toby — it's being seen to — don't go down!"

"What's happened?" I shook myself free of him.

"It's Ben O'Hara," said Albert Arse, coming up. "But the Combination men are seeing to it."

"Bring him in with us," said Annie, arms out to me, her hair in crackers.

"*Nanwen!*" I said, staring down the Row.

"It anna anything really speaking," said Mrs. Morgan, "an' it's nothing to do with us — come back to bed, husband."

I flung them aside and went down the Row at a run, and the first one I come across outside Number Twelve was Ugly Dic, the policeman, who, usually a man of dash and style, was now vacant and shivering. Guto Livingstone and his missus were there, also Bully State of Maine, who happened to be passing.

"What is it?" I cried, pushing in.

"It's the mad O'Hara," said Bully. "He's in there and bolted the door."

"Been screaming mad, she has," said Ugly Dic. "Don't you fret, Mrs. O'Hara, I'll soon 'ave you out, my beauty!" and he hammered the door, shouting for entry.

I pushed him away. My first shoulder charge splintered a panel, my next took the lock, and the frame split up; Nanwen shrieked my name as I ran at it again; the door went down, and I was in. And, as I rose, Ben came at me.

I ducked as he charged into me, overbalancing in bawling anger: his face, twisted and white, was not the face of a drunk, but a drunken madman. As I rose, his fist caught me on the shoulder, and I saw, in the moment before I squared to him, the form of Nanwen lying against the table, her arms protectively around Ceinie. People were thronging in now, women shrieking, men shouting commands. Ben came again, fists swinging, but I was up; steadier, I hooked him square with a right; it staggered him, but he shook it off and rushed again in the confined space, tripped over a fallen chair and fell headlong into me. People were pressing into the kitchen now; faintly, above their warning shouts I heard the baby screaming. Guto, with more sense than he owned, tripped Ben and held his legs, but he kicked and fought like a mad thing as I pinned his arms. Then Bully State of Maine hauled people out and knelt, adding his great strength to mine: I saw, in a flurry of arms and fists, the pale outline of Nanwen's face through the cage of her fingers as she slowly sat up against the wall: bruised and shining with sweat, I watched it uncover in the pale light of the lamp; her hands were stained with blood.

Blind fury struck me. Scrambling up, I took Ben with me. My first punch spun him against the wall, free of Bully's outstretched hands: and, as he gathered his failing strength and lurched towards me, I stiffened my legs and hit short: taking it full, he hit the floor like a sack.

Instantly, Nanwen was beside him, kneeling. Her bruised

face stared up from the floor as she turned him into her arms.

"Enough — he's drunk! Sober, he'd kill you!"

In a ring we stood; Bully State of Maine, Guto, Albert, Ugly Dic, and me. Ceinie ran to me and I lifted her into my arms. Our breathing filled the room; around the corner of the broken door Tommy and Rosie Arse, fingers in their mouths, peered in childlike contemplation.

"You all right, Mrs. O'Hara?" asked the policeman.

Nanwen nodded.

"And your husband?" he knelt.

Ben stirred in her arms, coming round. This is the trouble with drunks, they never go out though you hit them with a seven-pound hammer.

"He will be all right now. Thank you for your help. Go, please."

"You got a bad face there, missus — you want to prefer charges?"

"I tell you I'm all right," said Nanwen. "He just . . . just went mad. He wasn't hitting us."

She got up from the floor and took Ceinie from me, leaving Ben to amble up as best he could: sitting on the edge of a chair he stared at the boards in a glaze of hops, and I hated him. I hated all he stood for and all he ever was: it was all I could do to stand there and impotently watch him. He raised his swollen face to Nanwen and stupidly rubbed his chin.

"Ach, I'm sorry, me sweet colleen. Did I hurt anyone?"

She, with her face averted, said to all there, "We'll be all right. Go now — how many more times do I have to tell you?"

The policeman said, wagging a finger:

"All right, O'Hara, I'm going now, and for this ye can thank your missus. But any more rumpus and I'll 'ave you inside — it's a breach of the peace, ye know?"

After they had gone I fastened the door as best I could, and said:

"And understand this too. You're a mad drunk and you might have killed somebody. You hurt either of these two, and I'll have the liver out of ye."

"And you understand this," cried Nanwen. "It's only the drink — he'd die before he'd hurt us."

She was holding Ben now, her arms protectively about him.

"What the hell do you want of me?" I shouted.

"Now listen." She crossed the room to me. "This is my fight, not yours, and it's my responsibility, so leave it. Any damned lecturing will be done by me, too, and if you don't like it, you can go!"

Ben slumped down into a chair, grinned stupidly.

"Strikes me that'd be best," I said.

"Well, that's it, then, isn't it!" She glared at me.

In her temper, on the edge of tears, she still maintained her engaging honesty; I knew her better then, I think. Sometimes we reach our greatest understanding in the middle of our greatest loss.

Ben, vacant still, mumbled, "Jesus, me sweet man — what have I done to deserve all that thumpin'? I must have killed the Pope."

"It's all right, darling, I'm here," said Nanwen, stroking his face.

"That chap there comes storming in and belts me right and left. For God's sake, what for?"

I thought: as a man, O'Hara, you're about as useful as a fart in a breeze. What the hell did she see in you?

"Woman," said he, "what happened?"

"It's all right, Ben. I tell you, it's all right."

I left them to it.

It was freezing in the street; putting up my coat collar, I mooched aimlessly over the Ogwen and up to the Hole. The chasms and galleries yawned at me in the light of a fleeting moon; it was cold coming back, but the air, though sprinkled with icy points of pain, was like a cleansing solace to my loneliness. When I got in they had all gone to bed, and I sat in the empty kitchen for a bit, staring into the dead fire, thinking of Ma Bron and Sam Jones, and what a time it had been for them as well.

By the time I went to bed I knew what to do.

We weren't in step, Nanwen and me; we were hearing different drummers.

Best to go, before it ended in trouble.

I didn't bargain for the actions of the Quarrymen's Combination.

They came in black severity; these, the leaders of the Union. Late in the afternoon of the next day, they came — Henry Jones and Griffith Edwards, also Peter Roberts of Carneddi: William Evans came, he who had been dismissed by Lord Penrhyn for representing the men, also Robert Davies, the chairman of the 1896 Workers' Delegation. These, reserved and quiet, filed into the kitchen of Twelve Caerberllan.

And Ben sat before them, and would not meet their eyes.

They were ordinary workers like us, claiming neither rank nor privilege. But representing thousands, they had the right to order and dismiss; to complain and censure.

"Is it wise for you to stay for this, Mrs. O'Hara?" asked one.

Nanwen said, sitting beside Ben, "I want to be with my husband."

"And you?" The eyes of the committee turned to me; another said:

"There is a request that Tobias Davies be present; if necessary, as a material witness."

"You'll get nothing out of me," I answered.

"Let him stay," said Ben, cynically. "Can't ye see he's part of the family?"

They frowned up from the pages of the Combination books, and Henry Jones, the Strike Committee chairman, said:

"These accounts, entrusted to you, O'Hara, for the payment of relief to members of the Combination show a deficit of over fifteen pounds. The entries have been examined by the Strike Committee; all here are agreed upon the amount — do you admit the shortage?"

Ben nodded, his eyes lowered.

"And you cannot replace the money?"

Nanwen said, "We can sell the furniture, Mr. Jones, but it won't make fifteen pounds."

The shame of it had struck her in the face; she had the look of someone old.

"How much, then?"

Ben gestured emptily. "Say half?"

Silence. They rustled papers, glancing at one another; I hated the cruelty of it, but recognised the justice. People were on the starve; they couldn't let it pass. Mr. Jones asked:

"Has there been illness in this house?"

"None," said Nanwen. "The money went on beer."

"You knew this, Mrs. O'Hara?"

"She did not," said Ben.

I heard footsteps in the Row outside; the bass questions and replies of gathering men. Its money had been stolen; the Union demanded justice.

Mr. Jones said, "Then you admit to converting Combination strike money to your own use?"

"I stole it, man," said Ben, "is that what you want?" He grinned, rubbing his unshaven face.

I stared at Nanwen. You, I thought, will have to share your life with this. Sweat sprang to her forehead and she wiped it into her hair.

We waited. Outside the cottage door the hobnailed boots of men were growing louder, impatient for justice.

They assessed the furniture's value at seven pounds; the sum outstanding was eight pounds one and fourpence.

"In terms of ethics, it could have been a thousand pounds, you realise that," said the man Edwards. "At the time of the men's greatest need, you stole from them."

"Christ, get on with it, man," said Ben, sighing.

"They no longer need you in this community."

Nanwen's face was white, her hands clutched together in her lap.

Another said, "It would be in the interests of your safety if you left here . . ."

"Ireland," said Ben. "Out of this God-forsaken country."

"It is not God-forsaken," said Mr. Jones, "but it has been forsaken by the likes of you." He shut the accounts. "Right, then, let the Irish have you. A single fare for the two of you."

"Three tickets," said Nanwen, wearily, "I've a child asleep upstairs."

"Ah, yes."

They looked at each other with questioned finality.

One said, rising, "Leave everything as it is, Mrs. O'Hara. Take only what food you have and the clothes you stand up in. Be prepared to go this afternoon — the Committee is concerned with your husband's safety."

In the afternoon three men came and stamped their feet for warmth in the snow outside, waiting.

After helping Ben tie their bundles, I came down to the kitchen. Nanwen was standing there.

"You coming, too, Uncle Toby?" asked Ceinie, and I lifted her against me.

We moved awkwardly, contained by silence, Nanwen and me; words had vanished between us. The bruise on her cheek held me with relentless force. Above us Ben's boots were stamping the boards; the men outside were beating themselves for warmth.

"The Rhondda, is it?" asked Nanwen, empty.

"Aye," I said. "More'n likely."

"Best you go back to your father's country, eh?"

"Good people — Tonypandy," I said.

She smiled at me; her teeth were even and white against the pale curve of her lips. I said, "*Nan. . . .*"

Head on one side, she smiled at me, and I knew a sudden sense of wild joy, a strange and intimate knowledge that one day, despite all this, she would be mine: this hope, ever with me, had an uncanny will to survive.

I said, "One day I'll find you. One day, wherever you are, you'll be with me."

It was a sort of self-unity just to stand there within reach of her.

"You'll do all right, Toby."

"Aye, I expect."

"More than one you'll lead up the gospel path down the Rhondda. You go south and forget about Nan, eh?" She laughed with her eyes. "Poor old dab, like Grandad would say. Remember how he went with his trews half-mast?"

I thought desperately: *Come with me. . . .*

"Got to go," she said, taking Ceinie.

Empty of her, I stood while Ben came clumping down the stairs, and I closed my eyes to her nearness; when I opened them, hers were full on my face.

"Goodbye, my darling," she said.

I stood by the kiss-gate of Caerberllan, watching the three of them, with the Committee escorts either side, plodding through the snow to the station.

Ceinie, in Nanwen's arms, turned once to wave, but I could not wave back.

The wind was cold on my face, as I turned past Bodforris down the road to Betws, south, for the Rhondda.

Two

The Rhondda

19

If I'd had the railway fare, like others getting out of the north about then, I'd have landed in the Rhondda down in South Wales that much earlier. But, after leaving Caerberllan, and losing Nanwen, there didn't seem much point in going anywhere at speed, so I took the road to Betws and Swallow Falls at my leisure, sleeping in barns. Llechwedd called me, probably because it was there that I had first met Nan, and I stood in the snow outside One Bodafon looking at the windows, until I saw Bando Jeremiah Williams eyeing me from Uncorn, so I turned up my collar and tramped back down to High.

As the days passed into weeks I came to know myself better. A good day's tramp along an empty, winter highway, I was finding, did much to dispel my sense of loss.

I worked for a farmer for a month's lodging that saw out December; I jugged out ale in a little public on the slopes of Moel Llyfant to the collarless labourers of the old Welsh farms; listening in the candle-lit tap to tales of poaching and trespass. I wouldn't have changed them for gold, these haughty old Welsh crows of the land with their gravy-stained waistcoats and drooping whiskers.

Come next April I was still there in the tap, eyeing up the landlord's daughter and forking manure spare time, and there was a farm girl over in Dolgellau with plump round arms and hayseed on her breasts. She talked all through it about the coming Spring Outing; had she been quiet I could have imagined she was Nanwen.

The hawthorn was a shower of white blossom, I remember; and the heather blowing green waves in the wind as I took the road south again with the promise of the Rhondda and its coal slowly being forgotten in the fine comradeship of the cottage families, as I went from farm to farm, hiring out my labour.

This period of my life was like a peasant dance compared with the slog of Bethesda slate: the money was poor, the fare frugal, but my body thrived. I stayed a year in the Dolgellau country, taking labour and love where I found it, and life was good. I worked one harvest in Cross Foxes and another with a farmer and three daughters in Staylittle, and stayed eighteen months until somebody suggested marriage, and I was off again, this time south-west to Aberdovey; late winter found me with the coastal fishermen.

What is there in the sea, I wonder, that brings such a pull to the blood?

Looking back, I reckon my years between the ages of twenty-three and twenty-five, spent on the sea, were about the happiest of my life: on reflection, I've often wondered why I changed the sea for coal.

These were flounder fishermen, the sailors of the little gunter-rigged smacks that wallowed in the Dovey estuary, and, if the tide was running right, braved it east into Cardigan Bay, coming back with loaded nets and gunwales awash if the shoals were about — mackerel, herring and the little cousins of the big flat-fish — the dainty gold-backed wrigglers of the sandy inlets.

During the summer of 1909, after a year of wandering the quays as a longshoreman, I heard the shout of the Rhondda again, as if something deeper than the sea was stirring, my own people; and I kicked off my sea-boots and put on hobnails again, striking out through the narrow streets of lovely Aberdovey and up the sheep tracks of Cader Idris, the Mountain Chair of the Clouds.

Here, where the Roman legions formed after savaging Plinlimmon, I trudged in a new and marvellous loneliness, and washed myself in the tumbling brooks, the source of the Wye River; from its summit I saw the misted estuary and square-rigged schooners in the bay, where the barques and barges with slate from Portmadoc and coal from Barry lumbered into Tremadoc. South again I went, and into lovely Rhayader. Here, on a late June evening, I chopped firewood and swept out the stables of an old coaching station public on the road to Builth. It was rolling, lush farmland of fat sheep and buttocky cattle lowing for milking, and bright-faced young girls, pert and buxom. The landlord, I remember, was an old soldier from the Boer War; his missus thrived on cheek and customers — a boiling joint, if ever there was one, with a wicked eye on her and cherub lips.

It was here that I met the Wraith Girl of Rhayader: as this I still remember her.

There was a little room off the tap, and the woman was sitting on a chair in the middle of the floor. So still she sat that I wondered if she breathed; nor did she stir as I came closer with my tankard.

"You work here?" I asked; she did not reply.

She was no longer young; her face was pale, her gaze averted; I wondered if she were alive.

The sounds of the tap-room next door beat about us as I slowly circled her: amid the bass booming of men and the shrill laughter of women, this one sat as still as a fallen hand.

"You ill, missus?"

She was motionless, but I heard her breathing; a quick inrush of breath from one apparently transfixed.

I put down my ale.

She did not move even when I bent above her, gripping the back of her chair.

Her hands were clasped together on the coarse sack apron that covered her knees; her peasant's boots were cracked and broken. And then, suddenly, in the lights of a passing trap I saw her eyes fixed upon me. I had known a few women since my days with Nanwen, but none had asked me with her eyes, like this.

We fought in a passion of breath and kisses, and I drew her to her feet so that we were like writhing statues locked in the middle of darkness.

"You sleep upstairs?" I whispered.

She did not answer, but I saw her eyes, large and startled in the glow of the window moon, and again they spoke.

"Later, then?"

For answer, she loosened her hair of its clasps and let it fall over

her shoulders. Later, I saw a light go on in a room over the barn.
I tell of this woman in detail since she is often in my mind.

Later still, I helped the landlord and his blowsy wife ease out the
drunks.

He, stunted by ale, moved like a motivated corpse, while she, with
her great bare bosom pushed up like a whale in harness, winked at
me coy. Her baggy obesity and painted eyes made the ghost of a
woman who had died: pretty good pair, I reflected; strange house-
mates for the lonely little peasant.

In the cheeping of mice I left my bed and tiptoed down the
corridors. The house was as still as an undertaker's. The peasant
girl was awaiting me, her arms out to me from the bed.

In all truth, I never in my life had another night like it, but next
morning I remembered little of it because of the Rhayader ale.

She never saw the going of me as I cocked up my boots along the
road to Builth.

In a Builth Wells yard, taking the waters, I chanced upon a
five-foot dwarf with a face like a navvy's arm-pit, a cupboard of
obscenities, and he hadn't a decent leg under him: sporting leggings
and a dandy's yellow waistcoat was he, with a walking stick made
from the penis of a bull; he begged tobacco off me, but stole the lot,
for his clay had a hole in it.

"How're ye faring, me darlin'?" he asked.

"Come down from North Wales," I said.

"Through the city of Rhayader, was it?" and I knew him for bog
Irish, with the same tunes in him as Ben O'Hara.

"Ay ay — last night," and I started to get going.

"Then ye likely stayed at the inn, did ye not?"

Tiring of him, I was on my way when he called, "You enjoyed the
services of the deaf mute ghost, be chance, the Wraith Woman?"

It halted and turned me. Said he, "Ach, t'is a legend round these
parts — she gives of her favours if you happen to be under thirty
and six foot up — like you, me boyo. She's a bright lass for the
fellas, be God."

I stared at him and he rolled tipsy, adding, "Like a lover she once had, they say — a fine young sapling." He blew out smoke at me. "I've waited on her a bit meself, for she gives fine joys to a man, I heard say. But with me knocking sixty and five-foot-two, I've seen neither hide nor hair of her."

"I have," I replied, starting off again, "and she was flesh and blood."

The dwarf waved his stick at me. "There's nobody living there save the old Boer War soldier and his painted missus — think again, son!" He glared at me.

"As real as you, don't be daft," I said.

"O, aye?" and he spat. "Then I'll tell ye something — I'll lay ye twenty to one that ye've laid wi' the Wraith Girl of Rhayader, and the stain of it will lay upon ye soul. Now then!"

He crossed himself.

I went pretty fast along the road to the south.

In ancient Brecon, that still echoes to the clash of alien swords, I found employment, first with a wheelwright and then as a striker with a blacksmith in The Struet, and I stayed with him and his four-foot-high missus until the October Fair in the Bulwark. It was here that I laid out a pugilist from Swansea in the boxing booth, and collected a golden sovereign.

With this in my pocket and my hands still blistered from the anvil striking, I struck out over the mountains up to Merthyr, taking the old Roman road, Sarn Helen.

Snow was falling as I reached the Storey Arms, the half way house of the drovers, and the tap was full when I entered, with the pugilist I had laid out there well into his cups before me, and a blind clergyman drinking deep of a brandy flask, with his guide dog lying by the fire.

Here the drovers were arguing in the bedlam of the tap-room: fine fierce oaths they used, sinking their ale in shouted banter, with an Irish melodeon blasting and Merthyr gipsy women kicking up their heels in the sawdust while the clergyman beat the time.

Outside, staining the snow, were thousands of sheep being driven up to the high valleys of the Aberdare and Merthyr; a maggoty, moving mass bleating for food.

What went on in the old Drovers' Arms that night was nobody's business, for the place was rent with the squeals of women and the shouts of men. Come dawn, all was quiet. I never saw the going of them, save for the snow beaten into ice by countless tiny feet.

The clergyman, dozing by a cold fire, raised dead eyes at me from the folds of a fire-scarred face. That afternoon he was seen going down the old road to Brecon, which was the country of his fathers he had told me; later, he was found in the snow near Tregarth, with the guide dog strangled beside him.

A month later, while working as a haulier in the iron town of Merthyr, I saw a placard offering twenty pounds reward for the pugilist I had beaten at Brecon Fair, since he was wanted for the murder of the old blind clergyman, but I never heard of the end of it.

Unaccountably, during that month of labouring in Merthyr, I knew a clear and vibrant affinity with Nanwen; she appeared to be with me every hour. Such was the sense of her nearness, that I expected to see her around every corner, during my morning tramp from Abercanaid to Merthyr, where I worked. Later, I knew the reason for this.

I have never since neglected an inexplicable premonition.

I worked as a collier in Blaenafon, at the head of the Eastern Valley, as an ostler in Cwmglo, and a farrier over in Nanty; I lodged with a widow woman in Abertillery.

These were the great industrial valleys that ran over The Top to the land of iron and copper and the great rolling sulphur clouds; you could read a newspaper in the flashing of the furnace bungs.

Here worked the cosmopolitan communities that had flooded in during the earlier century; Europeans, and the endless columns of starving Irish who found their homes and graves in the iron towns where the beds, shift on, shift off, never grew cold. They were a bold people, their bodies hardened and enriched by intermingled blood — the dark-skinned Spanish, the gay Italians who courted the Celtic Irish, their folk-lore merging with the Welsh culture.

Spring had come to the land, and the Rhondda, when I entered it that sunny afternoon in April 1910, was as bright as a young girl out in her Easter clothes, with the wild flowers of the mountains a madness of colour in the sun. Dandy wet-a-beds grew in yellow carpets along the lanes; bluebells waved their heads off in the woodland as I strode into the Coal Country. And I thought, as I walked alone down from the mountain, of the generations of men who had come in before me, seeking new lives in the valleys of the Coal Rush.

I thought of my father; of how he had come here with a pack on his back, as I, to settle in the pits of Tonypandy. After a year or so, he had told me, he had hungered for a wife, so he took himself to Gilfach Goch where the women were known to be extra decent. Here, at the Fair, he had sought out my mother; sweeping his bowler in the gutter, she related, while she curtsied back, but my wicked old Grandad showed him the door because she was Congregational and my father was Church of England.

But next morning he missed a shift, did my father, and was straight back over to Gilfach Goch, and what with Grandad shouting on the doorstep and my mother howling, it was a choice bit for the relatives, he said, with neighbours chipping in and children swinging on the gate. And up and down Glamorgan Terrace (they lived in Number Six) people were scandalised, apparently, because my Grandad was proving an awkward old sod. But, after a while my grandfather repented, and my father, done up posh in his new suit and funeral bowler, called and asked officially for her hand, but he had to go to Congregational.

Within a month my mother had been pledged, banned and bedded in Tonypandy, and since my father never did things by halves, nine months to the day she brought forth me.

I sighed, smiling at my thoughts as I plodded down the mountain sheep track into Gilfach Goch. And I stopped for a bit outside Number Six, Glamorgan Terrace, and touched the gate that my people's hands had touched, until I saw curtains move.

Then, I was away to Penygraig, and along the valley road to Tonypandy.

God must have been in a good humour when He fashioned the

towns of the Rhondda, and had a great time inventing some of the names.

He must, I think, have made a fork of two fingers and laid them on the land, pressing them into the rich soil so that the big dividing ridges of Maerdy and Tynewydd rose up in between. The mountains, upon which He breathed in His labours, grew green; the land of His touch became fertile. One valley He called Rhondda Fach, the other Rhondda Fawr, and down each green belt He ran a foaming river.

It was a big country, like its granite sister-land up north; in the rounded hills lay unbounded wealth — timber, limestone, coal, and Man smelled its riches from afar.

The Coal Rush of the nineteenth century began.

Begging for food and money, the immigrants flooded in. Speculation mushroomed, leader-barons rose, and the twin valleys, divided communities of alien habits and customs, began to prosper. In the lust for wealth, pit after pit was sunk by imported navvies called sinkers. Little townships sprang up haphazardly around individual pits, often named after their engineers or owners — roughly a town to the mile by the year 1900, some overlapping; all joined in the south by a common road; here was the confluence of the two rivers, Fach and the Fawr. Communities like Maerdy and Ferndale rose in the Rhondda Fach; Treherbert, Treorchy and Trealaw darkened the sky of Rhondda Fawr.

Tonypandy, the town of my birth, lay near the end of the river confluence at Porth.

Now, with my bundle over my shoulder and whistling to have my teeth out, I strode through the Rhondda, past the two big Naval Pits and over the Adare Incline and on to Tonypandy square.

It was a gorgeous April afternoon and a Saturday long-pay day, too, and the place was crowded with people going about their business; broughams and traps, pony and dog-carts coming and going; melodeons playing in the gutters. Ragged tramps tugged at my sleeve for alms; wizened Irish, the refuse of the old Eastern Valley ironworks trudged in melancholy discontent among the poshed up, bowlered gentlemen bowing this way and that to hoop-skirted ladies: coloured parasols flourished, for the spring day was hot.

It was obvious to a stranger that the Rhondda, in the spring of 1910, despite its labour troubles, was doing well. With Glamorgan county sitting on a crock of gold, this was the end of the rainbow: over ten million tons of coal and coke were exported from Barry Docks alone that year, and most of it came from the Rhondda pits.

On I went, pushing my way through the crowded pavements — seeking lodgings first, then a job, and there was a new delight in me at being back among my father's people.

Most of the talk about me was English and the high lilt of the Irish; the Welsh I heard had a different song to the North in it, and I listened to a cheeky gaggle of women waiting on their doorsteps for the collier husbands. Sitting on backless chairs were they or leaning in doorways, their caps ready for their long-pay sovereigns. One of the younger ones, bright-eyed and generous in the breast, gave me a wink, and cried in a thick Irish brogue:

"*Arrah!* he looks a handy one. Irish, is it?"

"God, no Mary! — look at his nose — Welsh, for sure!"

"Wrong, missus," and I joined their banter, for God help you if you didn't. "I'm an Oriental Jew — where's Adams Street up by here?"

"Keep going — who're ye after, mun?"

"I tell you I'm after lodgings, Blod, and you'll be wiser than me!"

They shrieked at this, waving me down, and one shouted, "I can fit ye in, mind, if me old man turns over!" and she shouted laughter, slapping her plump thigh. "Lodgings, is it? Then keep off the Irish."

"What about it now?" I asked, meaning business.

They pondered this, their crackered heads nodding in secret whispers. "Ye could try Mrs. Smith up in Court Street?" said one.

"English?" said another. "Come winter she'd be sliding his dinners under the door. You'd be best off with us, son. Welsh doors are always open to hospitality."

"That's only so the blutty sheep can get out," cried the young Irish.

"You try Mrs. Best at Number One, Chapel Street — she'll feed ye, if ye pay. She always buys the best, she says. Most round here'll play a harp on your ribs."

"Or there's Angie No-Knickers, if ye aren't all that keen about eating!"

"*Diawch*, I haven't the strength."

They sent me down to Chapel Street with their shrill voices, and I wouldn't have changed them for gold; their men were lucky — girls to hang on to in a stiff breeze.

When the mother of God arrives again, she'll likely come in a Welsh shawl.

Mrs. Best was scrubbing the front doorstep of her Number One as I came down Chapel Street, and she was of a different ilk to the women I had left. Wiping her little plump hands on her apron, she peered up at me from a warm cherub face.

"Bethesda, did ye say?"

"Some years back, mind," and she gabbled, delighted. "Come in, come in — there's always room for a likely lad." But in the kitchen she saddened at me. "But I can't 'ave ye long, because the Company's taking the roof off me — I lost me chap, ye know. Lancashire born and bred, he were."

"I'm sorry," I said.

"Aye, well, that's that's the way of it. The chest took him. Gone to a better home, hasn't he? Now they want the house, so I'm renting a cheaper one for lodgers over in Senghenydd — you know it?"

"Senghenydd? No."

"Over in the Aber valley — good men there, too — easy lodgers. Welsh chaps who like the best. I never buy ought but the best, ye know."

We grieved together, both for her loss and the imminence of our parting.

"But I can give ye a week or so if you fancy?"

"It'll tide me over, missus," I said.

"Will ten shilling a week kill ye? You see, son, you got to pay for good stuff — in fact, I've just come back from Town with a pound of best neck from the Co-op — the divvie's handy, eh? I always sees to me gentlemen proper, you understand — Church of England, is it?" She peered at me with anxious eyes.

"Congregational."

She patted herself for breath. "Ah well, can't have everything. I'll get up and air your bed, son — I gave the place a good do through when me fella died."

"Much obliged," I said, and pulled my cap at her and went past the Square and along Dunraven, made a few enquiries along the way, and got myself signed on at the big Ely Pit; sixteen shillings a week starting next Monday morning day shift at six o'clock.

The Rhondda was paved with coal, right enough. It was all so easy that I couldn't believe it.

After settling myself in with Mrs. Best in Chapel Street, it was getting on for evening and with four shillings in my pocket I reckoned I deserved a pint on success, so I washed, shaved, brushed up and took me across the Square for a pint at the nearest public, the Pandy Inn.

The place was filling up with day shift colliers coming out of the two Naval Pits and the big Glamorgan colliery up at Llwynypia.

I had to shoulder my way into the big tap-room to get to the bar.

And the first woman I saw in there was Ma Bron, serving jugs behind the counter.

"Good God," I whispered.

But she hadn't yet seen me, and she tripped into the room with a pint in her hand and the other one out to a collier, and he turned her in a circle while his mates clapped a jig.

The same old Bron, I thought, making the most of life; a dream of a woman now; older, mature.

In a world that was changing all the time, she was constant. And then I remembered that, when I'd last seen her and Sam after the casting out, they'd intended to make south for the Rhondda.

Vaguely, I wondered if Sam was still with her.

Laughing, her head back, Bron pushed her way back to the counter. Time died in her eyes when she saw me.

"Ay ay, Ma Bron," I said.

I had the better of her. "You're surprised?" I asked.

"*Toby Davies!*" she gasped. "What you doing here?"

"Came in late today!"

"My, you've growed!" She looked me up and down in wonderment.

"That's what you always say."

"But . . . I can't believe it. You're a man!" She snatched at my hands, pressing them in her joy. "But it's eight years, mate — it must be — where you been?"

"Looking for you." I landed her a wink.

"I bet! Scotching up that old Nan O'Hara, the Irishman's wife, more'n likely! But what ye doin' here?" Her face was alive, her whole being consuming me; people were watching her joy.

"Where's Sam, then?" I asked.

"Why are you interested?" She went cool on me.

"He was my mate," I said.

"And mine, once." She poured a jug, adding bitterly, "But you didn't bed with Sam Jones, Toby, you only knew him."

"You've left him?"

"No woman leaves Sam — he left me."

"Another skirt?" I asked, and she drew a long breath like the well of life going dry.

"What d'you expect?"

"But you stayed as bright and clean as a wash-day!"

She smiled, but not with her eyes. "I ain't gone short."

"Don't change, do you?" I said, and there was a sudden warmth in us. But the customers were becoming impatient, pushing and shoving.

"Can't talk now," said she. "See you tomorrow. I'm off all day tomorrow — Sunday."

"Where?" I looked at the hostile faces around me and wondered if I was holding up their ale or imposing on their woman.

"On the Square by the fountain — two o'clock?"

"Are ye sure you're free?" I gave her a wry smile as she handed me a pint, and I sank it, watching her as she poured another.

"Now you're here," she said.

I pushed my way out of the Pandy and into the clear April day.

The stars were shining over the mountains; life was suddenly incredibly beautiful, and full again.

Yet even the act of meeting Bron again had revived in me my longing for Nanwen.

I stood outside the Pandy, rubbing my chin reflectively.

"Well, I'm damned," I said.

20

I LODGED THAT night with Mrs. Best; next day at two o'clock I was waiting on the Square as decent as my tramping clothes allowed; in my cracked boots and faded coat and trews I scarcely matched Ma Bron's magnificence. Done up fine was she in a white blouse and a long black skirt, with her fair hair shining under her pink spring hat. Spinning her bright parasol over her shoulder, she looked like gentry. We went together as old friends should — arm in arm — turning every head as we passed: the Pandy barmaid courted by a tramp, no doubt, but the least to care was Bron.

Past the Rink we went and over the Taff Vale Railway line, and behind the Glamorgan colliery we climbed Mynydd Trealaw, taking the sheep tracks up Tyn-tyle mountain to the slopes of Penrhys and St. Mary's Well.

We didn't talk much; it was enough to be alone in this newly discovered friendship, and the mountain grass was flashing greenness in the warm sunlight with the promise of May: scitterbags of sheep, stained black with coal-dust, roamed about us in baa-ing contentment.

Below us the Sunday Rhondda simmered and chattered on the still, cool air.

Below the Holy Well we sat, and there was a warmth in us; I sought Bron's hand, and we laid together, eyes clenched to the red-blooded brilliance of the sun; strangely, I again remembered Nanwen.

"Life's queer, isn't it?" said Bron, invading my mind.

I sighed, resting on my elbow above her, tracing each feature of her face.

Her fair beauty had flowered. Neither Time nor Sam Jones had begun to denounce the flawless quality of her skin; the girl had gone, leaving behind a woman.

"Good to be back with friends, I mean."

"God, you're beautiful," I said.

"That's what all the chaps say."

"And all the chaps are right — what's wrong with Sam Jones — what does he want from life?"

It stirred her and she came up beside me. "I know what he wants, and if I were a chap I'd blutty give it to him. All the time he was with me he was pickin' and choosing like a broody stallion, one skirt after another. There's no satisfying the fella."

"He needs his head read."

"That's why I took Bibbs-Two back up north to her aunt. She was born in Porth, bless her — down the road from here." Bron lowered her eyes, playing with her fingers.

"Sam was all right for a bit, after Bibbs-Two was born, ye know; he came off the beer, he even used to dig the garden — we had a company house then, till he put one on the foreman's whiskers and got himself blacklisted in coal for six months — then he went labouring." She sighed, "We had it tough, I can tell ye. I used to take in washing to make ends meet — scrubbed me hands into holes, and the first money he earned he'd sink a pint and chase a barmaid."

"When did you last hear of him?"

"Nine months back." She stared at me. "I haven't seen Bibbs for over two years you know — you can't keep a child in a house of bickering — she's coming up for eight now, would you believe it?"

She shook her head dolefully, adding, "I was like some little rag doll. One day he'd be all over me, next moment giving me a thumping — mind," and her eyes flashed, "he didn't get that all his own way, neither." Quieter, she said, "And so it went on, one year after another — job after job, back into coal one minute, on the blacklist the next — pit after pit — Treorchy, Wattstown, Treherbert — you name it, we'd been there; fighting it out and making it up — drinking, whoring — I never met such a man."

"And then?"

She emptied her hands at me. "He just vanished nine months back." Picking a dandelion, she held its beauty up to the sun. Faintly, amid the soft bleating of the sheep, came the sound of traffic down on the Tyn-tyle Road, and Mynydd-y-Gelli, on the other side of the valley, was stricken with swords of the sun. "Aye, plain vanished. I had a letter . . ."

"A letter?"

"From a woman in Porth at the end of the valley. Some kind soul — she didn't sign it. It was just after I started at the Pandy — a month or so after Sam left me final. It seems he was living with a Spanish piece in Hannah Street, near the station. I was over there like a rabbit, but the birds had flown. It was true enough, the neighbours told me."

"He likes a change, does Sam." I sighed.

"You know," said she. "I reckon he got hold of the only Spanish piece this side of Spain — I only ever heard of two in the Rhondda."

"And you?"

"You know about me."

"Tell me."

"I've been around." She glanced away.

"You'd be a fool if you hadn't."

"And what about you, then? What about Tobias?" She playfully tripped my elbow from under me and we lay together but apart, laughing at the sky. "I suppose you're the same old monk I rolled in the sheets in the Waterloo back bedroom?" She laughed gaily.

"Try me now," I said.

She cupped her chin in her hands and lay on her stomach. "Ay ay — what about that old Nanwen, eh? That weren't so innocent."

"You don't know Nanwen."

"You ever think of her?"

"Of course, but she's in another age." I sighed. "Now I'm tucked up with Mrs. Best over in Chapel Street, and butter won't melt in my mouth; least, not till I see an opportunity."

"Well, here's one coming up, and you can take it or leave it — there's room in my place!"

A silence grew within the day; the song of the birds was stilled; even the sheep listened.

Our smiles died and we faced each other, severe within the moment of decision.

"You really mean that?" I asked.

"It depends."

"On what?"

"On what you want from it. You've just come in, haven't you? I've got one of the Sinkers huts behind the Pandy — it runs with the job. Time was that Sam was there with me — now I'm alone." She paused, seeking words. "But perhaps you'd like to look around — one thing's sure, you'd eat better with Mrs. Best."

There was in her face such a tale of expectancy that I drew closer. It was the same magical Bron; the girl of Bethesda again. Of a sudden, I held her against me.

"Oh, God, Tobe — you come, eh? I got to put my arms round someone decent."

I heard her words as an echo. We did not kiss. I just held her. Later, we rose and went down into the valley.

We wandered as people uncaring, lost in the renewed friendship, and there was a fine glory in the day, with the wind blowing wild and free about us, promising summer, and this warmth was in the pair of us.

"It's been a lonely old time, eh?" said Bron, after I'd told her my history.

"It's been all right," I said. "Like Grandpa used to say — there's only one way to take life, and that's by the scruff of the neck — you haven't had it so easy, either."

"But easier than you; at least I had Sam for a bit." She nudged me secretly, screwing up her eyes and wrinkling her nose at the sun. "Dear me, now you've come me mind's as bright as a little girl's pinny."

"The deacons'll have us," I said, uneasily. "They can be pretty stiff in the Rhondda."

"And I'll have the deacons, down to the third generation. It's in the name of common humanity — a little bit of love and three square meals a day?"

"You were right the first time," I said.

She turned me to face her and I saw the old Bron, abandoned and carefree, as if the Sunday had touched her with a naughty finger; the wind, suddenly rising, had got her hair, blowing it out behind her like a wand of gold; her eyes were alight with the old mischievous way. There was a fine wickedness in her; part of the earth that seemed to beat about us in all its simple beauty, diminishing loss; bringing to us a oneness I had never known before. A curtain had dropped over the past and brought our lives together.

It seemed natural that I should kiss her.

"*Diawch*, no!" said she, pushing and shoving. "It's Sunday. But I'll make it up to ye back in the Sinkers, maybe."

"I'll keep you up to that."

We stood in each other's arms momentarily.

"One thing, though," said she, softly. "Come and go the best of 'em — and there's been a few — there'll always be Sam, ye know. I mean, he's my legal husband ain't he? If he lifts a finger, I go, mind."

"You're mad."

"Perhaps, but a woman can hope and I do me best to be honest."

I'd have lived with her had she offered nothing but cooking.

"We'll handle Sam Jones when he arrives."

"He'll arrive, he always does," said Bron.

Such was the quietness between us then that I imagined I heard, like distant music, the old rivers Fach and Fawr, the beating hearts of the Rhondda, boasting and laughing their way over the crags to the sea.

21

AND SO, THREE weeks later, on the morning Mrs. Best was moving over to Senghenydd in the Aber Valley, I packed my bundle, left Chapel Street, and moved in with Bron at Number Six the Sinkers Huts on the other side of the Square.

"She'll lodge you well, son — a good soul is that Pandy barmaid — don't touch a drop, ye know — though she works among it." Mrs. Best patted and smoothed me and straightened my collar like a mother. "Don't forget now, if ever you want a change and come to the Aber Valley, you can count on me — pay for the best, you're entitled to it." She bit on the sovereign I'd given her and slipped it under her apron, and I heaved up my bundle and took it over to the Sinkers, built years back for the navvies sinking the Scotch, the Glamorgan pit up the road in Llwynypia.

A lot asked me why I hadn't signed on at the Scotch, which was nearer, but I didn't fancy it. D. A. Thomas, who owned the Ely, wasn't the best of owners in the Rhondda, but he was a saint when it came to some. And in the three weeks I'd been on the Ely shift, I'd made good friends — people like Heinie Goldberg and Mattie Kelly.

The May morning I moved in with Bron was gay with sun; and even at that time of the morning the town was flourishing with people.

Every woman in sight seemed to be up and doing, scrubbing their fingers on the wash-boards, swilling out the tubs, cleaning windows, with happy good mornings right and left, and smells of frying bacon swept like perfume from the open doors of the terraces.

The Sinkers was alive with activity; biffs and howls coming out of the kitchens where children were being made ready for school; and the open drain down the back of the Huts was foaming with suds.

Already some of the older children were about — rushing around with their great iron hoops; urchins were fighting or playing Dolly Stones; black-stockinged little girls in white pinafores sucking gob-stoppers and hopscotching on the Square. Ancient grandpas and grandmas, pale with Rhondda's early hungers, were arranging backless chairs outside their doors; birds sang, cats arched to yapping dogs; the sun struck down from the mountains.

"Ay ay, missus," I said, coming through the door of Number Six, and there was Bron with the bed made and going round with a duster like a woman demented.

"Not so much of the missus," said she. "You're a lodger, remember."

I put my arms around her waist from the back and kissed her hair.

"*Jawch*, mun — one thing at a time," she said, elbowing me off. "How did you sleep?"

"Like a top if it hadn't been for Mrs. Best snoring."

"Remember how your old Grandad used to snore, you said?"

"*Ach i fi* — don't remind me!"

"By the way — talking about Bethesda — did I mention the Arses?"

"Who?"

"The Arses — come on, you remember Albert and Annie and the kids who lived in old Caerberllan. They're in Tonypandy. And the Livingstones . . . Guto and his missus — I met them in Porth — poor soul — she's got a cross, Guto's still addled."

She was at the sink now, tying back her hair.

"What takes you to Porth these days, then?" I asked.

"Is there a law against it?"

I said testily, "I only asked you what takes you to Porth?"

"What takes anybody anywhere? — go where I like, can't I."

"Because Sam is in Porth?"

160

Going to the table she began to cut my tommy box, sawing at the cottage loaf as if she had a coal owner roped to the table. "Bread and dripping suit you?" she asked, ignoring me.

"Aye, fine — I've just had egg and bacon with Mrs. Best — it's a higher standard."

"The standard's likely to drop," said she, "but I'll be waiting for you in the Pandy, when you come off shift."

"I'll slip in for a couple of pints," I said. "One to settle the dust, the other to settle you."

"That'd be the day. Best you go, or the lads'll be off without you." She heaved aside my bundle. "I'll wash this lot through and have it ironed by the time you're home."

I kissed her like a man going to work; it seemed the most natural thing to do, and she looked at me strangely.

"You act as like you've been here years, you do," she said.

"If I'd had any sense, I would have been." I went out to the front and leaned on the railings beyond the gate, awaiting the coming of the colliers for shift.

If there was one woman hanging around outside I bet there was ten.

Mrs. Rachel Odd from next door, I saw first, and knocked up my cap to her. Fat and wheezy was Mrs. Odd, a boiling joint, with her old man's cap on top of her head and her sack apron pinned up on her stomach.

"How are you?" said she. "Just off on shift, is it?" and the other women edged closer to get an ear in.

"Aye, missus," I said, wary.

"I didn't get your name, really."

"Toby Davies."

"Just moved in, 'ave you?"

"Aye."

"Down the Scotch, is it?"

"Ely," I said.

She gazed sightlessly at the clouds, saying, "I lost a brother down the Ely — lodging with Ma Bron now, are ye?"

"That's right."

"She's a generous soul, but the stomach don't come first with some of the young ones, ye know." She approached and patted me benevolently. "Still, I expect she do come up with other exciting things."

"I was just mentioning," cried a woman, "he's a real lovely fella."

"Do he play a brass instrument?" asked Mrs. Primrose Culpepper, coming up from Number Seven, and she was as hard to look at as the midday sun. "My old man's in the band, actually, and he's looking for recruits, horn players, mainly."

I shook my head.

"That's a blessing, I say — got to be thankful for small mercies, haven't we? We got Will Parry Trumpet down in Number Eleven, for instance," and she belched and pardoned. "He can keep ye awake any shift — like up in Adare Terrace — remember that musician up there Rachel? Nine till five, six days a week we used to get the horn whether we wanted it or not. Ah well," and she heaved up her stomach and set aside her broom. "Got to go and get a little bit of fish for my chap — good luck, I say. Tell your Bron I'll be bringin' her a bit of custard tart directly. You like custard tart?"

She talked more, but I didn't take much notice since I was looking out for the colliers coming on to the Square; every woman was out that morning, I should think, waiting for the shift going on, including Bron.

"Thank God you've come," I said, "I've been having a hell of a time."

"That's all right," said she, handing me my tommy box. "They dish it out, you hand it back — that's the way they expect it. Now you watch it, eh?" she gave me my tea bottle. "The Ely, I mean."

"Ach, forget it."

"I mean it Tobe — she's a bitch — watch it."

Every weekday shift the pit gangs collected; coming from different parts of Tonypandy and the valley towns beyond; each man aimed in his own direction, gathering mates on the way. On that first morning when I moved in with Bron, I was awaiting a gang from Trealaw; it picked up the Pandy men and was met by scores from Penygraig, on their way to the Glamorgan.

Near the Pandy it was joined by Heinie Goldberg and Mattie Kelly, the two mates I had got to know down the Ely.

"Here they come," said Bron. "You got everything?"

"Everything except you," I said.

I heard Primrose say as she nudged Rachel Odd, "But he's a well set-up fella, mind, and it anna any business of mine if folks ain't legally wed."

Expectations of twins had Mrs. Odd, by the size of her; imminent.

"You're right, missus," said Bron. "It ain't."

"Easy," I said. "Let them talk."

"As long as I don't hear," said Bron. "She needs a clean up, that Primrose Culpepper, her mind especially."

"See you later, lovely boy," said Rachel Odd, dainty.

Four abreast, the Ely colliers, my gang, came marching along De Winton, their numbers swelling as others joined the column.

Doors were coming open like magic all round the square; files of men ran out of Church Street, Pandy Terrace and Cwrt to shouted goodbyes.

"*Bore da' chwi!*" shouted Heinie Goldberg, my stall mate, and Mattie Kelly, an inch higher than Heinie's five foot, waved greeting beside him.

I took my place between them.

"Don't waste a lot of time, do ye, *bach*? I thought you was keeping Mrs. Best happy?"

"*Cythril!* Do you get around?" cried Mattie, his little cherubic face cocked up.

I ignored them, enveloped in the din of tramping boots and banter, and marched on, grinning.

"Barmaid at the Pandy, ain't she?" asked a third. "*Duw*, I'd rather have five minutes with her than the Chinese Strangler."

"She even kissed him goodbye!"

I made a mental note to see it didn't happen again.

You had to take it; if you didn't they'd give you a hell of a day.

"But how do you handle a piece like that?"

"He handles it, if I know him," said Heinie Goldberg.

"Reckon you'd be best down the Scotch," growled Ben Block, all seventeen stones of him thumping along in front of me. "Being nearer, ye could keep an eye on her."

"It'd need my missus to get me down the Scotch," said Mattie Kelly. "I wouldn't take a stall down there if they paid me a fortune, eh, Heinie?"

Heinie shrugged, "Mabon do think well of it, though."

"O, aye?" shouted another, turning in the ranks. "He wants to work it. Mabon himself's turning out to be a fraud, never mind coal owners."

"All I hear around these parts is talk of this chap Mabon," I said, happy at the change of subject.

This was the leader of the big Miners' Federation that was fighting to get better working conditions and pay for colliers. His true name was William Abraham, but he was better known by his Bardic title of Mabon. Member of Parliament for the Rhondda, he was the biggest thing that had happened to Welsh coal for a century, according to Heinie.

"Don't talk balls, Jew boy," said Mattie Kelly, now. "Mabon's like the rest of 'em — they start out all right but end in the pockets of the bosses."

"Aye," said a man nearby, and his face was that of a hawk, coal-grimed still, despite the bath; his eyes, black-laced, shone fiercely from his scarred cheeks. "Big in the stomach now, and that is all. Time was that Mabon was all for the colliers; now he's in bed in the south of France with a coal owner either side."

"I wish I was," said Mattie, "especially with a couple of their daughters, instead of going down the blutty Ely."

"You don't treat folks fair," said Heinie, bitterly. "When you negotiate, you've got to hunt a bit with the hare as well as the hounds, stands to reason."

I chanced a look at Heinie as we marched on towards the Ely. Fact was, I'd seen little enough of him, save for his little bald head popping up and down as we worked the stall in the light of the lamps. He looked to me more like an outsize gnome than a collier, with his little bits of cauliflowered ears attached to his skull, and his nose was as flat as a Japanese wrestler's; the Rhondda being a spawning ground for the Noble Art.

Gone was Heinie's first flush of youth, but he could fill a tram faster than any man on the five foot Bute seam, the new face causing all the trouble. Nigh forty years old, was Heinie, with the criss-cross tell-tales of hewing and fighting white above his cheeks. In his time he had held the great Shoni Engineer to a ten round draw at Scarrott's, but that was when he was young. When he was old he had taken on a lad called The Tylorstown Terror, a shin-bone wisp of a boy called Wilde: and the lad had laid one on Heinie's chin within seconds, knocking his eyes as crossed as Alfie Tit's in the Tonypandy Co-op. Down the stalls you had to watch him, too, since he'd eat out of other people's tins: once he had a wife, a slim-boned girl who died: Heinie hadn't eaten properly since, said Mattie.

"What was her name?" I asked early on, turning to face him under the eighteen inch roof.

"Leave me what I got of her," said Heinie.

Now the cage door slammed behind us and we were going down the Ely: she was a treacly mess of engine oil from the workings, and water fifty feet deep, had a sump at the bottom, and it always chilled me. One day the brake will slide on the drum, I thought, and we'll be down, down, past the Bute landing road and into that sump; oil, water, coal-dust. Sometimes, in dreams, I heard Heinie choking and Mattie Kelly gasping as the winding gear snapped and we dropped down, down, *down*.

In years of it, I never got used to the cage, least of all the Ely.

"One day it won't stop, ye know."

"Don't talk daft," said Heinie.

He was a philosopher when it came to consolations; perhaps life meant less to him than me, now I had found Ma Bron.

Stripped to the belts, we laboured; cutting the coal and bunging it back with our feet in the stall — Heinie, Mattie Kelly, Ben Block and me, and every time you lifted your nut you hit the top of the five foot seam, which was more like two-foot-six.

"You shift your backside like that again and I'll have this pick up it," said Ben, double bass; heavy in the chest he was, and sweating like a Spanish bull. Strong for his God was Ben, with drinking and fornication a long way down his list.

"I'm coming round," I said, twisting sideways under the roof of coal, and I thought of sunlight a couple of thousand feet up, and Bron, her bright hair shining, pegging out her washing.

"Get the muck back," said Mattie, working beside me. "Ben Block's by 'ere and he keeps filling my tram."

"You should worry," said Heinie.

"His eyes are going," said Mr. Duck Evans, a new man, crawling up with his curling box (with this he scooped up our coal and emptied it into our tram) and I thought of my old foreman, Dan Morgan, of Blaenau, whose eyes, I supposed, had long since gone.

"Ben ain't what he used to be," said Heinie, packing the gob, and I could hear the rats squealing inside as he hammered the rubbish under the roof to support it, replacing the coal we had taken out; forget to pack up the gob and the roof came down. "You heard what happened last week?"

I shook my head, pondering the roof for cracks. Heinie said, "Somebody down at the landing put a dead rat up the sleeve of Ben's coat, and he took it home to his missus for a kitten."

"Poor old sod," said Mattie. "His brain's gone, too — like yours, Heinie."

"More than likely," replied Heinie, grinning. "Last month — before you come in, Toby, the fireman sent Ben and me up to the junction to give the lads a hand; he was in one stall, and I was next door in the other. 'You in there, Heinie, lad?' he shouts. 'Ay ay, Ben, it's me,' I called back, and he yells, 'Then just swing us a bit o' your chalk over the wall, mun, I want to mark up for the foreman,' and I puts my head over to see what was happening and the sod clouts it with his shovel. 'That was my head, ye silly old bugger,' I told him, and I slid down the wall my side with a lump on me head as big as a duck's egg, and he comes over the wall and hits me with his shovel again, shouting, 'Half o' that will do, boyo — I don't need a bit as big as ye head, ye know,' and he still didn't get any chalk."

"Mind, your bald head, when shining, do look like chalk, Heinie," said Mattie Kelly, grave, and just then Ben Block sat back on his hunkers and said, "We'd best mark up for the foreman, Heinie — you got a bit o' chalk down by 'ere?"

"Christ," said Heinie, and got out and sat under the belly of Lark, our horse.

Really, she was only down for a lark, this old mare, that's why Mr. Duck Evans, the Stall Ten haulier, called her that. And it was a caution to hear him talking to her. 'Now come on, Lark, my girl,' he used to say, very educated, 'put your best hoof forward; you are such a lazy old mare, you shouldn't really be with decent horses, should you?' and he would feed her what was left of his tommy box or even give her a drink from his jack.

Everybody used to bring down scraps for the horses, and we were lucky with Lark since she was a canny old devil. We didn't do a lot of ripping the roof (making a wide groove to get the horse's head into the stall) because Lark used to bend her knees for us if the roof got low, and a mare like this is worth a few apple cores, instead of the whips, like some of the hauliers hand out underground. One down the Scotch used to hit his horse with a sprag. 'That horse'll bloody have you one day,' Heinie told him.

"Hit that mare with the nearest thing handy, he would," said Duck, "and the old horse just awaited his time. And one night shift, when there was nobody about, he got that damned chap in a narrow place and squeezed the blutty life out of him."

"Killed him?" I asked.

"You try breathing, with a horse leaning on ye," said Duck. "I always treats my animals respectably, don't I, Lark?" he cried, and threw his mare a piece of his cheese, but a rat scuttled out of the gob and took it before it stopped rolling.

I noticed that the lamps were going a bit dim as we settled in the stall with our tommy boxes. "You got much gas here?" I asked.

"Now and then," said Heinie, lying back with his boots cocked up. "The big Universal over at Senghenydd is the place for gas if you want it; down here in the Ely it's mainly roof falls and water."

"Mind, Lark will tell ye about the roof," said Mattie, biting into his bait. "Horses are better at detecting a roof fall chance than canaries are on gas."

"She turns up her eyes," said Duck, proudly. "I've seen my old

Lark going down the road wi' a journey of trams behind her like an express train, and the chap'd be a fool who didn't get after her. Twice in two years she's saved me on falls."

"And water?" I asked.

"The Ely's a wet bitch, some places," said Ben Block, heavily, and he bit out a great wedge of cheese and packed his mouth with bread. "I had water twice down by 'ere."

"You never said," mentioned Heinie.

"He never had it," said Mattie, "he's thinking o' somewhere else — now come on, Ben, come on!"

"Down this pit, I tell you — 'fore you lot kissed a collier's arse," grumbled Ben, wheezing fat. "I was getting out the pookings — working wi' an old slate Johnny North — and the face went down while he was picking, poor old bugger. He hadn't got a lot of breath as it were, and with water over our mouths he breathed less. I got him out, but he died. I was fourteen, I remember." He sighed deep and we chewed silently, thinking of the old collier who drowned. "Next morning, when I come up with his body, the agent stopped me tenpence for lost chalk. I used to get eight bob a week, those days, and had to keep me ma and two sisters. Christ, times was bad."

"They're not much better now," said Heinie, "on the old Sliding Scale." He sighed. "And we got trouble coming soon, sure enough."

I was just about to ask what the Sliding Scale was when Mr. Richard Jones came up and ducked his head into our stall.

"Trouble's just arrived," said Mattie.

Mr. Richard Jones, the Ely Lodge chairman, had a face of undertaker grey, a lanky figure to match, and tired eyes in his battered cheeks where years of coal had cut their lace; nobody spoke as he sat by the gob, opened his tommy box and took out his grub.

"You lot on a Roman holiday, then?" His voice was a surprise, being bass and beautiful.

"We was just working out who's pinched the Union funds," said Heinie. "How's Mabon?"

The Union man ate daintily, and his hands were clean; age had wearied him, but in him I sensed was a latent fire.

"Mabon is doing reasonably well for you ungrateful people,"

said he. "The fact that I don't think he's got our real interests at heart these days don't say anything for the old days — he was good in '77 when we elected him Miners' Leader."

"That was in 1877," said Ben Block. "I'd decapitate the bugger if I had him down by 'ere today."

I said, "I'm new, Mr. Jones, so I can't talk much, but it strikes me that what we want is more Union representatives and less Members of Parliament."

His eyes raised to mine.

"Nobody seems to think a lot of Mabon," I added.

"That's because few of us take the trouble to discover what he's trying to do." He sighed. "Paid Members of Parliament was one of the old Chartist aims, eh? — now you've got parliamentary representation, don't you want it?"

"We've got Lloyd George," said Mattie, "but we're still in trouble." He cursed silently. "Also, we've got abnormal places down 'ere, too. People like Mabon and Mainwaring want to try shovelling some of this lot."

This Bute Seam down the Ely Pit was the cause of most of the colliers' complaints, I was finding. Wherever you went in the Rhondda these days, there was talk of it, and argument was hot.

Mr. Thomas, owner of the big Cambrian Combine, had offered us a rate of one-and-nine a ton, and the Union was after two-and-sixpence, on the grounds that within the seam were abnormal places — rock and shale interspersed with the coal. Also, Mr. Thomas would only pay for large coal left on the screen; this was unfair: to get at the coal in abnormal places you had to break it up. "Two-and-sixpence is a living wage, Mr. Jones," said Mattie now, "it ain't asking much. One-and-nine means starvation."

"You know what'll happen," said Heinie. "We'll come out."

"Strike? And what about the Conciliation Board that's sitting now?" asked Mr. Jones politely, "Won't you give them a chance to bridge the gap?"

"Sod the Conciliation Board," said Ben, "all they do is talk — I got kids at home, an' they need feeding."

"It ain't fair, and you know it, Mr. Jones," cried Heinie. "From the time this five foot was opened, she's been abnormal."

"It is what has been agreed. Don't blame me," the old man said, "blame the Board." He raised his eyes to mine. "I've seen you before, son — have we got your Union contribution?"

"Contribution?" cried Mattie. "Up north in the Workers' Combination, he kept the funds, didn't you, Tobe?"

"I helped collect subscriptions," I said, "nothing more."

"The O'Hara business was it?" asked Mr. Jones, and it surprised me.

"You heard of that down here?" I asked, and he replied:

"Not much misses the Federation. Unless we keep a national blacklist, they shift their roots and try it again somewhere else — brothers in need, God help us — we've just got rid of one." He sighed. "So we're needing a new Lodge treasurer — would you care to give a hand?"

"He's an able scholar, aren't you, Tobe?" said Mattie, warmly.

I got up and wandered away down the heading and hoped that was the end of it.

That night, after my Ely shift, Bron and I came home from the Pandy hand in hand. Dusk was settling over the mountain, polishing the stars, and her room in the Sinkers looked pretty, save for its dividing blanket down the middle, which she was pleased to call the Walls of Jericho — nuns one side, said she, monks on the other.

Bron had rearranged the furniture too, apparently. On her side of the blanket — the larger room — were the chairs and table; a wash-stand, dolly and tub in the corner, and, of course, the grate for cooking — plus, of course, the double bed she had once shared with Sam. On the monk's side of the drape was the bed that had once belonged to Bibbs-Two — a narrow old cronk of a thing knocked up by Sam, and this bed of pain was now mine. So Bron was in feathers and I was on boards — and all protests were dismissed with an airy wave of her hand. Earlier, she had climbed the mountain and returned with wild flowers, decorating both rooms; they were as pretty as anyone could make a hut that was built to house navvies; even on the room door she had hung flowers, and her doorstep was scrubbed whiter than Mrs. Rachel Odd's next door, which was saying something.

"Good smell," I said, "What have we got?"

"Irish stew — they can keep their lobscows up North."

"I'd rather eat you," I said, but she moved neatly out of my arms and began to lay the table.

I thought she looked beautiful as I sat by the grate and filled my clay.

"Don't smoke now, Tobe — we're just going to eat," she said.

There was about her a grace that approached elegance: I had noticed this before.

She was not a small woman, and her red and white gingham dress enhanced her fine figure, which she made the best of in the right places, being Bron. She had done her hair in a different way, too; it hung in fair ringlets either side of her face. And suddenly, unaccountably, it seemed that she was Nanwen; she of the dark Iberian beauty that so contrasted Bron's.

It was incredible: as if Nan, smaller, dark, had entered the room and slipped into Bron's dress: that it was she laying the table as a ghost of the past. It was a phenomena I never explained.

Then the woman at the table turned and smiled, and she was Bron again.

"You're quiet for a change."

"One thing at a time — get your feet in first, eh?"

A silence came; you could have touched it. She added, going to the grate and stirring the pot. "You seen Nan O'Hara since you left Pesda?"

"No."

"Ever think of her?" she tasted the stew, gasping at the steam.

"Of course."

"You still love her?"

"Queer time to ask that — tasting stew."

"Come on, you've had my life story."

I got up and wandered about. "Aye."

"I'll say one thing, you were always honest." She sighed, ladling the stew into bowls. "God, we're a queer lot, ain't we? Sometimes I do think the human race is mad — you in here and in love with Nan O'Hara; me cooking you stew and dreaming of Sam."

"That's the way it goes. Got to make the best of it."

171

"You known any other women since you left up North?"

I brought a bowl to the table while she cut the bread. "You're looking at one of the original virgins."

"I bet!" She giggled like the old Bron, wrinkling her nose. "Dear me, you take me right back to Bethesda!"

"I used to throw stones at it then, but it won't happen again," I said. "Now tell me the truth and shame the devil — all that has happened to you these years."

We sat down and I faced her over her white tablecloth; it was going at the creases, I noticed, but no woman I ever met washed whiter than Bron.

"My business," she replied.

"One law for me and another for you, I suppose."

"Keep 'em dancing!"

"That one of your rules?"

The smile died on her mouth. "It is now."

"What do you mean by that?"

"Sam put me up on the shelf, but I'm not coming off it for anyone just like that — least of all you."

We ate in silence. The noises of the town were dying: mouse-dreaming, an owl shrieked from the trees as if awakened from slumber. Somebody was emptying a tin bath down the gullyway — a man off shift, probably a farrier; they kept queer times.

"It's Sam, isn't it?" I said. "We'll never be without the sod."

"Don't call him that! Sam's all right. It's just, well . . . just that he's a wicked old bugger. He can't help that."

"Why the devil did you take me in then?"

She raised her face. "Because I'm not having you lodging with anyone — I want to know you're kept decently, eating proper . . ." She faltered, looking close to tears.

"A sort of dogs' home then, is it?"

"You mean more to me than you think."

"It sounds like it."

She seemed to be slipping away from me for a ghost who didn't give a damn for her.

Parting the window curtains, I saw a few urchins lounging around the lamp-light; a man was sitting in the road close to the Pandy singing a faint, drunken song.

From the bosh, Bron said, "It's custard and apricots for afters, mind."

A faint memory whispered to me out of the past: I remembered the bedroom in the Waterloo at Bethesda, a love-making gone wrong. Trust her to humour the situation.

"Strikes me it isn't any more successful this time," I said.

Deliberately, she crossed the room and stood before me, then reached up slowly and put her arms about my neck. "I tell you what, Tobe — I can't explain why, but sometimes you mean more to me than Sam."

I made to turn away, but she held me, her eyes moving over my face.

"Damned women," I said, "it sounds like it."

Later, I said in the darkness, "You asleep, Bron?"

Etched against faint moonlight, like marble, was her face; her lashes dark on her cheeks. Strange about Ma Bron; her hair was like gold, her lashes black.

"Toby, go back to bed." She sighed in half sleep.

"Go on shift over, so I can come in, is it? You said that to me once, remember."

"Up half the night? — you'll miss the morning shift."

"To the devil with the shift — come on, Bron, be a sport."

"*Arglwydd!* Go *home!*"

A pattern of moonlight crossed the floor as I lay in the narrow bed and listened to Ma Bron's soft breathing — on the other side of the blanket.

I dreamed, I remember, of colliers and love-making. And, beneath my pillow the plaintive earth heaved; the mountain groaning to the lances in her side as the roof falls bellowed down the old workings and the water swirled two thousand feet below: colliers I dreamed of first, Bron later:

'There's gas about, lads — look at this lamp fading . . .'

'Slip up to the lamp room and fetch a blutty canary.'

'Aw, come off it, you're bleeding all over me knees.'

'He tells a good tale, though — reckons he was in the 1901 Senghenydd!'

'He do say that little boys burn blue — blue as the sky those little fellas burned down Senghy, according to Joe — about eighty caught.'

'And a hundred and forty-six died at Risca, a hundred and fourteen at Cymmer, an' a hundred and seventy-six over at Llanerch, remember?'

'I can't remember, mun — I was dead.'

I heard them talking; the colliers of the past. In my sweating dreams, when I should have been in the arms of Bron, I lived again my inner fears of the Ely sump; and the ghosts of a lost generation spoke softly:

'Two hundred and sixty-eight dead at Abercarn, remember — sixty at Ferndale — Christ, the Rhondda's had her share in her time — and the water'll come in down that blutty Ely one day for sure, you watch. . . .'

'Where did you collect it, Daio?' and the wraith of an answer, falsetto, came:

'I catched it down the Albion in 1894, with another two hundred and eighty-nine — and I'm still blutty down there — charred as the cinders of Hell.'

"Christ Almighty!" I exclaimed, and sat up in the bed.

"You all right, Tobe?" Bron this time, from the other side of the blanket; the living, not the dead.

"Aye," I said, sweating. "Just having a nightmare."

"Can ye have it quieter?"

I dreamed again; this time of happier things:

'Come on, Bron!'

'All the girls have got it and all the girls hang on to it,' said Heinie Goldberg in that dream.

And the voice of Bron from behind the blanket again, "Now stop it, Toby, go to sleep."

Up and down Tonypandy, over to Gilfach Goch, via Pentre, into the Trealaw Ward, I cursed Sam Jones.

The morning shouted his promise of summer. Stripped to the belt, I went out the back to the pump. The mountains were lying on their backs, rubbing their eyes and yawning at the sun: earlier, I had heard the early shift ostlers and farriers (being with horses they were always first on) going up to the Cambrian and Scotch. The two Navals were beginning to thump and whine their pit engines from the Adare Incline; trucks and railwaymen were clanking and shunting, and the statue of Archibald Hood still pointed the way to his colliery. If I had my way I'd turn that bugger round, said Heinie once. And Bron, looking gay and lovely in a summer dress, came out of the little privy down the back, and her hair was lying on her shoulders. Her fair, Brythonic beauty, fair as an angel, flowered before me.

Later, while I was whistling and blowing, diving my head under the pump, Bron began to comb out her long, bright hair in the sun.

"Have a good night, my lovely?"

"I had the wedding night of a Franciscan friar."

"But don't ye feel marvellous, now you've managed it?"

"Sure as Fate I'll have you one day, missus," I said, and tossed my towel across my shoulders and opened the door of the back.

All up and down the Row men were washing, bubbling and gasping; Moses Culpepper was in his tin bath on his cabbage patch, with his missus shricking for a pig-sticking and throwing buckets at him while he bawled and hollered. It was a sight for sore eyes, said Bron, seeing Moses in the bath, and I prefer him in bulrushes.

"Just been talking to Wendy Fourpence over at the De Winton," said she.

"Oh, yes?" I tried to ignore her.

"Got an eye for you, she has — 'Who's that big handsome collier you're living with, Bron?' she asked — the damned cheek of it!"

"A few more days of this and I'll be trying Wendy Fourpence," I said.

"You run Wendy Fourpence and you're not coming back here alive!" said Bron, her eyes flashing.

"Good for the goose, good for the gander," I said. "You have Sam, I'll spend fourpence."

"*Toby!*"

I ran for it, chuckling.

22

THINGS WERE GETTING tighter in the Rhondda a few weeks later; it looked as if I had dropped right into it; but not so tight that I couldn't take Bron out (even though I'd just been laid off for a fortnight) — this being Fair Day and her Saturday night off from the Pandy.

Heinie said now, lowering his glass at the bar. "Wages were all right on the Sliding Scale till they signed the Boer War peace."

"Come on," I said to Bron as she served the jugs, "don't get into politics!"

"Wages was all right till the Boer War started," said Mattie. "Now we can't afford the price of a pint."

"You killed that one all right," said Bron, taking his glass for polishing. "And most of you seem to have the price of a drink when you come in here." She was done up to the nines in a bright, pink frock, and I was eager to get her to myself. A man cried, "Stick to pouring ale, woman, and leave the wages to ye betters — it's worse'n being back home wi' my missus."

"Aye, and God help your missus, I say," countered Bron. "You don't go short, Billy Price, with your kids out working and your mother-in-law on the parish."

"Mind," said Mattie, chewing, "there's still good money to be had in the valleys."

"But not getting coal." An old ironworker from Tredegar, this one, with one blue eye shining in his scalded face where the other had been plucked out by fire. "Owners like Thomas should be gelded, I say — lest they start paying for small coal, the Rhondda's heading for trouble."

Bron smacked down a glass on the counter and put her hat on. "You hang down a rock face up north with Lord Penrhyn, laddo, and you'd go thinner in the belly on slate. Ready, Tobe? — this lot don't know when they're lucky."

"We'll vote you in on the Miners Federation," called Mattie. "With views like that you ought to be in bed wi' Mabon."

"If I work things right I ain't in bed with anyone," said Bron. "Where's my flower?" and she took my arm.

Very spruce and done up, me, that Fair night; boots to shave in, bowler polished like a real Heath hat; alpaca suit buttoned down the front, a wing collar cutting my throat, hair smarmed down with water. And Ma Bron, ankle deep in that ravishing pink, looking as exotic as an orchid with her hair piled high and diamanté earrings, and she treated me that night like I was the only man alive. Along De Winton we went arm in arm, turning every head on the street.

"You don't get any older," I said. "It's not fair on the others."

"Some people grow old inside," said she, bowing to people.

"Still got Sam with us, have we?"

"Many don't have a lot to show for their mistakes, Tobe; now I've got you."

"And what have I got that Sam Jones hasn't?"

"You're here," said she.

Because it was Fair night the Scarrott boxing marquee was in the fairground behind the Pandy, and was packed with people come in from the valley. De Winton itself was a jabber of foreign tongues, too — Welsh and English, French and Italian thrown in, and half the thick-eared fraternity from Bristol and Cardiff seemed to be there, queueing outside the chemist's for cobwebs and leeches for cuts. Some of the local boys like Snookey Boxer, Martin Fury and Dai Rush I recognised, also the ageing Shoni Engineer who had hit Heinie about, and talk was that Jimmy Wilde himself was in Town for an exhibition.

Beer parties were over from Gilfach Goch and Porth — even the dead rose in the cemetery, folks said, to hear the Salvation Army playing *Washed in the blood of Jesus* outside the Pandy Inn. Drunks were already on the streets; fancy folk from the big houses strolling with their parasols and canes, the gentry big hats going round at the sight of Bron's beauty, and Bound and Wilkins the milliners, were doing a brisk trade with the farm women down from the hills.

Patsy Pearl, leading light of the Vale harlots, gave Bron a slow, sad smile outside the De Winton jug and bottle.

"How you doing, Patsy?" asked Bron, stopping.

"Passable."

"Don't see you much down·the Pandy these nights."

"I used to come a lot before, though," said Patsy, pale.

"That chap still drinks there, you know?"

They smiled at each other. It was women's business; I looked away. There was in Patsy's face a light; later, Bron told me that she was in love.

"But she does better than a Turkish harem," I protested.

"Men don't understand."

Next door to the De Winton, in the little market place, the stalls of the home-produce women were end to end, for this was Fair night and everything was open, including the mortuary.

Cockle women were here in their black, nun-like habit, crying their wares: fat butterpat women, with red, chubby hands, the market wives of the mountains, and their language was pure Welsh: duffing up the great mounds of butter and slapping it into pats, shouting their banter at the passing people: here were the sweet stalls, the bawdy Irish confectioners with their bugs whiskers, bulls-eyes, gob-stoppers; Everlasting Toffee and Toffee Rex tins of gorgeous creamy mints, with liquorice by the yard.

Mrs. 'Catty' Ledoux was there on her meat stall, skewering up the horse-meat with wheedling flourishes of her claw-like fingers; Mrs. Mia Bellini was selling her ice-cream, yelling its quality in her shrill Italian. May Plain and Dora Dobie, the washer-women, were selling starch and hunks of conservancy soap. There was black pudding, faggots and peas and bright, red polonys sizzling and bubbling in savoury pans, and the smell sent my mouth watering.

"My God, there's style for ye," cried Mrs. O'Leary, pointing her ladle at Bron. "Where did ye get that rig-out, love?"

"Over at Wilkins, do ye like it?" Bron pirouetted, arms out.

"Sufferin' God, all you want is a man, me girl! Like me! My fella's out drinking, and me working me fingers to the bone!"

We bought steaming faggots and peas from her, watching her ladling it into the bowls. "Are you pledged to him, Bron? *Ach*, stay single, girl — he'll bed ye and land ye with six like mine — honest to God, t'is only me chap's drinking, ye see — he takes no comfort in other women, like some I could mention."

"Is that a fact?" demanded Mrs. Shanklyn, on the faggots.

The peas plopped and steamed and we got our teeth into them, jostled and bustled on the pavement, screwing up our faces to the scald of it, blowing to cool it, and Mrs. O'Leary whispered confidentially, "Don't ye know it, Bron — the Shanklyn chap's up to his knees in strange women — anna that right, Shanklyn?" and she slapped her mate on the shoulder. "Patsy Pearl, ye say? My fella, ye say? Sure to God, if Patsy took him to bed it'd need me over in Clydach to come and switch him on," and she bellowed laughter, her great breasts shaking.

With the faggots and peas down us, we bought a string of polonys, and Tonypandy, endlessly gay and endlessly in grief, flooded past us on the pavements.

Gangs of rowdies were pushing in and out of the crowds, and the language they were using took the skin off Satan: in droves came the children, the ragged, mufflered new generation following the Salvationist band, ear-deafening in its blasts of trombones and tubers. The Temperance Legion was out again, always on Saturdays, coming in single file along Dunraven and De Winton, holding high their banners of sobriety despite the catcalls of following urchins: feigning drunkenness came others, a tatterdemalion riff-raff, a thriving element of the Rhondda's soul: from the lodging and doss-houses came these, whole families; rickety children, some as bandy as hoops, paraded in shouting, jostling columns behind the Temperance banners. These were not the colliers of the Rhondda; they knew no trade. This was the human refuse that hangs on to the coat of Industry; living amid squalor in the slums, a livelihood of horse-minding, begging and stealing small coal from the patches; sheep-killing, when the opportunity presented.

"*Scarlet* woman," said a man, and handed Bron a copy of *The Trumpet of Temperance.* "Are you not the female who serves alcohol behind the counter of the Pandy?"

His age was saving him, but his battered elegance stilled us; education in any form commands respect.

"Get on your way, old man," I said, but he faced me with resolution, bracing back his thin shoulders. Speechless, I spluttered at him while Mrs. Shanklyn and Mrs. O'Leary shook with mirth as the band thundered past. Bron handled it better; opening the paper she read it steadily, then folded it and gave it back to the man.

"You know," said she, "every time a Welshman lifts a pint he looks around for John Wesley. The trouble with piety, old man, is that those who spout it are usually sods."

It quelled him: fuming, he snatched the paper from her and ran after the banners.

Strange, I thought, this mercurial ability of Bron to change; one moment she had the language of the educated; next, that of the gutter.

In a peculiar way it added to her charms.

Now, amid the yelling, joyful crowd we danced to the music of the merry-go-round; were caught up in the strident orchestra of the Rink steam engine with its ten feet iron wheels and boiler belching sparks; a harmonic pandemonium of sounds. Pickpockets were active, slouching through the packed bodies with sullen intent; rowdies out of the Pandy were trying to pick fights: there were coconut shies, target shooting: chairoplanes and swing-boats.

It was Tonypandy Fair, where pallid children wandered in search of dropped bread while fat buckeroos of men tumbled bank notes in total disregard. Here went the street hawkers, rock vendors and stall criers, the cats-meat men, muffin men, medicine quacks; every one knowing many reasons why this was the greatest town on earth, except Porth, if you came from Porth, or Maerdy if you came from Little Moscow, as it was later called.

Mrs. Annie Arse and Albert we came upon by the stalls, with Tommy and Rosie, the children. "Remember, I told you that the Arses were in town?" cried Bron.

"Well, I never!" I shook Albert's hand and Annie patted and softened at me, and it was good to meet old friends. But the years, if they had grown the children, had sullied Albert and Annie: poverty was written on their clothes. Tommy, now knocking fourteen, was a man before his time: dark handsome, indepedent and ragged, his fists were on his hips. Rosie was big in all the right places, her young face expectant with its inner joys.

"And Tommy growing up, Toby Davies — you noticed?" asked Annie, thin as a lathe. "Things haven't been too good with us, you know — skinny on the parish, but we managed to feed him, eh?"

"They're both a credit to you," I said.

"Take a bit of handling, mind — don't they Albert? — our Rosie especially — a caution, ain't you, Rosie?"

"She's a good girl, though," said Albert, meek.

"You heard from the O'Haras since they went to Ireland?" asked Annie of me, with a nervous glance at Bron.

"Not a sign, missus."

"Just wondered." Her face was vacant. "Things ain't what they were, though, are they? But Albert's going down the Ely soon — bit o' luck and we'll get Number Two at the Sinkers — that's near where you live, ain't it, Ma Bron? — where you lodging then, Toby?"

"With me," said Bron. "In Number Six."

"Living together, are you?" asked Rosie, delighted.

"Dear me," said Albert, flushed.

"Ah, well," said Annie, awkward, "we got to get going."

I said, "I'm down the Ely — might be seeing you, Albert?"

"You'll both have to come round to Number Two, when we move in." Annie faltered, looking sad. "Nothing like the old times, is there — and old friends?"

Rosie, with a faint smile on her rosebud mouth, looked me over as I took off my hat, and Albert added, "You'll 'ave to take us as you find us, though."

"When they move in to the Sinkers you ain't going out without a pass," said Bron afterwards. "I've sized that Rosie."

I laughed. "She's only a kid!"

"She'd handle you, mate."

"What you looking at?" demanded Bron, later.

"You're a touchful woman," I said.

"Half a crown would fetch you Patsy Pearl, you know."

"Half a crown when I got free ones begging me?"

"Mind, you're a cheeky old beggar, Toby Davies — what's wrong with you?"

"Give me two minutes and you'll see."

"Ay ay. You lay a finger on me, Samson, and I'll howl back home for a pig-sticking, and the pugs'll come in and show you the four corners of the room."

"I'll handle the pugs, missus, and you after," I said.

"What's happened to you, Toby Davies?" Her eyes swept over me; an urchin, chewing rock from a dribbling mouth, stared up in astonishment at her beauty.

"I've growed up, like you said, girl, hang on to your drawers."

"That's something to look forward to. Time was you knew where it was but didn't know what is was there for."

You couldn't better her. Hands on hips, she regarded me, and the fairground beat about us.

"No trouble from you, Toby Davies — you're in my place on terms. I'll open the window, mind, and yell for Snookey Boxer."

"And I'll have him, too."

"I believe you would — saucy old boy!"

"Now that Sam has gone."

It changed her; the spell was torn.

"Let's get back home."

That much cooler (with Sam like a ghost between us) we were going for the Sinkers when we bumped right into Guto and Mrs. Livingstone: it wasn't unreasonable — as Bron said later, for she had seen them in Porth earlier: the Rhondda being a homing ground for immigrants from the north, ever since the Big Strike (it was on for years) sent the quarrymen down to coal in thousands.

"Well, well, *well!*" cried Mrs. Guto, "it's just like being up north — Toby Davies, of all people!" and she smoothed and fussed me while Guto tugged at my sleeve for attention.

The fair crowds pushed about us. Bron, I remember, looked a gilded lily of a woman in that garish light.

Outside a meat pie stall the Livingstone's were standing; starved they looked, but Guto was normal.

"You ever been to China?" asked he as the crowds pushed about us.

"Away there for a weekend soon, my love," said Bron, holding his hand. "You ain't the only beggar off abroad, ye know. How're you doing, missus?"

"It be pretty dry for us, in a manner o' speaking," said Mrs. Guto, and her hands and arms were chapped with the suds. "But things'll get better, never fear." The people shoved us all together, knocking Bron's hat off, and she cursed and swiped at the offender: then she looked at the pies and at the Gutos. "You fancy a pair of them? Me and Toby was just having some, weren't we?" She gave me an elbow, brightening me up.

"Four, and make 'em big ones, I'm starved," she shouted, and the pie-man, white-coated and beefy, served them up with flourishes.

"It's his birthday Wednesday, isn't it, Guto?" said his wife.

"It's his birthday tonight — hot pies, indeed!" Bron paid the money.

"It ain't that we haven't got the price of things," said Mrs. Guto, taking her bowl. "Just a bit short, eh, Guto — getting our divvy from the Co-op Monday, see?"

Eager-faced urchins danced about us, making faces of agony at the savoury smell of it: broad-faced peasant women from the hills shrieked lustily from under their big hats, hitting off their men's bowlers; the organ music rose, discounting thought. Mrs. Guto yelled, nudging Bron, "Send him a card, Wednesday, if you think of it, love. He always looks for birthday cards, poor old dab. Mind," she explained blowing at her bowl, "I always manage to send him some — his old Gran up in Pesda, for instance — she's been dead years, of course — then his cousin down in Wrexham and his brother in Glasinfryn. None of 'em write to him, but he do look forward to cards."

I pitied her.

Snookey Boxer went by with Orphan Effie, the girl the Salvation

Army had recently saved, and Snookey rose his bowler, very polite.

"We got to go," said Mrs. Guto, her thin face pinched up. "Very good of ye, I'm sure. Our treat next, remember?"

"That's all right, missus," I said.

"Oh, Christ," said Bron, after they'd gone.

"What about home, then?"

The Rhondda sleeps: the fairground is silent, only the dying naphtha flares, like the wands of drowsy fairies, send beams of skittering light over the debris of the Rink.

The red-nostrilled stallions of the merry-go-round are stilled; stray cats, ever the scavengers of the Rhondda nights, pad the trampled mud in search of dismembered polonys and lick the savoury-sweet fish batter on truant fish wrappers; Mrs. 'Catty' Ledoux, the Frenchwoman who eats cats, is stroking a pet persian. High goes the moon, shedding silver on the roofs, where a handful of gravel against the stars would patter on slate under which Johnny Norths were sleeping: dreaming, making love in the fidgety, nerveless fits and starts of all the Rhondda loving.

The towns, huddled in the narrow gorges and gulches, link hands in the moonlight; the old urinal near the Empire, ancient then, guggles and gushes, mistaking shadows for customers; the unwashed quarts and pewters of the pubs, from the New Inn over in Blaenrhondda to the Pandy in Tonypandy, stand in sightless emptiness. Above ground all is dead; below ground the hearts of the towns are beating.

"Good night," said Bron.

23

THE YEAR OF the Riots gave us a glorious summer.

June had come and gone in all her verdant clothes, painting up the hedgerows, decorating the fields, and the children back from Sunday School made daisy rings and piss-a-bed chains.

July sent cool winds softly over the mountains, and the country clear of the industry was honeyed and golden; the Twin Rivers, Fach and Fawr, bubbled and leaped down to the plains.

August, far from cooling us off with threats of things about to die, packed her bag of mid-summer sun and heaved it over the mountains, and we simmered and broiled in the blazing days, with people like Ricardo Bellini making a fortune on ice-cream, and spending a lot of it on Patsy Pearl when he should have been laying it up for Maria, beloved wife.

"You can't blame Patsy, mind," said Bron now, "that's her trade. It's the men I blame, every time," and she went round the hut like something demented, as usual, hitting the dust from one place to another.

"I know who'll blame little Patsy if Maria catches her," I said over the top of my book.

"What are you reading?" asked Bron.

"Edgar Allan Poe."

"Good God!"

I liked to read; I had always done it. 'Read, Toby, read,' my mother used to say, 'everything you can get your hands on,' and, after starting, I could never get enough. Archibald Hood, once the owner of the Scotch Colliery, had done his colliers well in this respect; opening his Miners' Library, where you could borrow anything from *Coal Owners — Guardians of Poor* to *The Decline and Fall of the Roman Empire*.

"I think I'll bake today, being Sunday," said Bron, "you fancy a rhubarb tart?"

"I fancy you," I replied.

"It's Moses Culpepper's rhubarb, mind."

I didn't go a lot on Moses's rhubarb, especially since he used to water his garden night and morning, contending, as he did so, that this was good for rhubarb. The tricky bit about eating the Culpepper rhubarb was trying to forget about the watering can.

"I feel in a special light mood," said Bron, and she tripped happily around the hut. Mood, according to one of her relatives, played a large part in successful baking; the duller the woman the heavier the pastry, apparently — a sign that the Devil was in the house. Bron actually used to sing to hers, weaving her hands lightly in the air above it — mainly, *The Lass with the Delicate Air*. It was a bit of a palaver, really, getting hold of a rhubarb tart.

"He lost his glass eye last night, you heard?" she asked, sprinkling flour.

"Who?" I lowered my book.

"Moses — and his false teeth, too, according to Rachel Odd. Got himself filled up at The Golden Age; came back here, sneezed 'em over the Square, and lost his glass eye, the silly old faggot."

"I don't go a lot on the ale in The Golden Age," I said.

"He's going home, I reckon, is Moses. Last week he took his lad to the Sports ground to see the county cricketers — white flannels, see? They finished up among the new cemetery gravestones."

"He'd better keep his eyesight away from the Ely agent. Ben Block does — he'll get his ticket for sure, otherwise."

Tap tap at the door, the gentlest of knocks; Bron opened it, and Mr. Richard Jones, the Ely Lodge chairman, stood there.

"Why, there's a surprise!" said Bron, and bobbed a curtsy to his bow.

"Come you in, Mr. Jones." She wiped the flour from her hands. "I was just off next door, directly."

"Busy, is it? I can come back again, mind!"

"Ach, no sir, make yourself at home." She softly closed the door behind her.

I was wishing him to the devil; Bron, too. I knew what he had come for.

Gaunt and grey, Mr. Jones perched on the edge of a chair and peered at me with his red-rimmed eyes; his face was like dust, and dust was in his chest but not his big, bass voice. "You've given some thought to what I spoke of, Toby Davies?"

"Lodge treasurer?" I shook my head. "No."

"Good brothers are needed for the coming fight — stand or fall together, see? It is something to be offered the trust of the Union, lad."

"Didn't you say you knew what happened to me up in Bethesda?" I asked.

"Questions have been asked, and answered — O'Hara's dishonesty in the Quarryman's Union was nothing to do with you." Mr. Jones smiled faintly.

I saw beyond his ashen face the dim outline of the Pandy.

Dusk was falling. People, long from Chapel, were standing in little groups, the women with hymn books, the men laden with their big coloured bibles.

"A coming fight, you say?" I asked.

"To the death, if needs be." His voice raised. "The old Sliding Scale was once the miner's friend, now it's his enemy. The Boer War lifted prices on the Scale by seventy-five per cent; but, when the peace was signed eight years back, the cost of living cut take home pay by half. The Cambrian Combine's in trouble unless they raise to two-and-six a ton." He nodded sagely at me. "God will be on the side of the Federation in this, mark me."

"Strikes me that God's on the Cambrian's Board of Directors," I replied. "They deny us a united protest? You'll have to shift the county police before you shift the Cambrian Combine."

"You suggest force "

"You want a rise in wages, Mr. Jones, that's how you'll have to get it. The blacklist, spies within the Union, intimidation, bribes — the owners use force six days a week. Now they've got our agents in their pockets, force is all they recognise."

"They're grave charges," said he, his hands folding together.

"But true, and the Miners' Federation knows it. You won't get anything without a strike." I got up. "But the valleys are still doing well enough, aren't they? I've no complaints."

"Aye, but it is not today we're fighting for lad, it's tomorrow; not for this generation, but the next. We've got to get rid of the Sliding Scale; get payment for Small Coal and retention of House Coal at five shillings a ton."

"They'll call in the military before they'll sign to that, Mr. Jones."

"But you'll help, son? — new blood is needed. Thirty years I've worked for the Union, man and boy. Sometimes I feel as old as Methuselah. Tell me you'll serve!"

"If you think I can," I said, sighing.

"God bless you." The old man rose. "I'll bring the books round tomorrow. In my day we thought it a privilege to hold the Union's books. Honesty is the basis of unionism; men of honesty are hard to find and scallywags abound. They're kicked out of one place and turn up in another — men like Nairn, who disappeared with the Rochdale funds; Needham, who stole from Bridgend — these two went north — the Union rarely prosecutes, you know. The northerners come south, of course. Ben O'Hara, for one."

"Ben O'Hara?" I stared at him.

"He's settled up Merthyr way — Abercanaid, I think."

Realisation brought the old, obliterating emotion. I was fighting for the sense of it. "They . . . they've left Ireland, then? — *Abercanaid*, you say?"

The old man nodded, his eyes questioning my reaction. "The Federation checks the move of every scallywag — the quarrymen wrote that he moved to South Wales within the last year or so."

I reflected, bitterly, that Nan and Ben must actually have been in the Merthyr area at the same time as me; they could have easily been living in Nightingale Street. It was a bitter twist of Fate, the place being so small, that we had not met. I had a sudden and nearly overwhelming urge to walk through the door in search of her.

Bron entered, saying:

"One day women'll have a Union, you know. Then it'll be ten to five, and no baking Sundays."

After the old man had gone, she said, looking at me strangely, "What's happened to you, Tobe? Seen a ghost?"

Since I was on night shift that Monday, I went shopping with Bron in Town.

Mrs. Mia Bellini, the wife of the ice-cream man, we met on the steps of Paddy Ginty, the grocer; I hit up my cap to her, Bron bowed.

Dark and flashing was Mrs. Bellini, heaving bosom and hoop earrings.

"Seen my Ricardo, 'ave you?"

A direct descendant of a Corsican bandit was she, according to Ricardo, her husband, and God help me if she ever finds me with Patsy Pearl, he used to say.

"In the Scotch library," I replied.

"The library?" cried Mia. "What for the library? The fool cannot read!"

"Just seen him there, Mrs. Bellini."

She hit her forehead with her fist. "*Mama Maria!* When I catch him I kill him! The library, you say? you men, you are all the same — dirty boots, dirty minds — all the time it is women, women!" and she swept down the street.

"She's not far wrong," said Bron. "Is he in the library?"

"In Patsy Pearl," I said. "Number Eight, River Row. Monday's his afternoon off."

"You know her address?"

"I've heard talk of it," I said.

"And I bet Patsy's heard talk of you."

"That's a dreadful thing to say!"

"It's a dreadful thing to do," said she. "I tell you what, six-foot-three; if I ever catch you up River View, Corsican bandits won't come into it."

Despite the street criers and clattering trams the day was suddenly quiet.

"You're conquered territory, Bron," I said. "You belong to Sam, so why can't I get off?"

"Get it right. I belong to nobody now."

"That makes me free."

"Oh, no it doesn't — you belong to me."

"That's unfair."

"Of course." She glared at me.

Cooler, with sheet-ice like a window between us, we went into Ginty's.

A small dark, woman passed by on the other side of the street; it could have been Nanwen.

It was good enough for a Band of Hope meeting in Ginty's grocery shop that afternoon. And Paddy Ginty, as Irish as peat, was going like a steam-hammer behind the counter, while his missus, thin as a Galway ghost, watched the customers with her large, haggard eyes.

"I was just telling Mrs. Culpepper, if I never move from here," said Ginty, "it's the economics of the Rhondda's all adrift, sure to God. Don't ye agree, Toby Davies?"

"We've got no economics," I replied.

"That's right. If it wasn't for the Board of Guardians and the Quakers, the place'd be flat on its face. And if the Co-op carried the debts I do, it'd be in blutty liquidation," and he smacked up the butter pats. "Still, sure to God, we're all God's creatures."

"There's a heaven for ye somewhere, Ginty," said Bron, "though I doubt if it's in the Rhondda."

"One slice of bacon, please," said Primrose Culpepper, "and a little less old tongue with it, Ginty."

"There now — see what I mean?" asked Ginty. "A slice of bacon — all me clients are pantry blutty clients."

"Got to live from hand to mouth, haven't we?" said Mrs. Shanklyn. "It's just the same in the trotter and faggot trade — bowl to stomach, isn't it?"

"*Arrah!* Now ye've got it," said Ginty. "The place has got no larders — like India, if ye get me — nothing in reserve."

"No reserve for Union strikes, you mean?" said Bron.

"Exactly!" Ginty raised a boney finger. "You're all threatening strikes, but the town can't stand a strike. The time's wrong for it, your Union's not ready for it. You've got people like Ablett, Rees and Hopla in disagreement, the Naval Pit at the throat of the Pandy Committee and Nantgwyn knocking out the teeth of both. I'm tellin' ye — fight now, and you'll all lose blood."

"Mind," said Rachel Odd, "if there's going to be trouble, count me in. Six kids I got, and one in by 'ere," and she patted her stomach. "The way things're going I'll be breast-feeding this one through the school railings."

Bron said, "A cottage loaf and two ounces of liver, for God's sake, Ginty."

They spoke more, but I didn't really hear them, for I knew that Ginty was right. A dark cloud of threat was growing over the valleys: the old sufferings were about to return, and folks knew it. It was part of the inevitable cycle of Rhondda life.

Bron's elbow jogged me back to reality. "Come on, forget it, mate — it's far too beautiful a day."

Outside on the pavement the off-shift colliers and their wives thronged four abreast amid the clanging trams and strident voices of the street-criers; fiddles were screeching, concertinas going, and Tonypandy was golden with summer. Patsy Pearl we met, and Bron paused; then the new overman at my pit sought a path between us, and Patsy, I noticed, caught his eyes, and smiled. He was a man and a half, this new Englishman, John Haley, and the Scarrott heavy-weights were trying him for size. Returning Patsy's smile, he pushed on.

"You all right, Patsy?" asked Bron, who never passed her without a word.

"A bit tight, you know — it's a hell of a time about now, really," Patsy answered.

Aye, and you must have got rid of Ricardo pretty sharp, I reflected.

"Did you see Mr. Haley just then?"

I looked away in disassociation; not my business, women's gabbling.

I heard Patsy say, "Do he come into the Pandy still, then?"

"Aye," said Bron. "A lot."

"I'd go decent for him — you know."

"You'd best try it, girl," said Bron, "you never know your luck."

Up came Rosie Arse. Summerful and chesty was Rosie, her eyes alight with vitality, like a tiger hunting. "Seen my mam have you, Ma Bron?"

"Not today, Rosie."

"Changing me name, ye know?" She perked and pouted, looking gorgeous.

"I don't blame you, with a name like that," I said, and bright eyes switched over me; there was talk of boys and darkness whispers beyond the light of the fountain in Pandy Square; at fourteen she looked two years older. It was astonishing to me how Albert had fathered such beautiful children.

"Seeing one of the councillors about it, I am." Her beauty was comely, her puppy fat disappearing; soon, I thought, you will have shadows in your cheeks and jewels for eyes, and the colliers will see a woman. "Deed done, or something," she added. "Me name's Harse, really, see? Trouble is these Rhondda yobs can't pronounce their blutty haitches."

"Deed Poll?" said I, and spelled it into her questioning face.

"Dear me, legal profession now?" said Bron.

"Give her a year or so and she'll set this place alight," I said, after Rosie had gone.

"She's not doing so bad now," said Bron, eyeing me for shock. Turning, she switched on a smile for Sarah Bosom and Dozie Dinah who passed us, arm in arm, and I hit up my bowler.

"Funny pair they are," I said. "You know, come to think of it, they're a queer old lot living in the Rhondda."

"I was just considering that," she replied, giving me an eye.

We walked through the crowds.

Heinie Goldberg, we saw, alone as usual, with a little bag for groceries; Jimmy Wilde and his missus went past, all eyes turning to the pale shadow of a man who was knocking them flat all over the valleys — eighteen men in one night, at Scarrotts' booth, over in Trebanog: never more than nine stone, he took on men six stones larger; as much a phenomenon as the Rhondda itself.

"*Diawch*, I'm dry," I said, "you'd have to prime me to spit."

"I'm going on, then," said Bron. "I'll get the liver on."

"A glass of milk might soothe me," I said outside the dairy. "Got a cold coming, I think."

"You've a plaster for every sore, 'aven't you?" She put twopence into my hand. "Go on, I'll treat ye."

I kissed her, and passing people frowned, worried.

"Go on with you," said she, pushing, "get off," so I took her twopence and went into the De Winton.

Moses Culpepper was standing at the bar, parting his whiskers and killing a quart; most of the old-timers drank quarts, those days; the younger generation, being delicate, sipped pints.

"Old and mild," I said, and the landlord nodded: beefy and red was he, a change to Moses, who looked pale and drawn despite his eighteen stones. What with one thing and another, Moses had been having a bad time of late.

"Any news of your eye, yet?" I asked, and he shook his head, doleful.

"It's the marble season, mind," said he. "Anything could have happened to it. Now I've hit up me ampton — it never rains but it pours."

I said, "You poor soul. That's a tragedy."

"It'll teach him not to rub his knees with horse liniment," said the landlord, and I slid him twopence for the pint.

"But he's got my sympathy, sure to God," said an Irishman. "I'd not wish that on a duck."

Said Moses, glum, "Me missus thought the cork was in and poured it over me privates." So I'd heard; the whole of Pandy must have heard, with Moses charging around shouting murder.

The time went on and I ordered another pint. The talk was of horse racing and bets, and when the pits would come out; of Mabon, Bill Brace and Tom Richards, the Members of Parliament. Suddenly, the landlord said, "Hey, by the way, Toby, did you see that chap who were asking for you?"

"What chap?" I wiped my mouth and set down the glass.

"He was in here some time back," said Moses, writing a betting slip.

"Asking for me?"

193

"Well," said the landlord; "after Ma Bron, really, weren't he?"

A silence sparked within the din.

Both surveyed the room as if they had said nothing. It was crammed with noisy colliers, settling Tonypandy before they raised the dust.

"A chap asking for Bron?" I asked.

Moses, realising the error, shifted uneasily; the landlord adopted an air of studious absence.

"Made a right cock of that now, didn't ye?" said Moses, and the landlord said, uncertainly:

"Well, he'd been over to your place, see, and he couldn't find Bron in the Pandy. . . ."

"What did he look like?" I could feel my heart thudding in my chest and heard the clash of glasses, the hoarse shouts, as echoes. An Irishman cried, "Dark and tough, a great lump of a fella, so he was."

"Nothing to it, Tobe — a man's got a right to ask," said the landlord, plaintively, and I got him by his buttons.

"*When?*"

"Half an hour or so — come on, come on, hold your bloody horses!"

"What did you tell him?"

"I sent him back to the Pandy, that's what!" He shoved me away, brushing himself down. "Jesus, I ain't a home for lost dogs, ye know."

"You've got less brains than a horse's arse," said Moses. "Look, he hasn't even finished his ale."

I went over the Square and into the Pandy like a man out of a gun, and pushed the door back onto its hinges. I glared around, but Sam wasn't there. Something greater than intuition told me it was him.

"Just kick it open," said the landlord, "don't bother."

"A chap asking for Bron? Where is he?"

"You ask Bron, mister, no business of ours."

But I could see by his expression that somebody had been asking, so I shoved my way through the gaping customers and ran to the Huts, and there was Bron standing before the mirror, preening and

194

fluffing up, and she didn't spare me a glance. Slowly, I entered.

"Where is he?"

"Who're you after mate, the Pope?"

"Sam's been in here, hasn't he?"

"If he has he's been pretty sharp," she replied, "I've only just come in myself." Turning to me, she added, "Anyway, he's got the right, hasn't he? He's my husband, and this is my place."

It came as news to me; lately she had seemed so completely mine.

But it was the same old Bron, I reflected; Sam had only to wink an eye and she came running.

"Back in Porth, is he?"

She walked past me to the sink and began to fill a bowl. "At this rate you're going to miss shift — I haven't even got the tea on."

"Answer me!" I caught her by the wrist and swung her against me.

"You leave go of me or you'll get the frying-pan," she said softly, her eyes alight.

Tense, fighting to control myself, I released her, and she said, turning away. "According to you, he's in Tonypandy."

"You can't run the two of us, Bron."

"Right, then — you sod off."

"Don't swear!"

"Jealous, stupid beggar! — you're enough to singe a saint." In the middle of the room she swung to face me, saying, "Dear me, you've a reckless imagination, haven't you? Honest to God, you're the one chap I know who can make a monkey's tit out of nothing."

She was close to tears; only Sam Jones could make Bron cry, I remembered.

"You swear he hasn't been here?"

She walked back to the grate and poked it into a blaze.

"I'm swearing nothing, son — you'll have to take my word for it."

I didn't know what to do; how to handle her. Had Sam been there, it would have been easy — I hit my fist into the palm of my hand.

At the window, I bowed my head.

"Don't be unhappy, Tobe," said Bron, at the bosh.

I didn't reply; I hated the thought she that was lying to me, and said so.

"I didn't lie," she said, wiping her hands, and turned me into her arms like a woman cajoles a child, but I pushed her away.

"I can't stick this," I said.

"You'll have to, mun — there'll always be Sam."

"No man can bear being second best."

She held me away. "And what about me? — it cuts both ways, you know — what about Nanwen?"

"*Eight years* ago, woman? She's out of my life, and you know it!"

She made a face. "I'd be a larger fool than you take me for if I believed that."

Empty, we stood apart.

24

TROUBLE WAS COMING.

It was breathed on the mountain air, at the lodge meetings, and guzzled through ale in the publics. Acrimony over 'abnormal places' was developing between the colliers and the Owners. There was even talk that, if we didn't stop claiming the extra ninepence a ton and payment for small coal, the Ely management would lock us out of the Bute seam.

"That don't seem likely," said Heinie. "Cut their own throats? That isn't capitalism."

"It would make us an example to the rest of the Union, though," I said.

"You should worry, Toby — you've got it good," said Ben Block. "You, Heinie and Mattie — I've got six mouths to feed."

As a single man, I wasn't doing so bad in the Bute seam.

Even without payment for small coal, I was taking home nearly thirty shillings a week after stoppages, and Bron's twelve bob a week at the Pandy helped us to skin it out, for the rent at the Sinkers was only five shillings. In fact, we had six sovereigns saved in the tea-caddy.

But people like Ben Block, with a houseful of kids, were not so fortunate. Twice this spring Ben had been laid off for a fortnight, and gone on short time once; a couple of rejected trams a week — when the checkweigher refused to accept them because of shale content or small coal — and Ben Block and his like were in trouble.

Even at the height of the Rhondda prosperity, some colliers —

especially those with big families — were going on the Parish.

Take Albert Arse. Since coming to the valleys five years back, Albert had worked in practically every pit in Rhondda Fach, and, with a family of four, had known hunger when laid off.

The coal owners weren't particular about colliers; a cut in manpower meant a rise in profits. In the last seven years, with coal output steady at about two hundred and fifty million tons yearly, the value of exported coal had risen by three shillings a ton 'free on board' at the docks. But the colliers of South Wales saw little of this prosperity. The age-old jingle survived, but it was still only a colliers' dream:

> Eight hours to work
> Eight hours of freedom
> Eight hours of sleep
> And eight shillings a day.

At Mabon's rate of progress, men said, we'd likely get such a Utopia round about a hundred years hence.

Go-slows began in the pits by disgruntled colliers, who, working in 'abnormal places', and faced with the loss of small coal (also threats of the loss of their concessionary coal), begged in vain through the Conciliation Boards for a rise in wages to meet the leaping cost of living. The managements reacted by laying men off, and the old spectre of destitution began to stalk the valleys. Emigration began again, something that had not happened since the beginning of the Coal Rush fifty years back. Whole families could be seen trudging the roads to the west — back to the farms and the promise of sun. As in the Welsh iron era, the industries of Pennsylvania and Pittsburgh called, and people were spending their last savings on passages to America.

The Rhondda, once bulging with humanity, began to thin its streets; accommodation came vacant. What was once a landlord's paradise was ceasing to exist. Albert and Annie Arse, Rosie and Tommy, were a case in point.

At the beginning of September they moved in down the Row to Number Two, the Sinkers. Albert was prepared to work for a pittance on the top — carting rubbish for two shillings a day; then, with the prospect of Tommy beginning work, the family fortunes changed. At ten shillings a week the management put a premium on boys, making no indiscreet inquiries about their proper ages. But, despite all this, few colliers, and certainly not the Miners Federation, were seriously thinking about a South Wales strike to get conditions improved.

Indeed, on that bright, autumn morning when young Tommy started work, most people seemed more concerned about Moses Culpepper.

"He found his teeth, ye know, Ma Bron?" shouted Rachel from her wash-line.

"Who, Moses?" Bron, too, was pegging out, being a Monday.

The women gathered as usual; the Welsh being experts for a gossip over the wall.

"Last night a mongrel looked through the window of the Crown, and it was wearing 'em!"

"Wearing what?" shouted Etta McCarthy, leaning on her gate.

"Culpepper's teeth."

"*Gawd!*" shrieked Etta, "I don't believe it!"

"It were, I tell ye!" shouted Dai Parcel, the postman, at the gate of Number One; coming back down the Ely today, was Dai, an old collier; now moved in there with his mates Gwilym and Owen, all widowers. "Saw it myself, but he hadn't got his eye, mind."

"Very funny, I must say," said Primrose Culpepper, easing Moses off his chair with her broom. "Kindly raise your backside so I can sweep out. You can handle this blutty lot, I'm not stooping to pick up rubbish."

"It's me eye I'm after chiefly, though," said Moses, heaving up his stomach. "I'm not the same on the women, mind, with me eye absent."

"Lost your love life, Moses?" This from Dano McCarthy stripped for washing, while his six sons were bubbling and towelling over their buckets on the patch.

"He'll never be the same," said Primrose Culpepper. "Any spare chaps going loose round your way, Bron?"

"Not that I know of," said Bron, giving me a shove.

The cackling and banter went on all down the Row.

When I came out with my bait tin and jack, Tommy Arse was waiting at the gate, and Annie, his ma beside him, her hair in rags.

Bagged and belted was Tommy, nigh fourteen. In a pair of Albert's cut-down trews, he was quiffed and poshed up, ready for the Ely.

"*Duw*, couldn't you spare him another year, Annie?" asked Bron.

"His pa's on short, and we need the money," said Annie, thinly anxious.

"Does the new overman know he's under age? He's English and tough, they say."

"Got Willie Shanklyn's birth certificate," I said, "so he's fourteen and two months."

Bron said, turning away, "One wonders who's luckiest — Tommy or Mrs. Shanklyn's idiot — one thing's sure, the pit'll never get Willie."

"Got no option," said Annie, screwing her hands. "He's eatin' for a regiment, ain't you, Tom?" and Bron knelt and took the boy's hand in hers.

"And how does Tommy feel about it?"

"Christ, missus," said he, and his face became alive. "Down the Ely with Uncle Toby, I am, and coming for a farrier lad with horses, for the pay's good, and bring home money for ma!" I never again heard him say so much.

"God help you," said Bron, and tried to kiss him, but he pushed her away and came to me.

She wandered inside. Listening for the coming of the lads, I followed her.

"He could have been ours, Toby — you realise?" There was the strangest expression upon her face.

"Sam's, more likely."

But her smile, slow and sad, did not fade. "Well, he could have been, couldn't he? — ours, I mean. Like Bibbs-Two — she could have been yours — you ever realised?"

"One thing's sure, we'll never have one at this rate."

The knowledge that Nanwen was in the south was bringing to me

a new and vital independence; as if I had shed the cloak of my
necessity, making Bron of less importance.

"You've changed the last week or so, Tobe."

"Isn't that natural?"

"Do we have to share a bed, just because we live together?"

"Not necessarily, there's a lot more fish in the sea."

"You're getting bitter."

"What d'you expect?"

There was a pause; the chatter of the women outside invaded our
privacy.

Bron said, looking at her hands, "Suppose I fell for a baby?"

"Wouldn't that be natural, too?"

"I'm married, ye know — I got to think about babies. Not fair on
a kid, is it — taking its pick of a father."

"If you loved me and not Sam Jones, you wouldn't even think
of that."

Her voice rose, "And if you loved me you wouldn't be giving me
such hell about it — can't you wait till I'm free?"

"Free of Sam?" I laughed in her face. "You'll never be free of
him! In the last four months I've had him for breakfast, dinner and
tea. One day he'll come, give you a wink, and you'll be straight
through the window."

She wandered about, fists clenched. "I'd rather be yoked to a
pig!"

"Come on, be honest — lies never suited you."

"I would — I . . . I wouldn't give him house room. Life with Sam
again?" She strode about. "The beggar charms the honey out of the
hive, then skips off with the first queen bee — it wouldn't last five
minutes!"

She was nearly crying; I wondered if it was for Sam, or me. I
tried to turn her into my arms, but she shrugged me away and went
to the table, gripping it, head bowed.

"What a damned good start for a Monday wash-day!"

"I'm sorry," I said.

"What for? You're right, aren't you?"

And Tommy burst into the room, forgetting manners, yelling,
"The colliers are comin', Uncle Toby, the colliers are coming!"

Bron turned her wrought face to mine. "You bring that boy back in one piece, mind, or you'll never hear the end of it."

"That's better," I smiled at her and she dashed a hand at her face.

"Goodbye," I said, though I'd have liked to kiss her.

She was right, I supposed, as I hauled Tommy off to the morning shift. Bibbs-Two could have been mine, come to think of it.

All the Row was out to see Tommy Arse start work that early September day, which was the custom with a new lad starting, and a shout went up as the Ely shift wheeled into the Square, and there was Primrose Culpepper hugging Tommy to the ample breast, more dangerous on breathing than being down the pit: Rachel Odd ran after us, patting and blessing him, and watch yourself in the trams, lad. Will Parry Trumpet, always pushed but never late, galloped out of Number Eleven, and damn me, we're going to have that bloody bugle again, said Heinie, flies open as usual, when we joined him and Mattie.

Marching next door to me was big John Haley, the new Ely overman; handsome and aloof, he had about him the air of a man who wouldn't be tampered with. Patsy Pearl, I noticed, was standing with her baby Madog in her shawl as we marched past the chemist's: got it bad, had Patsy, her eyes, like saucers. But the English foreman, a widower, rumour said, didn't appear to notice her. Instead, he leaned across me in the ranks and put his fist on Tommy's shoulder. "New lad, eh?"

"Yes, sir," said Tommy, rigid.

"Easy," I said, "nobody's going to eat you."

"Name?" asked the foreman.

"Tommy," I said.

"Just Tommy?"

"Tommy Arse."

The foreman didn't bat an eye. "You're blessed with an original name, son — are you blessed with years?"

"Fourteen and two months," I said.

"The boy speaks for himself. Age?" He leaned over to Tommy.

"Got my birth certificate to prove it sir," said Tommy, stretching his thighs to keep our stride, "though Willie Shanklyn's name's on it, mind."

I groaned, closing my eyes.

"That's buggered that," said Heinie, and the foreman said:

"Once I had a son the same size as you, Tommy Arse."

I glanced at the man. I bettered six-foot-three, and he gave me inches. "You lost him, Foreman?"

He moved me over and marched with Tommy.

Past the Gethin we went and into the lamp room, and Tommy was all eyes as he got his first lamp and watched the lamp man light it.

"Right, you," said John Haley, the overman. "I'll have him," and he gripped Tommy's shoulder with a ham-like hand. "First time underground?"

"Yes, sir."

The coal-starched shoulders of the morning shift were all about us as we filed into the cage; the gate clanged shut. Near me, his head against the overman's stomach, Tommy's brown eyes stared with his inner fears. The cage dropped; the foreman's hand went out.

"Knees bent, stand limp. Don't fight it." Tommy came off his feet then, but Mr. Halcy held him down.

"Jesus," said Tommy.

At the Bute landing, John Haley said to me, "Did you make his application?"

"Aye, Foreman," and he said to Tommy, gripping him still:

"Properly introduced, officially taken on, eh? All in order. Now then, this business of the names — are you Tommy Arse or Willie Shanklyn — the owner of the Cambrian Combine has written in asking this personally — all the way from France."

"I'm Tommy Arse, really," said Tommy. "Shanklyn's only the fiddle, like Uncle Toby told me."

I made a face, turning away. Haley said to me, "They need the money?"

"As poor as ragged mice, Foreman," I answered.

"God, what a country!" To Tommy, he added, "Arse, you know isn't the best of surnames — how does Tommy Shanklyn suit you? — t'is a bit of both."

Bright and pleasured was Tommy's face.

"Or even Tom Shanklyn?" The foreman regarded the roof deep in thought; it was a matter of tremendous importance. "You see, you being a man now, you might even forget about the Tommy...?"

Tommy rose to his full height of four-foot-ten. "Aye, sir — Tom Shanklyn."

"Right," said Haley, and winked at me. "Get going with your butty and start loading — Mr. Goldberg'll issue you with your curling box. And lift with your knees together, remember?"

"I've told him," I said.

"Get going, then — are you hanging round all day?"

"There's water down here again," said Mattie, splashing around in the dark, and I brought our lamps up, and the water, six inches deep, swirled its oily blackness into our boots.

"There's always water in this stall," said Heinie.

I said, wading about, "What the devil was the night shift doing? Did they slacken off the pumps?"

"Pumps still going, I can hear 'em," said Mattie.

I didn't like it. In a warmer stall it wasn't so bad, but getting out big stuff under wet, cold conditions like this was worth a pound a ton, never mind one-and-ninepence. I stripped off my shirt, hung it on the roof and lay down in the stall. The water flooded over my arm, bringing icy fingers to my neck and throat.

I hewed and cut, kicking the coal back with my feet, and Mattie hauled it away with the curling box, emptying it into the tram. It was a hard seam, this Bute — five feet at its highest; about two feet high at the point where I was cutting. Beyond the face rats were scuttling; they'd scuttle faster, I thought, when Mattie packed the gob.

I had got used to the rats. Time was when the very sight of one would make me feel sick, but Llechwedd's Victoria cavern had broken me in: they were moving around more than usual that morning, and I mentioned it to Mattie.

"Taking over the Ely," said he.

In the silence of the face, when I was not breathing, I could hear distant shot-firers in other headings, raking the bowels of the mountain; the clanging beats of the sledge-hammers as they hit up the pit-props, and sometimes, I fancied, even voices in far away

204

galleries; the ghosts of lost generations, perhaps, talking out of the past?

Did unknown fish swim, perhaps, in the acres of static water? I wondered. Did the rocks three thousand feet under my elbow thunder to underground rivers? In the window of my mind I again saw Bron walking the shining face of Glamorgan; and us lying here, digging out coal for the fires of people to whom our deaths would mean nothing.

I brought up my knees to ease my aching back; sprawling around under the roof, searching for the seam.

"There's a dignified position for the new lodge treasurer," said Mattie.

"In this position I've given some of my best performances."

"Ay ay, well shift your arse over so I can come in."

I saw Lark, Duck's horse, turn up her eyes at the roof. The rats were squealing louder still.

"You are not chasing rats today, my lovely," said Duck, and he hitched her to the tram by dropping in the pin and gave her a slap, but Lark didn't move. Duck nodded and brought out his watch, peering at it in the lamp-light. "Just as I thought — snap, eh? This old mare can tell the time, you know?" and he opened his tommy box, eating delicately.

"Who's this coming?" growled Ben Block, squatting down on the gob.

"It's only me, lads," said Tommy. "Ay ay boys!" Black-faced and happy was he, coming with his curling box for loading.

"Ay ay boys, indeed!" said Mattie. "Cheeky little bugger. I thought you was down on Three Road with the new foreman?"

"I were," said Tommy, opening his bait box, "but he sent me down to be with Heinie."

"Mr. Goldberg to you," I said, crawling out.

"Is there going to a strike, mun?" asked Tommy.

"If there is, you won't be in it — you're not a paid up member."

Tommy looked suddenly close to tears. "A strike? But I've only just started!"

"Don't you worry, my flower," said Heinie. "You sit by 'ere with Uncle Heinie."

"Don't you call me a flower," said Tommy.

"Unofficial?" A prop trembled beside me; dust showered down from the roof.

"Unofficial strike? Talk sense, mun!"

"It could happen," I said. "People like Mabon will have to make up their minds."

"They would lock us out first, these owners," said Duck, biting into his bread and cheese. "But all the Cambrian and Glamorgan lodges would come out, too, they say. And we're twelve thousand strong in the Cambrian alone."

"Count in Maesteg, the Western Valley and you've got two and a half times as much," said Mattie, chewing, and he drank from his jack, eyes clenched against the sweat, and gasped. "Take the whole of South Wales and Monmouthshire and you're better'n a quarter of a million."

"They'd bring in the police if we start violence."

"And the military!"

"They shot the colliers down in Featherstone, remember?"

"Who's Home Secretary now, for God's sake?"

"Winston Churchill."

"He'll give you Featherstone," said Mattie. "Those blutty Suffragettes want to watch out with him about, an' all."

"Christ," said Ben Block, looking at his cheese. "She must have got this out of the blutty mousetrap."

"We'll be doing the breast stroke down here soon," I said.

"I'm reporting this pit to the agent," said Mattie.

"Poor little scratch, you'll frighten the arse off him."

"Or try Haley, the new foreman?"

"That's more reasonable," I replied. "Up north, we'd have seen to it long since."

"Are you talkin' of the North Wales Quarrymen's Combination?" asked Duck, polite, and I answered:

"Men like Mabon aren't a patch on people like the Parrys." I nodded around. "If we'd had W. J. Parry heading this Union, we wouldn't be wet-working."

"Give it a rest, Tobe," cried Heinie. "Sitting around on a tenholer privy with their shirt-tails out — just to duck the agent?"

"It do sound a pretty strange quorum — I'd like to have heard the speeches," said Ben Block, chuckling, and Mattie said:

"Success has gone to ye head, Tobe," and he stooped for his pick. "I'm prepared to bare me breast, mind, but not even for a quart of Allsops would I bare me arse." He got up, groaning.

"Can I have a quart, Uncle Toby?" This from Tommy, his eyes shining in the lamps.

"When we get up, son," said Heinie, cuffing him. "First smell o' the barmaid's apron, eh?" Fists on his hips, he surveyed Tommy. "Unions, Federations, Combinations? — it don't mean a lot to you, now, does it?"

"First quart, eh? Damn me!" said Tommy.

There came a silence of dripping water and a crescendo squealing of the rats.

"They're making an awful lot of noise these days," I said.

"Better than *Judas Maccabaeus*. You heard the tenors in Upper Trebanog?"

"They ain't paid up members, you know? They got no right to squeal without permission," grumbled Mattie.

"You bitter old sod," said Heinie.

25

I WANTED TO take Bron with me to the Rocking Stone meeting at Pontypridd that coming Saturday night, largely on the suggestion of Heinie Goldberg, who was an expert in certain matters, he claimed.

"You're quite sure that there's nothing wrong with you, then?" he had asked. "I mean biological — that's the word for it — biological."

"Not that I'm aware of."

"You live with her, but sleep apart?"

"That's the size of it."

"It's an awful waste," said Heinie, sadly.

It was three days later, and we were on our way home from the Ely shift.

"It . . . it's just that she's in love with this Sam Jones fella?" he asked.

"That's it." And he answered, surprisingly:

"Every woman's a virgin, Tobe, when she's in love." An amazing philosophy, coming from Heinie.

It was food for thought. Damned women! I thought; you can never get to the bottom of them.

"That's one way of putting it," said Heinie. "Look, *bach*, wheel her up to that Rocking Stone next Saturday, sit her on it, then stand by to fight her off."

I replied, "I can't — she says she won't come — she's not interested in politics. Anyway, that yarn about the Rocking Stone trick is an old wives' tale."

"Bet you a pint on it," said Heinie. "Do you fancy one now to settle the dust?"

"We'll set 'em up at the Pandy."

"And cast an eye on the sacrificial lamb," said Heinie.

We went up to the bar and hit it for ale, and Bron served us, looking gorgeous in her pink dress, but she had a face as long as a kite.

"You had much experience with women?" asked Heinie, quiet.

"Not a lot."

He drank steadily, watching Bron serving the customers; certainly, she wasn't her usual self that night.

"Have you ever run a woman that this one knows about?" he asked, reflectively.

I thought of Nanwen, and gave it a shrug. "Aye, once — but it was a long, long time ago."

"That makes no odds," Heinie grinned at Bron and gave her a wink; for reply, she put her nose up.

"That could be the trouble," said he.

In my desperation I'd landed among the witch-doctors.

I didn't stay long. Bron had got them on her, this was sure, and I wasn't in the mood to cajole her. It had been a harder shift than usual that day, with the engineers poking around the stall trying to find where the water was coming in, and I was soaked with sweat and oil. Bron wasn't off until midnight, so I had my bath and was towelling myself down when she arrived in the middle of it.

"Good God, there's a sight!"

"Keep the door closed, it'll upset the Welsh matrons," I said.

"One thing's sure, mate, it don't upset me."

"You make that clear. What are you doing?" I tied the towel around my waist.

"Pinning this clear a bit." She was standing before her little mirror on the chest of drawers with pins in her mouth, pinning up the front of her dress.

"You're too late, the colliers are halfway down it."

She turned her head, raising one eyebrow at me in disdain.

Gone was the girl in Clayton workhouse; vanished was her

immature prettiness. Life had moulded her into a vital womanhood; no wonder she drew the Pandy trade.

"Isn't good enough, Bron, you're setting the chaps alight."

"You had your chance and you didn't take it."

"We were kids, then. Why can't it happen again?" I approached her and put my arms around her waist, but she moved quickly away.

"Because Ma Bron, in the old days, didn't have the sense to keep her legs crossed."

"You can be vulgar, too, can't you?"

She crossed the room, and I watched her.

"Women face facts — that's what you want me for, isn't it?"

"I want you because I love you."

She swung to me. "And you broody about that Nan O'Hara all these years?"

"She's past history and you know it!"

I have often since wondered how easily a woman reads a man.

"*Ach*," she said, disdainfully, "you've still got her on your mind!"

"Wouldn't it be fair? It's the same with you and Sam."

She went to the bosh and began wringing out the dish-cloth, her whole being agitated, and I wondered at her sudden show of temperament; it wasn't like her. She was volatile and changeable, but rarely ill-tempered. "Upper class, wasn't she, eh?" She flung down the cloth. "Too high and bloody mighty to give a nod to the likes of me."

"Don't swear, Bron."

"There's a few of her kind round here, too — they think they piss port wine. And she was too good for poor old O'Hara, too, wasn't she? No wonder he went on the ale."

"Now, come on . . . *come on.* . . ." I was becoming angry.

She was flushed, and suddenly furious. "Rushing around like a pig in a fit, dancing her attention!"

"Suffering God," I whispered, "where did you find this sort of mood?"

"When you start gassin' about that Nan O'Hara!"

I shouted. "I never even mentioned her!"

"But you're broody about her, ain't you? An' that's just the same!"

Suddenly, she paused before me, her fingers twisting together.

"It ain't fair, Toby. I'm doing me best to be decent about Sam ..."

"What isn't fair?" I put out my arms to her, approaching again, but she turned and ran to the door and stood there momentarily, her head bowed. Then she said, "If you don't know, then you get on with it!" The door slammed behind her.

But, a night or two before the big meeting at Pontypridd, Bron's mood had changed.

"Didn't I tell you?" said Heinie, in the Pandy that night, "she's jealous. Jealousy makes 'em awkward. Though the cheese is usually that much sweeter when nibbled by another mouse. Next thing you'll know it's love and marriage?"

"You old faggot," said Mattie, joining us at the bar. "What d'you know about love and marriage?"

"He knows about sex," said Dai Parcel, coming up with Owen and Gwilym, his mates. "He hasn't the time to keep his flies done up," and he shouted at Bron for ale.

Gwilym said, his glasses on the end of his ring-scarred face. "Everybody's at it. What we want is a religious revival."

"Remember the Evan Roberts Revival, Dai?" asked Duck, leaning over.

"Remember it? He led it," said Heinie.

The day shift from the Scotch was coming in; bull-chested colliers as black as negro slaves were shoving to the bar, and Ma Bron was going demented with the foaming jugs in a thunder of coughing, for the lads were settling the gob.

I noticed John Haley, the Ely overman, sitting alone with a pint in a corner; nearby, Patsy Pearl, her eyes like stars, was giving him the come-hither, but he didn't appear to notice. And Evan Evans, the temporary landlord of the Pandy, beaming bucolic above his outsize brewer's goitre, opened his arms in blessing as the colliers flooded in. Ed Masumbala, the big Negro, had Precious, his baby son, on his shoulder; Albert Arse, on the other side of the room, was buying Tommy a pint. Beside him leaned Red Rubbler, the Irish mountain fighter from Porth; very interested in Bron, by the look of him and after trouble, too, by the cut of him; leaning over the bar, trying to weigh up her legs.

"Shall I ease him off gentle?" asked Heinie, anxious.

I shook my head. "Leave him, she can handle it."

"He's a groper, mind — done time twice."

"Up to her." I turned away.

Her pink dress was pretty, I thought, but I'd have liked it a bit higher in the front. Perhaps the pins had come out again, and Bron hadn't noticed. Also, it was well above her ankles, which was asking for it in a place like this.

"Ay ay, Toby!" shouted Bill Odd, from the crowd, and I gave him a nod; more than a nod would have cost me a pint. Coming in the door, Will Parry Trumpet was giving us the bugle; an ear-splitting, blasting sound, bringing yelled protests.

"Time was, the valleys were swept with a mass hysteria," said Gwilym, tugging at my sleeve. "It were Gabriel's horn all over again, just like that."

I sipped my ale, watching the fighter. I heard a man say, "Bron's got more up there tonight than the Nutcracker Suite," but Owen was after me again, commanding attention.

"It was the cholera chapels repeated, ye know?" said he. "The pubs was empty — it were a mortal sin to drink. Grown men were refusing to ride in the cages together — Non-conformists versus the Church of England — half the Rhondda was on its knees!"

"I'd rather chase her through the daisies than go down the Scotch," said somebody.

"A Baptist wouldn't share a stall with a Roman Catholic."

"Methodists wouldn't ride in the cages with Congregationalists."

"And if the cage-winder weren't Chapel, he'd give ye a blutty ride!"

"Processions were the order of the day," said Mattie. Over his head I saw Red Rubbler grinning vacantly at Bron.

"Drunkards were dressed in white, the lodges closed for lack of funds — everything was going into the offertory boxes."

"Pit ponies stopped pulling because hauliers stopped cursing."

"God was very popular," said Owen, dully.

"I prefer that barmaid to organised religion, though."

"The beer's gone up shocking since she appeared in the Pandy."

I was suddenly angry; not with the men, but with Bron.

"A good pair do have an effect on trade," said another. "She

212

weren't behind the dairy door when bottles was handed out."

"You randy old soak, Billy!"

"Mind, my woman's chest do take a lot o' beating, but I'm a leg man meself, personally speaking."

"Don't know what you're all on about," cried a third, falsetto. "I put my women up on a pedestal, I do."

"That's only so ye can see up their skirts, mun!"

I saw Heinie frowning at me. "You ready for off, Tobe?" he asked softly.

"No," I said.

I was watching Red Rubbler on the other side of the bar.

"Let him be, he's a professional," said Mattie. "He'd kill you."

"I'll see to it," said Heinie, and pushed through the crowd.

"A head taller than you? He's mine." I pulled Heinie aside.

The boxer was leaning over the counter, holding Bron's dress. She, with her back to him, wouldn't know what he was up to until she moved. Dano McCarthy and his six big sons had come in, shouting, and the sudden commotion had riveted Bron's attention. Now the jugs slopped as she moved, and her skirt went at the seam.

Instantly, she turned, pouring the ale over Red Rubbler's head.

In seconds, it was uproar. Drenched, the boxer wiped beer out of his eyes, gasping, then lunged at her.

"You bloody *bitch*!"

Bron hit him with a jug.

Bedlam. Colliers bawling, loving it, and the landlord shouting for order.

Reaching the boxer, I swung him to face me and hit him with a right. He was big, and it didn't floor him; instead, he staggered against the bar, then grinned, wiping his unshaven face.

"Ay ay," he said, and rushed. I side-stepped him and he barged into the men, slipped and fell; rising, he swung them aside for room.

"You big, Welsh bastard!" he said.

I got him with another right as he came lumbering in; it straightened him momentarily, and I saw his chin cocked up and begging as I ducked his swing and hit out with the left. Taking it full, he dropped.

"Christ," said Heinie.

"And I thought he didn't know a left hook from a coat-hanger," said Mattie.

"Come on, you," I said, and reached over the counter.

"All right, don't be rough!" cried Bron.

John Haley lifted an eyebrow at me as I steered her through the door.

Tonypandy slept. Furious, I lay in my bed on the other side of the Walls of Jericho and stared at the pattern of moonlight crossing the ceiling.

"I don't blame Red, I blame you!" I said.

"I thought I'd have the fault for it," said Bron. "But, it was a good punch though — never seen a chap done better."

"He's a poor, ignorant oaf! What do you expect from a man like that? You set the Devil alight — low and behold in that dress!"

"They're mine, I can do what I like with 'em." I heard her sit up in bed. "What's wrong with you, anyway — you taken the cloth? That Nan O'Hara got some too, if you're in luck."

"You leave her out of this!"

"She's in here every day, mate — what's the odds?"

I was about to shout something back; strangely, my conscience stopped me.

The thought that Nan was close now — as near as a few hour's walk — was bringing me to a new if uncertain warmth.

Earlier, I had gone out to the back, believing Bron to be already in bed. But she was still undressing; her fair-skinned beauty had caught my breath.

Now I lit the candle behind the Walls of Jericho and started to work on the lodge accounts. They had been kept meticulously by Richard Jones; every payment entry made in his copper plate handwriting. I smiled, thinking of his fanatical dedication to the Union. Perhaps, I reflected, it needed men such as he and Parry — the unpaid slaves of ideals — to make the industrial world go round.

Later, in bed, I listened to Bron's breathing.

Strangely, at such quiet times, my thoughts invariably turned to Nanwen; she, the epitome of all my dreams, I thought, could never be replaced by one like Bron.

Vaguely, I wondered if this was a true love; if my desire for Bron was purely physical. Certainly, I'd have killed Red Rubbler if he had laid hands on Nanwen. . . .

"Toby . . ." Bron now, from the other side of the blanket.

"Yes?"

"Did you hit out that boxer because of me?"

"I'd have done it for anyone."

She giggled. "Didn't know ye had it in ye — fisticuffs, eh?"

"Aye, and you want to watch it, or I'll be starting next on you."

The room went silent; an owl was crying faintly from Mynydd-y-Gelli.

"Toby. . . ."

"What now?" I suitably humped and heaved, to discourage her.

"I've changed me mind about next Saturday — I'm coming with you to the political Meeting." She sighed in half sleep. "What's it all about, anyway?"

"I'll come over there and explain in detail."

"You come over here and you'll get more than you handed Red Rubbler."

"Good night, then." I turned back again.

"Best to know where you get to these days, perhaps," said she. "Lest you end up in places like Abercanaid."

"Abercanaid?" I cocked an ear to the blanket between us.

"Merthyr way, isn't it — or ain't you never heard?"

Somebody had told her about Nanwen being there, of course. I'd half expected it — nothing much missed Bron.

"Nice having your Nanny around again, is it?"

It angered me.

"You might have mentioned it, you rotten bugger," said she.

As I said to Heinie later, I couldn't make head or tail of her.

"So if I catch you up in Abercanaid, you won't know what hit you — d'you hear that?"

I smiled to myself: Bron fell to silence.

The night went on. All down the Row the huts were whispering to each other in the dark; faint snores and groans came from the sleepers of Tonypandy.

"Good night, lovely boy," said she.

215

26

WE WERE A lot warmer together, Bron and me, when I took her off that Saturday to the political meeting. The fact that I hadn't mentioned about the O'Haras being up Merthyr way and she holding out on me about Sam, seemed to even things up between us.

"Was it Sam who came that day?" I'd asked her.

"You'll never know, will you, ye poor soul," said she.

And so, the difference put on the side of our plate, so to speak, I was trying another tack, for the Walls of Jericho were still firmly up in the Sinkers.

"You'll likely find that golden bugle under the Rocking Stone at Pontypridd," said Heinie, "that's where they sit the barren wives, you know."

"Come off it!"

"Then you ask Rachel Odd. Dry as a desert was Rachel, before Bill took her up to Ponty. He sat her on that Rocking Stone and she brought forth sprightly."

"Triplets," said Mattie. "Nine months to the day."

"Bill got her home by a fast train."

"I don't believe it!" I said.

"Put a little Welsh bakestone in her oven."

"Don't be disgusting," said Mattie.

So I made great preparations for this political meeting. Taking out my Sunday suit I ironed the creases to cut my throat: I got Dora Dobi, the washer-woman, secretly to starch me up a collar, with Reckitt's Blue on the shirt and lavender water under its arms.

I took half a sovereign out of the tea caddy — sixpence for flowers, sixpence for tea in Ponty, twopence for a buttonhole as big as a bride's bouquet, and five shillings to hire a pony and trap. Doing it proper — I'd even invested money in it.

"She won't know what hit her, poor little dab," said Heinie.

The autumn smiled on the valleys that gorgeous Saturday evening.

It set the neighbours back a bit to see that pony and trap outside the Sinkers, and folks were pretty forlorn: standing around with never a word while I handed Bron up and climbed in beside her, for it's not often you get gentry behaviour round Tonypandy square.

Most of the hard cases came out of the Pandy Inn too, standing with their quarts respectfully under their bowlers, and I was proud indeed to be stepping out official with the prettiest barmaid in Town. And, as we clip-clopped that little nag over Trealaw bridge and past the station, we set every head turning.

Hundreds of the lads were here, catching the train to Pontypridd, and Heinie and Mattie were present on the edge of the crowd, also Duck; ever the perfect gentleman, low he bowed, sweeping up the dust with his new grey bowler, and a great cheer went up from the colliers when Heinie cupped his hands and bawled, "Good luck, Tobe!"

"What does he mean — good luck?" asked Bron.

She eyed me, but I made myself busy with the reins. Then, suddenly, she began to sing, hands clasped before her, looking as lovely as a picture under her broad-rimmed, summer hat. Bron sang, the pony clopped along and I gave Sam Jones a thought as we entered Porth, and was anxious there, for Bron was silent.

"You still around?" I asked her.

For reply she reached out and silently gripped my hand; Sam and Nanwen, for once, were pale, unsubstantial ghosts.

"I'd work for you, girl," I said.

No reply; just held her face up, smiling at the sun.

"Will you come away with me then — to some new place? And forget about everyone except us?"

She'd gone so quiet I thought she'd dropped off.

"Two pints, please," I said, and it opened her eyes, and she laughed gaily so that people waved and urchins cheered from the gutters as we took the valley road to Ponty.

"London, even — I'd dig the roads for ye," I said.

When the cottages thinned a bit after leaving Porth, I stopped the pony and tried to kiss her, and her hat fell off and her hair came down and she was pushing and smacking as gay as a virgin maid: very sweet, it was, trying to kiss Ma Bron on the road to Ponty. Birds sang, the hedgerows flourished in the wind; the corn in the fields was so golden that you could have pinned up angels' plaits with it.

I thought desperately, in my wish for her: I'll settle the dust under this one for good. If she wants Tonypandy, she'll have it. I'll wed her, bed her and bring out sons, but not for the pit, oh no! No boys of mine are ever going down the Ely. Tell you what, I told her — I'll buy me a job on the local council from eight till six every day except Sundays, with a black stock and a wing collar — macassar oil on my hair and powder under me arms — flavoured sweet as a nut.

She laughed all through this, hitting me about. "You're as daft as a brush, Toby Davies! Don't you know I like you as a big, sweaty collier?"

In that ride after leaving Porth, where Sam had once lived (and lived even now, perhaps, I reflected) a new gaiety and charm came between us, like a blessing from the sun.

The market was in full swing as I reined the pony into the narrow streets of Pontypridd, and urchins were hanging like sheaves on the arched bridge, waving us greeting.

Every collier in South Wales must have been in Ponty that evening, for the trains were shunting in from the Great Western and Taff Vale Railway like strings of centipedes, and the lads were pouring out into the streets, raving for the publics.

They came by canal barge, too, and three to a dray; in brewers' wagons, dog carts, and they climbed the hill to the Druids' Circle that overlooked the town, and surrounded the famous Rocking Stone in thick wedges of black.

"There's a lot of police around," said Bron, as I tossed a penny to an ostler lad to mind the pony.

"Yes," I answered, "and they're watching every move."

In the market the stalls were end to end, with everything man can buy since the Creation.

There were poultry stalls with feathered necks swinging and ducks and geese being executed in squawks: pig-stickers were at work on the cobbles, carcasses being swilled in boiling vats. There were button and silk mercer stalls, quacks up on boxes selling potions for constipation, cauliflower ears and womb disorders.

"God!" exclaimed Bron, "I've never seen anything like it!"

Drunks were already on the streets in rolling gangs, arms linked and roaring their bawdies; here went the riff-raff of the old iron-works and the worked out refuse of the Coal Rush; in pacing groups, hands cupped to their ears for harmony, went the collier choirs, their sweet-sounding hymns ignored in the rush and tear that was forever Pontypridd. Snookey Boxer, still wearing his boxing boots passed us, holding Effie's hand, and by the expression on their faces there wasn't a brain between them. Looking for the boxing booth and a quick guinea was he, and Effie well stuck up with a toffee apple.

"Can you see the Rocking Stone?" I shouted to Bron, and pointed upwards to the mountain.

"Is that where we're off to later, then?"

"Give it till dusk."

"For the Union meeting, is it?"

"Got to be dark, see."

"To sit me on the Rocking Stone?"

"*Diawl!*" I exclaimed. "Who told you that?"

"Mun — do ye think I'm daft? It was me who put old Rachel up to it!"

"I'll skin that Heinie Goldberg," I said.

She kissed my cheek. "You change my mind about Sam Jones, Toby Davies, an' I won't need rocking!"

"Right, then, we'll see, for you're a devil of a woman for promises." I took her arm and hurried her through the crowd. "What I can't get down the Sinkers, I'm trying for under the stars."

"You'll be lucky," said Bron.

Mabon had already delivered his Union speech, apparently, when we had climbed the hill to the Rocking Stone.

Here were the big-wigs of the Union; chairs and tables were set within the Druid's Circle about the Stone, with rank on rank of colliers a hundred deep. And Mabon, great in stature, was standing on the Stone, head and shoulders above everybody, his thick arms flung out to the crowd, for his usual biblical text before departing, and he cried:

" 'I will go before thee,' saith the Lord, 'and make the crooked places straight' — Aye, men! Isaiah 45 — remember, you who know the Book? 'I will break in pieces the gates of brass, and cut in sunder the bars of iron. And I will give thee the treasures of darkness ...' " and he flung upwards his great hands to the lowering sky, "Come men, come — you know the Word — quote it with me!" and a great murmur came from the men as they spoke:

" '. . . And hidden riches of secret places that thou mayest know that I, the Lord, which call thee by name, am the God of Israel!' "

A silence grew on the mountain, as if the town itself was listening.

This was William Abraham the bard, now nearing seventy years old; time could not taint his marvellous presence. He stilled his colliers now as he had done in 1877 — thirty-three years ago, when they first elected him as a miners' agent. For a third of a century he had represented them in Parliament, bringing to the Chamber his marvellous gift of oratory.

Possessed of astonishing *hwyl*, the unusual Welsh eloquence, he could hold a thousand men on the tips of his fingers.

But these days, Mabon's influence with the Miners' Federation was on the wane. His domination of wage negotiation had gradually evaporated, as had the miners' confidence in his integrity. Lodge leaders now openly complained that he had become an 'employers' man; one unfit to lead the new younger legions who were bent on social and economic reform.

The miners' distrust had now extended from the coal owners to Mabon, who was once revered, and one cried hoarsely, his hands cupped to his mouth, "Now we've had the biblical, Mabon, what about a rise?"

The colliers began to chant and stamp their feet.

"How further can I serve you, then?" shouted Mabon, his arms opening to us in astonishment.

"By telling the Conciliation Board that we'll never make the Bute seam pay!" cried a voice, and I recognised Mr. Jones, my lodge chairman.

"Isn't it up to the Bute colliers to prove it can be made to pay?"

I left Bron and ran to the edge of the crowd, calling, "Let D. A. Thomas strip down the Ely, and try."

Men turning now, craning to find the speaker. I shouted, "Four months now I've been working the Bute. Give me a wife and kid and I'd be on the Parish."

"Come nearer," called Mabon, and I did so, pushing through the men, shouting:

"Isn't it roundabouts and swings, Mabon? One pit is a loss, another's a gain. Hang us all on what can be earned down the Bute, and they'll crucify the coalfields."

Applause clapped into silence, and Mabon said, "See the Union's position, young man! The Owners claim you're going slow on the Bute. Unless we come to some agreement, they'll lock you out."

"Lock out the Bute colliers and the Combine pits down tools," cried Mr. Jones, now beside me.

"Pledge your best efforts to make the Bute seam pay, and nobody will be locked out," replied Mabon. "Weeks back this threat was made. Come autumn, unless output improves, they'll shut the Ely gates." Hands on hips, he surveyed me. "You speak for yourself, collier?"

"He speaks for the Ely," shouted Mr. Jones.

Mabon raised his hands for silence as the commotion grew.

I yelled, "There's not a married collier who can live on Bute wages, and the Owners know it. That's why they want the Cambrian pits based on this seam. Betray us now, and you'll have a strike on your hands that will break the Federation."

I never expected what ensued. The men recoiled like pent springs, roaring assent.

Torches began to spark and wave in the crowd. Men were being hoisted up on to the shoulders of comrades, yelling their individual complaints. And Mabon, as if in answer, put a chair on to the Rocking Stone and clambered upon it, his hands again upraised.

Within the thunder of shouts and boos, his lips began to move soundlessly; the crowd ebbed into silence, and a collier shouted:

"Christ, lads, here it comes — the tonic solfa!"

Strangely, nobody laughed. Not a sound they made, once Mabon began to sing.

Pure and beautiful, his bass voice echoed in the dusk. Arms wide, he sang, softly at first, to command attention. The mountain whispered; the flickering torches bathed red and black in skittering shadows, the faces of the listening men. Resonant and powerful was that voice that had for forty years commanded silence. When all else failed, Mabon sang: we listened now to *David of the White Rock*, in Welsh.

"Tell me what you want from me, and I will serve you," cried Mabon, after the song.

Arms flung up, his great beard trembling in the red light, he looked as Moses must have looked before the people of Israel.

Sick of him, I turned and went back to Bron.

"Is there going to be trouble?" she asked.

"If there is, you won't be in it. I didn't bring you up here to listen to the politics," and at that moment Heinie, Mattie and Mr. Duck came up.

Four sheets in the wind was Heinie, and Mattie not much better, with Duck holding them up, and the pair of them stinking of Allsops to dry the mud on a navvy; Heinie with his flies undone, as usual.

"Watch it, Heinie, there's ducks about," said Bron.

"We're just off," I said.

"Come on, come on," said Duck, and he staggered, holding up his mates. "This is the Union at work, my beautiful," and he tipped Bron under the chin.

"I've seen enough of the Union to last me a fortnight," Bron replied. "Arguing, threatening — why does everybody want strikes and lock-outs?"

"Striking against a lockout is the only thing we know," said Heinie, rolling.

"The trouble with Mabon," said Duck, indicating the Stone where Mabon was still speaking, "is that he's too damned old.

222

Young blood like yours is what we want, Toby," and he clapped me on the shoulder.

"I'll be that much older if I hang around here," said Bron, testily.

"O, aye?" and Duck fixed her with his eye. "Stay and improve your mind. Women will benefit, too, you know — political freedom."

"I don't want political freedom," said Bron.

"Easy, Duck," I said, and eased him aside, but he swung me away, with just enough ale in him to make him quarrelsome. "Doesn't she know that we're fighting for her most of all, then? Let her speak for herself! If we don't get paid for small coal now, she'll starve in her kitchen on big stuff tomorrow!"

"I'll starve, too, if me missus catches me in this state," said Mattie.

"You're riding a greasy pig, Duck," said Bron, "leave me be — I don't understand the politics," and she shook him off.

"She's right," cried Heinie, falsetto. "Keep the women out of it. It's a sad old house when the cock's silent and the hen does all the crowing."

"To hell with the lot of ye, I'm off," said Bron.

Darkness had fallen over the mountains.

The meeting ended, the hill of the Druids was empty save for discarded political pamphlets and sandwich wrappers blowing in the wind.

Standing together on the Rocking Stone where Mabon had stood, Bron and I looked down at the blaze of Pontypridd below us, where the market, despite the late hour, was still in full swing.

"Best get down there," said Bron, "before somebody walks off with that pony and trap."

"No hurry," I said. "Sit," and I drew her down on to the Stone, and we rocked together, looking at the moon.

"If this puts me in the pudding, there'll be the Devil to pay rent to in the Sinkers, you realise?"

"You don't get puddings just by sitting on a stone." I drew her against me. "Other things have got to happen, too — your ma never mentioned it?"

"I read about it somewhere, I think," said Bron.

There was a new sweetness in her face for me as we rocked together, like statues in that moonlight.

"I'll read it to you again, if you're interested."

Her eyes were incredibly bright, like a woman in tears, but she was smiling. "Spring heather can do queer things, they say, if ye get it up your garters."

"Don't you fret, missus, I take good care of my women."

"*Arglwydd!*" And she looked at me very old-fashioned. "Cocky old boy, aren't ye?"

It was the strange, lilting look in her face that took me; she was the Bron of Bethesda again. Head on one side, smiling; hands on swaying hips. "You know, Toby Davies, I'm getting a shine for you. Now ain't that strange? Last one down the hill is poleaxed," she cried, and pulled up her skirts and ran demented, with me after her.

I caught her near the bottom of the hill.

Flushed and breathless was she, and I kissed her in the thickets where the moon had hidden. Nearby were the ashes of a dying fire where Irish gypsies had camped for the market. Sitting in its glow was a woman feeding a child, so we up and walked again.

She disdained to cover herself as we passed, this woman: when I bowed to her, her chin went higher; the baby hammered her and sucked.

Later, perhaps, when the market was over, those of her tribe with young children would return and spark up the bonfire, and the men would bring out the wine, and there'd be dancing to the guitars and castanets. Heinie Goldberg reckoned he'd had a night with one of these girls and he'd never known such an outing, but there was always a palaver if one of them came full, with Pedro this and Mario that rushing around the Rhondda, sorting out the father.

There was a place of moonlight nearby where the wind blew soft and here we sat in an arbour of the bushes, Bron and me, and she must have known what I intended since I'd done my best to make it clear. Yet here she was acting the virgin surprise.

This women do, I find, when they're keener than most.

"Dear me, no," said Bron.

"Just remember that old Rocking Stone, my precious," I said.

224

Amazingly, I think we both knew strange shyness, which was difficult to explain, since we'd shared a room for months. But we were closer here, in this foreign place, than at any time with the Walls of Jericho between us; or was it that the business of making love (which begins with the eyes and passing the cheese) had all been done before?

Now there grew between Bron and me a bond that fused us tight; and, gypsy bonfire sparks started blowing up between us.

I came nearer; Bron lowered her face.

"Best not, Tobe."

Which is only really a woman's way of calling you on.

"We'll be sorry tomorrow, mind," said she.

The breath of the wind is like a swig of gin; time suddenly paused and pushed us through its door.

There is a freedom in the wild places that does not spring from beds, and little rivers are running in your head and flowers make the hot, anxious perfumes. It was being like children again, lying there holding hands in the heather, and my heart was thumping as I bent above her.

"Do not make it hard, precious," said Bron, and I saw the moon in her hair and her eyes were narrowed as she turned away her face. So big that moon, triumphant brilliance — having a good look at me kissing Bron, and now I touched her breast.

"Hop it, Tobe."

The shock of my coldness took her breath.

A lifetime back it had come to this. I remembered the heart-thumps of the lad in the Waterloo bedroom; the crumpled dress, the moonlit window, Bron's whispers.

Now I heard her voice again, the voice of a woman, the soprano turned contralto:

"You need me that much?"

"*Diawch*," I whispered, "I'm in a terrible blutty state."

She giggled, being Bron, and I needed her more. "Easy, mun, ye've got to let 'em breathe. Careful with me, is it? — I ain't usual, you know."

I did not reply, for this business of loving is an obliterating chord of sound in the breast. "Dear me," said she, "what's happening. . . ?"

Bron was warm and soft beneath me and now willing. There grew in me a giant need of her; a forging of heat and strength.

No sound then but the rushing of the wind and a gasping of kisses, which is a stillness when the world ceases.

It was love come alive in the body, a tumult of chaotic movement; bringing to me expression, in word and deed, beyond my understanding.

Light flows here, in the darkness of clenched eyes; a fusing of the mind and heart. And, as my strength tightened about her, there came a breathlessness of kisses I had never known before.

The wearing of that love was like a garment. At first there was no compulsion. Locked in the womb of her arms I knew an ecstatic oneness.

Transported from the present, I no longer laid with Bron on the mountain above Ponty, but in some strange place amid a galaxy of stars. And I saw, in the voice of her eyes, the message that lovers understand. Others I had taken, and enjoyed, like the Wraith Woman of Rhayader, but even Bron's merriment was beguiling; bringing to the ridiculous posturing a purity. No pillows lurked here, no formal bed seduced it and her breast was white under the moon. And even as she became one with me in that fragmented second of time, there was a yet a newness in its joy; lithe and quick was Bron beneath me, in the dance of life.

In a passion of coolness, the moment transported me to another distant lover . . . a sudden betrayal I did not understand.

"How did all that happen, then?" asked Bron, opening her eyes.

"Largely done by mirrors," I said, "and bits of red paper held up to the light."

I spoke again, yet did not hear my words: Bron replied, her voice clear, yet I did not hear her.

I heard only one voice, suddenly, beyond the flax of the dream, and this was the voice of Nanwen.

So clearly I heard her voice, as if she were beside me; it came out of the night, from nowhere, a counterfeit.

But Bron had not heard it, and she twisted her body so that, locked together, we rolled slowly down the slope as one, while the night stepped over the petticoats and lace-trimmed drawers and trews in all its stumbling breath.

"Oh, that were gorgeous!" Bron whispered against me. "Do it again?"

The moon dropped her Sunday dress over the night, hiding us from gipsies.

So I loved Bron again, seeing before me Nanwen's face; even feeling on my mouth Nanwen's breath.

27

AND SO, TOWARDS the end of August, when the painting was gold on the trees of the mountain, I took myself down the Sinkers Row and fished out Will Parry Trumpet.

"You got your trumpet?" I asked.

"Aye, and ready," said he, wonderingly.

"Then bring it along here," and I positioned Will outside the window of Number Six where Bron was washing up and singing like an angel. "Sixpence," I said to Will, "for six good blasts."

He stared at me, rocking in the wind, being as thin as a starved ferret. Six good blasts, I thought, could be the end of him.

"On this trumpet?"

"On that trumpet," I said.

"T'is right good payment," said Will. "I reckon they don't get more in the Household Cavalry. When do I start?"

"This minute," I said, and the neighbours gathered in anxious concern and the night shift colliers put their heads out of their windows, cursing flashes, as Will Parry Trumpet gave them six blasts of his trumpet, and I paid him sixpence.

When I got back inside the kitchen Ma Bron was at the bosh, pretty glum, but the Walls of Jericho were removed.

That room looked as palatial as a Victorian mansion with its tattered old blanket down.

"You won't lose by it," I said, and put my arms around her waist and kissed her bare back above her chemise. "The matrons of Wales would give a lot to be in the position you're in now."

"And I won't gain a lot; ought to have me head examined."

"We'll see about your head later," I replied.

Moses Culpepper put his face through our kitchen window, shouting, "What's all this trumpeting, then?"

"Has Will Parry got his sixpence?" cried Bron from the bosh.

"Ay ay missus," sang Moses.

"Then kindly remove your chops from my window sill or you'll end up in blutty hospital."

"No offence, mind," called Moses.

"None intended," said Bron. "Now go to hell from here." She pushed past me, looking gorgeous, her hair tousled with sleep. "The damned cheek of it — give you an inch and you takes a yard."

I was combing my hair and gave her a grin.

"Walls of Jericho, indeed!" she said at nothing.

"Took them down, didn't you?"

"Some people think they own the place, too."

"Possession's nine points of the law." As she passed again I got her and tried to kiss her, but she slapped me away.

"Just because you pop something into the pawnbroker's it don't mean he bought it — I told you before, I don't belong to anyone."

"*Duw!* Where did you find this sort of a mood?"

She ran to me; I held her and we did not speak.

It's a strange old business, trying to understand women.

"You all right?" I asked at length.

"Aye." She was hard against me, her face hidden, sniffing and wiping, and I knew she was remembering Sam.

Scratch scratch at the door then. With a glance at me, Bron opened it, and a little sheep stood there. It did more to change the subject than I could.

"Well, I never did!" Bron ejaculated. "If it isn't our little Arabella!" Her mood vanished, she bobbed a curtsey and opened the door wider, and the thing walked in daintily.

"Toby Davies," said Bron, "this is Arabella, friend of the Culpepper's. But you've got the wrong house, Arabella! — Primrose lives next door!" Bending, she untied her red hair ribbon and put it around the little ewe's neck. "There now, go to see them pretty.

Out, out. . . !" and she swept it through the door with her apron, saying:

"She's Primrose's really. She's known her since she was a lamb. On her way to the slaughter-house, she roamed away from the flock, and just popped in. Primrose pays the farmer a penny a week to keep her out of the abbattoir."

I wasn't really listening. Through the kitchen window I could see the town hemming in the dusk, and the misted, roving shapes of off-shift colliers.

"It took a sheep to cheer you up," I said.

Bron sighed. "Well, I always reckoned that animals were better'n humans."

The coming of Arabella had broken a sad, empty spell.

Ever since the Rocking Stone meeting some eighty of us had been laid off from the Bute seam — over a week now, because the sea-coal demand had gone down at Cardiff, or something; I never did get to the bottom of this supply and demand, neither did the Union.

"I've got to hurry," said Bron. "Will ye be calling in to the Pandy for a pint?"

"I haven't the necessary."

"You can rob the tea-caddie." She opened her purse. "Tell ye what, I'll stand you?"

"I'll earn my own money," I said, and she sighed at the ceiling. "Oh, for God's sake, don't start that! We share, don't we?"

"I'll have an early night. Besides, I've got Lodge books to do."

"Please yourself."

I lay on the bed and watched her at the mirror.

She was doing a bit of pruning and preening, I thought, for somebody off to serve ale to colliers. Wearing a white blouse and long, black skirt pulled in as tight at the waist as a Church of England dog-collar, she looked lovely smart; it was sad to think that only part of her belonged to me.

"Don't take any old buck off anyone, remember — if Red Rubbler's around, you shout," I said.

Making faces in the mirror above the bosh, she said:

"Expect you'll be asleep when I come back, then — don't forget your supper. Lobscows, remember." She pouted and painted, a woman absent, her expression as changeable as her mood.

"I can smell it," I replied automatically.

Strange how I knew that Sam Jones was in the offing.

Now she began to comb her hair and I watched its tumbling waves in the faint light from the Square.

I could sit for hours watching a woman do her hair, seeing the business of the fingers, hearing the scurr of the comb, the gentle tearing of the brush.

"What's happening at the Ely, then?" she asked, hairpins in her mouth. Earlier, I had found one of these in the bed; part of a feminine sweetness that seemed to speak of a bond between us.

"Difficult to say," I answered.

"Voted on to the Union committee now, aren't you? — don't you know if there'll be a strike?"

"Nobody wants a strike, but we'll likely come to it." I sighed. "The Owners reckon we're going slow."

"And are you?" She was brushing down her dress now, trying to see the back of her skirt in the mirror, I replied:

"You go slow down the Bute seam and you draw no wages, mate. It's wet, it's abnormal, it's full of rock and shale. And they're trying to force the rates for the Bute on all the pits in the Combine. It won't wash."

"So what next?"

"We're trying to get the backing of all the Welsh pits."

"And will you?"

"Miners have always stuck together; I expect they'll do it again." I sighed at my books on the table before me. "Half the trouble is that the Owners won't arbitrate."

"*Diawch!*" She was walking about and patting herself with finality. "There's new words cropping up every minute."

"Accept an independent decision," I said.

But she wasn't listening, and I sensed in her a private anticipation she was trying to suppress.

Bron's inborn honesty always betrayed her; she was no actress.

The Sinkers was waking up for the evening; the colliers of the Scotch were making ready for the night shift; children were bawling

231

— always a palaver as they were threatened into bed. Pablo, the Mexican parrot belonging to Bill and Rachel Odd gave his usual cheeky whistle, a sign that Rachel was getting into the bath, and it's very disturbing, mind, Rachel used to say. But it was enough to make anybody whistle, said Bill, her husband, for it takes me five minutes to get her in and ten to get her out, when she's expecting.

"He's a cheeky old bugger, that parrot," said Bron.

"Got red ticks on him, too — unhealthy for children."

There was growing between us a new barrier of coldness fed by words of nothingness.

It was like the siege of Jerusalem going on next door now, with a lot of swishing and swoshing and the kids shouting; Bill Odd booming bass while Rachel shrieked soprano. Farther down the Row the McCarthys were at it again, Etta throwing the pot of aspidistras at Dano and giving him stick in her rich, Connemara brogue, and nine times out of ten, one of the family caught it. Will Parry Trumpet was practising for the brass band — giving Handel the cornet, and I know where that cornet would end up if he was mine, Primrose Culpepper used to say, for it's the children of Israel sighing for reason of their bondage, Exodus 2; 23 — a great one for the biblical was Mrs. Culpepper.

"She's a bloody cough-drop, that one," said Bron. "Her pa was a Seventh Day Adventurer, ye know."

"Adventist," I said.

"Aye, she's a good one though — got a lot of love — that's what's wrong with this place — not enough love!"

She was ready to go, standing by the door.

"Here?" I raised my pen. "Don't be daft — the valleys are built on love."

"Still?"

"Of course — the *people* are the valleys. Folks don't change."

"Hope you're right." She came to me at the table and bent to my lips; her perfume drifted over me. I said:

"We might be in trouble with the Owners again, but the people will stand together; they're changeless." I looked at her. "Like us?"

She smiled into my face, her eyes dancing. "Dear me, poetry now, is it?"

"When I look at you."

She brushed my mouth with hers; it was scarcely a kiss. "Don't wait up. I'm late shift tonight, you know — Mrs. Evans is off, so I shouldn't hang by the neck waiting up."

Momentarily, she was the old capricious Bron, and I liked her better.

Pouting a kiss at me, she closed the door.

Through the kitchen window I watched her running towards the Pandy.

I did the books for a while; made mental notes that people like John Haley, the Englishman, and Albert Arse, both new members, hadn't paid their subscriptions, then packed the ledger away, had my supper and lay reading on the bed.

When I got up to light my pipe I found that Bron had left an ounce of tobacco on the mantel as a gift for me.

All down the Row the night was strangely quiet, and there grew within me, in the noisy loneliness of the darkening room, an elation mingled with an unaccountable dread. Bron wouldn't be back for hours, of course, but her nearness, I reflected, never failed to banish my insecurity. Her almost masculine air of self-sufficiency served to strengthen the bond between us: living with Bron made a man two against the world. Now she was gone I felt empty and uncertain.

Normally, this richness of belief served to dispel my nagging worry of Rhondda's approaching disasters; it needed no crystal ball to foretell that trouble was coming.

With the issues at my own pit, the Ely, unresolved, the confrontation between the Union and the Cambrian Combine management was widening to a chasm; this could have been the root cause of my enveloping depression.

Also, in the uncertainty of Bron's absence, my visions of Nanwen returned; even while in Bron's body, this was happening with stunning insistence.

I lay on the bed and listened to the trams going down De Winton. Had I been in the money, I'd have been out there forgetting it all with people like Mattie and Ben Block; sinking a pint up at The Golden Age; perhaps giving the wink to Annie Gay, the barmaid there (whom I fancied) or listening to Heinie's boasting talk of being a ring professional when the legendary Shoni Engineer was knocking them cold.

Yet tonight this only battered on the outer portals of my mind.

I was lying as a fake on the bed; a man removed.

At last, after eight years of loss, I had been given news of Nanwen. Now that I'd heard she was near me, my need of her was rising like a panic within me, despite my love of Bron. Sometimes a wraith of myself discarded the rough cast now living in Tonypandy and sailed to Abercanaid.

Bron and Sam Jones, I thought; Nanwen and me. . . . It was a concourse of lost loves, make-believe, and snatched joys, the living of lies; and I cursed myself for my own responsibility in the scheme of it.

If I really faced the situation, I'd know the truth, I reflected.

Sam lived as much in the Sinkers as did Nanwen: he always had, from the moment I'd entered here. A lover might hold Bron in his arms, but she was as unsubstantial as a cloud; never could I capture her wayward, roving soul; this part of her still belonged to her husband.

Four of us living in the hut.

Bron, Sam, Nan, and me.

I must have dropped off because the mantel ticker said midnight when I awoke and put out my hand for Bron. Then I realised that I was still fully dressed, and rose.

Going out into the Square I saw that the Pandy had closed; the late drinkers of this and other publics were wending homewards amid the usual bawdy choirs. A great autumn moon lit the criss-cross, crazy roofs of the town and men stood in clutches around the fountain lamp, arguing rapaciously: others slouched in shadows like prospective footpads.

I tried the back of the Pandy, but it was locked, and I was just going round to the front when Evan Evans, the landlord, seeing out the last customers, came to the side door accompanied by Fang, his outsize Alsatian. Fang, normally as gentle as a spring lamb, became like a dog afflicted with rabies when once Time was called: setting about the clients until the bar was cleared, since his supper depended on it.

He was loping in my direction when the landlord called him off.

"Where's Bron?" I asked him.

"Search me, I haven't seen her." He turned to go but I gripped him and swung him to face me; the dog snarled deep in its throat.

"When did she leave?"

"Leave, ye ask? I've been managing on me own — she didn't even arrive."

I said, lamely, releasing him, "She . . . she said she was on late duty . . ."

He shook himself free of me. "Not here, she's not."

"Sorry, Mr. Evans."

"You'd best be. This is the second time you've been here causing trouble. Now away with ye, before I whistle up Fang and he lifts the seat of your arse."

It was fair. I pushed past him through the door and strode off down De Winton.

It was as if the Rhondda, sensing privation, was having its last fling of pleasure before the coming of hunger.

Rowdies, arm in arm, raked the streets, clamouring at the beer-houses as landlords fought them off; harlots stood in corners, surveying the prospects of payment; wives were collecting husbands, ragged children pulling at fathers. Among the roughs went the more respectable; the home-going visitors of the little terraces after the Victorian evenings of tea and song. With their Bibles under their arms, the God-fearing closed the chapel doors.

Sarah Bosom, the persian cat-breeder, went by with Dozey Dinah, her mate, on her arm, and Dozey, half asleep, gave me a wink. They kept house together in One Church Street, these two, with Sarah breeding and Dozey on her needle. Kept to themselves, too, though nobody got to the bottom of what kept them together, for they were as different as chalk from cheese. I touched my hair to them as they passed with bowls of faggots and peas.

All the Rhondda was coming alive in the individual, passing faces. Mrs. O'Leary and Mrs. Shanklyn I saw then, packing up their stall, and O'Leary waved to me with a fat, bare arm.

"Seen Bron?" I asked her.

"*Gawd*, what a life," said she, sweating, "I haven't had time for a scratch. Me old man sinks the profit, you know — but he's good otherwise." She turned to Patsy Pearl who was standing nearby with Madog, her baby. "Seen Bron, pet?"

Shanklyn, I saw, was adopting an air of distinguished absence, washing up with gusto.

I knocked up my cap to Patsy, and she said innocently, over her bowl of faggots, "Come off the last tram, a few minutes back, she has — you've just missed her."

The women exchanged glances, I noticed, and I didn't want to appear too put out, so I hung around talking to Patsy for a bit.

The Penny Bazaar was closing down; cockle-women, as straight as Amazons with their baskets on their heads, were homeward bound with a marvellous dignity. The jug and bottle customers were thinning out around the side entrance of the De Winton; pale-faced children, the sacrifice to ale, waited in line of their parents' night-caps, clutching jugs covered with bead-trimmed muslin. Solly Friedman Pawnbroker tiptoed past us, raising his bowler to Patsy, his smile wider than a barmaid's bum: little Annie Gay stepped by with a fine independent air and a cheeky swing to her hips — recently she'd moved to lodgings opposite the Glamorgan colliery, and I'd made a mental note of it, since it's a good idea to have something in reserve.

"She's a good 'un, mind," said Patsy, lowering her bowl, and she shifted Madog more comfortably in his shawl on her back.

"Annie Gay?"

"Your Bron. She'll love you when you've got pennies on your eyes, remember, Toby Davies."

"I hope so."

"So you treat her decent, eh. Try to understand?"

I looked at her. Madog had his thumb in his rosebud mouth, slobbering, and he gave me a toothless smile. "Understand what?" I asked.

"Nothing — just treat her decent. She's the best you'll ever dig up."

"Don't lose sleep, she gets treated all right."

"You seen the Three Road Overman?" she asked. There was about her face a wan, anxious loveliness.

"John Haley? Not the last ten days — the Bute seam shifts are laid off, aren't they?"

She shrugged, empty. "Just wondered — no sign of him in the Pandy again tonight?"

"No sign of Bron in there, either."

"Course not — it's her night off."

"Is it?" I smiled at my thoughts. "Both gone short, haven't we, Patsy!"

I heard Mrs. O'Leary say to Mrs. Shanklyn as I strode away, "Oh, Gawd, now she's blutty done it."

Everybody appeared to know what was happening, except me.

I met the Livingstones on the edge of the Square. Dribbling, Guto was staring at the moon, and his wife said, "Out late, aren't we? We've just been down for a little bit of fish — he do like a little bit o' fish, don't you, mun?" She nudged me confidentially. "You heard the O'Haras are down in these parts, Toby?"

"Ben O'Hara?" I didn't believe her. Nor was she having me as easily as that. Mrs. Guto was all right, but she'd got a handy tongue. I said, "Last we heard he was somewhere up Merthyr way."

"Didn't Bron know, either?"

"She will by now," I said.

"Just arrived in the Aber valley — he's working down the Universal. Funny you ain't heard."

"When . . . when did that happen?" I tried to keep calm.

"Last week, according to Albert Arse — he met 'em in Senghenydd."

The full implication of the news had now taken my breath. She added, "Albert was over there shift-hunting — the Bute seam's stopped temporary — but then, you'd know. Poor Albert, he'd only just started — and Tommy off as well." She sighed at the moon. "Bumped into the O'Haras, did Albert — they was out shopping."

The knowledge that Nan was now only a few miles away was

having an astonishing effect on me; I cursed the brightness of the moon.

"Thought you'd be interested," said Mrs. Guto, with a wink.

It was a drama of irony that was slowly being played.

As Nanwen moved nearer, Bron seemed to be moving away.

I knew where she'd been that night, of course.

The last tram into Tonypandy came in from Porth.

The lamp was on in the kitchen when I got back; it was plainly one of those things — as I'd gone out Bron had come in.

Her face was pale in the lamp-light as she glanced up from the stove. "Ay ay, Tobe!"

"Aye, mun." I tried to sound normal.

"Thought you'd be abed — been cooking the Union books again?"

I sat down at the table with the *Labour Weekly*, watching as she filled the kettle and poked the grate into a blaze. She had taken off her hat and her hair hung in tight ringlets down her back; there was in her an unconcealed weariness.

"God, I'm tired," she said. "What you been up to?"

"Been asleep. Put my head down and just dropped off. Had a hard night at the bar?"

It was unfair, but I couldn't help it.

"Never damn stopped from the moment I got in," she said.

"Is there that much money about?"

She made a wry face in the mirror as she waited for the kettle. "Mainly the Scotch colliers, now the Ely's locked out and a lot down from Clydach." She smiled. "Patsy Pearl was in again — looking for John Haley."

"O aye?" I was surprised to hear her complementing the lie.

My tone evoked a glance from her; she said quickly, "Like a cup of tea?"

I nodded. "Working to this hour, they ought to pay you overtime."

She turned; her hands were clasped together, the knuckles white.

"I haven't been working in the Pandy tonight, Toby."

"I know you haven't."

"If you knew, then why the *hell* didn't you say so?" She swung to me, furious.

"And why the hell did you have to lie about it?" I got up and flung the paper down. "What's more, I know where you've been!"

"That makes it easier," she said, empty.

"Sam again, isn't it?"

"If you know, why trouble to ask?"

"Christ, what a bloody great fool I am!"

The kettle was singing. Going to it she stood staring down at it. "I'm the fool," she said.

"But why? *Why?*" Crossing the room I turned her to face me. "Aren't I enough?"

Her lips were bright, as if fevered; her cheeks were blooming red, and faintly scratched, scurred by a man's beard. She looked drained of vitality.

"Can't help it, Tobe," she said, faintly.

"Is that all you can say? Woman — what's wrong with you? I thought we were doing all right!"

For answer she shook her head; she was beaten; I had never seen her in this state. Moving lethargically to the window she drew the curtains, looking out into the night.

"For pity's sake, Bron! You go straight to him from me. Is that fair?"

She bowed her head. "No."

"He's back in Porth, isn't he?"

She nodded.

"But not with that woman?"

"No."

"She's gone, so he's after another skirt — he snaps his fingers and you come running. For God's sake, where's your pride?"

She turned her face to mine. "I lost that a long time back."

I said, desperately, pacing about, "Well, we can't go on like this can we?"

"I'll . . . I'll go if you like?" she said.

Amazingly, the thought that I would lose her brought me fear; a frightening sense of impending loss, and I could not bear it. Bron was looking at me, as if awaiting my agreement. We faced each other

over the room. The kettle was boiling its brains out, as if crying for
the pair of us. I didn't know what to do. I wanted first to hit her and
then comfort her, and I was terrified that she would start to cry. If
she started that, I thought, the farce now being enacted would turn
into reality and the parting would have to be faced.

She said, "Do . . . do ye want me to go, Tobe?"

I crossed the room and took the kettle off the hob, seeking escape
in practicality.

To break the tension more (for she still hadn't moved from the
window) I clattered cups and saucers about and made a great play
of finding the milk.

Coming slowly, she joined me at the table; her hands were
shaking; there was upon her face an incredible sadness. Softly, as I
poured the tea, she said:

"My Gawd, Tobe — he ain't like you. He can be a bugger."
She twisted her hands together. "I ain't never known such a man
like Sam Jones."

I didn't reply. I dared not trust my voice. There was burning
within me a mounting hatred of everything he stood for.

"I suppose you went to bed with him?"

She took the cup and saucer from the table and turned her back
upon me.

"*Did you?*" I yelled at her.

"My husband, ain't he?"

"And where do I come in on this?"

She smiled sadly. "You don't, Tobe — I've always told ye that —
not while Sam's about."

"God almighty!" I put down the cup.

Outside on the Square a drunk was singing, a faint, high-pitched
song of shouts and grunts; it seemed the only sound that Tonypandy
had to offer.

"You . . . you'll have to make up your mind then, won't you," I
said gently.

The kindness seemed to revive her. "You need me here?"

I nodded. "Of course I need you!"

"Because you love me?"

"God knows why!"

Her face became suddenly agitated. "Then say it — say it now?" She came to me and caught my arms, gripping hard. "Go on, say you love me?"

"I love you," I said.

She stroked my face. "Good old Tobe — such a pity, isn't it — getting hooked up on me?"

"But I'm not sharing you — it's Sam or me from now on."

I wanted to kiss her, but could not. It didn't seem right to put my lips on hers.

So, there was an emptiness between us as we undressed that could not be bridged by words; we moved as strangers in the moonlight of the window, together, yet alone.

With only her petticoat upon her, Bron went to the bosh and poured out the hot water left in the kettle. There, stripping to the waist, her back turned to me, she began to wash herself.

After a minute or two I became aware that she was scrubbing herself with an almost desperate vigour. I looked from the bed. Red and blue patches stained the fair sheen of her skin. Like a woman possessed, she was scrubbing at her body, as if hating it.

Getting out, I crossed the floor and turned her to face me.

"What's all this?" I said, touching her. She held the towel against her and I pulled it away. Half naked, she stood before me, her face low.

"Who the hell did that?" I asked, and touched the bruises of her arms and shoulders, even her breast.

"Ach, Tobe, it's nothing!" She turned away, discounting it.

I knew a chain-reaction of anger; it contained me, forbidding speech. I snatched at her wrist and twisted her nearer while she clutched at the towel in a vain attempt to hide herself.

"Was it him?"

"Aw, forget it — he don't mean any harm!" But she was uncertain; furtive in her fear of me, and I pulled down her sheltering hands.

"Look at you — just look at you!" I swung her around; her shoulders were swollen by clutching fingers.

"God in Heaven, woman — is this what you want?" I stared into her face.

241

She said, cajolingly, "But . . . he's always been like that, Tobe — doesn't know his own strength, see? He don't mean it, honest . . ."

"I'll kill him," I said. "You go to Porth again, and I'll make you a widow — d'you hear me?" I turned from her, trembling. "The bastard!"

"Don't say that, Tobe."

"Well, he is — a bloody bastard. Do you call that love?"

When I turned back to her again she was standing with her hands by her sides; there was upon her face an expression of infinite understanding. "But he doesn't love me, I know that. Sam'll never love anybody, as long as he lives."

"Yet you waste love on him? — a man who treats you worse than a whore?"

She nodded.

"Then you make the best of it, I'm going to bed."

"Put your arms round me, Tobe," she said.

"Go to hell."

"Please?"

I got into the bed and turned my back upon her.

I was acting like a child, but it was the best I could do. It was sickening to find her so weak — he'd taken everything off her — self respect, pride — she no longer seemed like Bron.

"If I wash myself all over again Tobe — will ye?" There was in her face a contrite beauty.

"Oh, Christ, come on," I said, and got out of the bed and held her.

"He ain't so bad really," she said. "Honest, Tobe — not when you get to know him."

For a long time Bron sat at the table by the grate, her face in her hands. The night went on.

"Come on, come in here," I said, pulling aside the blankets.

She did so; we lay apart in the bed as strangers. She said:

"Expect I'll get a letter from Bibbs in the morning."

"Look, it's late . . ."

"She usually writes every month, ye know. It's really the aunt, of course."

"Go to sleep. It'll be a different kettle of fish in the morning."

"Why? I'm not on till afternoon and you ain't going anywhere."

Her change of mood, her sudden, almost flippant attitude to what had happened angered me, and forced upon me new thoughts of Nanwen.

Lying there, I reflected that I had always been Bron's second string: she loved Sam, she'd never made any bones about it.

I chanced a look at her in the room moonlight. She was lying with her eyes wide open, her hands clasped before her, as one in prayer, and I pitied the conflicting emotions with her, knowing in my heart that even this apparent flippancy was an attempt to normalise our relationship. The dishonesty of the situation was grieving her: she was in love with Sam but in bed with me; the immorality would never bother Bron, the betrayal did: everything she did was naively fair.

I began to wonder how I could relieve her. If leaving her would give the balm, then I would go. Yet this could only bring her to more loneliness. A month or two with Sam, and she'd be back on her own again.

She said, "Tobe . . ."

"What is it now?"

"She'd think a lot of a proper father you know — my Bibbs, I mean."

"Not my kid," I said.

"Sam don't care about her."

"Whether he does or not, it's him she'll want, not me."

"Don't say that," she said.

"Bron — look, for God's sake go to sleep?" I heaved over in the bed and turned my back upon her to widen the chasm between us.

Softly then, she began to cry, stifling the sobs in the pillow.

This brought me near to panic, but I did not turn to her.

I thought, desperately: if I went to Porth, found Sam and reasoned with him, he might, perhaps, take her back permanently. Or better, I'd get out and he could return here, to the hut. He wasn't living with anybody now, according to Bron, and the hope that I might be able to smooth things over between them — perhaps get Bibbs down from the north to renew a bond — brought me relief. It was inconceivable that even Sam would exchange Bron for some fancy woman on a permanent basis.

And then, without apparent cause, fear swept over me at the thought of losing her. It was a ridiculous situation. I was suddenly furious. Had Sam appeared in the doorway then I'd have had the pair of them with the same fist.

"Toby. . . ?"

"Will you go to *sleep*?" Up on an elbow I thumped my fist into the pillow.

She touched my shoulder with the tips of her fingers, whispering:

"You . . . you remember that day in the Waterloo? You know, when the landlord was away, the men were on the march, and you came in. . . ?"

"Don't remind me."

The room grieved within its silence. I'd hurt her, and was glad.

"Nanwen's over in the Aber Valley," she said then, softly.

It was as if all she'd been saying had been leading up to this, such was the finality of her voice.

"Yes, I know — Senghenydd." I answered curtly. I wanted her to shut up and leave me to my despoiling loneliness; a hatred of Sam Jones and everything he stood for was searing me.

"You knew she'd come recent?"

"Yes."

"Then it would be fair, wouldn't it, if you saw Nanwen again?"

Conscience, I reflected, uses strange concoctions in the art of human healing. I'd have preferred her stronger. Why the hell couldn't she be as honest as she was supposed to be, and call herself a whore? All she was doing now was offloading some of her responsibility.

After a bit, because she was crying again, I took her into my arms.

Within moments, she was asleep.

She'd had me up half the night.

Trying to obliterate thoughts of her love-making with Sam, I held her, watching a pattern of moonlight cross the boards.

If only she were happy, I reasoned, there could even be a small, if sad sublimity in the loneliness . . .

28

THE DAY BEFORE the Cambrian Combine management locked out nearly a thousand of us from the Ely Pit, I took myself over to the Aber Valley, about ten miles away, to try to see Nanwen.

It was about a week after Bron had been over to Porth to see Sam, so I had no conscience about going. Like as not, I reflected, Bron would take the opportunity to go to Porth again in my absence, for now a chasm that could not be bridged by words had come between us.

It was ironic, I thought, that, at the very moment of possessing Bron, I had entirely lost her; as if the action had made her spirit free.

"Off, then, are you?" she had asked, when I got up early.

"Aye, for a few hours."

"Going to Senghenydd?"

"Why not? I'm not much wanted round here." It was childish and ineffective, but I could not help it. "Good chance for you to kick over the traces again isn't it?"

"You want me to go?"

"Please yourself."

At the hut door she said, with a whimsical smile, "Give her my love."

I said, evenly:

"Pity, isn't it, Bron — we were doing all right."

"We could still do all right, mate — it's you who're making an elephant's cock out of a pig's ear."

"I don't share my women."

It was pious, and I regretted it.

"Tell that to Ben O'Hara."

She always managed to better me when it came to words.

For the first time since I had come to live in the Sinkers I felt I had truly lost her, but brushed the emotion aside, being filled with an expectant joy now, at the prospect of seeing Nanwen.

These were the days when I'd go to the Athletic Ground and lose myself in rugby; soon after I'd arrived in Town I'd joined the local club, the Ystrad Stars, and there was a fine comradeship of knocks and lads of an afternoon off shift, and knocks mostly, for my rugby was like my cricket — what I couldn't get my bat to I got my head to.

But today I took the early tram to Porth and got a lift on a brewer's cart to Caerphilly; sitting with my back to the ale casks, dozing in the sun.

I walked from Caerphilly and got into Senghy, which was the local name for Senghenydd, before midday. Even the bleached trees of the mountain, tortured to death by the rubbish of the tips, seemed to beckon me with leaf and flower as I strode into the village. In the Square I asked for Ben O'Hara and got sent to a nearby pub, the Gwern.

"Big Irish fella with a thirst like a desert?" asked the five-foot landlord, peering over the bar like a stoat at a rabbit.

I sank my half a pint, all I could afford. "That's right. Just come in, they say — got a wife and little girl."

"Try Four Windsor Place," said he, and wiped his whiskers. "You his butty?"

"Sort of."

"Then settle his slate — he already owes me."

By the look of things I'd got the right O'Hara.

Number Four had a front I would have expected of Nanwen, and she always kept a marvellous upstairs.

Ceinwen, aged nine, was standing near as I knocked on the door; she regarded me with unspoilt eyes; long plaits, ink on her fingers and school books had she.

"Senghenydd Board School?" I asked her, and she nodded, shy. "Don't remember me, do you?" and she shook her head.

I'd have known her among marching thousands; Nan's serenity and dark-Welsh beauty, in miniature. The door opened and Ben stood there, filling it.

"Sufferin' God!" he ejaculated. "Is there wind of ye?"

"I told nobody," I said, and he reached out and hauled me into the narrow hall, crying:

"Devil take me!" And he shouted to Ceinie. "D'ye know who this is, me lovely? It's your fine big Uncle Toby, that's what! Hey, Nan — come on here — it's the lad from Bethesda!" He shouted bass laughter. "It's ye sweet fella!"

She arrived with flour on her hands, wonderment on her face. "*Toby!*"

The sight of her stopped my breath. With Ben bellowing nonsense between us, we stood and stared, and it was wrong that I could not take her into my arms.

There was no change in her, save a gentleness of years, and then she smiled, and beauty, as always, flew to her face.

"Christ!" roared Ben, pulling me through the narrow hall. "You're a man wi' a weak nut, for sure. Didn't I hear tell you were over in the Rhondda?" He thumped my back. "Why the hell didn't ye come before?"

"Hallo, Nanwen," I said.

The girl came in behind us and we went into the kitchen to a smell of baking and warmth, and Nan took off her apron with agitated fingers and patted and smoothed her hair and there was talk of a cup of tea, though as Ben went past me I smelled his ale.

There was about him now a brutal strength, and a coarseness born of drink.

Later, we sat at the kitchen table and talked of Bethesda.

"So Mrs. Livingstone told you we were here — she gets all the latest news, that one!" laughed Nanwen.

Ben roared, "Albert Arse must have told her — we met him out shopping, down the village. Talk about tom-toms. Is that right they're living down the same Row as you now?"

"The Sinkers," I replied, "moved in recent. You should see

young Tommy — he's working, you know — coming on in leaps and bounds — handy with 'em, too."

"And young Rosie's a jewel of a girl, too, Albert says," shouted Ben. "When she was toddling she was coming for a caution! Remember the Love-Jenkins?"

"Aren't they round here somewhere — in the Aber Valley?" I asked.

The words were flying now.

"Not come across them yet," said Nanwen, and lowered her eyes as they met mine. From a corner of the room Ceinie watched me with an unquiet stare.

Despite Ben's occasional surly silence, Nan and I chattered on about Dan Morgan, my old Llechwedd foreman, who had now gone blind; of Grandpa with his trousers half-mast and Sam's mother, who had died. We talked of Sam Dickie, whose wife never came back to him — all this according to the Livingstones; we laughed together, remembering old Dick Jones, the miser who bottled his water.

"He wouldn't give a bit of cheese to a starving navvy," shouted Ben, thumping the table with his fist, but I sensed that the atmosphere of renewed friendship was dying between us, despite the old memories.

"Tom Booker died, you know," said Nanwen, softly. "Tom Inspector, too — killed in a fall at Penrhyn Quarry."

It quietened my thoughts, bringing life into perspective. A young woman hurried past the kitchen window with her basket; she was greeting somebody I couldn't see; her hair was fair, her smile beautiful; she was vibrantly alive, unlike this forced and artificial conversation: strangely, I remembered Bron.

"And Dick Patagonia — remember Dick? And Harri Ogmore, too — they all caught it," growled Ben.

"All four?" I gasped. "God! Poor old Harri taught me to fly on the chain!"

"He's flying with a harp now, me son!" Ben rubbed his stubbled chin like a man needing ale. "Shot-firing — the usual. No warning. Sam Jones's father was on the fuse — he took all four of 'em." He settled his elbows on the table and grinned at me. "Don't you see

Sam Jones these days, then?" Taking a hip flask from his pocket, he swigged deep from it, eyes clenched at the ceiling.

Nanwen's movements quickened, and I realised that Albert must also have told them about Bron and me. I realised, too, that Ben was tipsy. Meeting his eyes, I shook my head, and he grunted deep, pushing himself up from the table to knock out his pipe. "Ach, what the hell — does it matter — any of 'em? Every man jack o' them were bloody *bradwrs*."

"But they didn't deserve to die," Nanwen added, quietly.

At the grate, with his arm around Ceinie's shoulders, Ben said:

"So ye say ye haven't come across your mate, Sam Jones?"

Nan said, "Another cup of tea, Toby?" and she flashed a warning glance at her husband.

"No," I answered, replying to Ben.

"Which is a wonder, considering you're living wi' his missus, according to Albert Arse."

"People need to nurse their own troubles," said Nan, angrily. She poured the tea and handed me the cup. "Not our business, is it?"

"It's simple enough — Sam didn't want her," I replied.

"How's Bron's little Bibbs, Toby?" Nan asked, quickly.

I laughed. "Growing up, like Ceinie. She's up north in Caernarfonshire with her aunt. The aunt writes occasionally."

Ben said, "She's out of the way, so to speak?"

"Ask Sam Jones, mate, not me." I met his eyes.

"So you ringed up with Bron after Sam left her?"

I said, "Bron needed a friend — that's how these things start," and Ben replied:

"Ach, stop coddin' us along, lad — t'is a pretty romantic business, ye know, and I always approve of love. You had a fair glance for Ma Bron when she was up in Pesda, for she's a well set-up lass." Stooping, he knocked out his pipe in the grate and said into Ceinie's face, "Which goes to prove that you have to watch the opposite sex, me sweet child, since ye never know where ye are with 'em — on your backside or your elbow."

Ceinie did not move. She was staring at her mother. Nanwen's face was pale. I drank the tea, inwardly cursing myself for coming.

"Are ye marrying the wee soul?" Ben asked, filling his pipe and grinning aimlessly in my direction.

"Ben, please," said Nan.

"Dear God, I forgot — she's married already! Does it set ye fair, Toby, me son — lyin' wi' another's man wife?"

There was no time for reply because two colliers came and hammered on the window; codifiers of Welsh ale by the look of their stomachs, and Ben shouted:

"I'll be with ye directly, me darlins'." He turned to me. "I'm away on shift, ye young skut, so I am. D'ye fancy a light pint with the lads before making your way back to the Rhondda?"

I shook my head, watching him. The shame of it was in Nanwen's face, and I hated him.

"Your tommy-tin's in the back," said Nanwen, cold.

Laughing, he waved to the window, got the box and his bottle and crossed the room to Ceinie. Taking her hands in his, he stage-whispered:

"Now, hearken, treasure. The fella in here is after ye ma, understand? So you keep an eye on him for the sake of your pa, is it? And, if they step anywhere together, it's up to the pit and three pulls on the hooter."

Nanwen said, "Ben, how dare you!"

"Aye, woman, I do." He straightened, no longer smiling. "Because, with one man's wife in the cupboard, he's bound in this direction now."

"You watch your mouth," I said.

"And you yours, me son, lest this time I shut it. How many women do ye want?" He pushed past me to the door, pulling it open. "Give him a piece o' your cake for the journey, missus, and send him on his way, for I'll have the balls off the bugger if he's here when I get back."

Nan gasped, "Ben, for God's sake, Ceinie's listening!"

"Let her hear! A man never knows where he is with you two from minute to minute — damned Welsh! When she mixes the Godly with the ungodly, she'll have a stew to feed the world." He stared at us. "What the hell do you two see in each other?"

"Nothing that you'd understand," said Nanwen, and I flashed a glance at her. "You'd best go, Toby."

"Out, ye big lanky bastard," whispered Ben, and pushed wide the door. "And don't come back, me lovely boyo."

But he feared me; I saw it in his face.

His two mates, awaiting him on the road, watched us with beery apprehension: tipsy on shift, I reflected, and these would never set foot down the Universal where drunks weren't needed to raise the danger.

Joining them, Ben marched off, swaying. All his movements, like his lust for ale, had become misshapen by the years.

Ceinie went back inside the house, but I noticed her watching us through the window.

"Got to get her dinner," said Nan, and waved to her, calling, "I'll be in directly."

And then she turned to me. "Oh, *Toby!*" she said.

I moved to the gate. "I shouldn't have come."

"I'm glad you did." She was close to tears and I wanted to put my arms around her. All down the street the curtains were moving, doors coming open; women greeting each other.

I said, "After all these years, we're still in the same mess, aren't we?"

She made a gesture of emptiness. "But you're happy with Bron, surely?"

The big Universal, the distant Windsor pit, whispered between us in smoke, brought on the mountain wind.

"I love you, Nan," I said.

She looked at me. "And I love you, Toby. It's like being alive again, seeing you."

I said, "You need me, you send for me, remember?"

"Aye." She had upon her face a beautiful expression.

"Goodbye, then."

Strangely, Ceinie waved from the window as I went.

Bron was still at the Pandy when I got back home.

Dusk was falling, for I'd walked the whole ten miles, stopping for a few pints in Caerphilly, trying to sort out my thoughts.

Perhaps it would be best to go from the valley and start a new life, I considered; there were other jobs, other places for a man without attachments.

I wandered into the empty hut. Bron's hand was everywhere; the ironed washing on the fireguard, the grate like polished ebony, and not a speck of dust. The bed was neatly made, the blankets meticulously folded; bacon was in the frying-pan, an egg on the side.

And in the middle of the kitchen table was a little vase of wild flowers; beside it was a note.

'I love you,' it read.

Damned women.

Didn't know what to make of them.

Nor men either, come to think of it . . .

29

"WE'RE LOCKED OUT," said Heinie, as we reached the gate of the Ely, reporting for shift the following month.

The colliers crowded up behind us, bawling unanswered questions at the locked colliery gate, trying to read the notice that the management had posted up. For a month now the Owners had been promising this; now they'd done it.

"Read it out, Heinie!" yelled a man from the back.

They fought for room as the crowd increased, swinging their comrades aside, and Heinie shouted, "We're bloody locked out — can't you see the gates?"

Silence while he read the notice. High above the motionless pit wheels of the Ely, a lark sang, his voice cadent in the still September air; the morning sun bathed the valley in a golden radiance.

Nearly a thousand men waited, pent.

Heinie cried, "You're out, I say! All eight hundred and eighty of ye — they've shut the Ely," and a voice cried:

"You blind fool, read it again — give him his glasses! *Eighty*, you mean — the Bute Five Foot teams — that's what the argument's about, not the whole shift!"

"You're out, it says — every man jack — every Ely collier — underground and on the top!"

"They can't do that!"

"They've bloody done it," said Ben Block.

They cursed in a rising tumult of threats, and Tommy Arse, standing near me, shouted:

"But I'm starting a new stall today — I anna anywhere near the Bute seam, sir!"

"You're out just the same, young 'un," said Moses Culpepper.

I saw Tommy's stained face; the only collier I had seen shed tears.

"Now there'll be trouble," this from Bill Odd, and he gripped the gate with his big fists and rattled it. "Nine hundred out, eh? And over one seam?"

"It'll bring out the whole of the Cambrian!"

"And the Scotch Glamorgan, too — Christ, we'll show 'em."

"We'll have that Mabon for this — him and Mainwaring," cried Dai Parcel.

"Don't blame the Union representatives!" shouted Richard Jones, and he stood on a plinth. "Calm, now men — keep calm!"

"They lock us out — nine hundred men and boys — and you say keep calm!" Boos and insults rose; the colliers heaved; the gates clattered, but held.

"Break down the gates!"

And there arose in the crowd a man of good height; the sight of him standing with Richard Jones on the plinth momentarily stilled the mob.

"Break down these gates," said John Haley, the English overman, "and they'll bring in the Glamorgan police to crack your skulls: take a single cage down the Ely by force, and they'll send in the troops — remember what happened up in Featherstone? Now then — easy, and *cool*. . . . Richard Jones here is right," and he put his hands on his hips and grinned about him. "Can't you reason why the owners lock out nine hundred men, with only eighty of the Bute Seam in dispute? To bring the place to violence!" They stared up at him, muttering like bulls at feed, and he said, in the silence, "Go home. They want us out, they shall have us out. But, by God, when we're back it will be on our terms!"

The colliers rose to this, cheering and shouting. The door of the Gethin went back and they flooded into it, stamping for ale, while every spare skirt the landlord could muster went round with jugs.

"Dear me," cried Annie Gay, with a saucy eye at me, "what a lot of lovely men!" and she clapped her hands. "Gets right up my nose when folks run 'em down."

"*Duw*, look at them," said Mattie. "I like a pint, but not at eight o'clock in the morning!" He pinched Annie's bottom. "You come down from your pub special to see me?"

We clustered together, penned by the mob at the gates. Trams were clanging their bells for passage; tradesmen standing up in their carts, cursing and cracking whips. Dano McCarthy cried in his thick Irish, "Go home and fret, is it? *Ach*, the skuts! St. Paul himself never thought so wrong," and he crossed himself. "And I come from Ireland to get a fair deal from Wales?"

"This place is mad daft, Pa," said Shaun, his youngest. "We'd be best back home in Galway."

"Sufferin' God!" cried Dano, lanky and thin, "that's where Etta will land me in the Sinkers, for she don't approve of the striking."

"Do any of us?" asked Mattie Kelly.

"Me, for one," I said. "If they want a lock-out, let them have a lock-out. The owners have the money, but we've the strength. All for one, is it? Aye, then — one for all — they'll think again when the Nantgwyn and Pandy drop tools."

"And the Aberdare and Ogmore lot, remember — us first, them later," said Moses Culpepper, soprano. "I said it before — strength in numbers — two hundred thousand colliers in South Wales, remember!"

"You got to ask your missus first, though," said Mattie.

"Aye, but he's right," said Ed Masumbala, the black man, and men went quiet, for he rarely spoke; much respected was he, like Beli, his black missus. "Strength is right; we got to stick together."

"Tell that to Mabon," said Heinie Goldberg, and he shouldered a path into the free. "We pay our money in the Miners' Federation, don't we? Conciliation boards and half-cock committees, is it? Now we can watch them earn their wages."

I looked at John Haley the new overman. He was standing with Tommy beside him, wrapped in thought, as in a leaden shroud.

I crossed the road and pushed through the men to him. His fine blue eyes, ringed with coal, moved slowly over me; no wonder Patsy Pearl was curdling Madog's milk.

255

"Haley, Haley?" I asked. "There's not much Welsh in that." I gave him a grin.

"Is it a crime?"

"*Diawl*, no, mun — we'll sign a Chinee into the Union."

"No Unions for me, mate." He looked beyond me, a man removed.

"You don't believe in collective bargaining?"

"I do not."

"But you take the Union's rises and stick to Union's rules? You can't have it all ways."

"I take what's coming. The stewards don't force pay awards, Welshman, the colliers do — the power lies at the coal face. There's too much money and career prospect in the Union, that's why you're lumbered with people like Mabon. Negotiate with this Owner? They crawl under stones better than him."

"What will come of it?"

He looked at the sky for words and said: "Trouble."

"Real trouble?"

"The place is going to starve."

Snookey Boxer, bulky, flat-faced, came up and pestered me, pulling at my sleeve, making incoherent sounds; night-time, on the steps of the Empire, he cut out dolls with scissors and brown paper. I shook him away, but he came at me again, rolling on his heels. I said to the overman:

"We'll fight, then?"

He looked me over, sighing, as if he had never seen me before. "God Almighty," he whispered, "won't you people ever learn? We've got to fight, there's no alternative."

"The business is getting them all to fight," I replied.

"God help you if they don't."

I watched him going up Dunraven with his hand on Tommy's shoulder.

Unless I was mistaken, I thought, we were going to see more of John Haley.

So the whole of the Ely Pit (not just the Bute Seam) was locked out — nearly a thousand colliers; it was an act of violence that was uncalled for and unnecessary, and the Management refused arbitration on the price of coal per ton. Four days later, the Nantgwyn and Pandy, two other Combine pits stopped work in sympathy with us in the Ely, and the fingers of hatred for D. A. Thomas spread outwards through the Rhondda like the fingers of a hand. As grievances against other Owners were aired, more pits dropped tools — the Lower Duffryn in Mountain Ash and the Lletty-Shenkin in Aberaman — when the police stopped colliers taking home waste wood for their fires — a custom long accepted by managements.

One by one the shutters went up in the tradesmen's windows, for lack of custom; the doors of the little terraced houses were shut tight to keep in the warmth. Aye, said Bron, the doors are closing against hunger like the slamming of coffin lids.

Within weeks, because we were all pantry clients, like Ginty said, the children began to cry for food — while Mr. D. A. Thomas — Mabon's mate, the colliers said — was tucked up fed and warm in the south of France.

"This place is going mad," said Bron, at the hob.

"Well, what d'you expect?"

"I expect some blutty sense!"

"The Ely didn't strike, you know — it was locked out," I retorted.

"The Ely isn't Nantgwyn, the Pandy Pit, Lower Duffryn and Lletty-Shenkin!"

"We stand together or fall together."

"Folks'll be on the starve." She swung to me. "Where's the sense of striking when you could negotiate? That's what you've got men like Mabon for, isn't it?"

"But the Owners won't negotiate, woman!" I sat on the bed. "What the hell can you do with Owners like Thomas who lock their workers out? We were in the middle of negotiations for fair rates for work and they slam the door and go off home — how do you handle people like that?"

"And what are the women of this town going to do, eh?" White-faced, she bent towards me, making points with her saucepan; she had never looked so fiercely beautiful. "It's all right for you lot, you know — it's the women and kids that do the scratching. You men are a lot of bloody kids — like an Irish parliament — everybody talking, nobody listening; shouting your heads off in the publics — you should hear them in the Pandy — will that bring negotiation?"

"You've got to have two for a negotiation!" I was getting angry. "What the hell can we do if Thomas won't talk?"

"Ach, come off it, ye bugger — you've been hitting up for a strike for months. And now you've got one, it's the Owners' fault."

"Because families can't live on one-and-nine a ton!"

A silence came; there was no sound but Bron's breathing. At the grate, she said over her shoulder, "You'll go back, you know."

"Aye, and on our terms!"

"On masters' terms — with your tails between your legs. Union or no Union, that's how it's always been."

"Don't talk rubbish, woman — we'd be half dead by now if it hadn't been for the Union. And that's what's happening now — the Owners are trying to break it." I strode about. "The trouble with you is you've been reading too many newspapers."

"Does nobody tell the truth except the Union?" she cried. "What about the pits flooding out if there's nobody down there to man the pumps? What about the ponies?" I was too sick of this newspaper bogey even to reply to it.

I said, "Tom Mann's got an article coming out soon. Class solidarity in the face of oppression is what's wanted now, he says. So let the capitalists look after their own property or let it go to hell, and he's right." I went to the door. "If you want the truth you should read the Union pamphlets — the newspapers are run by the Owners."

"Who's Tom Mann when he's home?"

"God Almighty!" I said.

I put on my coat and muffler: the night was star-lit cold in the window, an early raw, even for the Rhondda, God being a Tory and working for the masters. I said, "If you don't know who Tom Mann is, there's no sense in continuing this stupid conversation."

"Now you're off, I suppose!"

"Aye."

"Got money for beer, have you? Ten bob a week strike pay? You'll find your mates in there. What the hell would happen if women went on strike?"

I closed the door and leaned against it, facing her. "What's wrong with us? We've had trouble before, haven't we?"

She said, with cold practicality, "Same as is happening all over Town. Colliers fighting Owners; wives fighting husbands."

"Not true. The women are behind us — why not you?"

"*Listen*, I'm like the rest of the women if I think there's chance. But you haven't got one. I've seen all this before — in Clayton workhouse, in the mill country — I've seen it in Bethesda. Later, when there's big Union money behind you, you can fight. But the Owners have a union of millionaires! Unless you sink your pride, you'll pull this town into the gutter."

"You've missed your vocation," I said. "They'll call you to the bar."

I slammed the door behind me.

Sad was my town that October.

Silent, deserted, were the streets of Tonypandy; the empty trams rumbled through a place of loafers; the front and backs were shut tight to the world. Shawled, mufflered and cosseted, huddled over their dead fires or bedded in groups for warmth, the people began to starve in earnest.

No longer the Salvation Army pumped and blasted on the Square in Pandy; Will Parry's trumpet was put in cold storage. Instead, the trundling soup kitchens of the Quakers appeared; gentry people, too, served us, and they will be remembered. Up on the hillsides the old levels were opened in secret; on the 'patches' small coal was scrabbled; men and boys working like blacks; women and girls dragging it down in sacks, watching for the police patrols. Pickets were posted: magistrates threatened with anonymous letters.

And, as up in Bethesda in the strike against Penrhyn, out came the blacklegs.

"Every community's got them," said Mattie Kelly.

"The dregs of a community," I said.

259

"Oh, aye?" said Heinie. Thin and pale he looked already. "Men with sick wives, more'n likely."

"Bollocks to 'em," said Moses Culpepper. "We stand or fall in sickness or health."

"Even the chapels are against us."

This wasn't unusual. The chapels and the Church of England had vested interests in the south of France, people said; when it came to economics, God went out of the window. Yet we all clung on to God in our hearts.

"If I had a starving child, I'd kill that bloody D. A. Thomas," cried Mr. Richard Jones. Things were changing when he talked like that about the Owners.

"They won't let the Quakers serve soup in the vestries."

"Who won't?"

"The Elders."

"I'll give 'em head deacons when this strike is over — the toe of my boot in the arse."

"And Jesus fed the five thousand? Is it Christian?"

"Changing my religion to agnostic, I am."

"Mind, starving kids do weaken a man," said Bill Odd. "Mine cry in their sleep, you know."

"No more peaky than my lot," said Moses, "you seen 'em?"

"At her wit's end, is my missus."

"And my little Willie needing special food, and all?" said Mrs. Shanklyn.

"When there's no more faggots, feed 'im on the peas, love," said Mrs. Leary.

"Sod these coal owners."

"It will end," said Patsy Pearl. "Nobody's wanting love."

"I'll give ye a tanner for it," said Solly Friedman, pawnbroker.

"And Dozey, Sarah's mate, goin' to a shadow?"

'Oh Lord, my God, hearken to our call,' they sang in the chapels.

'Thou who watches the sparrow fall,' rang out from the Church of England.

"You get more religion in the inns and publics," said Bron.

"Mrs. Catty Ledoux seen up in Penygraig yesterday, you heard?"

"And she ain't the only blutty cat consumer. Got slanted eyes, you noticed?"

"Gives me the shivers, she do," said Bron.

"Mind," said Primrose, "French, ain't she? — I never did trust the French, not since the Battle of Waterloo. But fair's fair to Ledoux, I say — got mouths to feed, ain't she? Though Sarah Bosom's persian were worth a fortune; she ought to restrict herself to tabbies, I think."

At night, if the wind was right, we could hear little Madog crying up near River View, Patsy coming thin in the milk with her, according to reports.

"They eat rats in China, you know, when things get skinny."

"*Ach y fi!*"

"You can say that again," said Bron, and shuddered. "I've got to be a lot more hungry before I drop to cats."

"They dropped to rats once, up in the Eastern Valley," said Richard Jones. "In Dowlais they cooked them on shovels and quarrelled over the gravy."

"Ten bob a week strike pay?" cried a woman in the De Winton. "Six mouths to feed? If I had starving kids I'd feed 'em Ginty, never mind cats."

The world, I thought, holds no better teacher than adversity.

In places like Caerphilly and Senghenydd, and down the Rhymney Valley, the pits still worked, being out of the Cambrian Combine, for this was not yet a National strike. But, in our part of the Rhondda, the Cambrian, the strike was total.

"You fools, you're playing right into the Owners' hands," cried Bron. "They're after breaking your hearts. And you'll be back on their terms, as I said before."

"We'll die first."

She glared at me. "Probably."

The strike went on.

In the pinch-pale, coal-stained witch of a night; in the sparkling air of Tonypandy with her glinting roofs of frost: under the eaves of Court Street, Ely Street, Adare Terrace and Church Street; in the empty pantries, the bare front rooms, the foodless kitchens, the bellies rumbled as I went on my rounds, with Union strike pay — as I had done with Ben O'Hara years back.

They had stomach trouble in Number Two, the Sinkers, for a start, but it wasn't much to do with the lock-out.

"Oh, *Duw*," whispered Rosie Arse, twisting on the sofa in the kitchen. "I got a pain and a half in my tum."

"Come in, come in," Albert greeted me, and sat me at the table.

"It's strike pay," I said. "If Rosie's that bad I'll come back later, if you like." I opened my ledger on the table. "How long's she been like that, then?"

"She'll get worse, I reckon, before she gets better," said Annie, coming in from the back. " 'Evening, Toby."

"Is it something she's eaten?"

"Oh, *Arglwydd!*" groaned Rosie, holding her middle.

"She ain't eaten at all — that could be the trouble," said Albert, worried. "Or what you think, Annie? Perhaps we got another woman in the house, really speaking?"

"She's a woman these past two years," said Annie.

"Is she going to die?" asked Tommy, her brother. He was getting bigger every day, shaving, a man before his time.

"They don't usually," said Annie. "What can we do for ye, Tobe?"

"Ten bob, missus, sign here — strike pay," and I slid them the silver.

"Strike pay, is it? — you always was an angel," said Annie.

"Shall I fetch the doctor?" asked Tommy, dark-eyed and serious.

"We got no money for doctors," said Albert, and knelt by the sofa, soothing Rosie's head. "Where does it hurt, my precious?"

"Cor, love us," whispered Rosie, going cockney. "I am 'aving a turn," and she moved her great dark eyes to mine.

I looked around the bare room. Everything had already gone into pop; there was nothing left but the table and chairs, the couch and the crockery.

"Anything I can do?" I asked, getting up.

"Nothing I can't handle," said Annie.

"Shall I go and fetch Farrier George?" asked Tommy, his eyes like saucers. "He's good when horses have pains . . ."

"She's my daughter," said Albert, flushed. "She ain't a mare, ye know."

"She's a mare, all right," said Annie.

The wind was howling for a Wake as I plodded up to Court. Will Shanklyn was out looking for firewood, according to Mrs. Shanklyn, so my baby won't die of the cold.

"He won't die of the cold, ye understand, Toby Davies?" said she. "All the time there's an Owner's mansion with teak on the stairs, says my Will, my Willie's dying warm."

I followed her into the front room where her idiot son was lying; cold as charity he looked, with his little white face pinched up.

"Isn't fair, really, you think of it, Toby Davies?"

The lad snuffled in sleep; I held her against me while she wept.

"I got the strike pay — ten bob, missus."

"We don't like the charity," said Mrs. Shanklyn, blowing her nose.

"Strike pay isn't charity."

"My Will reckons it is. He don't mind the five bob Benefit Club money, you understand — he pays twopence a week for that, see — but he won't take strike pay."

"But it's an entitlement — and you need it for Willie."

Her obesity was thinning out. The flesh hung on the pin-bones of her gaunt face, her breasts sagged on her stomach. She wept in blueness and shivering, the tears running down between her fingers. "Oh, God in grief, what am I going to do? Mrs. Change, the midwife, reckons he's dying. Ye see, Toby, Willie needs special food. Milk, mainly — he never could keep down solids."

"Then the ten bob will help you, Mrs. Shanklyn — please take it?" and I pressed it against her, but she pushed me away.

"Will would go mad," she said.

"He'll go worse if Willie dies, girl. Where's the sense in it?"

She said at the window, "There's milk in the Co-op and eggs and butter. We could make a go of it when I ran the faggot and peas. But now there's no money about. That's how we kept our lad alive

263

— milk and eggs. They builds him up fine, you know — he's big for fifteen, actual."

I thought of Tommy Arse, vibrant with health and muscular; I thought of Willie Shanklyn, born lop-sided, who had been dying since birth.

I said to her, "Need Will know, girl? All you've got to do is to sign your name."

"He'll kill me," she said at nothing.

I knocked on the back next door to us and Rachel Odd appeared at the window in her night-cap, at three o'clock in the afternoon, and all the kids about her, standing with their fingers in their mouths, all six except the last two, being twins, recently delivered.

"Hallo, my son," said Pablo, the parrot.

"Strike pay, is it?" asked Bill, and he eased his great bulk into the kitchen where Mrs. Odd was cooking with a candle.

"That all you've got to cook on — candles?" I asked.

"Just till tonight, when Bill gets back with small coal from the 'patches'."

"The police are up there — you mind you don't get caught," I said to him and put the strike money on the table. "Sign here, Bill," and he did so with a flourish.

"Stay for bread and dip, will ye, Tobe?"

"No thanks, Rachel — got to get back to Bron directly."

"She at the Pandy? I thought she was stopped."

"She still goes, but custom's small — no money about."

Mrs. Odd, watched by the children with spit on their mouths, carefully laid a slice of cottage loaf in the lid of a biscuit tin and held it over the candle; fat spluttered. The aroma coming up from that bacon dip never smelled so sweet in the Café de Paris.

"Christ, mama, hurry up," said Ianto, aged nine. "I'm first, being eldest."

"Any news?" asked Bill at the table.

It was as cold as a workhouse yard in that kitchen; blue-faced, pinched, the children shivered in their bare feet on the boards. I shook my head. "None. The Federation's doing it's best to bring the Owners to talks, but they'll have nothing of it."

Bill hugged himself against the cold. "They're mad! Nobody struck, ye know? — even on the one-and-nine a ton. What are they trying to do to us, for God's sake?"

"Beat us to our knees."

"That'll be the day," said Rachel. "Who's next, my charmers?"

"Me," cried Blodwen, aged eight, and she grinned at me with her teeth missing in front; hands cupped, she received the bacon dip like a woman at communion.

"I'll be up to that Owner's mansion first," said Bill, bassly. "My kids starving and bloody D. A. Thomas on steak and chips?" He thumped the table with a fist. "The Union's big now, me lad, and the Union'll handle him. I say stay out."

"And you with eight kids?"

"Who can break strike if we stay out, eh? Next?" cried Rachel, the bread and dip held high.

"Me," said Olwen, aged seven, and her tiny blue feet slithered on the floor. She ate delicately, for all her hunger, kittenishly, her green eyes watching me.

"Eat it slow," said Rachel. "Thirty-two chews, remember — make it last. They haven't shut down in the whole of the Rhondda yet, I notice. . . ."

"It'll spread." Bill picked up Ruth, aged three, and put her on his knee. "And serve them right! Look, I only want to feed my lot, nothing else. They can keep their ale, their smokes, their chews — I just want enough to keep a table — for Rachel and the kids — not much to ask, is it?"

"It's too much for the share-holders. They've got to have profits."

"And Thomas a millionaire? What else does he want?"

"My wedding ring," said Rachel, "and I'm putting it in pop tomorrow. Growing kids can't live on bacon dip." Suddenly angry, she busied herself about, picking things up and hitting them down again, and Bill said, "Ach, don't be daft, woman, there's no bloody need for that."

"Married to you, there is!" said Rachel. "Or this blutty Pablo will 'ave to go; plucked and feathered, he'd make a dinner."

"What you going to do for decency, then?" asked Bill, and they had suddenly forgotten me.

"All we're worth is a damned old curtain ring, anyway," said Rachel, and in passing, kissed him.

It seemed wrong to stay longer. The children were watching them with deep apprehension.

"That's right, you sod off," said Pablo the parrot.

Mr. Richard Jones breathed frosted air at me when he opened the door of Number Fifteen, Court.

" 'Evening, Mr. Jones," I said. "The Union hand-out's arrived."

"We don't need it," said he, and his watery eyes regarded me. His missus came then, peering over his boney shoulder. "Who is it, love?"

"Toby Davies," I said, "come with the funds. Ten bob for spending — the Union's compliments. What will you have, sir, a flitch of bacon or a hamper from Ginty's?"

Hand in hand, they smiled at me. "How're the lads doing?" he asked.

"They're alive."

I saw the kitchen behind them, the bare room, the dead fire.

"You need it, too," I replied.

"Children need it more. Take it down to Mrs. Ledoux." Mrs. Jones clasped her mittened hands together. "Breaks my heart to see those little mites, it do. Her husband's left her, you know?"

"The Brittany onion-sellers aren't very dependable," said Richard, archly.

I closed my ledger. "You're a good one."

"How's Bron?" he asked.

"Middling."

They shrugged; hunger was helping age to give them the pallor of workhouse ghosts.

I took off my hat to them and went down the street to see "Catty" Ledoux.

There were enough cat skins curing in the scullery of Mrs. Ledoux to make fur coats for the matrons of the Rhondda.

Through the cracked window of the kitchen I saw the children — all seven — up at the table and banging their spoons, with a brown,

266

sizzling corpse that could have been mistaken for a rabbit, and Mrs. Ledoux was basting it with ceremonial flourishes.

Nobody got the proof of it, for dead pussies tell no tales, but there was a distinct shortage of pets in Tonypandy at the time, especially in the vicinity of Court Street where the mice were getting away with murder.

I gave Mrs. Ledoux the ten shillings and she took it in a purring gratitude of French and feline grace. And I saw through that window, the caterwauling children, amber-eyed and bewhiskered, their spoons clutched in their paws, tails erect in a chorus of mewing.

Mrs. Ledoux, with a clawed hand, clutched the silver against the furry front of her.

Her iris eyes glinted at me in the dusk.

"*Entrez, s'il vous plaît, monsieur?*" she purred at me.

I got going, and didn't stop till I reached the end of Court Street.

There I bumped into Sarah Bosom and Dozey Dinah: lanky and thin was Dozey; Sarah was the short of it, lavish in the hips and breast, and in tears.

"We had our Timmy this morning," grizzled Dozey. "True, she were out all night, but she came in for her breakfast," and Sarah wept openly into a tiny lace handkerchief.

"We'll 'ave to slip down to Church Street and ask Mr. Goldberg about it — he'll know what to do."

"Seen to us individually, if ye understand," said Dozey, "in times gone by."

"Has he, now?" I said. I knew Heinie had a past but I was doubtful if he'd got a future.

"Meanwhile," sobbed Sarah, "if you see a lovely big white persian, you'll let us know immediate?"

I bowed to them.

Bron wasn't in the Pandy when I called for her; the landlord raised a flushed, heavy face to me as I came in; the bar, once full of the shouting, rollicking shifts from the Big Glamorgan, was as bare as an Eskimo burial ground and twice as chilly.

Even the Square was empty. It was as if the strike had come in with winter brooms and swept up the refuse called people.

Bron wasn't home, either.

I threw down the ledger, counted the money I had left, and lay on the bed; later, I undressed and got in properly. After a bit, I slept.

Bron came home near to the dawn: she did not light the lamp. I saw her but dimly, as a man lying within a husk of dead love.

30

SOME, WHO WERE wrong, said that the Rhondda blew up when Winston Churchill, then Home Secretary, sent soldiers into the valley: others who were right, claimed that the violence really began when police, under the leadership of the hated Captain Lindsay, their Chief, began to beat up our coalfield picketers, who were acting peacefully and within the law.

"You know," said Heinie, after this, "all the Cambrian management has to do is to make its own laws, see the police carry them out, and sit on its backsides until the colliers' children begin to fail."

They failed all right.

Up to now, they were children confined to the Ely colliers. But, on the sixty-third day of the Ely Lock-out (when we weren't allowed to work though we wanted to) the Miners' Federation made its call to the rest of the Cambrian colliers. These, after a mass meeting of assent, came out in sympathy with us of the Ely.

More than a dozen pit wheels in the two valleys stopped turning.

The battle was on. And, according to Bron we were on a hiding to nothing. As things turned out, she wasn't far wrong.

Poverty, deep and true, stalked the valleys.

Famished in the little bare bedrooms in an icy bitch called November, the children died, and the little white coffins, always the first, began their drab processions to the mountain cemeteries.

Later, though toughened by earlier privations, the old ones began to falter: the poor, the ailing; women with consumption, men with miner's asthma. Then the big yellow coffins with shining brass

269

handles, beautiful with flowers, passed the curtained windows in a clattering of black-plumed horses, and the Hibernian band played *The Dead March in Saul*.

But, according to the popular newspapers, these did not die of starvation: they died, it was said, of a score of diseases from tuberculosis to scarlet fever, 'flu to whooping cough, croup to pneumonia. Few took account of the truth that the Rhondda was starving. Our constant applications to the Owners to recommence work at the Ely and put the Bute Seam to new arbitration, was met with rejection: unless the colliers accepted one-and-ninepence a ton, said the Management, the Ely would stay shut.

And so, one by one, with the pumps silent, underground workings began to flood. Engine-house fires were put out in Tonypandy, which brought Mr. D. A. Thomas back from the south of France.

"God help us," said Bron. "The strike will be total."

"It'll only be total when the blacklegs are dealt with," I said. "That's up to us, it has nothing to do with God."

"You know," laughed Heinie, "when you talk that way, you sound like a communist."

"He's in good company," said Dai Parcel, come over to visit us. "Jesus was the first."

"I wish you lot wouldn't talk like that," said Bron. "We're in need of God now, that's certain sure."

We were in despair.

The Combine management had brought in outside labour; these joined with scabs to keep wheels of some pits turning, and our attempts to picket the colliery entrances were again broken up by the police and strong-arm volunteers working for the Owners.

The colliery up at Clydach was a case in point; they were still taking out coal and running it in trains past our noses. And Chief Constable Lindsay, known as 'The Roman Centurion', had taken more pit ponies underground; then he gave newspaper interviews telling of the heartless attitude of the colliers to their animals, who were in danger of drowning now the pumps had stopped.

"He's been taking ponies underground every day this week," said

Mattie Kelly. "If there's one horse down the Scotch there must be four hundred."

"Why do they want ponies down the pit if there's no work for 'em?" asked Rachel Odd, come in to borrow bread.

"Wake up, woman," I said.

"For the sake of public opinion," explained Heinie. "One drowned pony and the whole country'll be against us."

"King George is losing sleep already," said Mattie. "If pit ponies drown they reckon he'll abdicate."

"What about us — won't he abdicate for us?" asked Bron.

"You're not important compared to a pit pony," said John Haley, who had joined the Union now and come with Richard Jones. "Keir Hardie'll be in trouble, the way he's talking — anti-patriot, they'll call him now — criticising the King."

"Christ, what a world," said Rachel. "You heard about the Shanklyn boy?"

"The doctor gives him a couple of days, at most."

"The Shanklyns'll give 'em pit ponies if that boy dies, including God save the Prince of Wales."

"And that's been tried before! Remember the Chartists?"

"So what's the Union doing about it?" asked Haley. "What's our weak-kneed Federation got in mind, now the kids are dying and everybody hates us?"

"The Federation's been more active than you think," said Mr. Jones. "So listen, and spread this to every Ely lodge member. The Union has called for a mass meeting and demonstration of strength tomorrow. All of you — get the buglers out at dawn and rouse people up. All committees and stewards are to be responsible for turning out in force."

"Just a demonstration?" asked Heinie, innocent.

"An official Federation mass meeting, man — everybody up at the Athletic Ground by seven o'clock. Discussion first; the total strike resolution repeated, and then a march to Clydach to drown the engine-room fires. We're to shut down every pit still working with blackleg labour."

"Now you're talking," said John Haley. "But what about *positive* action?"

"Isn't drowning fires and closing pits positive action?" asked Richard Jones. "What more do you want?"

"Drive out the Metropolitan police, for a start. Attack the newspaper offices — run out the lies!"

"Cool heads will win, Overman," I said.

"Violence will win — it's the only way!"

"With Captain Lindsay spoiling for a fight and a hundred and fifty Metropolitan police billeted in Town? — talk sense!"

"You fight now," said Haley, softly, "or you might just as well let this generation die, wipe the slate clean, and start all over again."

"Every time I fought outside me weight I got a hiding," said Heinie. "We're featherweights compared with the London government."

"And even if we drove out the police, they'd bring in the military — do ye want another Merthyr?" asked Richard Jones. "Sixty shot dead and hundreds wounded?"

"God alive, man, that was eighty years ago; come up to date!"

"It could happen again," I said. "The Owners can call in the military at the drop of a hat."

"You've got the right Home Secretary in Winston Churchill, that's for sure," said Richard Jones. "Right now he's getting practice in by beating up London suffragettes."

"Who are they when they're home?" asked Bron, making tea.

"Women rebels trying to get the vote for women."

"They must be pixilated," said Rachel. "I'd beat 'em up meself."

"One of them died, did you hear that?" asked Haley. He took the tea Bron offered him and warmed his hands on the mug.

"Winston Churchill knocked her off?"

"Same thing," said Heinie. "The London police again, the big brutal swines, but Churchill gave the orders. Give them a hard time, he says. That's nothing to what the bugger'll give us."

"The all-time enemy of the working class," said Haley, staring out of the window.

"Rosie Arse has fallen for a baby — you heard?" asked Primrose Culpepper, just come in.

"Don't change the subject!"

272

"A boy, ain't it?" asked Rachel from her corner, sipping her tea. "Grand little bouncer — ain't it romantic?"

"It is when you know the father."

"And changed her name to Rosie Jenkins. Rosie Arse weren't good enough for her, I suppose — Arse was good enough for Annie."

"Rosie Arse-Jenkins it'll be for sure, and she's called the kid Llewellyn."

"Llewellyn Arse-Jenkins," said Mattie reflectively.

"Send her dada soft, it will — doted on her, he did, poor old Albert."

John Haley rose and put down the mug. "Well, I'll see you all tomorrow. Got to do something, haven't we? Best do it quick."

"The Federation's calling this mass meeting, not you, Overman," said Richard Jones, "let's have that one straight."

"As long as they act," replied Haley. "When the Owners start importing blackleg labour, we've got to move — with or without your bloody Federation."

"You damned rabble-rouser!" said Bron.

He bowed to her, smiling, as he went through the door.

"He'll cause trouble before he's finished, that one," said she.

"He won't if you all follow the Union's lead," said Richard Jones. "Only unity will help us now — independent action by anyone tomorrow and the police will come in."

"So you're starting trouble in the morning, are you?" asked Bron, undressing. "You start easing out scabs and blacklegs and the police'll be in — or have you forgotten all about Bethesda?"

There had come between us a sense of isolation. She was going to Porth now with growing regularity; I had almost accepted it. We did not discuss it; it was as if it had become an unspoken agreement between us — she went to Sam; I could go to Nanwen.

We no longer made love. Had I made approaches to her, I suppose she would have acceded; offering me the husk of a woman out of pity. But, although my need of her was great, I could never have used her as a mere receptacle: possibly, I thought, lying there in the dim lamplight, this was a proof of love.

273

Try as I may, I could not isolate this emotion: it was hating and loving simultaneously. I said, answering her:

"If trouble comes, mun, you won't be in it."

She made no attempt to cover herself while undressing, and across the shivering room, I briefly saw her nakedness. The sight brought to me the old, parching need. And perhaps some telepathy flashed between us, for she turned holding her nightdress against her.

Strange, I thought, the sudden warmth in all that coldness; smiling, head on one side, she stared at me over the ocean of the bed.

"Poor old Tobe," she said, "poor old lad."

The winter night seemed to beat about us; the moon in the hut window was sighing with the cold: frost was on the Square, icicles hung spiked glass from the eaves.

"You need me?"

It seemed like weakness to take her offering of second best. I thought of Sam wanting her over in Porth; also, I thought of Nanwen in Senghenydd, wanting me.

"Not particularly," I replied.

"Not particularly, eh? Dear me — *hoity toity!*" She made a face at me. "Ah, well, perhaps it's best, since you've got to be up in the morning. *Damn* men!" She got in beside me and thumped the pillow, like I'd have thumped Sam Jones if I'd had him then. "Right you are, boyo — you chase off to your fancy Nanwen, though you'll find she ain't got nothing better'n me, though she might have bells on it."

I awoke once in the night because I thought I could hear her crying, but it was probably the wind.

31

To MAKE SURE he was early, I knocked Will Parry Trumpet out of bed next dawn, and, while Will was tuning up his bugle down the gullyway at the back of the Huts, I ran over the Square to Heinie's room in Church Street, behind the Pandy.

"Come on, come on!" I cried, hammering his door, and he up and opened it and scurried around in his combs, shouting:

"Sound the alarm! Strike up the trumpet — give it hell, Will Parry — D. A. Thomas'll hear that Angel Gabriel!"

Meanwhile, the town was beginning to wake for the earliest shift in months. Peal after peal of that bugle echoed over the Square; answering bugles were sounding in every corner of the valley.

This was the morning of the Federation's mass meeting; the Rhondda was responding as to a call to arms.

Tonypandy spun into life like a whipped top. Colliers, engine-men, farriers and ostlers, top workers and face workers poured in black streams from the doors of the terraced houses, many dressing as they went.

"Get a move on! We've got to get Richard Jones up on the platform," I yelled at Heinie, and he ruptured himself into his trews, bare feet hopping on the boards, and waved his arms into his shirt: slop water into a basin, down with his face to come up streaming: in front of the mirror now, roaring with pain to the scur of the razor.

"You're undone in the trews again," I said, and the moon put her fingers through the window and did up his flies for him.

The bugle blasted on while I waited for Heinie; Will Parry making a meal of it. Dogs were howling to kicks as we eventually made our way up to Court where Richard lived, cats slamming down the alleyways, children being scolded for wetting the beds.

The old people, the tortured refuse of the old generation, opened their eyes to a misted dawn. Babies were being potted, vests lifted for furious mouths, aunts shaking uncles, lovers covering their ears to the blasts of Will Parry's bugle, and "the daft nit wants to get hold of himself, raising Cain at this time of the mornin'," cried Mrs. Change, the Pandy midwife, with her night-cap bobble out of her bedroom window. "Stuff up that blutty bugle, Will Parry, or I'll tell on ye!"

"You stuff up, missus," yelled Will, blasting away. "I'm waking the town by orders o' the Federation, that right, Toby Davies?"

"Just go on bugling, *bach*," I commanded, passing him with Heinie.

"It do surprise me where he gets his breath from, mind," as Mrs. Change told Bron later. "I'm the medic round these parts generally, and one good rallentando ought to have him over. And he's impotent too — though I don't make it public — medical etiquette, and all that. Anyway, I don't go a lot on this conjugal palaver myself. Come on, come on, get back," and she eased a relative away from the window in his nightshirt.

"*Jawch*, what a life it is," cried Primrose Culpepper from her door. "Out to make trouble, are you? Come to a bad end, you will, as God's me judge," and the mob swept past her, cheering and hullabalooing.

"No, not you, my lovely, you can't go," said Mrs. Livingstone, her arm round Guto. "You got to be sane for this one, boyo — I keep telling him, eh, Toby?" and I knocked up my cap at her.

"Where are you off to?" I cried, gripping Tommy Arse as he dashed past me, for everything seemed to be happening at once now.

"Not to Union meetings," cried he, pushing me off. "Not, leastwise, till I've 'ad him. . . ."

"Had who, mate? Who's for it now?" asked Heinie, bright-eyed.

"That Shaun McCarthy, the swine!" Tight-fisted was Tommy,

looking for a murder. For weeks now, they'd been trying to get the father out of Rosie.

"One of Dano's lads?" I asked. "You're bonkers, Tom!"

"Our Rosie just told us — he anna getting away wi' it, mind — laying my sister."

"Don't be daft," called Heinie, swinging him back into the crush of men. "All the McCarthy boys are virgins, Ma Etta sees to that."

"Not Shaun, the young one — took Rosie's advantage, he did — she just told us."

"Won't it wait for the revolution?"

"It won't," shouted Tommy, and went.

"God help us," said Heinie.

Like packs of starving dogs the men of the town were pouring over the Square now, making for the Athletic Ground beside the Incline, as Heinie and I fought our way up to Court for Richard Jones. And still the bugles were calling, calling.

Bron we met next, confronting us as we organised the stragglers. Her black shawl was scragged tight over her hair, her face pinched with cold.

"I'm coming, too," she gasped, lifting her skirts.

"You're not, mate — this is no place for women!"

She tried to catch my arm, but I shook her off.

"Haven't women got rights, too, then?"

"Now come on! You don't agree with all this — you said so!" I shouted.

"And now I've changed me mind, haven't I?"

"Since when?" asked Heinie, wryly.

"Since the blacklegs came in, you said, and the police started beating up our pickets."

I strode off, but she followed me, picking and pestering, and she nearly fell once as the men surged about her. "What happens to you happens to me, Tobe," she shouted, one fist up.

"O, aye? That's a new one. A few days back we were rabble-rousers — remember?"

"Not now. There's nothing left to do but fight. I realise."

"Go and tell it to that fella in Porth." I pushed her away.

"Keep your moss on and your hands off me!" The men closed about her. I swung people aside for a path, and Heinie followed.

"And what was all that about?" he shouted.

Furious, I didn't reply.

"I thought you two were mates!"

"We were."

"And now she isn't good enough? That it?"

I glared at him. "Our business, Heinie."

"And mine." Stopping me, he hauled me back to face him, his little flat face glowering up into mine. "She's a good one, and she's my mate, too, so try shoving me!"

"*Ach*, she knows what she can do."

"Right, then, but don't you rough her up."

The men were swaying about us: Lodge leaders were being hoisted on to the shoulders of others: the colliers thronged in a great black wedge of humanity towards the dais where Federation officials were waiting to address them. I shouted at Heinie. "You'd have roughed her long before this — if she were yours."

"Well, she's not mine, worse luck." He grimaced. "The way you're behaving, you just ain't fit to clean her boots."

We glared at each other.

Saddened at the first rift between Bron and me, I waited with Heinie on the doorstep of Richard Jones's house while he took leave of his wife. All down Court the doors were coming open and colliers rushing out with flung goodbyes.

"So you're going to put out the engine room fires?" asked Mrs. Jones and it seemed as if, in her misery, she was unaware of us.

Thinner and paler than Ginty's colleen was she, and worried about her husband's breathing.

In Welsh she spoke to him, thinking I did not understand.

"Give us a couple of hours, woman, don't make a meal of it," said Richard.

"Do you really have to go? What about the young ones?"

He said, looking past me, "I'm on the Standing Committee. Mainwaring and Rees will expect me. I'm down to speak first for the Ely Lodge."

"They expect too much," she replied. "They always have. Give it all up soon, will you *bach*?"

"*Ach*, missus, see sense. The Union's my life."

He did not resist when she tied his muffler, for he was looking at the sky, where a clutch of ravens were flying.

His wife said, "All our lives it's been like this — married to the Union, aren't you, in a manner of speaking. Besides . . ." and she stroked his arm. "You aren't fit to go, *bach* — you should be under the doctor."

He fought for breath, saying huskily, "Talk properly, woman — even at a time like this — Dr. Lyon's tops eighteen stones," so, in English she said, warmly:

"I think a lot of you, Richard . . ." and she leaned against him.

He stared anxiously around. "Ay ay, but loose me, girl — not in front of people."

And, as if the cue to a drama in coal was given, he coughed, eyes closed, to inner soundless explosions.

"I got to go," he said in wheezes. "Young Toby's waiting."

I behaved as one disinterested. "You ready, Mr. Jones?"

"Aye, son," and he turned to his wife.

They looked at each other, smiling, with empty resignation.

"*Yn iach! Ffarwel. . . !*"

Strangely, he kissed her.

With Heinie on one side of him and me on the other, we fought a path for him through the packed ranks of roaring colliers, and took him up to the platform where the members of the Workmen's committee were waiting. The chairman, William John, spoke first, ending with the words:

"We will not lower our banner now! This committee will strain every nerve to bring the fight to a successful issue, and it is our intention to stop any man from working on in the collieries now the Federation has said stop. With your help, our pickets will prevent any official — including our much respected Chief Constable Lindsay — from entering the colliery yards. . . !"

His speech ended in thunderous cheering, and he added, his arms high, "Now I ask Richard Jones, the chairman of the Ely Lodge, which spear-heads this fight, to address you," and Heinie and I helped old Richard up the steps of the platform.

Thin and pale he looked standing there surrounded by the big-wigs of the Federation committee, but the very sight of him brought the men to instant silence: his fine voice rang out:

"Well, we are come to it! On this day, the sixty-third of the lock-out at the Ely, we are joined by the strength of the Miners' Federation! Think of it — all you who have starved with your women to keep your children fed! The whole of the Cambrian pits have struck in sympathy. Count in Aberdare, Maesteg and pits in Monmouthshire, some thirty thousand men have laid down tools against tyranny!"

Not a murmur. The wind, ruffling his thin hair, was the only sound of the morning, and he continued:

"So, as William John says, we must not lower our banners now — it must be a fight to the death with this tyrant — we quote W. J. Parry, the great Union leader up in Bethesda. Today we will begin by drowning out the engine fires up at Clydach, which is still working on, though the Federation has said stop!" He raised his voice. "By this time tomorrow every pit in the Combine will be idle — not by our wish, mark me, but by the decree of a management which has locked out a thousand colliers on a whim."

They bawled mass assent at this, but he conducted them into silence. "And by this time next week the Winding Engineers' Union, the Stokers, Enginemen and Surface Craftsmen's Union will have joined hands with us in this fight against evil. *For we did not call this strike*, remember — we were locked out of a pit which was exploiting us, yet one we were still prepared to work!"

They roared, waving a forest of arms. Richard cried:

"But one thing I beg of you — no violence! Let the violence shown by this vicious management never be matched by ours! Unionism is negotiations, conciliations, argument — violence is the business of employers! What you do in the next few days will be known to history, remember. Unions, federations of workers all over the world are watching. Picketing has begun at all the Combine collieries — let it be peaceful, despite police beatings. Let the blacklegs and imported labour be persuaded against working, in an orderly manner. . . !"

A man yelled from the crowd, "*Persuaded*? Persuade bloody blacklegs? Aye, Richard Jones, we'll persuade 'em!"

Another shouted, "And you talk of a fight to the death? What is this, a Sunday school outing?"

"Men, *men*. . . !"

They jostled about him, raising fists as he cajoled them:

"I beg you to stop and think," he cried. "The police are here in force. And not all Welsh police, but the London Metropolitan drafted in. . ."

"And we'll bloody show them!"

"Get him down!"

"The ailing old fool — take him off the committee!"

And Richard shouted, his voice piercing their bass lowing, "The Ely men — my own Lodge — are already starving. Do you prefer to starve in gaol?"

"Talk sense, they can't gaol all of us!"

"Give us a pint o' your blood, Dick Jones, I want to water me garden!"

Laughter mingled with the jeers; I could have wept for the old collier. Then a man cried, "You're talking Owners' language, mun — we're talking colliers' talk, and we've been meek too long!"

"Negotiations within the law. . . ."

"Sod you Dick Jones and sod your negotiations! We've had enough!"

"Then blood will be spilled on these mountains!"

"Not yours, old man, that's certain. What the hell do you want of us, you and your committee? We've got William Abraham who calls himself Mabon, Vernon Hartshorn and D. Watts Morgan and biblical buggers like you left right and centre — when are we goin' to get some Toms, Dicks and Harrys — men at the face?"

"No violence, you say? I'm up to me ears in pawn!"

"I've got five kids starving — ain't that violence?"

"Mabon says . . ." Richard tried to quieten them.

"To hell with you! Does Mabon starve?"

281

"Stop talking, mun, and get us up to Clydach Vale — we'll give 'em blacklegs."

Hoots and catcalls drowned out words and sense. They jostled about the platform and, with Heinie beside me, I worked my way closer to the steps, climbed up, and brought Richard down.

Little and old he looked, as if the mob had touched him.

We held him between us while he fought for breath.

It took the authority of Noah Rees, the secretary of the Cambrian Lodge, to regain order.

"God help them," said Richard, leaning against me. "They'll take you to the devil, d'you realise?"

"Empty bellies raise tempers, old man," said Heinie.

"But why vote me in if they don't do what I say?" He stared about him, gasping. "Listen to them! Hundreds have died to build the Union . . ."

"They're tired of words, Mr. Jones," I said, and he turned his ashen face to mine, saying:

"It'll come to words in the end, it always does. Too young you are to see good sense, but you'll understand when the police come out. Have you seen the big Metropolitans with the batons up in front? Have you heard their stamping?"

"Time enough when it comes."

"No time at all. Too late then," he said.

"Best get him home?"

Slowly, clearing a way through the mob of howling men, we took him back up to Court Street and gave him to his missus.

The colliers were organised by the time we got back.

Columns were being formed by the Federation stewards; tempers were regained. They even raised a cheer for us as we took our place in the Ely Lodge ranks.

Urchins and pit boys were handing out Tom Mann pamphlets and colliers' newspapers like *Justice* and *Labour Leader*; a brass band came from nowhere and formed up at our head.

Women and children were running out of their doors, pent with excitement, the wives black-shawled and capped, hopping about us like frock-coated undertakers. Bang, bang, on a big bass drum, and we were off up the hill to Clydach. And we were but one such mass meeting.

All over the Rhondda the colliers were answering the Union's call; snake after snake of men marching in the mountain towns in search of blacklegs and imported labour — the old, old stick which was used to thrash miners.

Up past River View we went to the colliery, bringing families to their doors, waving to Patsy Pearl who was feeding her Madog on her doorstep (and I saw Ricardo, the ice-cream man, fashioned on the bedroom window) and on to the colliery where we chased out the blacklegs and hosed out the engine fires, stopping the cage.

One blackleg we caught, wrapped him in a bedsheet, and marched him like a ghost at the head of the band; another we hoisted to the top of the pit-head, leaving him swinging there, yelling for a pig-sticking.

Down the valley road then, and along the railway to the Nantgwyn Naval colliery; here we did the same, then marched on to the hated Ely through Penygraig, making sure it was shut. Back down Amos Hill we went, singing and cheering, with half the population following us now, some said twelve thousand. To the two Pandy pits and the Anthony we went — all of the Cambrian Combine, with whom we were in dispute. Here we gave the blacklegs a run, sending the women and children after them, and Primrose Culpepper and Rachel Odd in the van, had a field day, hitting the daylight out of them.

It was nearing dusk and we were tired by the time we got back to Pandy Square, leaving behind us a trail of wet fires and halted cages; the wheels of shunting engines jammed, trucks derailed.

The police, mainly Glamorgan Constabulary, watched at the entrances to colliery offices or agents' houses, arms folded, and did not move against us.

"What of the county police now, then?" called someone.

"And what of the big Metropolitans?" asked somebody else. "Skulking behind the curtains of the Thistle Hotel, are they?"

"They'll stop skulking when we go down there tomorrow," I replied. "Big trouble will arrive when we tackle the Scotch."

"You can say that again," said Bron, when I got back to the Hut.

283

"Well," said she now, "have ye had a good day setting the world aright?"

I kicked off my boots and lay back on the bed. "One thing's sure — you didn't contribute."

The meetings and demonstrations weren't really over, but I'd returned early because I was worried about her. Now she said, caustically:

"I tried to help and nearly got me eye filled up."

I had to grin. She was at her best in this mood; her mercurial ability to change disallowed any vendetta; she never sulked. When something went wrong between us she behaved, in minutes, as if it hadn't happened.

Now she was ironing, with a blanket on the table. Nothing interfered with Bron's ironing — weekday, strike day, it had to go on, and she reckoned she had the whitest washing in Tonypandy, never mind the blutty Sinkers. She even lent me a wink as she held up her drawers; lace-trimmed were these but with a rip across the rear, and she flapped them at me and made draughty noises and big eyes.

"That'll tickle your fancy," I said.

"Chance'd be a fine thing!"

"*Ach*, go on with you," I said. "There's nothing in them."

"You never know your luck," and she pouted prettily. "I know a few who'd be interested."

"So do I." It was meant to hurt her and it stilled her hands momentarily, then she smiled. "Ah, well, back to the convent. Meanwhile, you've drowned the fires, stopped the pumps and settled the blacklegs, is it?"

"Aye, in all pits but one."

"What about the Llwynypia Scotch? Why does she get off?"

"She doesn't. We're down there first thing tomorrow."

"Ah, well, I suppose that's progress."

"Don't you agree?"

She spat on the iron and whistled at the steam. "I didn't once, but I do now. We've a right to peaceful picketing — that's the law. When the police change that law, I'm with ye." She ironed vigorously. "But I tell you this, you'll be in trouble tomorrow when you tackle the Glamorgan pit."

284

"We know all about that."

I was hungry; with it came the usual irritability. She seemed so composed. Getting up, I went to the tea caddie; it was empty.

"I took the last eightpence to Ginty. Bread and mousetrap suit you?" she asked.

"I'd prefer roast chicken."

"That's the main course — didn't you eat at the soup kitchen? I did."

"Too busy chasing blacklegs."

"Aw, me poor sweet boy!" Smiling, she wandered towards me at the grate, her arms out to me.

I didn't know how to handle her. Every time I looked at her these days I saw Sam Jones. She walked into my arms and there was a kindness in her against me. I held her; we did not speak. Then:

"Hell of a time we're having, ain't we, Tobe?"

I did not reply.

"Thank Gawd little Bibbs ain't here, eh?"

I nodded against her. She said, "It . . . it's the people with kids that get me. If a kid started to cry — one of mine, I mean — I'd go mad."

"It'll pass. Bron . . ."

She looked up into my face. I said, "Don't go to Porth again — not till we get through this bad patch, anyway."

Perplexed, she held me away, staring. "Christ, man, what do ye take me for?" She searched my face.

"Well . . ."

"Listen," she said, "if you've got trouble, I'm in it, too. Bugger Sam Jones."

"For better or worse, you mean?"

She made uncertain gestures. "Well, not that. It's just . . . well, it wouldn't be decent if I walked out on you now, would it?" She lowered her face. "Anyway, Sam don't want me."

We stood apart. "Any more than that Nanwen really wants you," she added.

"You don't know that."

"I got a fair idea, or she'd be over here to get you. I would." She shook her head at me as one does to a wayward child. "Dear me!

You're a regular cuckoo in the nest, ain't you? Like me, you're a loser."

I nodded, sighing, and she said:

"You poor old sod. I just don't know what I'm goin' to do with you, I don't. Come on, come by 'ere." She put her arms around me and smiled capriciously up into my face. "Look, if you can't have that old Nanwen, would it ease ye any if you tumbled me on the bed?"

I said, "You just don't understand, do you, Bron?"

"You're a man, and I've been up against a few in my time, but mate, you take the biscuit." She stood away, opening her hands at me. "Oh well, if you ain't all that keen on me, would some bread and Ginty cheese warm ye?"

"Now that's talking!"

She ran to the biscuit tin and brought out the food, spreading it with relish on a corner of the table. "There now! I got that special for my old Tobe!" She cut me a hunk of bread and a wedge of cheese and I attacked it, a man famished.

"Come on," I said, my mouth full. "Where's yours?"

"I'm all right," she said. "I ate on the Quakers. I told ye."

Smiling, she watched me bolting it.

"You sure you don't want me after?" she asked, head on one side. "Like a sort of second course?"

I was well into the bread and cheese. "Quite sure."

Her eyes narrowed with suppressed delight and she reached out and squeezed my hand. "That's all right, then! The way to the heart's through the stomach, they say — friends again now Tobe, ain't we?"

For a long time that night (for we were abed by nine) I lay half dreaming of Nanwen. I wanted her; she wanted me, yet she had to live a life with a drunken Ben O'Hara. It was an impossible situation, I thought, to be so close to her, yet so distant.

"What you thinking about?" asked Bron.

"Nothing much."

"About how the lads are going to do the Scotch tomorrow?"

"No."

286

"What, then?" But I didn't reply.

She was up on an elbow; the cold of the room swept into us and I pushed her down. Frost was on the window; icicles hung from the downspouts and gutters.

"Thinking about that Nan O'Hara, is it?"

Her eyes were large and beautiful in the soft light of the window. "Yes."

"You in love with her, Tobe?" She leaned above me, looking into my face. "Really, truly in love, I mean — like dying?"

I did not reply. There was no point in hurting her.

With finality, she said at the ceiling, "Always loved her really, 'aven't you?"

"It's just the same with you — you've always loved Sam Jones."

"Hell," she said, softly. "A woman just can't help loving Sam Jones. He's a bad bugger, I know, but ye can't help lovin' him." Rolling over to me, she said, "But what you going to do about it? Loving that Nanwen, I mean?"

"I don't know."

"You could always knock off Ben O'Hara!"

"Don't be ridiculous."

We lay in silence, then she said, "Love's a very funny business, you know, Tobe. You take these policemen beating up our pickets — somebody loves 'em, I suppose." Distantly, I heard the sounds of a gathering mob. Sleep was claiming me after the exhaustion of the day.

"Bron, go to sleep. Why d'you always wake up at this time of night?"

"And then old Richard Jones — he's half dead, poor soul. And his fat old missus waddles around like a ram with foot-rot, yet he loves her, don't he?"

"Good night," I said.

"Aye," and she sighed deeply. "Love's a funny old thing, you come to think of it." She touched me gently. "Like me loving you, for instance."

I listened, and she said, "Mind, I do love Sam — I just said so, didn't I? But I love you, too — all at the same time. Anybody hurt you, mate, I'd batter 'em."

"You'll have to make up your mind then, won't you?" I replied. "Sam or me."

"Like you with that Nanwen." She kissed my cheek. "But you'll always be friends with me, won't ye, Tobe? Even if you start poodle-faking wi' her?"

We lay together, her hand in mine, and I listened to the sounds of the night. The mob noises were pulsating on quick flushes of the wind, but I tried to ignore them. Memories of Nanwen's dark beauty was invading me with persistent force.

When this lot was over, I thought, I'd go over to Senghenydd and bring things to a head; it would be Ben O'Hara, or me. Life was just a mess of conflicting emotions and frustration, continuing like this.

"Good night, son," said Bron, and kissed my face, and I remembered the perfume of Nanwen's hair. "You all right, are ye?"

"Aye."

She whistled against my ear. "Don't take it all so ripe, mun — that's your trouble, ye know — you take it all so serious, and cupids ain't like that — they're just, well . . . little old dancing chaps with flowers behind their ears . . . you listening?"

I breathed so steadily for her that I nearly dropped off.

"Eh, my, you're a sweet thing, Tobe — just like a little lad you are — come on now, cootch up to me, is it? And anything you fancy in the night, mate, you just give aunty the elbow. . . ?"

32

WE HAD BEEN asleep for about an hour, I suppose, when I was aware of a gathering of people in the Square. Bron awoke, too, sitting up beside me. "What's happening?"

"It's the Glamorgan pit — hell's setting alight."

"But you're drowning the Scotch fires in the morning!"

"Earlier, it seems," I said, getting out on to the boards and peering through the frosted window.

Men were thronging to and fro on the Square under the light of the fountain; I heard bass shouts and the high voices of women. And just then the door nearly came off its hinges under Heinie's fist. He entered on a rush of words:

"The Cambrian management have taken over the Scotch," he cried. "Word's just come out."

"But what about our pickets?"

"Flung out by the police. There's three outside with split heads — one's a hospital case."

"And Lindsay's occupied the colliery?"

"That's it," said Heinie. "And Llewellyn, the Combine manager, has gone underground with eighty blacklegs."

"We'll soon dig them out."

"But there's a hundred policemen guarding the top — they're all over the yard, and in the power station."

I was dressing hastily. "If there is there'll be trouble!"

"There's trouble already — it never really stopped. A lot of the lads are at Llwynypia now. And another fifty Cardiff bobbies have come in overnight to the Thistle Hotel."

"So they're making the Glamorgan Scotch a show-down, eh?"

"That's the size of it," said Heinie. "A gang of our boys tried to talk to the blacklegs, but the police drove them off."

"I'm comin', too," said Bron. She was pulling on her drawers, unconcerned about Heinie.

"You're not. You're staying here," I said.

Heinie said, "The Management's taken the scabs underground, they say, to save the ponies."

"Yet they took those horses down themselves especially?"

"But it works," cried Mattie, appearing at the door. "Now there'll be talk about the brutal miners, though Manager Llewellyn don't give a sod if all four hundred ponies drown."

"You're dealing wi' some lovely people," said Bron.

"If he isn't careful he'll drown his eighty blacklegs," and I flung open the door.

Bugles were blowing in strident blasts as I ran out on to the Square.

Word had gone around like a prairie fire blazing. The Combine Management had got control of the Big Glamorgan colliery, known as the Scotch. Blacklegs were working the engines underground. Chief Constable Lindsay had thrown out our pickets and a force of constables were now guarding the colliery pits.

The colliers were infuriated.

Out of their beds rolled the children, out of the doors poured the men, grabbing their tools as they went — mandrels, axe-handles, shovel hafts, brooms.

Followed by their shrieking women, they came pell-mell on to Pandy Square, raising the roof, and even the dear departed in the cemetery must have cocked their dusty ears to listen, said Bron.

From Court Street to Chapel Street they came; up from afar as The Golden Age in Williamstown; rushing in streams from Gilfach, Maddox, Primrose and the Bush, and they packed the Square — the centre of all Town activity — like sprats in a cask.

Moses Culpepper and his Primrose were there, also Rachel and her Bill. The McCarthys came in force, led by Etta, wielding a poker and shrieking like a Sioux Indian. All the Arses came, save Rosie and child; I saw Dai Parcel, Gwilym and Owen; also John Haley and Will Shanklyn with the O'Learys. Diving into the mêlée of the swaying mob, they joined the chorus of yells and threats, for the Town was maddened by the management's occupation of the Scotch.

Where, earlier, there had been organisation and purpose, now it was anarchy, without a Union leader in sight. All the thick-eared fraternity turned out this time, too, with famous people like Tom Thomas and Martin Fury crowding in with the likes of Dai Rush and Snookey Boxer, their blood up at the prospect of battle.

Mr. Duck, lately returned from exchange work over in Senghenydd, fought his way into the crowd beside me.

"Toby, this is madness!" he cried, cultured.

"Try telling them that," I shouted back.

"Where's Mabon at a time like this?"

"Or Noah Rees, Mainwaring — Watts Morgan — where's anyone?"

The men were swaying in a body, shoulder to shoulder, across the length and breadth of the Square, chanting, amid cat-calls, "The Scotch, the Scotch, the *Scotch!*"

I yelled to Mattie and Heinie, "Raise me, get me up!" and they swung me high on their shoulders, turning me in the crush of men.

I shouted, my hands flung up, "Listen, *listen!* Don't act like a mob. Wait for Mabon?"

A man yelled above the rest, "We're always waiting for bloody Mabon — we don't need the Union to dig out bloody Llewellyn."

"Pelt out the scabs — run them out of Town!"

I shouted, "The police are waiting for us, remember?"

"Bloody bad luck for them!"

From my swaying perch, I saw the face of Bron among the infuriated men, with John Haley beside her, barging and shoving for room, trying to protect her.

"*Bron!*" I fought myself down and ploughed through the men towards her, but the sheer weight of their numbers swept me away.

"Bron, *go back!*"

The falling of a leaf will start an avalanche.

In hundreds we started the march on Llwynypia. Meeting other columns coming down from Clydach Vale, Dinas, Penygraig and Trealaw, we marched up the the Llwynypia Road and on to the Big Glamorgan colliery. Some lit torches, and from these other firebrands blazed. The pale moon was rolling on billowy, wash-day clouds, her light dimmed with the redness of the waving torches.

Now that we were committed to drown out the Scotch by force, there came upon the marching men an unearthly quiet.

"My gran's milk," said Heinie, beside me, "I've never heard colliers as quiet as this."

Doors were coming open along the road; whole families standing there, their faces pale with apprehension. The torch-light shot shadows into the eyes of the women. This move spelled more hunger: some, like the Ely people, had been eating skint for three months already; their bellies gnawed.

"How are you, Toby?" asked John Haley, pushing into the ranks with Tommy Arse.

"No better for asking," I answered. "This business stinks."

"But time we stopped the Scotch isn't it? She's on the list."

"We should have done it this morning, before the police made it into a fortress."

"Time comes when you've got to fight, man," said he, tersely, and his eyes were shining. "Like loving when you've got to love."

"Ye don't usually get your skull fractured, just for loving," said Duck behind me.

"The women don't hold with it," said Mattie. "My wife's playin' Hamlet, first act."

"She ain't usual," replied Ben Block. "My missus is behind us — she says give 'em hell."

"Time'll come when we'll be behind the women," grumbled Dai Parcel, over to my left. "Under their skirts, me, when the batons come out — Toby's right, this business stinks."

"Then why are ye here?" shouted Tommy Arse, and I chanced a look at him in the tramping of the boots; big and handsome he looked, a boy made into a man.

"Because colliers stick together," I replied.

"And fall together likewise," said Heinie. "It won't be the first time I've had a baton on me nut."

Lock and Company, the grocers, had barricaded their doors and windows to protect their hams, for the best money hangs from ceilings. Studley's Fruit Shop, in the process of getting out the apples and pears, hung a drape over the photograph of the late lamented Queen Victoria, since loyal subjects appeared few and far between. Watkins the Flannel had got his bales inside; the Monument Chemist slammed shut, with Tailor Jones going demented to save his Union boss frock coats, and the roars that came up from the Square that night eased the slates off the workhouse roof, according to Solly Freedman, the pawnbroker, raising dust up Zion Hill with his trunk on wheels.

We marched on.

There grew an accompaniment to the stamping thunder; a low chanting in the ranks, like cattle lowing; by the time we neared the Big Glamorgan we numbered thousands.

We of the Ely were in the van. Behind us, I saw a massive column now, snaking back to Tonypandy, a great wedge of torch-light. The chanting rose higher as we spilled along the railings of the Scotch.

Many women had joined us, their faces wild, their shawls scragged back over their hair; many armed with pokers, for women fight to kill.

Urchins were darting through the ranks of men, their shrill cries sparking the growing of shouts and bawls.

Before us the road lamps were bright; the pit-wheels of the six pits of the Big Glamorgan stood black against the stars.

A man in the crowd yelled, "Pull up the railings as weapons. If we get the power house we'll stop the Scotch!" and the men about me spilling out of the ranks and began to tear up the wooden fencing surrounding the colliery. Stone-throwing began; glass clashed and tinkled as windows shattered. Then came quiet.

Before us on the road the police began to mass. Led by a mounted figure, Chief Constable Lindsay, the 'Roman Centurion', they formed up out of the shadows silently, without command; no sound came but the clattering hooves of the horses and their slithering hobnails.

And they stood like a black barrier between us and the power station.

Big bastards, these; we feared them. They might have been ordinary Welsh policemen, but they were hand-picked in anti-riot, from Cardiff and Swansea mainly, and no bloody truck with the black-faced yobs of the Rhondda.

The silence grew in strength and power.

Stock still these policemen stood, and it was clever. Even Lindsay's horse was motionless, with Lindsay astride him, his sabre stiffly upwards.

As black marble statues, they were motionless: the night was as shifty as a monastery in Lent.

"Christ," said Heinie beside me, "now we're goin' to blutty 'ave it."

We hesitated.

From within the colliery came shouted commands. More police poured out, breaking the tension; others were forming up on the east of the colliery, also behind us, boots clattering in the eerie silence.

Then a new leader swept to the fore of us, John Haley, and he shouted, wielding a fencing post, "Right, follow me! Come on — get the power house, stop the pumps!"

Bedlam came loose in a chorus of cat-calls and shouts; men lacking courage.

"Dig out the manager!"

"Beat up the blacklegs!"

"Bring up the ponies!"

A new chanting began, "*Scabs, scabs, scabs!*"

Stones began whistling overhead; the windows of the power house clashed as urchins got the range. Ed Masumbala I saw, his black face shining with sweat, as the rush at the police began. Hair down, fighting to be free of men who tried to hold her, Rachel Odd was like a mad thing, swinging her fire-tongs; behind her came Primrose Culpepper and half her brood, darting forward from the crush, baiting the wedge of policemen barring our way.

But, though I joined John Haley and reviled them, the mass of the colliers did not shift.

"Wait till they charge, then," I shouted. "And pull out these damned women!"

Stones were hissing over us now; empty windows, stab-toothed, were grinning at the moon, truck buffers ringing as the stones pelted down. The grass slope above the road was thronged with children and ruffians, but the police, so far, were out of their range.

Men hauled the women and children out of it: the road was clear for a charge.

But the police charged first.

I have never seen anything like it.

They came in a solid box of blue. Tense, gripping our weapons, we awaited them.

They came in a phalanx, the centurion attack of another age; stamping upright, like automatons, faces lifted, expressionless; knees bobbing up, with mechanical precision; approaching slowly, their short, hardwood truncheons held upright at their belts, big fists gripping white. Wide-shouldered and burly, their domed helmets made them gigantic.

Their pace quickened to a rasped command as the distance closed. Seventy yards.

A collier bawled. "Come on, then, Bobbies, and God help ye!"

Fifty yards.

"Christ!" whispered a man beside me.

In the front rank, I crouched, waiting. Mattie was one side of me, Heinie on the other.

Twenty yards.

I could see their big faces now; jaws thrust out; some split wide in joyful anticipation. Some of these Bristol bastards were just delighted by the Welsh.

Ten yards.

Gleaming red, on a command, the batons flew up.

"*Charge!*"

In dervish yells, they leaped at us.

295

Our front ranks bulged upward to the impact: the mandrels went high, the truncheons smashed down.

Instantly, as pole-axed, men fell sprawling; the colliers stayed down, but all the policemen rose, as if commanded. And their truncheons rose and fell again and again in smashes of pain.

Men about me were howling, clutching their red faces; others were crawling among the stamping boots, yelling from bloody mouths. Heinie was down, pulling a policeman with him; Mattie was flailing away at bobbing heads. Helmets were being tipped off, chin-straps torn away; amid a sea of struggling, cursing colliers and policemen, the palings and batons, mandrels and axe-handles rose and fell in flailing, crunching thuds.

Men with broken limbs reeled out of the fight with disjointed cries. A face loomed up before me as John Haley struck out; I elbowed him for room and hit blindly, and the punch caught a policeman square. Instantly, he slipped down the front of me and I lowered him to the ground; next moment the bugger was on my legs. Dull blows were thudding all over me now as my companions thinned out around me; two policemen at me, now three, and the weapons were thudding down on my arms, an old trick of the anti-riot: a baton actually splintered on my shoulder as I ducked and brought down my fencing post on to an unprotected head, which disappeared, as if by magic. It was a bawling mêlée of a fight: Tommy Arse leaped to my side, hooking with his fists and shouting madly, and I had to fight to save him from a six foot Bobby; then Haley grabbed his collar and dragged him out, a moment after somebody felled the boy from behind.

"Get him out!"

We fought for room in a chorus of yells and screams, taking the stabbing blows on the fleshy parts of our bodies, blows that brought a numbing pain.

I saw the furious, snarling faces, yet knew no anger.

Strangely, I fought in a comradeship that embraced even the police. The agony of it all seemed to stitch us together; it was neither my fight, nor theirs. Removed in time and space, in reality I was not there. Amid the cries, the blood, there was an astonishing cleanness . . . until I saw the truncheon come down that felled Moses Culpepper. On top of Sam Rays he fell, soundlessly: men trampling on the mounding bodies now.

I saw another baton coming and hooked my fist into the body of a constable; he grunted and doubled up; I felt my knuckles crack on the big buckle of his belt. Another baton descended, a weapon in slow motion; step by step towards Heinie's unprotected face it came. I saw it, but could do nothing: it hit Heinie on the cheek, breaking the bone, spinning him sideways.

"Collar him!" shouted Mattie.

"Haul him out," I gasped, and barged into them with Mattie Kelly and Bill Odd beside me.

One-handed, shouting to the pain of my broken hand, my desperation drove them before me.

Will Parry was near me: there was Albert Arse, Shanklyn, O'Leary. Ed Masumbala was with us, pulling policemen aside, clubbing them down with his fist; there was Dai Parcel, Gwilym, Owen and Duck; also Snookey Boxer and Ben Block, gasping fat, but fighting like a demon beside the McCarthy lads (though Dano was down). Moses was on his feet again, his face a mask of blood. And then somebody bellowed:

"Look out, lads — look out, behind you!" and we swung to a new enemy.

Rhondda policemen were coming over the Taff Railway at our rear. They came in a tearing, swaying clutch, arms reaching for us — their capes streaming out behind them like flying witches.

"These sods are real Welsh mind," yelled Mattie, and head down, clutching his face, he bolted.

I paused in my flight to grab Tommy with my good hand while John Haley helped me; together, dragging him between us, we ran, while Ben Block, Albert Arse and Bill Odd fought off the police like a rear party.

"Somebody will pay for this," said Bron.

She bathed Tommy's head while Annie and Albert, nearby, screwed their hands, and watched, weeping.

"The skull's split — God, I can see his brain," said Bron.

297

Said Heinie, "That's unusual — brains in the Arse family? He'll pull through."

"Can I help, missus?" asked Patsy Pearl, at the door with Madog shawled.

"If you're cool on blood," said Bron. "Where's Primrose?" and she indicated Moses lying half-conscious at the door. "Christ," she added, "it's worse than blutty Inkerman."

"Primrose coming now just," answered Rachel, and Mrs. Kelly, Mattie's bulldog wife cried:

"*Diawch!* Wait till I get my hands on that Mattie — I'll give him riot!"

"God bless the King, is it?" asked Bron. "Don't be daft, woman. He was doing what he had to do."

The bulldog face went up. "Mad dogs, I say — nothing but a contaminated set of ruffians. I don't know how I'll face the vicar next Sunday."

"You've changed your tune, 'aven't you?" asked Annie Arse, kneeling beside her Tommy. "A week or so back, Kelly, you were all for castrating D. A. Thomas."

They argued, groaned, commiserated with each other in the pain of it; they fought the battle all over again, but I did not take part in it. I saw Bron's eyes raising and lowering at me from across the room as she bandaged and bathed and comforted.

"Can you stick it for a bit, Tobe?"

I nodded, but could have wept with the pain of my broken hand; my other cuts and truncheon bruises were as nothing compared to this searing pain where the knuckles were vanishing in swelling blueness.

"I'll be with ye directly, mun," she said, and she stiffened beside Moses, I noticed, as Patsy Pearl came over to me, carrying a bowl. Madog, used to men, examined me with his great blue eyes from the confines of his shawl.

"I'll see to you, Toby," said Patsy, and with her small, deliberate fingers, she bathed my hand with care.

"You've made some enemies tonight — Chief Constable Lindsay for one," said Mrs. Kelly. "Remember that!"

"He's not an enemy, he's an enema," said Bron, watching Patsy.

"But he'll be awful high down with us after this, God help us,"
said Mrs. Shanklyn.

Patsy, as she bandaged, was watching me with her mind.

I knew what she wanted, and she wasn't having me easy; none of
my business where John Haley had got to.

"You seen 'im, Toby Davies?"

"On the palings by the Scotch, but not recent," I said, cool.

"All right, was he?"

"Got young Tommy through, didn't he?"

Quietly, now, Patsy said, "I got a budding for him, Toby." She
smiled wanly. "Mad, ain't it?"

"Likely he's married," I answered.

People talked in the room, and she bent closer, whispering, her
eyes like offering plates.

"No, not married — his woman's dead, don't ye know?"

"In the heart still," I said.

She looked at the window where torches were glowing from the
Square. "He's a well set up chap; I come warm inside when I sees
him in the Pandy."

"You got it bad."

"I tell you, Toby Davies, I ain't a pearl no more for anybody now
but that John Haley."

I protested, "But you're still at it, woman. You're still on the
game!"

"Aye, I know, mun, but me heart ain't really in it, if you get me."

"Good God," I said.

It was like a Turkish battlefield, with bodies lying round and
women crouched over them with scissors and knives.

"I'll have that hand over by 'ere, if you don't mind," said Bron
now, with business. Blood never sorted Bron out; they could have
done with her over at Rorke's Drift. Patsy Pearl said, as I left her:

"You'll speak for me, Tobe?"

"Likely so."

"Just for old times, is it?"

"*Heisht*, you, for God's sake," I breathed.

"One good turn deserves another, remember. And you never paid,
ye know?"

I left her pretty smart, for Bron had ears to hear brown grass growing.

Now Bron took my hand with her usual couldn't care. "*Ach y fi!*" she exclaimed. "What happened to the Bobby on the end of this one?"

The noise of the misery beat about us, but we did not hear it; my pain seemed to sanctify us, and she made large eyes at me saying:

"Don't let that Patsy touch you again, you understand?"

"Just . . . just an old friend," I said. "No harm in it."

"So I gather, but I'll shuffle you off this mortal coil if I find you white-mooning with anyone, all right?"

"But that doesn't apply to you, does it? — you just do what the hell you like, don't you?" I glared down at her as she retied the bandage.

"That's right. The fella in Porth's a relative, or don't you remember?" Eyes flashing suddenly, she glowered at Patsy and weighed me up for size. She'd got fierce bangle earrings on her; give her a pair of castanets and she'd have gone round a bonfire: even Moses was watching her, and he was semi-conscious.

"This hurt?" she gave me back my hand.

"Like hell," I said.

She got up. "Go on, get on with ye."

Mattie came bursting into the room then; blood down his muffler, and red in the face with him.

"And where might you 'ave been?" cried his bulldog missus

"Murder's being done," cried Mattie. "There's bodies all over the road from here to Llwynypia. And the police are beating up folks in their houses!"

"I'll believe that when it's signed for," said Bron. "Even Lindsay isn't as bad as that."

"Aye, well, I'm tellin' ye!" shouted Mattie. "Just now they're clearing the Square again, and stone-throwing down De Winton and Dunraven — smashing shop windows."

"Tonypandy folks?"

"Tonypandy people!" cried Mattie.

"Go and buy yourself a tin of Toffee Rex," said Heinie, coming to.

"I tell ye, I saw it! Running wild and busting windows, hitting out the lamps and stoning Bobbies."

"Must be the Irish again," said Dai Parcel, sitting up. "Or those rough clods over in Porth, eh, Moses?"

"More'n likely." Pensive was Moses, with goose egg building up behind his ear, and sparking.

"I hope they keep away from the Co-op," said Mrs. Shanklyn. "We're shareholders — sure as fate it'll affect the divvy."

"What's happening now, then?"

"We're after 'em again, that's what," I said, getting to my feet.

Bron said, pale with anger, "You'll risk your lives again for payment for soft muck?"

"It's more than that, and you know it," I replied. "I was more tired going to work than rioting, and the pay's the same — we'll end it once and for all. Who's coming?"

"Ay ay," said Moses, "let's finish it," and those who had legs, got up and trooped to the door, and Bron said, backed by the other women:

"Of all the idiot men! Your brains are in your arse!"

"Likely so," said Bill Odd. "You coming, Dai?"

"My brains must be misplaced," said Heinie, "or I wouldn't have worked the Ely in the first place."

And, as we opened the door to go out, the London police flung it back on its hinges, and came in.

They did us then as they did the Morgan house later, over in John Street, Penygraig.

Tonypandy will never forget it, said Keir Hardie later, and neither did we.

"Blood," said Winston Churchill, in Parliament, later still, "may be shed, though most of it will be from the nose, which can be subsequently replaced."

"If we'd had the bugger down here in Tonypandy," said Bron, "he'd have seen some blood, and not from his nose."

With mounted policemen clattering up and down the Row, they came into our place like men demented — six London constables

301

with their batons flailing, and the first to stop one was Bill Odd.

Dai Parcel ducked the next baton, and Bron, turning, took it full on the side of the face, and dropped.

Keir Hardie said, in Parliament, that he possessed factual, eye-witness accounts of the bludgeoning of solitary individuals on the streets; of the police knocking them down and kicking them, and he called for an inquiry into police brutality.

They tripped over Tommy as they barged their way in; they hauled Annie out of it and got Albert in a corner, hammering him with their batons and fists until his face was covered with blood.

Churchill said, officially, "The people of South Wales owe a great debt of gratitude to the police."

With my good hand I got the leading policeman: as he stumbled in, striking with his baton, I hooked him to the jaw; the second policeman, in his onward rush, fell sprawling over this man's body, and I got him as well, as he rose, staggering him; Rachel hit him with a chair, the first thing handy. Two down, four left, and one of these punched Mrs. Kelly in the face, sending her flying.

"You bastard!" I shouted, and rushed, with Bill Odd one side of me and Dai Parcel on the other.

Keir Hardie wrote later, "Mrs. Morgan, of 45 John Street, Penygraig, has had her house forcibly entered by the police when the whole family were indoors. A most brutal and savage assault was committed on two young men. One of the policemen broke his truncheon, half of which is in possession of Mrs. Morgan."

Churchill said, "As Home Secretary, I have been greatly blamed for my conduct in this matter, but I am quite ready to defend my action . . . If disorder does arise, it will be repressed by the police, if they can possibly do so."

It was repressed all right; they were at it now.

Old Dai Parcel was down from a baton across his shoulders, a favourite target; and while he was down they started to kick him in the fork, the idea, they said, being to lower the birth-rate: and the kicking went on while Gwilym and I, penned by five of them (for more had come through the door) fought in a chorus of women's screams.

They were big men, and handy; we hadn't a chance. Out of the corners of my eyes I saw Patsy Pearl hanging on to a boot with another policeman kicking her off; Primrose was lying over her Moses, protecting him; Mattie, with Tommy in his arms, was backing away through the door.

But Bron lay still: white-faced, she lay, like a woman dead.

"Bron! Christ Almighty, *Bron!*" I cried, ducking the truncheons on one side and taking them on the other; the lamplight swam as Gwilym staggered against me. Moses was calling faintly, but I didn't hear what he said. I remember only hooking my good hand to a policeman's chin in the second before I was dropped.

"I claim a public inquiry," said Keir Hardie, in Parliament.

"On what grounds?" asked Winston Churchill.

"On the grounds of the charges against the police," said Hardie. "Charges of having ill-used women and other unoffending persons, not during a baton charge against a mob, but under circumstances in which revenge could be the only motive."

"But, be fair," said Heinie, when he came to again. "Nobody can say we're unoffending persons — after all, we're Welsh."

"Are ye?" asked Mattie. "I thought you was with Moses when the sea divided off Porthcawl."

"I'm Welsh," interjected Dai Parcel, smiling through split lips. "And right now I feel a bit anti-English."

John Haley said, "Count ourselves lucky — so far we've had it easy. If Lindsay keeps pestering Churchill, he'll send in the military."

"I anna waving to brass bands any more," said Bill Odd, while his wife bathed his face; black and blue was he from truncheons — mainly those Metropolitan swines, said he — and if it hadn't been for his boots I'd never have known him, poor old dab, said she; but I'll have them, mind — knocking my fella about.

Kneeling beside Bron's still body the minute my senses returned to me, I tried to get my good arm under her to raise her against me.

"*Diawch!*" ejaculated Pru Natal, hurrying over the kitchen floor. "Put her down, man, we think she's cracked a rib."

I screwed up my good hand and put it against my face, and said. "I'll kill someone for this!"

"I got the one who did it, though," said Heinie, sitting up against the wall. "He's got a different nose to when he came in, the bugger."

"Get her on the bed!"

People moving about, urgently whispering; the palaver of the accident.

I staggered about, trying to help.

"Sit down, Tobe — you're only in the way," said Primrose.

They gathered up Bron's still body and I could have screamed and flung them away; all I wanted was to hold her.

She shrieked the moment they lifted her.

"Bastards, bastards, *bastards!*" I said, my hands over my face.

"There, there," said Patsy Pearl, "that'll do you a world of good. They've gone, Tobe — that's the main thing."

Bron started to cry like a little girl. It was more than I could bear.

"But beating up women!"

Patsy and Mrs. O'Leary held me away from her.

"Bron asked for it, mind," said Dai Parcel. "Two she got with the handle of the mangle."

They laid her on the bed and she groaned, twisting herself to the pain of her body, and hatred, deeper and purer than anything I had known, ran like a flame in me. I bent over her trying to kiss her face, but they pulled me away again.

"Now look, Tobe — hop it. Leave her *alone!*"

I went to a quiet place of the room, and wept, my good hand over my eyes.

"Well, I suppose we all asked for it," said somebody, while the women undressed Bron and got her into the bed.

"I only asked for two-and-six a ton," said Heinie.

Along Dunraven and De Winton, they collected broken heads; also in Pandy Square, strikers and police; the massacre of the batons and shovels. From Gilfach to Hughes, the side streets had been torn up for the Irish confetti; three hundred staves were brought to Llwynypia to replace those broken on colliers' skulls; this was official, according to the Coal Owners.

"Mind, we could have got into that power station if we'd a mind to," commented Ben Block. "We let 'em off light, sort of."

Rumours, like scandal, can outrun a prairie fire.

"Somebody saw Winston Churchill riding a horse up Court Street, you heard?"

"You saw him yourself?"

"Aye, well not personal, but he were seen all right. As certain as me name's Kelly — riding with Chief Lindsay, he was."

In the darkened sawdust of the four-ale tap, they crouch like conspirators over fires, manufacturing rumours.

"Where did ye hear that, then?"

"I tell you, I saw him — with these two eyes."

"Who?"

"Winston Churchill."

"In Tonypandy?"

"In Tonypandy — I swear it!"

"Man, you're nothing but a blutty gas leak."

"I tell you, I saw him — riding along on a horse with Captain Lindsay."

"Holy Mother of God, is that true?" gasped Mrs. O'Reilly. "The devil of Gehenna's among us!"

"*Ach*, stop coddin' us along, Pat. Tell us the Pope's truth, now!"

"But I am, ye blitherer! As large as life, he was — frock coat, top hat, just like ye see in Parliament, be God — and with a truncheon five foot long in his hands, cracking Welsh heads."

"Aye, well, I'm all for that meself, d'ye see, being Irish."

"But ye don't believe me, do ye? Jesus, you've more suspicions than teeth, man — I'll swear it on the Holy Water!"

"Och, give him a wee drop of the hard stuff, Mike, for the fella's started seeing things."

"And he was holding the English rose aloft in his hand, an' all! Are ye off now, Paddy?"

"That I am."

"You're going, so you are, eh? — then tell me when you're gone."

"Holdin' up an English rose, indeed," said Mrs. O'Reilly, in disgust. "The bugger wants brainin' with a Welsh leek." And I had flash visions of the entire Rhondda population bowed in sniffing grief.

The rioting went on. All down the main street most of the shop windows were out, excluding Ginty's. I was in there begging for Bron, having run out of strike money.

"Sure," said Ginty, "if this goes on I'll be scratching a beggar's arse, so I will. Half the population's on the soup kitchens and the other half's on tick. And now the military are on their way to set fire to the place."

"Not true, Ginty," said his missus; thinner than a plasterer's lathe was she, and worried about the hunger. I saw Ginty's eyes then, and read his mind.

He saw her face as that of a cemetery ghost, and remembered her then as she was when young; in summer, wearing a cotton bonnet on a hill near Galway.

"*Ach*," said Ginty. "What with one thing and another I'd be best knocking timber out in pit time, and take the narrow squeaks; I used to rip it from underneath, ye know. *Arrah!* I was a foine collier."

"You're too old for coal now, Ginty," I said.

"And too daft to be a grocer. There's money in sweets, you know — Bug Whiskers and Everlasting Strip, liquorice and dolly mixture — who's this comin'?"

"Mrs. Shanklyn, with her Willie?"

"Can't be — he's dying."

A loaf of bread, a pound of marge, two cold faggots and a basin of drip.

"On the slate, Mrs. Shanklyn?" says Ginty. "God, woman, not again!"

"Nigh four hundred horses starving down the Scotch — terrible, isn't it?" whispered Sarah Bosom.

"Bugger the horses," said Ginty.

"They say the King's worried about 'em, too," said Dozey Dinah, sad.

"And bugger the King," said Ginty.

"Ludlow the Sweep do say the soldiers are comin'," remarked Sarah, vacant.

"All got our little crosses, haven't we?" says Mrs. Shanklyn. "The poor always help the poor, I always say — thank God my Will ain't here no more. Prosperity do always discover our little vices, don't it?"

Frost is on the cobbles; the wind is howling down Dunraven; even the corpses are chattering.

"Just this once, Ginty? I'm flat broke," I said. "And Bron's that ill. . . ."

Up to his elbows in his trews, huddled against the wind, a collier mooched down Dunraven, and I thought it was me.

Ancient faces, too old to die, watched from cracked windows.

"Please," I said, waiting.

"Jesus, man . . ." whispered Ginty. "Would ye break me?"
Uncertain, he looked about him for escape.

"Give it him," said Mrs. Ginty, "*Mark, Mary* and *Joseph!*"

"Three saints," I said, "and you're the fourth."

"Who's this arriving?"

Guto Livingstone, it is, going like the wind. Tattered and defrauded, he goes, with his hollows of eyes black in the light of the moon; knapsacked and bundled is he, with urgent looks over his shoulder for Mrs. Guto: the skeleton had found the key to his cupboard, and unobserved, crept out.

In the witch-howling night he goes, making for Penygraig, to catch the inland steamer.

"You seen my Guto, Ginty?" asked Mrs. Guto, coming into Ginty's, hair awry and breathless.

"Just gone by, this minute, girl," I replied.

"Got away from me, see?" said Mrs. Guto. "Off to Santa Rosa

in British Honduras — he's got relatives there, he says, poor little soul."

Shocked, Mrs. Ginty waited, telling her beads.

"You spare a bite for me, Missus?" asked Mrs. Guto.

"No," said Ginty, coming to the door.

"Being spare in the attic, my chap do get hungry . . . I don't eat meself actually." ·

"Oh, *God alive*," said Ginty, barring the door. "We got to live too, remember?"

"I beg ye — look, I'm begging ye." She pleaded with her hands.

And a cheese got up on its hind legs and walked out to meet her, assisted by Mrs. Ginty. Said Ginty. "Where's the sense to you, woman?" and he elbowed his wife. "I'll be as skint as me brother Shamus, and he's got his bum in the county jail."

"But folks are starving, bless 'em," said Mrs. Ginty.

"A month more of this and you can bless me, too, Pope and cardinals included. Bad cess to ye, woman — send the sods to the Co-op."

"You don't get much out of boards of directors, mind," said Mrs. Shanklyn. "But you always was a good soul, Ginty. Got a spare tin of pilchards, 'ave you?"

"*Ach*, dear God, she's tryin' me for the miracle of the fishes," and Ginty crossed himself.

"I won't forget this," I said, hugging the top of a cottage loaf against me.

"Neither will I," replied Ginty. "Now bugger off."

As I said to Bron when I got home, folks varied at a time like this: Mrs. Ginty was all right, but her old man didn't give a lot away.

"Sam's the one for generosity, though," she replied. "He never denied anyone. He was always giving away little bits of himself, especially to the women."

I cut thin bread for her, with a scraping of marge, worried about her mentioning Sam.

The man was a walking blemish.

Even in a joke, I didn't want him here.

33

WITH EIGHTY POLICEMEN injured, some seriously, and more than five hundred strikers wounded (according to an official Glamorgan Police report) Winston Churchill, the Home Secretary, after a lot of palaver about not wanting to, sent the troops into the Rhondda.

"It's because he loves us," said Dai Parcel, bathing his cuts, "that's why he doesn't really want to."

"He don't really want to because he's got a General Election coming," interjected Heinie, while Primrose put a new plaster on his skull. "And soldiers are bad for politics. They start shooting people down here like 'Featherstone Asquith' told 'em to up north, and we're likely to call him 'Tonypandy Churchill'!"

"But did he really send them in — the soldiers, I mean? Didn't he order them to stand by at Pontypridd?" This from Richard Jones.

"The Secretary of State for War, Mr. Haldane, halted 'em at Pontypridd, after he'd heard Churchill had sent them," I said. "Let's get it straight."

"Does he need to send soldiers?" grumbled Ben Block, bandaging his shins. "Sent the London Metropolitan Police, didn't he? — them's worse than soldiers."

"And didn't he tell the squaddies to 'mow the Welsh buggers down'? — what about that?" asked Heinie.

"Lies," I said. "He said no such thing."

Lies, rumours, apologies, white-wash.

And mainly white-wash, as history will relate.

"One day," said Richard Jones, "the tame historians will start their bleating, you watch. By the time they're finished he'll be the hero of the Rhondda."

Nobody replied. But one thing was sure.

The name of Winston Churchill, then, and later, stank in our valleys.

It was the middle of November. The town steamed with mist in its uneasy truce, while policemen were carted to hospital and colliers were carted away: away to anywhere, their relatives said, before the courts begin to sit. People with bandaged limbs were moving very sprightly around the Rhondda about now — slipped on the ice outside the Pandy, I did: mending one of the windows, I fell off a chair, these were the general excuses. And it was more than your life was worth to send for a doctor.

The big London policemen, marching in squads, were all eyes; hammering on doors for searches at two o'clock in the morning, beating up people they found in the street.

Within a week of the riots starting, the soldiers came marching in.

I was sitting at the table in the Hut, days after the Llwynypia riot, getting the Union strike pay ready, when they marched across the Square.

Bron heard the tramping boots, the clattering hooves of the cavalry and turned her white face to me from the bed.

"That the English soldiers?"

I got up and pulled a curtain aside. "Aye, they've arrived."

"Criminals, ain't we?" She sighed. "God, what a life!"

Splendidly, they came, the pride of the Army.

With fluttering pennants they marched, preceded by Captain Lindsay and his foot constables. Sitting astride their chargers, in full uniform to impress the rebel Welsh, they went in a hoove-clattering, jingling of harness fit to raise Egyptian mummies.

Finger-sucking urchins stared in awe at the fine authority of the English. In a tarantella of head-tossing plumes, they went, a spectacle of brilliance and power in the midst of our indignity.

A few black-clad women were on the Square by the fountain, in hen-clutches and whispers, shawl-scragged against the wind. I heard one shout, her shrill voice piercing the day:

"Bugger off back to England, where you come from, ye rubbish!"

It seemed to sum it up for us. I went to Bron on the bed, smiling down.

"How do you feel?"

"Better when I'm up and at that lot."

"You've done rioting for a bit."

The baton had taken her across the face; one eye was still shut tight; the other shone brilliantly from the fevered flush of her cheek. Worse, though, was the rib she had damaged. The police, for what they had achieved down Sinkers Row (for others had been beaten up, too) studiously kept away.

Dr. Walker had said it was a greenstick fracture, and bandaged her, but I had my doubts.

Sometimes, in a fit of coughing, Bron was in agony.

Mrs. Change, who reckoned she'd broken ribs on bad deliveries, was worried about her catching cold, and I wondered, since I had it up in Clayton once, if she had pleurisy.

"You ought to have the doctor again," I said, touching Bron's damaged face.

"Can't afford him twice."

Her beauty had gone; I cherished her the more when her face wore this parched, anxious frown of pain and hunger.

"You see to the face, I'll see to her stomach directly," said Primrose Culpepper, coming in to visit. "Just saying to that old Rachel, I was, how I'll fry up a nice bit of sirloin for that copper-fighter lying next door," and she beamed down at Bron. "You could do with a bit of raw meat on that eye, mind."

"Chicken, if ye can manage it," answered Bron. "I've gone off sirloin."

"By the way, my Moses's set fair for a good feed when I've got the makings. Don't expect he'll get his glass eye back till the end of the marble season, though." Waddling to the door, she hitched up her sack apron and winked at me, so I followed.

"What's up?" I asked.

"We're sheep-killing tonight in Rachel's," said she, looking

311

around for listeners. "We're doing it down the Row — there's no real danger knocking the beggars off, ye know — it's transporting 'em home where you hit the police."

"I agree."

"Will you help, Tobe?"

"I'll do my best," I said, holding up my bandaged hand.

"What was that all about?" asked Bron, when I got back to her.

"Been invited to dine out."

She turned her face away and closed her eye.

"Sheep enticing, eh? Six months if you're caught, remember?"

"Aye, but we won't be caught, will we?" Hunger was making me as edgy as her.

Even while looking at Bron's wan face, I wondered how Nanwen was getting on over at Senghy, and knew a fullness of relief that the Aber valley wasn't on strike in sympathy with the Rhondda — least of all, not to date.

Somehow, I couldn't have borne the knowledge of Nanwen starving.

They were risky times for sheep these days; every ewe and ram on the mountains had minor strokes when the colliers came out on strike, for the Rhondda Welsh weren't tardy about a bit of mutton on their Sunday plates when times were thin, like now. And the sheep themselves didn't help a lot, putting temptation in the paths of Christian people. These days there were more sheep window-shopping than shoppers: shoving their noses into women's baskets, whipping carrots and bananas off the stalls; generally getting above themselves.

So the anarchists were abroad that night when I stole next door into the Odds's hut, and a few other criminals were already present, such as Bill and Rachel; Duck (who was partial to lamb and green peas) Heinie and Mattie, and Ben Block, who was once vegetarian before he became the Camarthen slaughterer. All were sporting head bumps, black eyes or sticking-plaster cuts from their battle with the police.

Primrose closed the door behind me like a nun in a catacomb and peered at me with her shadowed eyes.

"Police are about, mind," she breathed. "Blutty Glamorgans, too."

She brightened the lamp the moment I was in.

Everything was ready to execute the crime; saucepans were bubbling on the fire and Primrose, pale as death, was standing over them like a witch with a brew, stirring big spoons with her hair hanging down. Moses was sharpening knives; Rachel stitching up sheets to hide the dismembered corpse.

"I've got me da's Irish shillelagh," said Mattie, bringing it out from under his waistcoat. "Used to pay the rent wi' it back home in Connemara."

"Now it will pay a little fat ewe," said Heinie, who possessed no soul.

"Six months if we're caught, mind," said Ben Block, wheezing. "Fifty years back they'd have hanged us down the well of the stairs."

"The Bobbies don't go short on much," said Bill Odd. "Least of all these bloody Glamorgans. I expect a hiding from the Londoners, but not me own Welsh."

"The Bobbies don't go short on anything, ask me," replied Rachel. "Over in New Inn, Ponty, the police and colliery officials are putting it down with champagne while our kids starve. Agents and owners are stinking food like Roman emperors; any legs o' mutton walk up my way tonight, I'm going to clout 'em."

"Like I'm clouting you if you miss," said Bill.

"Where are all the kids?" I asked.

"In Primrose's place, out of the way. You think they'll catch us? The military's on patrol now, ye know. Talk is that they flog ye first, before prison. That so?"

"Not true," I said. "Compared with the police, the military are all right."

Duck asked, "Bron still poorly, Tobe?"

"Be another week or so — she's got pain with breathing, mainly."

"I'd crack a few ribs, half a chance — beating up women," growled Ben Block.

"Reckon you should have had the doctor again."

"What do I do for money?"

"Lot of things we should have had," interjected Primrose. "Never mind, a cut or two off a shoulder should cheer her up no end, eh? How's those saucepans doing, Rachel?"

"Better for a bit of meat in them, lest we'll have to boil the ornaments."

I said, "I reckon we ought to be doing this up the mountain. If folks see sheep walking in here it's bound to rouse suspicions."

"One thing's sure," chuckled Ben Block, bass. "They won't see the buggers walking out."

Primrose prodded Heinie at the window. "See any coming? Their time's about now, every night regular — scavenging, ye know, upper-cutting the dust-bin lids — poor beggars are hungrier than us."

"There's a fat one feeding on the doorstep of Dano's place right now," whispered Heinie, and we all went peering through the curtains behind his ears.

"Put the oat pan out on the step."

Porridge oats for sheep; I could have eaten it myself.

"Is she still down on Dano's door, then?"

"Aye," said Heinie, peeping through the chink. "The biggest blutty ewe I've seen."

"Whistle it down by 'ere."

"That animal's nearly ninety," added Duck, at the other window.

"Here she comes," whispered Heinie.

"Turn out the lamp!"

In darkness we crouched, gripping weapons, and there came from the flags outside the patter of little feet.

Mattie and Duck were either side of the door with mandrels gripped; Heinie was standing above them, his Irish shillelagh swung up both hands.

"Right you, Tobe," whispered Primrose. "You're the youngest — when the door comes open, look lively and haul one in."

Outside in the night the oatmeal basin scraped the flags.

"Ready?" I saw Rachel's big eyes in the window moonlight while Bill peered out.

"Right," said Bill. "Fetch her!"

The door went back; I grabbed the sheep by the ears, hauling

314

it in. And the way Heinie clouted with his shillelagh should have settled the thing for a fortnight, but this one went demented.

Getting between Primrose's legs, it brought her down on top of Heinie, and these two floundered about in the dark, cursing and hitting out solid. People were bawling, Rachel begging everyone to mind her furnishings, and next time I saw her she was legs up waving, with the sheep in her skirts. Ben Block went down, taking people with him, and Duck caught Bill Odd one behind the ear with his mandrel, sending him howling. *Bedlam*. Everybody was shouting and the animal baa-ing and rushing blue murder.

"What the hell have we collected?" yelled Heinie, staggering up, but the thing was like a raging tiger, and it butted him flat again. Lights were going on along the Sinkers, and what the hell's happening in Rachel Odds? Over the kitchen floor raged that sheep, head down, barging everything in sight — chairs, table, the Welsh dresser, Grandma's chiffonier, and mainly Primrose, by the sound of her; taking it bad was she, halfway over the mangle.

"Get the devil out!" yelled Moses, coming to.

"Light the lamp!"

"Christ!" exclaimed Duck. "It's a ram!"

"Serve you right," said Mrs. Etta McCarthy, opening the door. "Sheep killing, indeed! Common thieves now, are we, Culpepper?"

Half the population of the Rhondda present now, peering through the door at us, but they scattered when that ram came out berserk, butting everything, including the door, which we managed to shut, and Ben and Moses slammed the table against it, lying back exhausted.

"Ought to be ashamed of yourselves, all of you!" cried Etta, knocking on the window. And neighbours were banging and threatening, fists up, red-eyed.

"You piss off," shouted Primrose, "or I'll come out there and cut the throats of the lot of you!" Hands on hips, she glared around the kitchen. "Now, what prize idiot picked the ram?"

"It were dark, mind," said Heinie, sheepish.

"Sorry," I said, my head going down.

Silence after the damned fools and recriminations were over.

We sat in a monk quiet at the table — Rachel and Bill, Primrose

315

and Moses, Ben and Mattie, Duck, Heinie and me, and thought of roast mutton, mint sauce and gravy.

Then, suddenly, Primrose giggled; Rachel started next, hands clapped over her mouth; Mattie Kelly wheedled soprano: this set Duck off, then Moses and Bill, and me and Ben Block came last, he booming bass, and he had a laugh from his belly to raise roof tiles.

Sitting round that table, we thumped and roared, and the lights started going on up and down the row again and it's that daft lot in Rachel's place again — when are we going to get some sleep? And folks were wandering around in nightshirts and sleeping bobbles, scratching their ears and what the hell's happening.

Then, when we quietened, Rachel said, "Mind, I'm against eating flesh myself — it ain't natural, really, is it? — eating our comrades, you come to think of it."

"A good slice off the shanks do go down good, though," enjoined Moses. "I could do with a pint or two just now, a loaf, and a pound or so of leg."

We rumbled in unison, thinking of spring lamb, roast potatoes and gravy, with bread to polish the plates.

"The old Greeks used to sacrifice a hundred bullocks — I read somewhere," said Ben Block. "Just imagine that. That must have raised a sizzling."

"It is in accord with the laws of Nature," replied Duck, educated. "The little innocents have to die, so that we can live. . . ."

"But, it's wrong," I said. "If I had any strength of character, I'd never eat meat."

"Says it's all right in the Bible, though?" suggested Rachel.

"We shouldn't have done it, biblical or not," whispered Primrose, damp. "Cannibals, ain't we? You come to think of it, we acted like blutty savages. Old Etta McCarthy were right."

"I'm ashamed of myself, really," added Rachel. "I'm not eating flesh again, not after that palaver. Shameful, that's the word for it." She glared at Bill. "And you put me up to it in the first place, remember."

We sat in a new silence, enveloped by shame, and from the door came a little sound; louder now, louder.

Scratch, scratch . . .

316

Ben got up and opened the door.

Arabella stood there with her little forefeet together and Bron's red hair ribbon tied around her neck, and I reckon she was smiling in the light of the lamp.

Arabella, arrived for her weekly oats.

Up with Duck then, in his best courtly manner. Removing his bowler, he bowed low before her. "My little four-footed friend, pray enter," said he.

"Oh, *Gawd*," breathed Primrose, and hid her face. "Not *Arabella!*"

Many sheep went to their ancestors about now, for the colliers were quick with knives and buckets: and pigs, many devoted family friends, fared little better: nor did colliers, come to that. For the crime of being caught, scores went to prison; Will Shanklyn, for instance. He wouldn't take strike pay, considering it charity, but he took the life of a ewe up on Mynydd-y-Gelli, and, while he was in Cardiff gaol, his son Willie died.

Sad in my heart I was for Mrs. Shanklyn, losing two at a stroke, as it were. "Anything we can do to help her?" asked Bron.

"You tell me," I said.

It was thin.

In our hut, with Bron lying ill with suspected pleurisy now (according to Mrs. Change) things were thinner than most. She had been off from the Pandy since the riots, so there was no money coming from there. All I had was the ten bob a week strike pay, and this didn't go far on milk and eggs.

It was strange indeed, going to the bank every Friday night and drawing strike-pay money from the Union funds; about five hundred pounds me and Mr. Richard Jones collected weekly, with Heinie, Mattie and Ed Masumbala as bodyguards, yet we hadn't the price of a pint between us. And we would go the rounds of the Ely Lodge members, doling it out to the half starved colliers, with their wan, pale wives and children peeping round the doors.

I was worried about Bron.

She had been in bed a fortnight now — ever since the police had beaten us up.

317

The only medic I had now was Mrs. Change, the midwife at sixpence a time, and she was scarcely welcome.

"You keep the old hag away from me," said Bron. "There's talk about her, ye know."

She was rapidly losing weight, but her spirit burned with the same old fire.

"Talk?"

"I've known women handled by midwives 'ave conceived that moment."

"That can't be the midwife's fault."

"O, aye? You think again — take that Effie over in Cynon, for instance. Just a common cold she had, till Mrs. Change handled her — now she's in the basket."

"Don't be *twp*," I answered. "Snookey Boxer had a finger in Effie's pie, they reckoned. He's been activating her for months."

"Snookey was over in Gilfach, picketing — now, come on!"

"So the beggar sneaked back, didn't he?" I slammed the ledgers shut.

"He didn't — he was away six weeks an' she was only one month gone, you ask Effie. Mrs. Change of Life, it were."

I got up. "Don't be daft, it's an old wives' tale."

"All right, then, but you keep her away — she's not selling me puddings."

I had to smile; I liked her best in this mood. When low, or in pain, Bron reverted to her peasant roots; a contrast, I reflected, to Nanwen's warm practicality.

It was difficult, at times, to say whom I preferred.

But there was growing in me a burning need to see Nanwen again; it was a sort of clean necessity that seemed divorced from the dirty old strike.

I used to change my ten shilling Union pay into pennies and spend it like gold on a daily dole-out: with the rent five shillings a week, this cut me in half before I began the budget, for you've got to keep the slates, like my old man says, said Rachel Odd; lose the slates come winter and you're on a hiding.

Like the O'Learys, for instance, up in Court Street; they were evicted after losing their stall, and Mrs. Shanklyn, with whom they went to live, was right on the edge of it herself, with Will in prison. No messing, as Heinie said — just bloody *out*. The Management didn't give sympathy to striking colliers.

It's amazing what you can do on five bob a week when you come to it.

I only begged once in those first four months, and that was off Ginty.

Reading was free, so I used to read. Tolstoy's *War and Peace*, Engel's *The Condition of the Working Class in England*, and everything written by Hilaire Belloc I could get my hands on; I used to read and re-read his *Path to Rome*. *The Girondin* came out in the year of the strike, but they couldn't get it up at the Scotch library, though I read about it in *Labour Leader*, in which Keir Hardie used to write, telling us how much Winston Churchill hated the Welsh, and what a sod he was for sending the troops into the Rhondda. Belloc must have agreed with Keir Hardie at the time, because later he called Churchill a 'Yankee careerist'.

"The soldier boys are all right," said Bron from the bed. "It's the police are the trouble. And Welsh police, too, remember?"

The Rhondda will remember the Glamorgan police for a century.

"The London police are bad enough," said Bron, "we expect rough stuff off them. But if ye want a real good hiding you can bank on your fine Welsh brothers."

For my part, I blamed Churchill for sending the Metropolitan Police, not for sending soldiers.

They were empty old days, just sitting reading, or doing the Union books.

The Rhondda was as deserted as a bankrupt workhouse. Little happened on the frosted streets. The colliers lounged on the pneumonia corners; the walls of corner houses were stained black with their coal-starched shoulders.

Sometimes they would sit on their hunkers, playing Fives, or fight with their mates just to keep warm. The police were everywhere; in the colliery offices, guarding the pit-heads, wandering the Taff Vale lines.

Not a lot happened, really, especially in those early weeks after the Riots.

Rosie Arse-Jenkins's baby died on the day that Noah Ablett and Tom Smith first demanded a South Wales strike. So far, only the Cambrian Combine Pits were out — about 12,000 men. Elsewhere, such as in the Aberdare and Western valley of Monmouthshire, a further 20,000 were idle either in sympathy or go-slow and lock-out, for longer or shorter periods, for some men had drifted back to work. But had a South Wales Strike been called and the Minimum Wage demanded as a body, then nearly a quarter of a million colliers would have downed tools.

But the Miners' Federation of Great Britain wouldn't support us; the Cambrian Dispute, they said, was a local affair — settle it locally.

"The truth is that the British Federation don't give a sod for us," said Heinie. "You can prate all you like about the Union, but we'll never have a Union worth calling a Union, unless it stands together. Now we come off Irish stew and begin to eat the leek."

We ate the leek all right, and only in dreams did I taste Irish stew.

Hunger, I find, is something you can't get used to.

First come the billious attacks, then the gnawing pains, then the heady swims that blind you into collisions; last, the dangerous time, comes apathy, a listless emptiness.

"The Management's offered us two-and-a-penny a ton, remember," I said. "It was in last week's *Labour Weekly*."

Said Richard Jones, "But the issue's greater now. The South Wales Federation wants a minimum wage of 6/9d a day for all colliers, never mind the Ely."

"They'll never get it."

"There's new men coming on to the Executive," said Richard. "Strong, firm men like Noah Ablett, the Maerdy check-weigher — and Tom Smith. These are new leaders who are ousting Mabon. Now you'll see sparks."

"All I want is a good Sunday dinner," said Bron. "You know, Tobe — a good round of beef, baked potatoes and cabbage? You reckon such dinners still exist?"

She had been in bed a fortnight now and was sweating badly, as usual; I didn't know what to do for her.

"You got trouble here," said Heinie. "She's ill."

"She's starving — do you have to tell me that?" I paced about. He stood by the bed screwing his cap.

"Aye, she's just plain hungry, that's all," said Rachel. "Rachel's here, me little love."

"If I give her solid food she only brings it up," I said.

"Then she'll have to have more milk and eggs, won't she?" said Primrose Culpepper. "We'll just have to share more."

"Share what?" asked Moses.

The children of the Culpeppers and Odds stood around Bron's bed in a ragged disconsolation, their grimed faces staring.

"Get the kids out of it, Primrose?" I said, gently.

"Aye. Hop it, you varmints!"

"You tried the Parish?" asked Rachel, and she bent above Bron. "Have you pain, my cherub?"

"Of course I've tried the Parish and of course she's got pain!" I whispered.

"She's declining — you're goin' to lose her, lest she eats."

It was Heinie who had the answer after the others had gone.

He entered the kitchen like a ghost with a purpose, on tiptoe, lest he should awaken Bron, but I knew she wasn't asleep.

"The oven door's open again, Goldberg," she said from the pillow.

"Sorry, missus," said Heinie, and did up the front of him. "How you doin'?"

But Bron didn't reply.

Later, when we were sure she'd dropped off, he said, softly, "You got to do something, Tobe."

He stared around the kitchen. "Anything else you can pop?"

In the past month most of the furniture had gone into the Three Balls. All we had left was the bed, the table and chairs.

"I'm popping nothing else," I answered. "Now I'll have it coming in."

"That's the idea." He sat down in wheezes and grunts. "She's worth it, isn't she? Mine was, too, you know. Did I mention her?"

321

"No," I answered.

"Died of T.B." He grimaced. "It were about eight years back. I was twice her age — she were only a kid, really. The Ocean Coal Company strikers marched over and fetched us out for a rise of twenty per cent — there wasn't a hope in hell of getting it. We struck for a month, and starved — me mostly, for my girl was delicate." He made a wry face. "We went back, of course."

"Got nothing out of it?"

"Nothing at all — like now — a blutty waste of time."

There was no sound but Bron's hoarse breathing.

Heinie said, with hopeless dejection, "People were good, but she were too far gone in the chest, and she needed good food." He looked at me. "They killed her, ye know, like they'll kill your Bron."

I stared back at him. He said, "If they'd come in and knifed her — the coal owners, I mean, they couldn't have done her better."

"I'm sorry," I said.

Heinie smiled, empty. "One's enough between us — you see your girl don't end up the same? You need money for her, you go and fetch it. I did for mine."

"Steal?"

"Why not? I remember Isaac Evans, one of the Committee at the time my Hannah died — saying that Mabon was taking employers' bribes. Him drinking wine and smoking cigars — getting his son a job in the coal office — and my girl dying. Pretty good, eh? So I hoofed it down to Swansea and stole a fob watch for food."

"You got away with it?"

"No, I got six months — but it were right, wasn't it? Property's theft, anyway — it says so in the *Labour Weekly*."

Later, Patsy Pearl called in, wanting to come with me up to John Haley's place, for the story had it that he'd been batoned in fresh rioting over at Cynon recently, and I promised to meet her later.

But first I saw to Bron.

Mostly, when her fever was high with the pleurisy, Primrose or Rachel would come in and sponge her down for me, but tonight I wanted to do it myself.

"You'd make a good nurse," said she, her good eye dancing at me.

"It isn't the only thing I'm good at, woman."

I noticed that she was thinner, and her weakness had increased: probably, I reasoned, the fortnight in bed had done that; get some good food into her and she'd be up and about again, giving everybody hell.

Bron began to cough when I restrapped the bandage the doctor had put around her ribs, and I noticed some tiny blood flecks on her pillow.

"What do you want for supper?" I asked.

"Keep it down to steak and onions."

I bent to her, drawing the bandage tighter; she must have been in agony, but made no sign of it.

"You're a good one," she said.

"That's what I keep telling you."

"Sam wouldn't nurse his grandma."

"I'll nurse the bugger if he comes round here. Doesn't he know you're poorly?"

"I expect so. News gets around."

I washed her face and combed her hair, and she said, "You're on the wrong horse, you realise that, Tobe?"

"More than likely." I was at the stove now, making her bread and milk.

"I mean — you'd best know — I'll be up and away to Sam for sport, the moment you get me on my feet."

"That's nice to know."

"You don't mind?"

I was stirring in the bread and sugar. "Up to you, isn't it?"

The night was silent beyond the kitchen window; faintly I heard the rumbling of a tram; empty, mostly, they came and went up and down the valley in illumined discontent and with ghostly precision.

"You'd be best off with that Nanwen, really speaking."

I poured the steaming bread and milk into a bowl. "Chance would be a fine thing."

"I'd do the same for you, mind . . . nursing, I mean, if you was ill."

"That's all right, then."

Sitting on the bed, I raised her on the pillow, then spooned the food to her lips, blowing on it first.

"You make me feel a bitch," she said, swallowing, her face turned away.

"That's good."

"Perhaps if you hit me around sometimes, like Sam does, I'd treat you better."

"I'm trying that next."

She swallowed like a woman swallowing chaff, and said, "I . . . I can't help it, Tobe. It's . . . like being mad."

"You're the one who keeps on about it."

Her single eye suddenly blazed. "And why are you so blutty pure and holy? Given the chance you'd climb all over that Nanwen!"

"Of course."

"Then what do you stay here for?" She made a fist of a hand and thumped the bed, instantly groaning with pain. "Christ, I hurt. Somebody's been gnawing at me with gumboils."

"Then don't get yourself so excited."

She lay silent. Tears filled her good eye.

"Oh, hell," I said, "don't start that!"

"Cootch me up a bit, Tobe."

"Finish your bread and milk . . ."

"Come on, be a sport. Hold me?"

Sighing, I did so, bending over the bed.

"Don't you fret, my beauty," she said, "I'll make it up to ye." She gripped me, whispering, "That blutty Sam Jones — he's bound to know I'm ill, but he don't come. He was always the same — wouldn't spit in me eye if I were on fire. Do . . . d'you think he knows about me, Tobe?"

"Of course he doesn't, or he'd be here on the next tram," I said.

It placated her, and she slept.

It was cold in the room and I thought about getting in with her to keep her warm, but blackness was on the window when I finished reading. The clock said eight, and I was due to meet Patsy outside John Haley's room at half-past.

Meanwhile, Bron was asleep and breathing at peace, if noisily.

I wanted to kiss her, but thought it might wake her up.

She'd have given birth to a set of jugs had she known I was going to meet Patsy, so I made sure she was really sleeping before I left her with Primrose sitting guard.

I walked slowly down De Winton to the Gelli Road, and the house on the corner where Haley had a room. Rumour had it that he entertained women there, which I doubted: a pint, a smoke, and John Haley seemed at peace.

Others were not at peace, though they were sleeping; young Shaun McCarthy, for one.

Shaun, once the beloved and youngest son of Etta and Dano, had been thrown out into lodgings for taking the starch out of Rose Arse-Jenkins's bloomers, but nobody (including Tommy, who handed Shaun a hiding) had the proof, for Shaun denied it. I paused at the window where he dozed in his lonely room like a boy embalmed. Dreaming of Rosie, perhaps, with whom he was in love, they said: and properly in love, I reckoned. I watched, pitying him, for he was a regular good Catholic lad: behind him the flickering candlelight on the wall made shadows of fornicating rabbits.

"Dirty old thing, ain't he now?" said Sarah Bosom, going past.

"Ought to be put away," said Dozey Dinah, holding her arm. "Regular sex maniac. Etta won't 'ave him back, ye know. How's Heinie?"

This was the scandal at its noblest and best — farted round corners, bubbled through beer. I pitied young Shaun, in lodgings, when he wanted to be back home with Etta and his brothers.

"Good night," I said.

It was a pity I'd met Sarah and Dozey; later, it wouldn't be possible to testify that all that night I'd been sitting in with Bron ...

Life, at best, I thought, was a savage hunger for food and love, of one kind or another.

On the way up De Winton I met a gang of English soldiers coming down: a boisterous, laughing lot were they, their bodies muscular under their grey-backs, and I liked their cheek and banter: they were towing a cart of coal from the Ely, and one was riding the donkey.

All down De Winton the doors and windows were barred to them. English soldiers on Welsh streets; the Welsh didn't like it.

"Ay ay, Taff!" cried one, taking me off.

"Ay ay, rough stuff," I said.

Coal carts like this one were travelling up and down the Rhondda about now, by special orders of General Macready, the English Officer Commanding, a man the colliers respected, even if the Irish rightly hated him later for commanding the Black and Tans.

Starting full at a colliery, these carts would arrive nearly empty at the barracks, and there was never any official inquiries as to how the coal got lost. So on they'd go, spilling coal with such carelessness that the valley children could sneak out and collect it up in bags: the police might send you down for a month for stealing coal off the tips which belonged officially to the Owners, but nobody got sent down by Macready for stealing off the Army.

"You got a fire at home, mate?" called one.

"Don't need it, boyo; got a warm missus."

I walked on. I respected them, but I didn't want a lot of chat with them.

But you got to give them credit, said Heinie.

The Lancashire and West Riding men gave concerts during the Cambrian Strike; they organised food kitchens in defiance of the Owners, shared their rations with the children, beat us at football, took hidings at rugby. In the early days of their coming, a Welsh girl seen out with a squaddie would likely get her head shaved. But now a few soldiers were being invited home, and, when they had the money, would drink in the pubs. One or two actually married Welsh girls and stayed on as colliers.

Not so the police. The sight of blue instead of khaki was enough to send a Rhondda Welshman raving mad.

Churchill's stupidity in sending in the troops, said Richard Jones, was only matched by General Macready's integrity; he was firm, but kind. He didn't hob-nob with the coal owners; he put his officers under canvas, away from the clutches of the local squires. With the police at large in the valleys, it could have ended with another blood bath like the old Merthyr Riots; Churchill had used a sledgehammer to crack a nut, people said, and his orders to the police will be remembered by the Rhondda. Blood from the nose, indeed? Blood from the brain, and Macready cooled things down. But it was the indignity of having soldiers in the Rhondda — this is what we hated, not their presence.

They were singing some tuneless song of home, these soldiers, as they went down to Pandy Square.

Mr. Winkle, the cockle man, went along Dunraven with his tray on his head, bawling his wares. His lava bread, they said, was the best in the valleys, though Bron reckoned he grew it under the bed. And even the official cockle women come up from Port Talbot couldn't match the plump, delicious cockles he stored in his two gallon china; peeing over them in winter to keep the beggars warm, said she, for cockles, being cold-blooded, enjoy a warm environment.

"You fancy a pint, Toby Davies?" asked he, stopping.

"Not cockles," I said, and turned down Gelli.

Patsy was waiting in the hall of Number Thirty-Nine, just down from the Empire.

"Hallo, Tobe," said she, faintly.

John Haley's next door neighbour was standing in the doorway, a broom with elbows, and she turned her wasted face to Patsy, saying, "Mind, his landlady weren't all that good — went off with the other lodger, she did — always a fancy man round the corner, isn't there?"

"He's in there?" I asked. "Mr. Haley, I mean."

"Ay ay," said the neighbour, barring the way. "Wait till his friends come, I said to my Girt — we've been doing what we could for him. She were the peak of low taste, his landlady ye know — ye could skate to Trebanog on her dish-cloth. Do you know she used her old man's bottom set to mark the edge of her tarts?"

"Can we go in?" I asked, taking Patsy's arm.

"Didn't even feed him; got no maritals, some people. D'you know she cooked his Christmas pudding down the leg of his long-johns? He's been used to a lot better, I'd say." She stared at Patsy. "Ain't I seen you before?"

"Come," I said, and led Patsy into the hall.

Somebody said that the police had batoned John Haley; it looked like the entire Glamorgan constabulary had been at him, with the London Metropolitans thrown in.

"Oh, God," whispered Patsy, and went to her knees.

"They just come in here after him and did him up," said the woman from next door. "Six of 'em — day before yesterday."

It was a tiny room; a bed, a table, a chair; on the mantel was a fading photograph of a dark-haired woman with a child. And John Haley, his face a dramline of cuts and bruises, was lying in the bed.

Patsy wept.

"That won't help. Get up," I said. Then, to Haley:

"John, I've come with the strike pay," and he opened the slit of one eye at me. "And Patsy's come to feed you."

The blood-shot eye drifted to Patsy, and closed: he looked like a twin to Bron.

I put the ten shillings into Patsy's hand and she rose, a woman with a new demeanour.

Before Patsy went to Ginty's for food, Haley drank warm milk from the cup she held to his split lips; thirstily, he drank, demanding more.

"What's good enough for Madog ought to be good enough for anyone," said Patsy. "It stands to reason, don't it?"

"She fed him breast milk — I tell ye, I saw her through the window," said the woman next door. "If I hadn't seen it with my own eyes . . ."

"It was the best drink a man ever had," said Haley, and put out his hand to her.

One thing was sure — it was all Patsy had.

For my part I was off to the New Inn, Pontypridd a few nights later, but not for ale, it being after closing hours. Once last year, at a Rocking Stone meeting, I had killed a pint in there with Heinie.

This is where the colliery officials caroused: roast chicken and stuffed pork dinners, with wine to wash it down.

Ponty was in a midnight darkness by the time I got there. The town snored behind its shuttered windows, and the full-drunk moon was courting her tipsy stars above the slated roofs down High.

Nobody about save me and a few stray cats in the streets and alleys, enough to feed the Rhondda, for Pontypridd wasn't on strike.

I walked slowly through the town with my eye out for policemen, then vaulted the wall at the back of the New Inn, which was shut.

The cold, bare yard stared up; blank windows awakened, fluttering winks at me and the moon. I stood for a bit listening to the sleeping house.

With the banks shut after the Saturday festivities, like as not the till would be full . . .

Deeper in the town, a dog dismally barked: close to me, tiptoeing on bottle glass, two cats eyed each other on a wall, jet shadows of hate against spindrift clouds.

A window facing the yard slid up with a wheeze to the lever of my chisel; I swung a leg over the sill and stood within the warm, sweet smells of a kitchen; red bars grinned at me from the grate: somebody had left a kettle on and it sang a tearful song of hope to me. Come morning, the bottom would be burned out of it, so I took it off the fire.

Through the kitchen door now and over the hall like a wraith, till I came to the tap. My heart was thudding away at my shirt as I stepped silently over the sawdust and ducked under the counter flap, but the till was gone.

In window moonbeams I stood listening to the beetled, mouse-scuttling talk of the house. Smiling, I uncorked a bottle of gin from the rack and drank deep for courage: I drank again until I realised that I hadn't eaten all day. Later I reflected, I would search the kitchen for food, and take some home for Bron.

Standing there, I saw her face with astonishing clarity.

Back through the tap-room now, and into the hall. At the bottom of the stairs a black cat was sitting. Purring, unafraid, she arched her back as I stroked her, her amber eyes addressing me with night prowling, friendly regard; her very presence brought normality and allayed my apprehension.

Now up the stairs I went. On a landing, I listened again, followed by the cat.

Soft-carpeted, the bedrooms growled and grunted the insensitivity of humans, and I saw, in the eye of my mind, florid-faced agents lying flat on their backs in colly-wobbling, steak and kidney dreams of bubbly and naked barmaids. A door ajar; it magically swung wide to my touch, exposing the room within like a touch from a fairy wand.

A woman was lying in the bed.

Her white face upturned to the ceiling, her hair lay in staining waves over the snow-white pillow: the moon from a skylight immediately died, bringing darkness to her face, which possessed the sheen of jaded alabaster.

I came closer to the bed, staring down at her, as one does at a corpse. Outside, the town was striking the hour; one o'clock, two, I did not count.

So still this woman lay that she intrigued me; the shadowed eyes, the paling crimson of her mouth: she could truly have been dead.

On the table beside her was earrings, a little graven necklace and rings. Of these, I took the necklace, which was of gold. In a flash of the moon, I saw it, but the room was dark again when I turned to the woman in the bed.

Her eyes were wide open.

It was as if she had watched me in the act of theft.

Watching her for movement, I turned to a dressing-table.

Drawing the curtain, I peered down on to the blackness of the flagstoned yard. Money, gold and silver, was scattered on the table; silently, I gathered it up. The room swam suddenly, like a drunken dancer pirouetting, and I held on to the table, cursing myself.

When I turned, with the money in my hands, the woman was no longer in the bed. And the moon, as if in answer to my question, swung over the skylight, bringing the room into sudden shape.

She was standing in front of the door, and I knew her instantly. As a statue of white, she stood in her long nightdress, her hands held out to me in greeting. Clearly, I saw her; as clear as on a sunlit day.

I could have shouted with fear: it was the Wraith Woman of Rhayader.

Some money spilled from my damaged hand as I tore aside the curtain.

330

Throwing up the casement window, I swung over the sill and dropped down into the yard.

Here, a man was standing; a groom by the size and smell of him, a misshapen gnome of a man. As I went passed him he waved his stick at me, which I knew was the dried penis of a bull, and he cried in his thin, Irish falsetto:

"Bad cess to ye, me lad! And wicked cess indeed for turning her down! Ye'll be travelling faster than Barney Kerrigan's bull, sure to God, before ye're rid of her this time," and he cackled laughter, stamping around in the yard. "She'll be laying her curse on your fifth generation."

It was the man I had met on the road to Builth, years back, on my way to the Rhondda.

The street was awaking; lamps were glowing in windows, curtains going back, doors coming open.

With my hobnails sparking on the cobbled road, I went pretty fast up the road out of Ponty, cursing myself for drinking raw gin on an empty stomach, as the laughter of the Irishman echoed in my ears.

Mind, said Heinie later, it's happened to me a couple o' times as well, for raw gin from the bottle plays hell with the constitution — "mine's mainly pink elephants."

O, aye?

Something was telling me that I'd pay dearly for that trip to Ponty, if the woman of Rhayader had anything to do with it.

Clear — as clear as day I saw her that night again, as I can see her now.

34

It was Christmas, 1910.

As an undertaker's cloak, the old anxious sighing for food dropped over the valleys.

No longer the sounds of children echoed down the gullyways and alleys; rain erased the chalkings of the hopscotch flags; the running chimes of the hoop and iron, whip-lash and spinning tops died in memories of bountiful summers.

All down the coal-grimed streets, where once black-shawled women chattered, the doors were locked; the windows barred to the black intruder Starve.

The High Street shops gazed their brown-papered windows at the frosted streets; the Empire was shut, so was the little Market in Tonypandy: the publics were gated or on short time: dogs, too thin to howl, dozed on wet Sunday afternoons.

Weary old people, the grandparent rubbish of earlier generations, turned their sallow faces to the Rhondda sky and wondered where God had got to; the present generation, the mufflered, moody, still volatile Welsh, turned their eyes from the god called Mabon and the Union, which, they said, had betrayed them.

But the masters, Chapel deacons and the Church of England pastors were still eating, as Heinie mentioned, though larders, like bellies, were empty. And the old people, without asking permission, as usual, began to die.

In the grip of a bitch of a winter, up to their knees in snow, the little black processions, dew-dropped, in creaking boots (a sure sign they weren't paid for) and Sunday alpaca, began the old bible-hugging journeys. Hymns were sung outside blind windows and at gravesides.

In ragged, dejected columns or in white breath before the trundling soup kitchens of Lady This and That, the scant-thin families waited, bowls in blue fingers. Scitterbags of women, once capped and noisily defiant, now stood in dejected lines before the Quakers boilers with their babies on their backs, and did not speak: or crept out under the diadem, Rhondda nights to thieve coal off the tips under the noses of the big Metropolitans.

The children sickened, the youngest first, as always.

Blood on coal, said Mattie; now you Rhondda fools, try licking off the blood in the name of Mr. D. A. Thomas.

Slowly, the workhouse filled.

All down Sinkers Row the babies had ceased their crying; up Court Street, down Eleanor Street, Charles and the Bush Houses it was the same: no babies crying: always a bad sign, said Primrose — it were the same in the Ocean Coal strike — remember, Rachel?

"Things are serious, mind, when the babies stop crying," said Patsy. "Will Bron be all right now, you reckon?"

I looked at Bron's thin face on the pillow.

"Aye, and thanks for coming," I replied.

"Feels more settled, she do, after a blanket bath, see?"

I nodded. At the hut door, Patsy said, "Don't take it hard, Tobe. She don't know who's washing her — except that it's a woman . . ."

"Yes," I said.

"And it's only when she's dreaming that she calls for that Sam." She smiled at me. "You've always got to reverse your dreams, you know — it's you she means."

"Of course."

"Good night now." Patsy humped up Madog and gathered her shawl about her. "I'm away up to Mr. Haley, then."

I gave her a penny for Madog's supper.

"Happy Christmas, Tobe. You want anything, you send for me, is it?"

I nodded. "Happy Christmas, Patsy."

For a long time I sat at the table, watching Bron's pale face.

It was over six weeks now since the police had batoned her; after the pleurisy came pneumonia. With the help of the women, and the money I had stolen from New Inn, Pontypridd, I'd managed to keep her alive.

It was Christmas Eve, 1910.

Earlier, I had torn up pages of the *Labour Leader* and painted them in various .colours, making paper-chains, and these I'd suspended across the hut: I'd whipped a Christmas tree off one of the estates and had put it in a pot beside the bed with a candle on top, decorated like a fairy. There wasn't a lot to celebrate, but I'd got hold of a bit of under-belly pork, and this, after Patsy had gone, I was roasting for a treat; it was no bigger than two fingers, but it smelled sweeter than the hanging gardens of Lebanon. The idea was to surprise Bron when she woke up; it had cost me half our capital, but I wasn't letting Christmas go by without tickling her fancy.

I was just getting it out of the oven when she stirred in the bed and opened her eyes at the ceiling, and I got the joint out in the pan, still basting it and wafted it to give her the smell of it, but I reckon she wasn't ready for a Christmas Eve joint and paper-chains.

"Sam," she said, "you there?"

I closed the oven door.

"Aye, I'm here," I said, and sat back on my heels.

Christ, I could have done with a pint.

At the turn of the year Bron was still very ill.

Normally, every New Year's Eve, folks came in throngs from up and down the valley to see the New Year in, and there would be dancing and drinking, and a gay old time, with the publics spilling out of the doors. And Tonypandy Square would be packed with revellers making the best of it. At near midnight, with the old year dying, people would dance in rings of joy, hands clasped, singing *Old Lang Syne* at the top of their lungs, old and young all mixed up together. And then, on the stroke of midnight, every colliery hooter in the Rhondda would blast out its message of goodwill, howling stridently down the valleys — the distant ones echoing over the frosted mountains, making the Rhondda, in all its neighbourliness, one with itself in love.

334

But this year, standing beside the window, I saw but a few straggling people hugging themselves against the wind: no singing, no laughter sounded from the Square; indeed, there was no sound at all but Bron's quiet breathing.

And then, as if in defiance to strikers, a siren sounded from the Scotch; then another from up Clydach way, then another, a growing chorus of discord wailing and sighing around the empty streets.

I screwed up my hand and put it against my face. Bron stirred in sleep and I knelt by the bed, holding her. Coal owners, I thought, had a marvellous sense of humour.

"What's that, love?" she asked faintly.

I could have gone down to the engine fires and taken the steam cocks to their faces; a hatred, deeper and purer than I have ever known, surged within me.

"*Heisht*, you, it's nothing," I whispered.

As if brought back to life and reasoning, Bron smiled then; a woman coming out of a dream of death, and whispered something incoherent.

"What's that. . . ?" I bent closer to her lips, listening.

"Happy New Year, Tobe," she repeated.

The sirens wailed on tunelessly while I knelt there, holding her.

What with one thing and another, between coal owners and strikers, the Rhondda had something to answer for, I reckoned.

For the first month or so of the Cambrian strike I'd done little else but read; now I was can-making, something more constructive. It appeared a sort of intellectual chicanery to improve one's mind in the face of people starving. Empty milk tins, refashioned, polished, made good drinking mugs in the absence of crockery, and I sold them down in Porth at twopence a time, my eye constantly out for Sam Jones, but I never came across him. Had I done so, I'd have taken him by the scruff and hauled him up to Bron.

Now, with February chasing out January, and Bron sitting up in bed, I was still at it — the finest can-maker in the Sinkers, self advertised.

"Give you a bangle earring and a fiddle and you'd make a good tinker, Six-foot-three," said Bron.

"Got an eye for the fellas again, eh? Sure sign you're better," I said, polishing.

But it was the ghost of Bron, sitting there in the bed.

Her hair, regaining its old flashing lustre, was tied back at the neck with a bright red ribbon — stolen from my old gran's wedding box, said Patsy: over her thin shoulders she was wearing a baby-wool turnover, knitted by Primrose for Rachel's last confinement. And there was about her an air of wistful contentment; no life was in her, although she was young. The skin was stretched tightly over her high-boned face in a Dresden china beauty; her eyes, once sparkling, were large orbs in the shadowed darkness of her cheeks; as if the merriment of the old Bron had flown away on wings. Left behind was the winter counterfeit of the summer Bron I knew.

"What's all this about Senghenydd, then?" she asked.

Her curiosity, however, hadn't diminished.

I put down a can. "Heinie suggested it — I can tackle it now you're better. According to Mattie, he knows a chap who has a pull with the foreman of the Downcast; we'll try for signing on."

"At the Senghy big Universal?"

"Why not — there's nothing doing here?"

"Isn't the Universal on strike, then?"

"Of course not — she isn't in the Combine."

Pick pick pick went her fingers on the blanket, always a sign of trouble.

"And that's the only reason why you're shovelling over to Senghenydd?"

"Would there be another?" I got up and put the kettle on the grate.

"You know what I mean — come off it, Tobe!"

"Nanwen, you mean? Ben's got her barred, shuttered and chained, don't you worry."

"But if you had half a chance — I know ye!" She was watching me.

"Stuck it out here so far, haven't I?"

A squad of Glamorgan police were marching across the Square; their tramping boots beat between us. Most of the soldiers had gone now, but the police remained to deal with the uneasy peace.

"Don't like you going down the Universal," said Bron. "She's like Mrs. Change — a gassy old bitch."

Gas had never worried me; only water, and a distended death in bubbling suffocation disturbed my sleep; talk did have it, too, that there was water down the Universal . . .

"Didn't they have a gas flow down there recent?"

"Coal isn't a fancy parlour job, you know — one has to take some risks."

She turned away her face like the old Bron, saying flatly, "You're blutty toop, the lot of you — they'd never get women down a pit."

"Years back, they did."

"Now they've got more sense, I reckon. When you trying Senghenydd, then?"

"Give it a week or so; Mattie's going to fix it." I got up again and made the tea. "You'll be all right — Primrose and Rachel will slip in from time to time." I held a brightly polished can up to the lamp. "Now then, what d'you think of that?"

"You're the best gipsy can-tinker this side o' Maerdy."

"And this?"

I danced about to happy her, one hand on my hip, a can held high, snapping my fingers.

"Oh, Tobe," she said in tears, and put out her arms to me.

"Don't be daft," I said. "Drink your tea."

It was over four months in all before Bron was back on her feet, and Mattie landed us the big Universal jobs.

April was into us, after eight months of the Ely lock-out; the actual Combine strike being in its twenty-fourth week.

I was in the bath by the fire when the urchin called, handing out what the police called subversive literature. Bron picked up the pamphlet from behind the door.

I sat in the bath with the soap tufting up my hair while Bron read falteringly, sitting on the bed:

'Through all the long dark night of years
The people's cry ascendeth.
The earth is wet with blood and tears,
But our meek sufferance endeth.

337

The few shall not for ever sway
The many who toil in sorrow.
The powers of Hell are strong today
Our kingdom comes tomorrow.'

"Is that in the *Labour Weekly*?"

"Aye," she replied. "Part of the Cambrian Strike Manifesto, it says. What's a manifesto?"

"Just keep reading," I replied, and she held the newspaper up to the lamp:

"It says here that Noah Ablett, John Hopla and Noah Rees wouldn't take part in agreeing to a return to work on Management's terms; they said that the colliers had been jockeyed and sold . . ."

"That sounds like Noah Ablett right enough."

"Listen to this," said Bron, "he says," and she read: " 'We have been deliberately and foully misrepresented by a large section of the public press. We have been bludgeoned by the police . . .' " She glanced up. "Well, I can tell 'em that . . ." She continued, " 'One of our comrades lost his life, two committed suicide, many have suffered imprisonment — some are even now in prison. If we could tabulate even a part of the suffering and misery endured by our women and children, we would say that our suffering has been too great already for us to be handed over to the mercy of D. A. Thomas, who is one of the greatest despots these valleys have known.' "

"Good stuff," I said.

"What does it mean?"

"That the Strike goes on." I stood up in the bath, towelling myself down. "And it should go on, until the South Wales Federation gets either a guaranteed Minimum Wage for colliers, or calls for a national stoppage."

"Meanwhile the valley starves?"

I got out on to the floor. "We've no option."

Now that the riots were over, we were beginning to see the bailiffs for the rabbits, as Heinie put it. The only man to come out of it all with clean hands so far was General Macready. He had left the Rhondda now after a job well done; soon, more of the soldiers would follow him, and their names would ever be respected by the Welsh.

338

But not that of Winston Churchill, the man who sent them in, despite the efforts of Haldane, the Secretary of State for War, who insisted to him that they be held in reserve at Pontypridd.

For a century Churchill would be remembered, also, for sending in the Metropolitan Police, over whom he held sole control. Their brutality (he consistently refused to allow an official inquiry into police behaviour) was matched by that of the hated Glamorgans, our own constables. The importation of blackleg labour, the free rein given to the despised Chief Constable Lindsay who hated the Welsh; all contributed, in measure, to the Tonypandy Riots.

And the Rhondda will remember.

"When that Churchill bugger goes down," said Bron now, "we'll dance in the streets."

"Dear me, Tobe," said she now, coming nearer the bath, "you've got shoulders like a barn door and a waist like an Egyptian queen." She kissed the top of my head. "And another hair on your chest. *Jawch!* I haven't seen this one before — must have grown while I've been away."

"Hop it, you're supposed to be ill."

"Old Rachel's ill, I reckon. You noticed her lately? Dropped stones, she has — a lazy wind would go right through her." She sat on a chair beside the bath. "Fancy your back washed?"

I took the towel from her. "Sure sign you're up and about."

"Tell you what, son — cross me pillow with silver and I might let ye make love to me." She praised me with her eyes.

"Ach, I'm not much good at night, girl."

"And not that much better in the morning. Hark, what's that?"

It was the Odds next door, singing, 'As pants the hart for cooling streams . . .' "What they got to sing about?" asked Bron.

"Bill's not doing so bad, remember," I said. "Things got better for them after he went to the brickfields."

We all had little bits of jobs about now to stretch the Union money. Moses Culpepper, who was once a chippy, was making coffins for Dai Up and Down, the undertaker, and was going around measuring up his friends, for old Dai always made his money in advance, so to speak. Ginty, who had closed his shop, had also gone back to the tools and was knocking up emigration chests for families sailing off to America and Patagonia, the new craze. Albert and Tommy Arse had been hauling for the Army; Dano McCarthy had returned to his trade of slaughterer and Mattie and Dai Parcel had jobs as spare-time postmen.

Bron said, civil, "You've been pretty good to me, mind, since I been ill."

"You'd have done the same for me."

"Wasn't your job really, though, was it?"

She was sitting in front of the grate now, her hands held out to the glow. I'd always managed to keep a bit of a fire for her; it was only a week or so in the jug if you got sent down for stealing coal off the tips, and it was worth it. I towelled down and pulled on my clothes. "Of course it was my job. We live together, don't we?"

"It was Sam's."

"Oh, God, do you have to bring him up?"

She frowned at her fingers, looking like a sickening child, sitting there with the glow of the fire on her thin features. "I . . . I expect he didn't hear about me being ill — that's why he didn't come, eh?"

"I suppose so." I was tying my boots.

"Perhaps he was away — he's a hell of a chap for going off somewhere, you know."

I grunted reply, and she said, turning:

"What you got dressed for? Time for bed, isn't it?"

"Got to go out."

"This time of night?"

"There's a duchess told me to report to her bedside over in Maerdy — I'll be in with her directly."

"Don't be daft!" It didn't amuse her.

"I've got to see Solly Freedman, Three Balls," I said.

"He's closed."

"Not to me, he isn't."

She rose. "What are you popping that's so special?"

"If I tell you, you'll be as wise as me," and I kissed her. But she stood, unmoving when I reached the door.

"Don't get us into trouble, Tobe."

I gave her a wink to discourage her curiosity; buttoning me up

340

against the cold, for it was a night to make monks out of brass monkeys. Crossing the Square, I went down De Winton to the back of Solly Friedman Pawnbroker.

The little golden necklace I had stolen from the New Inn, Ponty, gleamed like molten brass in the palm of my hand.

I got eight sovereigns off Solly for that necklace, which astonished me, but he agreed that it was solid gold. One thing about Solly, he never asked questions.

It would have been better for everybody, including Solly, if I'd stayed at home and starved it out with Bron.

A new spring came dancing down the slopes of Mynydd-y-Gelli and Penygraig — come over from the Brecon Beacons, folks said, with sunlit hair, dandelions behind her ears and white crocuses on her feet. And the twin valleys, thumped into white iron by the fists of winter, grew warm and soft to the touch.

Snow-drops, sleeping since Christmas, put their noses out of the frosted ground and yawned at the sun; the primrose (always shy of humans) hid her face lest she saw a drunkard, and Primula, her shameful cousin, rose from the rich, warm earth to peep up passing skirts.

Feather-duster winds came greeting down the valley, kissing the dereliction of the unquiet dawns; motionless stood the pit-heads against billowy wash-day clouds. And the twin rivers, Fawr and Fach, stretched their quicksilver radiance through the greening country.

Sometimes, that early season, when Bron was still sleeping, I would climb to the top of Mynydd Trealaw and look down on to Tonypandy.

Of all valleys, this, I thought, was surely Welsh best. Where exists such loveliness as my Rhondda in springtime? The mountains are sylvan here, the country gold; the hills, bracken-crested, are hot cottage buns, the rivers milk, the sky honey. God knows why exile Welshmen search the ends of the earth when Heaven is on their doorstep.

Sometimes that April, sitting up on Mynydd Trealaw, I would listen to the sounds of spring, and wonder about God and His profoundly bitter humour. Anger assailed me, so that, even had He confronted me, I would have remonstrated: 'But why build cottages on vineyard slopes to desecrate them with fire? Why cast limbs of strength and beauty for mutilation? Why sculp lovely faces merely to chastise them into ugliness? Why, most of all, create in my lovely Wales a vision fairer than belief, just to ravage it with pit-heads and strikes?' And why, indeed, I thought, sitting there, build a love as great as mine for Nanwen O'Hara, and then bemuse it with a fierce emotion . . . the one I held for Bron?

Strange, the conflict on that April day. Even while bargaining my soul for a moment in the arms of Nan, I suddenly remembered it was nearly five; that Bron would be awake and looking for her tea.

If I didn't get moving, Rachel would come and make it, and she hated Rachel's tea. And, on the way back, I would try for a seedy-cake from the Co-op — with the money I'd got from the necklace, we'd celebrate, I decided.

After I'd got her on to her feet proper, I thought, I'd take a trip to Porth, find Sam Jones and try to get them together for good — this would settle everything: she'd have Sam and I'd be free to make a run at Nanwen — to hell with Ben O'Hara.

Rising, I went down into the valley.

After walking for a bit, I imagined I could hear Bron calling me; and then the thought struck me that Sam Jones might have come in the moment my back was turned and removed her, so I ran.

And I didn't stop, except for the cake, until I reached the Sinkers.

Throwing open the door, I stood staring down at the bed.

"Hallo, my lovely," said Bron, and opened an eye at me.

Kneeling, I kissed her. She was plainly surprised; I didn't kiss her a lot these days.

"Hey, get off!" she said, gasping to breathe. "Tea, is it?" She stared at me, wide-eyed, holding me at arms' length. "*Gawd!* Seedy-cake!"

"God knows why I'm back," I said. "I was doing all right with that duchess."

Mattie reckoned that he'd heard of the Senghenydd jobs from

Dinny Gnatshead, one of the drinkers in the Pandy before the Strike. Turning an honest penny, Dinny called it, with his cap sitting on his ears and the peak down over his eyes. He used to buy a side of bacon and sell it to his wife by the slice; steal coal from his neighbour's bin and sell it back to him at fourpence a bucket: tighter than a duck's arse was Dinny, according to Mattie, who paid him a week's strike pay to get wind of our jobs.

These jobs turned up in the middle of April.

"So you're off to Senghenydd at last, then?" asked Bron, that afternoon when I came in from coal stealing.

"Aye, meeting Heinie on the Square."

"Will you be back tomorrow?"

"Yes, if I don't get the job."

"And if you do?"

"Back at the weekend," I said.

I couldn't manage my collar stud, so Bron dried her hands at the sink and came and fixed it, and I sensed her ill-ease.

"Think you can manage by yourself now?" I asked.

"Ay ay — Rachel and Primrose'll be in from time to time."

Ever since we'd got up, words had evaporated between us, as if our lives, like the Rhondda, were gathering to a climax of doubts and fears.

Over her shoulder I saw the bare hut: the town, like us, seemed to be dying, too, for nothing moved on the empty square. People were starving properly now. Some over in Trealaw were selling their insurance policies for nine bob in the pound, and the money-baggers, as always, were moving in: the slick city boys with polished shoes and double-breasted waistcoats, while half a million British miners watched our agony from the touchlines.

"What will you do with yourself all week while I'm away?" I asked.

Her smile, as she stood before me, was like a small celebration of love.

"Hang around till Saturday night and you come home."

I turned from her, going about my business of packing things in my brown paper bag. Bron said:

"What will you both do for lodgings in Senghy?"

"I'm tackling Mrs. Best — I don't know what Heinie's up to. Can't go wrong with her, she always buys the best."

We laughed together, but it was forced. If she had cried a bit, it might have made things easier.

Solly Friedman Pawnbroker went past the window; in his black astrakan coat he looked like an avenging angel. Bron said — out of context:

"You heard about that copper up the valley?"

I shook my head. She said, "Rachel reckons they tied him to a lamp post and poured chamber pots over his head. And him in his best suit, too, and his missus done up in her Sunday braveries."

"Serve him bloody right."

"We ain't finished with it yet, ye know, Tobe. Trouble, I mean."

"Yes we are, it is ending."

I opened the door of the back and looked at the sky. Rooks were cawing at the April afternoon, circling like burned ashes — carrying in their beaks, like carrion crows, I thought, the poor, sad dead of the Rhondda. Leaving Bron at that moment seemed like a part of this dynasty of death: all down the Sinkers doors were slammed shut as if to keep in the poverty and allow things to die.

I made a mental note to hand the Union books over to old Richard Jones before I left the valley.

"I got to go," I said, finally, picking them up.

"Why can't I come?" Bron stood apart from me, looking lost.

"If I can settle on a place for us, I'll come back for you later, eh? Besides . . . you've got to work it out — Sam Jones or me, isn't it?"

She lowered her face. "Like you, with that Nanwen, really speaking?"

"Come Saturday night I'm back by 'ere with you," I said, "if you're still around."

"Don't you worry!" She straightened before me as the sun came through the door, curtseying our shadows. Bron, as usual, had an uncanny will to survive. "You don't chuck me over that easy, you'll see!"

"So you won't hop over to Porth the moment my back's turned?"

Although it was early, the rag-and-bone man was coming, singing his rag-and-bone call; his missus was having a baby; it would be a little rag doll for sure, folks said, so I mentioned it.

"I reckon we're all rag dolls, sort of," said Bron, empty.

"Goodbye, then," I said.

The world came through the door and stood between us.

"There's a pain in me for you, Tobe."

"That's good, hang on to it," and I kissed her.

I think we both realised that the time had come to part.

Bowlered and polished up, boots creaking for a funeral procession, Heinie came like a man to his bride, with buttonholes either side, stocked and waxed, creases to cut his shins and buttoned up in the flies.

"You losing Bron, Toby?" Heinie always had possessed an unfathomable ability to read my thoughts.

"Likely she's lost me."

"You leaving her alone won't help, mind."

"So we'll have to sort that out, won't we? I got her up and about again, didn't I? Now it's up to her."

"She's a sweet swansdown woman, ye know, you'll not find the likes of her."

"Aye, well, perhaps there's too many people around; Sam Jones, for instance." Together we strode down De Winton. "What about you?"

"Me, son?" Heinie turned his little flat face up to mine, his crossed eyes twinkling. "I come simpler. New job, new place! All I want now is a little plump widow with a weakness for whiskers and a guaranteed minimum wage. I've always wanted a daughter, ye know."

"At your age?"

"Ay ay — you start new, Heinie, I said. Good ale and wicked girls — I'm a primitive methodist when I've got me clothes off. But I'd treat a woman good — I did my little Hannah, you know? Two I want, a son to keep me, a daughter to bounce on me knee."

"You've got to make up your mind," I answered. "A good time, or a family, you can't handle both."

"The good time first. I'll have the family after."

He spoke more as we strode on, but I wasn't really listening.

"Dear me, I hope old Mattie's cooled those jobs," said he. "I don't trust Dinny Gnatshead, really."

"One thing at a time."

Dusk and bats were dropping over the Aber Valley when we got into Senghenydd, and there was an excitement growing in me again at the chance of catching a glimpse of Nanwen. Instead, the first women we saw was Sarah Bosom; plumper than ever was she; faster to jump over her than walk round her, with Dozey Dinah on her arm as skinny as adversity.

"Well, I never," said Sarah, contralto, and she patted her chest for shock. "Look who's here — that Heinie Goldberg gentleman who helped us!" and she dropped a curtsey low, with Dozey down beside her: pretty it looked.

Down with Heinie, too, hitting his bowler on the kerb; up with him then, expansive. "I heard you was over here, though," said he.

"Just visiting, actual," said Dozey, thinly. "Come to open a lodging house in Senghy — you working here?"

"Expecting to," I answered.

"Good clean beds at ten bob a week, all found," said Sarah, comely. She sniffed and wiped daintily, smiling at Heinie. "Though kind offers of lodgings are often misrepresented, if you get me?"

Heinie, in a trance of joy, was gazing up at her, a man with fearful ambitions.

"You're welcome, remember — both of you," said Dozey. "There'd only be the four of us to start with, see?" and she tightened her gloved fingers and fidgeted her hips at me.

"I'm fixed with Mrs. Best, more than likely," I replied.

"And you, Mr. Goldberg?" asked Sarah.

Delusions of grandeur were Heinie's; Sarah, in turn, was weighing him with a honeying touch; Dozey pierced me with eyes like phials of poison. She said, "Lodging with Mrs. Best, eh? Now that Ben O'Hara's out of the way, so to speak, I'd have thought to see you honouring his missus."

I lifted my eyes to hers.

"Well, Mrs. Guto Livingstone mentioned the connection, if I

may call it that." She beamed at me. "Likely you'd manage to give her some comfort . . . at a time like this?"

"Why?" I asked. "Has he left her, or something?"

"He's left her, all right, mister — permanent. He's dead."

The publics were filling; the colliers strolling in arguing, dismal groups in the moonlight and the wind had April shivers in him. I saw the faces of the women before me as white, embalming masks.

"Dead? Ben O'Hara?" I stared at her.

"Ain't you heard? A journey of drams hit him underground . . ."

"*When?*" whispered Heinie.

"About a week back."

"While we was over here negotiating for the lodgings," said Dozey.

Gladys Bad Fairy, locally known in the amateur dramatics, I learned later, went past us with her feet at ten-to-two and a bottle of blue ruin tipped up against the stars. Sarah said, "Jones the Death had him last week, poor soul. Good on the Irish, he is — all burials executed with great deference and respect."

"Mind, I only met him once, but he weren't my cup of tea exactly."

Others spoke, but I didn't hear them.

I ached for Nanwen.

"You mind if I go, then?" asked Heinie, tugging at my sleeve.

"Where?"

"With Sarah for lodgings?"

"Aye, of course," I answered. Realisation was sweeping over me in waves of increasing intensity. I thought, *Nanwen!*

"See you later down the Universal public for a pint?" asked Heinie.

It seemed impossible that Ben could be dead: the wheel of Fate, it appeared, had turned full circle: in fact, as I discovered later, it had only just begun to move.

"Yes," I said, looking at the sky.

"Coming, my lovelies," cried Heinie rubbing his hands, and went.

The curtains of the terraced house in Windsor Place were drawn for mourning, but a dim lamp was burning on the glass of the door: knocking gently, I waited.

347

It was difficult to believe that, such a short time back, Ben had opened this door to me. Now I expected it to swing back again, exposing him as a wraith in all the mutilation of his accident: I expected to see, in his bloodstained face, the same accusation as I had known in Bethesda.

Instead, when the door opened, Nan stood there.

We stared momentarily, unspeaking.

Her brow was high and pale. Deep shadows embraced the once brightness of her eyes, which looked sick of tears. It seemed as if, in Ben's death, there was bequeathed to her a new countenance; one that left her empty, bereft of life. And then, as realisation grew, she smiled, and she was Nan again.

"*Toby!*"

But she did not move to me. Beaten, she lifted vain hands to me in futile explanation.

I nodded, words being useless.

"I've lost him."

"Aye, Nan, I heard."

We stood contained by the embarrassment of her grief.

Ceinie appeared soundlessly beside her from the kitchen darkness of the hall. The child's dark eyes moved swiftly over me in woman-like assessment. Nanwen said, softly. "It . . . it's Uncle Toby — you remember Uncle Toby?"

Ceinie did not speak, except with eyes. Nan said, touching me, "I knew you'd come. I told Ceinie you'd come, didn't I?" She caught my hand and drew me within.

"I . . . I'd have come to the funeral if I'd known before," I said.

The three of us stood in the kitchen with its smells of human warmth and cooking. She'd got pretty women's things on the table and the iron was heating on the grate; Ben's slippers were on the fender; on the hearth lay his pipe, as he had left it. Over Nan's shoulder, in the scullery, I saw his shaving things neatly laid out on the copper. It was an abysmal ritual of life in death, I reflected; why the hell couldn't she let him die? Perhaps Nan noticed the emotion of my face, for she said:

"Can't get used to it, see?" She gestured, adding vacantly. "He was here such a little time ago . . ."

348

"It was quick," I said softly, and gripped her hand. "Be thankful."

Ceinie's eyes were bright with unshed tears. When her lips trembled, I released Nanwen, and turned away.

"Best I got going," I said. "I'll come back later, if you like."

"Oh, no, please stay! Look, I'll make a cup of tea. We can't let Uncle Toby go without a cup of tea, can we?"

Nan bustled about, flashing me looks of tearful apology.

"Come on now, sit you down."

The activity of the tea-making, the very tears of the kettle, the cup-rattling, seemed to sustain us; I have often thought since that the therapy of making tea surpasses its quality of enjoyment.

And Nanwen was smiling at me over the brim of her cup; that smile took me right back to the white starched cloth on the table in Caerberllan; to Ben, the Union books, and to Grandpa.

"Good to have friends about one at a time like this, isn't it?"

For the first time, Nanwen wept.

Going to her chair I stood above her, holding her while she sobbed. She put out her hand to Ceinie, who did not come; instead, her child's eyes, as startled as a faun's, held mine from the other side of the room.

Ben might be dead, I reflected, but there would always be Ceinwen.

Later, at the bar of the Universal, the pub next door to the pit and named after it, I called to Heinie as he came through the door, entering the throng of working colliers.

A Union meeting was going on upstairs, they told me; a cock–fight was squabbling in a corner of the tap-room. Harpies and harridans, the usual refuse of coal, were shrieking to pumping blasts of an Irish melodeon and an old navvy, the aged, human dross of the Universal pit-sinking, did a Connemara clog dance to a thunderous beating of time. Pushing aggressively up to me, Heinie thumped the counter for ale.

"Two pints, boyo," said he: blowing off the froth, he killed his alive, then elbowed me. "How did it go?"

"The usual funeral parlour — what about you?"

"I'm in," said he. "Supper tonight and feather-down bedding — ten bob a week, all found."

I said, "If they dropped you into a piss-pot, you'd swim out smelling of ashes of roses. I'm off back, bugger the job."

"What d'ye mean, mun — Mattie's got it fixed!"

Heinie's voice was the only sound in a sudden, intense silence; the music, dancing, clash of glasses and shouting had snapped off the world like the slam of a hand. I lowered my ale.

Two policemen, Metropolitans by the size of them, were standing at the door. The pit-head lights gleamed momentarily in the moment before it closed behind them, then they moved over to the counter.

"Anybody here by the name of Davies? Tobias Davies?"

The landlord repeated, raucously, "Is a Tobias Davies in here?"

I pushed past Heinie. "That's me," I called.

The constables approached me, gently handling Heinie aside.

"You're Tobias Davies, lately of the Hood Huts, Tonypandy?"

"Aye, the Sinkers," I replied.

One said, looking at his mate, "As big as a door? A collier? — this is him." To me, he said, "Tobias Davies, I am arresting you on a charge of feloniously entering premises known as the New Inn, Pontypridd, on the night of December the 3rd, 1910, and stealing money to the value of eight pounds two shillings, and this . . ." He opened his hand. The little golden necklace I had pawned with Solly Freedman glowed dully in the lamp-light. "You recognise this article?"

"Yes," I replied.

"You were silly to pawn it, weren't you — unprofessional, eh?"

They spoke more, cautioning me, but I was thinking about Nanwen and what she would do if I didn't return, as I'd promised: also of Bron, if she didn't have any money. I said to Heinie:

"See to Bron for me, eh?"

"Christ. . . !" whispered he.

"Get moving," said somebody, pushing me.

I said, "Heinie! Please. . . ?"

"Are you coming?" asked one of the constables, "or do we have to carry you?"

"If you take your hands off me," I said, shoving him away, "or you won't get me as far as the bloody door."

The bar went silent; people were crouched about us, like animals about to spring. Vaguely, I wondered what would happen to Solly Freedman: it was scarcely his fault . . .

Heinie came outside with us; the April night was cold.

"Goodbye," I said. "Remember Bron. . . ?" I gripped him. "*Please. . . ?*"

"Aye, mun."

I pulled up my coat collar against the wind.

Three

The Aber Valley

35

DURING MY TWO year sentence for the theft of less than thirty pounds, I didn't see a lot of the next two summers, except when out with prison working parties in the Rhymney valley; a far call from my beloved Rhondda.

But the spring of 1913 beckoned with promise of an early release. I recall (dressed in gaol grey and my head shaved as clean as a billiard ball) leaning on my shovel with the rest of the convicts, listening to the birds going mad with joy. It was a good spring too, green and fruitful; one far removed from the coming threat of war. And I saw, in the shovel-clatter of the working party around me, daffies and tulips waving their heads off in the nearby gardens while we trenched and ploughed the fields.

All the earth on that bright morning seemed to brim with beauty, and the distant mountains, lying on their backs under the sun, waved their heather, green and gold, in great, rushing swathes of the wind.

"All right, Davies, get on with it," cried a warder, and I tore my eyes from the sky beyond the mountain, where Nanwen lived.

A lot had happened during my two years in Cardiff gaol.

Peace had at last come to the coalfields: the national strike for a Minimum Wage had ended by last year's spring and the Cambrian dispute of the Rhondda Valley had been settled six months before that: a return to the pits on Management terms.

With starvation facing them, they had no alternative.

"A year of idleness since the Ely locked us out," said Heinie, on one of his monthly visits — "you had it easy in gaol, mate — you worked it good."

Heinie came to visit me with expected regularity.

"And then back on D. A. Thomas's terms, eh?" cried Mattie, who had come with him that day. "What the hell did the Rhondda die for?"

"The Rhondda's been dying since they first discovered coal in the valley," I replied. "Tell me something I don't know — is there still no news of Bron?"

"Still over at Porth — far as I know," said Heinie.

"She knows where I am, and she knows why — the least she could do is drop a bloody card."

A week after I'd been sentenced at the Cardiff Assizes, Sam Jones had come over to the Sinkers and collected her, according to reports.

"Never see hide nor hair of her since," added Mattie.

"But your Nan O'Hara's still activating," said Heinie. "I see her most nights when I come off day shift from the Universal. They ain't never had a prettier mistress at that old Board School."

It was difficult to talk privately in the prison meeting hall, with the other prisoners and their relatives chattering about us.

Mattie whispered, "Keeps to herself, she does, though. A tuneful little piece, she is — no followers — give her credit. And you can't say as much for some." He looked at me.

"Just her and the girl," said Heinie. "You reckon to settle down with them when you get out, Tobe? You could do worse, mun."

I didn't reply. Perhaps, I reasoned, my own sense of insecurity was being shared with Nanwen. She had written every week for two years with astonishing punctuality; every Saturday morning her letter would arrive, telling of the happenings in Senghenydd, and in Windsor Place in particular; the comings and goings of people; of her work as a mistress in the Board School where Ceinie attended. Her composition flowed with the serenity of her nature, uncompromising, kindly; constantly looking to the future and our new life together. And yet I sensed, within the lines, her innate fear of the future, an apprehension that was a part of myself. It was not that I

356

doubted our ability to find a new happiness; it was as if some act of Fate would sully such happiness: Nanwen appeared to sense this, too.

It was a complication fed by absence; letters, at best, can be awkward things, she wrote.

Bron, for her part, sought no such complications; she didn't write at all.

And yet, despite the knowledge that she was now completely lost to me, the Rhondda, that old, dark mistress of coal, black-faced, was calling me with a vibrous, fiery impetus; it was impelling, forcing itself into my being, and I wondered why. Mattie said, "Mind, some are doing all right in Senghenydd. They can keep the old Rhondda, I say. I'm on me jack with Mrs. Best, perhaps, but some 'ave nice warm feet, don't they, Heinie?" He nudged him. "Any happy events comin'?"

Glum, looked Heinie. Things in the Sarah-Dozey establishment hadn't turned out exactly as expected, apparently.

"Why don't you marry the girl?" I asked. "One of 'em at least."

"That's what I say," interjected Mattie. "He could do worse, I reckon. Or even living together in sort of marital accord. Sarah's a well set-up piece — I'd rather be in her than in the Glamorgan Constabulary."

"She ain't what she looks though," muttered Heinie, sad. "Her legs are botherin' her."

"They don't seem to bother nobody else," said Mattie. "You want to get moving, son."

I said, "Well, if there was one chap I thought I didn't have to worry about while I was inside, it was my poor old mate, Heinie Goldberg."

"Aye, but lodging with Sarah and Dozey ain't all it looks," Heinie answered. "They'd get no promotion in a harem — it's like a resolution of virgins — they're very fond of each other, you know."

"Oh, dear."

"You poor little soul," said Mattie, patting him. "I thought you was gettin' dozens. But it's not doin' it that does the damage, it's thinking about it that knocks your brains out."

We sat in a holy silence, grieving about Heinie's conjugal complications.

"Oh well," I said.

We all got up. "Next Saturday, then?"

"Two o'clock, outside the main gate — and don't be late."

"That's unlikely."

"And straight over to Senghy?" asked Heinie, hopeful.

"Straight over to the Rhondda," I said. "Come on, it's a prisoner's request. I want a quart at the Pandy."

"With that beautiful Nan O'Hara awaiting ye in Windsor Place?" Mattie sighed. "Don't be daft, mun — start the way you're intending."

"Tell her Sunday," I said. "Lads, I've just *got* to see old Tonypandy?"

I stared at them, and Mattie came up and put his fist under my chin, saying:

"Saturday night, then, and we'll give it Hamlet, like my old girl used to say." He sighed. "Six pints of Allsops embalming fluid!"

"She were a good one, mind — Mattie's wife, I mean," said Heinie, glancing at me meanfully.

"The best," I said. So far we hadn't discussed the death of Mattie's wife.

Mattie moved awkwardly, grimacing. "She was all right. Just that she didn't make the best of herself with folks, that's all. Also, I kept her to myself a lot, so to speak — I was never one for bumming a woman up to me mates. She made very good gravy, ye know. Mind, I still got me pigeons."

"His Milly's in the family way again," announced Heinie. "And got third prize in the Pandy to Gelli race, didn't she, Matt?"

"Ay ay — lucky, isn't it?" Dried of words, he stared, vacant.

The cacophony of the room, the relatives' chatter beat about us, bringing us loneliness in the face of Mattie's loss. He said, pulling his cap to bits:

"Come to think of it — us lot are all widowers really, in a manner of speaking."

"We'll give 'em widowers next Saturday night," said Heinie.

"We'll give 'em hell in the Pandy!"

"Then straight over to Senghenydd, last train?"

I nodded. "Anywhere you like — after I've seen the Rhondda."

" 'Cause that little woman'll be waiting — Nan O'Hara, remember," said Mattie, persistent. "Mrs. Best told me to remind ye . . ."

The following Saturday I was standing outside the main gates of Cardiff prison, looking out on to the sunlit city and the traffic clattering along the cobbled road before me. The sun was hot, and grey-faced rooks (You got Cardiff, you got to have rooks, said Heinie) were shouting their heads off in nearby elms. And starlings, a great perplexity of numbers that spring, were rushing in black swarms across the caverns of the sky as if in haste to mate on the rich, warm earth. And, as the clocks struck midday and I waited with my brown paper parcel of belongings, the people I expected got off a tram and started piling over the road towards me — Mattie and Heinie, Mr. Duck and Ben Block, with Dai Parcel, Gwilym and Owen bringing up the rear. Noisy and purposeful were they, swilled with enough ale already to refloat the lost *Titanic*; if I'd been released an hour later they wouldn't have had a leg between them.

Men for comrades; women for kitchens and beds, said Grandpa once; Grandpa was right.

"*Toby!*"

They nearly hoisted me off my feet in the rush, and we finished up off the tram down the back streets of Tiger Bay with our back teeth awash and pledges of eternal friendship, till Mattie started to cry. Back on the tram then and off to the station, Rhondda colliers setting Cardiff alight; dusk found us coming off the train and thronging along De Winton, in Tonypandy.

It was all I had dreamed about, the town at its best.

Poshed up and pretty were the little shop windows, like peacocks come alive after a long, winter sleep. And the pavements were thronging with black-faced colliers and wives; the children at it again bowling iron rings, and whipping tops and bawling. Great brown drays clog-stepped along in a flash of painted wheels; dog-carts trotted, gay little cobs showed sprightly heels; arched glances from painted ladies, lifting their needless parasols; blushing glances from girls growing into women. Ginty's shop was open under new

359

management, for Ginty, like hundreds of others, had shifted to the Aber Valley during the Strike. And the muddy little market, where once Shanklyn and O'Leary had their stall, was alive again and steaming its pigs' trotters, black puddings and faggots and peas. Arm in arm with Heinie and Mattie, I strode on, remembering the old nights when I made love to Bron, and thought I saw the sway of her amid the coloured dresses.

The visions came stronger when once I was in the Pandy.

The Scotch colliers were in there, cramming it to the doors; Red Rubbler, the mountain fighter, eyed me as I pushed to the bar; Annie Gay was serving the jugs, and I reckoned I could see three of her. But John Haley wasn't in his usual corner, neither was Patsy opposite, watching him.

"You go to Senghy sober, mate — we've booked you in with Mrs. Best, and she's respectable," said Heinie.

"So am I, you're sleepin' with me, God help you," said Mattie, five sheets in the wind.

I was seeing Annie Gay now through the hop-reeking haze of old and mild.

"You want to watch him, he's bowlered," said Red Rubbler. "Last time I saw him he was a fuzzy-wuz — now he's a blutty baldikin."

"So will you be lest you stop pattin' the top of his bald head," said Heinie. "You ain't lost your punch just because you lost your hair, 'ave you, Samson. Beside, you're still sober, ain't you, Tobe?"

"Sober enough to take you, Red," I said, and saw in Annie's youth and gaiety the smile of Bron: fair hair replaced Annie's Welsh darkness; blue-green eyes lowered admonishingly from Annie's oval face, and, when she spoke, she made the sounds of Bron.

"You sober up, Toby Davies, and I'll be off duty directly," whispered Annie, filling my pewter.

"He won't be sober this side of Easter," said Red Rubbler, and caught my arm, but I pushed him aside.

"God knows how he's standing," said someone, and I think it was Mattie.

"Tell him to take his eyes off my woman or he won't be standing no more," said Red Rubbler.

"Bron. . . ?" I said to Annie.

I heard somebody say, "Abraham Lincoln had a soft spot for the Welsh, too, did you know?"

"Bugger Abraham Lincoln," I said, and reached for Annie. "*Bron. . . ?*"

Red Rubbler swung me to face him. His large, bald eyes, heaped with old cuts and bruises, regarded me as he drew back his fist. Everything seemed to be dying about me. Even the daffodils on the shelf behind Annie looked as if they'd been out all night.

"Christ," I said.

I heard Heinie say as he dragged Red Rubbler away, "Touch him, and I'll kill ye, Red — I'm givin' fair warning."

"But she's got a husband — that Bron," said Annie. "It just ain't good enough, really speaking, Toby Davies. Time you left her off, ain't it!"

"You seen her?" I tried to focus her, and failed.

"I don't know, rightly . . ." said Annie. A man was saying into my face, and God knows who he was, "Things are never what they seem, ye see, son? Even some stars ain't there really — the light still shines, though they was burned out longer than a million years."

"Blutty remarkable," said Mattie, weeping.

"He'll see stars if he don't loose my woman," said Red Rubbler.

"Two pints of skull attack," said a voice, and it was Dano McCarthy with Shaun, his son.

"Mind, I'm glad Etta's goin' to take him back in," said Ben Block, wheezing up.

"Och, don't be daft," said another. "God only listens to saints."

"Bron . . ."

"I tell ye again, me name's not Bron," said Annie Gay, and Dano cried:

"And I says to him, sure to God, I says, 'D'ye call that religion, do ye?' Ach, the fella had a face like a bunch of laughs, and I never trusted him — if a boy's face shines, examine his knees."

" 'Will ye come to communion, Patrick?' asks me wife. 'Aye, I will,' I said. 'And if you loved Jesus as much as I do,' I told her, 'when it came to the communion wine, ye'd sink the lot.' Aren't ye drinking, Shaun?"

361

"Aye, Pa," said Shaun, and drank. "You all right, Mr. Davies?" His young, fresh face smiled at me, and I wondered about Rosie.

"Best you're away, lad," said Red Rubbler, " 'cause there's going to be trouble."

"She'll find her own level, that Rosie Arse, never fear," said Dano, "forget her, son. Is it good being out of clink, Tobe?"

"If he don't let go of my Annie's hand he'll be out on his backside," said Red Rubbler.

People were pressing about me, Red was pulling at my coat. Aunty Boppa Hughes, the new Pandy landlady, said into my face, "Ain't you met my old man then — Exalted Ifor? His ma used to wash the dishes in the lodger's po, but she were good otherwise, mind. Eh, she were a card! 'To my beloved husband I leave the back rent,' she says in her will, but then, all lovers die broke, don't they? Used to live round here, did ye?" Her powdered face stared up into mine. Very urgent was this Aunty Boppa's need, apparently, but I never got to the bottom of it.

"God Almighty, Bron . . ." I said. "Where you got to?"

"Right you," said Red Rubbler, "you're off."

And I was. I don't remember making a raw suggestion to Annie Gay, but I suppose I must have done, for next moment I was sailing through the air of the tap room with Heinie close behind me and Mattie following rapidly. And we hit the cobbles smartly, all three of us, outside the front door of the Pandy, with Ben Block and Dai Parcel arriving shortly afterwards, and Red Rubbler brushing himself down, after he'd tossed out Duck.

"All right, we can take a hint," said Heinie, sitting up, and he grabbed me as I moved. "Where you off to?"

"I'm going over to the Sinkers to look for Bron," I said.

"You're going to Senghenydd, mate," said Mattie.

I but vaguely remember the train ride back to Senghenydd, and I was vaguer still about the walk down to Woodland and Mrs. Best in Number Ten. But she greeted me like a long lost lover, ushering me in with matronly chatter, despite the hour.

"There's been certain inquiries made, mind," said she, lips pursed.

"Inquiries?" It had been a good night, but with sobriety came remorse, mainly alcoholic. I sat down in the best kitchen in Senghenydd and held my head.

"It's the prison, mainly," said Mattie, fearing repercussions. "After two years it's natural — he ain't himself."

"Feminine inquiries," said Mrs. Best roundly. She wasn't going to make it easy.

"Nan O'Hara?" I asked.

"Mrs. O'Hara, the widow of Windsor Place. She had supper prepared for you tonight, especially."

"God," I said, repentant.

"I'd just slipped out for a best bit o' scrag end and bumped right into her. You was due there tea-time. Flowers with beauty, that one, when she's got something under her apron. Wouldn't be in your shoes. Twelve bob a week suit you?"

Mrs. Best was a woman of economy where economics were concerned.

"Yes, ma'am."

"And you've been fighting, too, just look at that eye! Dear me, Toby Davies — stealing, prison, fighting — ye've been on the slide since last I saw ye, so ye have."

"They knocked him about something cruel in prison, though," said Mattie.

"I'll believe ye — thousands wouldn't — see you in the morning — sharp to table, money on the nail, and no camp followers, remember."

I bowed as I went past her in the kitchen, granting her a grudging, reluctant respect. I even tried to kiss her hand, said Heinie, in bed. "Get the pair of us blutty shot, you will, ye drunken bugger."

"Go on, get on wi' you," said Mrs. Best.

Sod women, I thought, and Ma Bron in particular. I'd have been drunk, even if she'd come to meet me. Two years in jug and not a single letter . . .

Side by side with Heinie on the white, starched pillows I listened to his raucous, belly-raking snores, and watched a wild salacious moon lifting her petticoats over the lush Aber Valley: yet even this beauty failed to move me; I *longed* for the Rhondda.

363

As Mattie put it (he was simple-minded but in no way a simple-ton) being here was like worshipping at some lovely foreign shrine.

But for me, Senghenydd had an overriding compensation.

Nan was here, and at last was mine. This is where the value lay — *sod Ma Bron.*

It was gone midnight when I awoke.

Getting out of bed, I looked out on to a sleeping village.

Faintly, I heard the old familiar sounds of the shot-firing from a thousand feet below, as the Universal night shift got going. Standing there, sober, I knew a sudden and intense desire to see Nanwen.

Dressing silently, I tiptoed downstairs to the kitchen and through it out into the silver night.

Woodland was blank and deserted under the baleful glare of the April moon; a stray cat watched me from the shadows as I went down the hill past the glimmering lights of the pit-head; here wagons were shunting to a hiss of escaping steam and commands. On through the Square I went into Windsor Place; slowing to a stroll, head down and up to my elbows in my pockets, I came opposite the door of Nanwen's house.

It seemed another life since Ben had opened that door to me.

I don't know to this day what took me there at that time of night, save an overwhelming necessity to belong. My life, at that moment, seemed to have made a full circle: if Nanwen rejected me now, I decided, I'd turn my face from the valley, walk out and never return.

It was nearly one o'clock in the morning; a neighbour's clock chimed the three-quarter hour. Silently opening the gate, I went up to the door, and quietly knocked.

I waited, tense; a faint light glimmered in the hall, then brighter. Brighter, brighter it grew, then spent itself in exploding brilliance upon the glass of the door.

"Who's there?"

"It's Toby, Nan."

She made a faint, inarticulate sound. I heard the door chain fiercely rattling in her fumbling hands, then she pulled the door open.

She was youth and beauty, vividly aware, stepped out of a grave with a lamp of life; like one of the original virgins, dressed in white, and her hair was tumbling over her shoulders. She was just as I had imagined her in dreams.

"*Toby. . .!* "

Here was nothing of uncertainty, and I despised myself for doubting our ability to love. Her arms were instantly about me, her lips reaching up for mine.

She swiftly drew me within, closed the door and set the lamp down, whispering abstractedly:

"Oh, God, I've waited *all day!* — I thought you weren't coming! I nearly died!" Her eyes searched mine with lovely ever-changing expressions; she was laughing and crying with pent joy; never had she looked so beautiful.

"And Ceinie?" I glanced towards the empty stairs.

"Ceinie isn't here, my love! She's staying in Brecon. See how I planned it?" She held me at arms length. "Oh, come, let me look at you again." She showed mischievous astonishment, a hand clapped to her mouth. "But where's your *hair*?"

We laughed together, softly, so as not to awaken neighbours.

It was a destiny fulfilled; Bethesda, Tonypandy, all the long years of waiting, the doubts, the anxious fears, were magically swept aside. We stood together, enwrapped, and there was no sound but the torment of our breathing.

"Oh, Toby, it has been so long — so *long!*" she gasped against my face.

And, even as we stood there, the siren of the Universal wailed faintly for an accident, the sound eerie, crying on the wind like a witch in tears. Nanwen stiffened in my arms. I could almost feel her reliving the loss of Ben. "Listen, there it is again!" she said.

I did not reply; my arms went about her hard and strong, drawing her against me.

It was enough, at that moment, to be needed.

The siren faltered, and stopped.

"Come," she said, and drew me within the hall.

I hesitated, knowing unaccountably in the gain, a sweet, sad sense of loss.

"Nothing can part us now," Nan whispered.

"*Come. . . ?*"

36

LIE BACK IN the pillows, eyes half closed. It's amazing what comes to pass when you pretend you are sleeping. And there can appear before you, in an actuality removed from dreams, a vision of loveliness in pantomime — the palaver of a woman getting up in the morning.

Here's a curtain-raiser if ever there was one.

"You still sleeping, Toby?"

Bron's face, but an inch from mine.

Breathe on steadily, like something dead: open one eye the moment she's away.

Watch!

One leg out now, careful not to wake you; up she stretches, yawning, in the middle of the floor; like a young faun, bare arms waving (and shivering chilly, April being late this year). Off with her nightie, and she's as bare as an egg. A glance around for confidence, then a bit of a scratch (mainly where the elastic catches) looking ecstatic; a lift to the breasts, to give them a start for the day. Hitch up the bloomers, knees akimbo; on with the stays, pushing up the front like a little French countess. Now, here's a performance (doing up the laces at the back now) — wandering, stooping, like a mare with a load on; down on to a chair to pull on black stockings; carefully examine each shapely leg: upright again and on with three petticoats, the last one flannel; flop out her hair and drape it down her back. Faces in the mirror now, this way and that, looking for blemishes, and over her shoulder she cries:

"Tobe! Now come on — time to get up!"

Breathe on, deep in sleep.

"I won't tell you again, mind!"

I watched her, one eye open, and she saw me in the mirror, swinging round.

"You've been awake all the time! *Diawl!* You rotten thing!"

"And got an eyeful!"

Turning, she dived full length on top of me, fingers scrabbling, searching for tickles while I yelled and shrieked; and I caught her round the waist and rolled her, and her legs went up and so did her petticoats, till we slipped off the bed and bumped on the floor, me on top, entangled in her long, bright hair.

There upside down, I kissed her in a sudden, quiet communion of lovers: no sound but our breathing. And Bron's eyes moved over my face.

"I love you, Tobe."

God, I thought, I'd very nearly believed her. A couple of weeks later, after I'd gone to prison, Sam gave her the eye and she was off again to Porth.

But did I love her? I wondered. Had I ever loved Bron in the face of my worship of Nanwen? Infatuation, perhaps? I didn't really know then; perhaps because I didn't know a lot about love, which takes a lot of schooling.

One thing was sure; it all seemed to have happened fifty years ago.

But this was a very different business — Nanwen getting dressed on the morning after the night before, after I came out of Cardiff gaol.

Here she was, peeping around the bed-rail when I opened that eye.

"Oh, no, Toby — that's *unfair!*" Her eyes admonished; the redness flew to her cheeks.

"Does it matter?" I asked. "Don't you belong to me now?"

"Why, yes, darling, but I'm entitled to privacy."

I closed my eyes at the ceiling. And the room where I first made love to Nanwen, the crucible of former dreams, was painted on my mind.

I saw the little casement window that overlooked the road; the night of a fractured, opal moon, brilliant on his sea-scape of blue-bagged clouds. The little wash-stand in the corner I saw, its marble top, the ingrained figure of the little white mouse: the wardrobe frowning down at people making love, as wardrobes do, being celibate; the Bible on the table by the bed, and *God is Love* on the wall above it.

Strange, I thought, that in this bare place should be consumated a love I had held so long in chains: and such an unerring formality, too, after the fierce midnights I had planned in youth.

And Nanwen? I wondered. What had it meant to her? Hers it appeared, was but a resigned communication, when I wanted so badly that I should bear her gifts of pleasure.

Hours back, she had lain as a woman removed; a fraud of death: a still, vague counterfeit of my manhood's joy: stifling her breath when I forged with her as one: an animal trapped.

Thus had we lain until the night sounds intervened; the barking of a dog, the thumping of the Windsor pit's engines. Compared with the sweet, unchaste wooing of Ma Bron, this was a dowdy immolation.

"Toby . . ." Nanwen stirred faintly on the pillows.

The moonlight, flooding through the casement, seemed to chain her.

"I . . . I'm sorry," she said.

"That's all right, love, we've plenty of time."

She whispered, "It . . . well, I suppose it's because we're not married, isn't it?"

"We've been married since I met you; in the heart."

"Will you never understand?"

"Only that I love you. Don't you love me?"

It sat her up. "Oh, God!" she said miserably. "I knew you'd say that."

Getting out of bed she drew a sheet about her and went to the window, looking like some wandering goddess of a lost mythology, of whom I once had read.

Somewhere down the street, a baby was crying.

"Look, it's all right, Nan — come back and sleep."

"Do you think it could be because of Ceinie?" She turned from the window and faced me.

"What's she to do with it?"

"Well, you know — snatching at this behind her back, as it were."

"We'll ask her tomorrow, and see if she approves."

She didn't reply, but wandered back and sat on the bed. "I can't help it — I know it's ridiculous, but I really can't, Toby. I love you, and I want you, but . . . well, it's the way I've been brought up, I suppose. Do you understand?"

"To some extent. But God is love — it's up there on the wall."

Her eyes, her whole being, beseeched me.

"Yes, I know, but there are certain conditions, Toby, certain rules. . . ."

"You don't have to explain."

She stroked my face. "If we were married, it would be so different." She stared around the room. "This . . . this seems so *wrong* . . . !"

Amazingly, it induced within me a growing humour. I thought of Bron and the first night of love we had spent in the Sinkers. At this stage of the proceedings, she'd done a fan dance with her nightie, and put me into stitches.

Perhaps there is a difference, I thought, between a lover and a wife.

Strangely, I recalled, I'd always looked upon Nan as being my wife . . .

"Nan, it's *all right*, I tell you," and I put my arms about her.

Off shift next Sunday, a May morning, we knew, Nan and I, the advent of summer.

Hand in hand above the scar of the big Universal Pit, there came to us a peace that, I thought, could never be bought by coal.

And it had the promise of a pot-bellied summer, this one, with the first corn thick and green in the valley and the back gardens of the colliers ripe with young plants; everybody digging and hoeing and the spring flowers waving their hands to the warming winds of the mountains.

Time and loss had brought to Nanwen a mature loveliness: as

Bron had turned the heads of Tonypandy, so Nanwen did in Senghy: grief seemed to have transmuted all his haggard ills to her advantage. But her beauty that Sunday morning when we walked together, was not as Bron's: in Bron lay freedom and youth, being a girl. The sway of her dress, the provocative cut of her, shouted of vitality. Nanwen possessed the elegance of a woman.

She was wearing a dark brown dress that day, as if still remembering Ben (while, Bron in or out of mourning, would likely have been in pink). The early May was hot; the old sun glowing his contentment at being over Wales so early. Great cumulus clouds towered vertically above us like smoke from the pillage of distant cities, and I mentioned it.

"You're a poet these days, Toby," Nan said, smiling.

"When I look at you."

"Indeed," said she, "you think as a poet, I notice. Everything you read, you quote. If you'd had a decent education, you'd never have been a collier."

"Make the most of it, girl, that's all I'll ever be."

"Oh, come, you're not yet thirty! — there's always time to improve yourself. Besides, you're very well read — Voltaire, Belloc. . . !" She laughed softly as we sat together on the mountain grass above the village, and kissed my face.

Laughter, I think, is a signpost: Nan's was a smile in sound, Bron's like a mating cry. Sitting there, all the spectres of our past misunderstandings appeared to vanish, yet I knew the chill of a slight reserve; a small chasm existed between us which, somehow, I could never cross. For the past three weeks (I had been lodging with Mattie at Mrs. Best's in Woodland, but visiting Nan almost daily) since we had been together I had but once enjoyed the fiery excitement of a new lover; but I could not help doubting if Nan found much satisfaction in me. Indeed, I wondered if Ben had discovered also that the possessing of Nanwen's body did not ordain the possession of her spirit.

Now she said, with a laugh:

"Of course you could improve yourself if you tried, Toby. Come, you're far too modest. With very little effort you could become a good teacher, for instance."

"Ben didn't make much of an attempt, yet you seemed happy enough with him."

"But Ben was limited, bless him — you have the potential. Why are you so unsure of yourself? Don't you want to get on?" She smiled, her head on one side.

She was wearing the same, broad-brimmed, summer hat she'd worn when I helped her to move from Blaenau, and I thought she looked beautiful. "Besides," she added, flatly. "You are here, and Ben has gone."

I was a little surprised.

"Has he?" I plucked a blade of grass and lay back, eyes closed to the glory of the sky.

She was peremptory. "Of course."

I said, from the grass, "And dead two years, Nan, so only old crows should still be wearing black."

"It isn't black!" she examined her dress with obvious concern.

"It's as near widow's weeds as doesn't matter. Are you still going to Ponty market tomorrow?"

"Aye, if Ceinie doesn't arrive."

"I thought your friend was bringing her back on Tuesday?"

"Could be a day earlier. Her last letter said she was just dying to come home."

Faintly, I wondered what it would be like with Ceinie, now aged thirteen, pottering about us, and said, "Well, buy a new dress when you can — pink, perhaps?"

"Bron used to wear pink, didn't she?"

"Not that I remember."

"I do. I'll buy blue — I'm not in competition."

I smiled admonishment. "Oh, come on, that's not like you — it's just that you can't keep paying bills of mortality. I read that somewhere, too." I gave her a wink.

Her eyes didn't falter on my face. "Like you, perhaps, Toby, I need more time to lay the ghosts."

We lay in silence, still hand in hand.

I have often wondered at the power of humans to be perfectly in love, simultaneously, with two people. Love is a sister to pity: pity could be the basis of my love for Bron, I reasoned, but the love I held for Nan was as commanding now as in its callow youthfulness. And yet, why was it that even these few sacred moments with Nan had been invaded by Bron? — the sound of her instant in the quiet day. And I think I understood better Bron's love of Sam Jones — a transgression of the noblest moments of her love for me.

Bending above Nan, I kissed her lips, her face, her hair. "Do we have to talk about it?" I whispered. "Bron's a life and a thousand miles away."

"Face facts, Toby — it's this life and a few miles away — she's living in Tredegar."

I raised my face from hers. "That's wrong! — she left the south."

"Aye, but now she's back."

"When?"

"About the time you came out of prison."

"You're sure?" I sat up.

"Of course. School teachers get all the news — we're walking newspapers."

"Funny the lads didn't mention it," I said, reflectively.

"Perhaps the lads didn't know."

"They know, all right." I sat up, staring around.

High above us in the cloudless blue a lark was teaching the world to sing. Intent, we listened, and Nan said, watching me:

"Bron's married to Sam, Toby — you must accept it?"

"I've always accepted it."

"Is that completely true?"

I laughed. "Now you're being ridiculous! Come on, don't spoil it! We've got our lives to start anew."

"And preferably back up North?"

"Up North? Why there, for God's sake?"

"Because that's where we *belong* — it's your home as much as mine!"

"You'll always be a Johnny North, won't you?"

"Of course," she said simply, "and so will you."

"I won't, you know — me pa was Tonypandy." We laughed, but the laughter died.

By some strange trick of refracted light, the sky was suddenly overcast, and from its billowing cloud-darkness, immediately overhead, two beams of light began to form, a strange configuration. Brighter, brighter this grew in the noontide glare, then shut off with searchlight rapidity. It was startling in its suddenness; it left us silent.

Nan spoke first, her face against me, but I did not hear her words.

In a gap in the rim of the distant mountain, where, but a moment ago, these twin beams had burned, I saw a sphere of blueness stretching away to infinity, as beyond the daylight stars. And, in an instant, my mind went back to my meeting with Grandpa up in Deiniolen; when he and I, lying in the tram-bucket, slid down the slate Incline into the valley of Llanberis. I knew now, as then, a marvellous affinity with the world through the joy of sight; it transcended all other values with its power. Sight, limited in the dark sequestered places of the mind, could be confined within the walls of coal; shut off in the choked galleries a thousand feet underground; shaded in approaching age, obliterated by death. But here, on this mountain, it was unencompassed, save by the orbit of the meteoric stars.

"You still with me, Toby?"

It was as if, quite suddenly, a chill wind blowing over a blind man's grave, had touched me with an icy finger.

"Darling, you're shivering!" She was troubled.

I got up, brushing myself down. Always, in the face of visual beauty, this terror of blindness engulfed me.

Down in the valley the fields, chequered patterns of green and gold, flashed their sovereign brilliance under the midday sun. Nan said, "Best we start back, anyway, if we're going to get any dinner. I've got Sunday School at three o'clock — feel like coming?"

It was suddenly imperative that I should not be alone. I said:

"Couldn't you give it a miss this Sunday?"

"But the children are expecting me! Tell you what," Nan said, secretly. "You go back to Mrs. Best for dinner, then come up to the house for Sunday tea, is it?" We began the journey back to the village.

"And after?"

Her eyes held a charming, whimsical expression. "Now come, darling — I'm a respectable widow!"

"Isn't it respectable, being in love?"

We walked in silence, contained by thought.

I thought of Bron and her capricious wantonness; it possessed in all its abandonment, the virtue of a perfect gift. Perhaps Nan read my mind.

"We're not living together, Toby, and I'm not Bron, remember."

"There was nothing wrong with Bron!"

I wasn't handling it well, but one thing was sure; I wasn't begging off any woman. Now, approaching the streets, we lowered our voices.

"Oh, dear, do try to understand!" She would have touched me, but people, severe in Sunday clothes, were passing with sidelong glances or short bows of greeting. We stood together, lost, while Senghenydd watched us in a timorous silence.

Nan said, apologetically, "Well, it . . . it's just that you simply can't expect to begin again with me where you left off with her, that's all."

"That wasn't my intention."

"Oh, God . . ." She looked around her as if for escape. "This is all so cold."

"Come away with me, then."

"Where?"

"Anywhere, as long as we're together." I added: "Marry me, then. Now?"

"*Cariad annwyl!* Give me time, Toby. We've been through all this before!"

"*Duw*, missus," I said with a grin, "you don't give much away."

"But my position's different from yours — I've got Ceinie to think of?"

"And I don't count?"

"Of course you do — don't make things difficult, love."

Suddenly, incredibly, she sounded like Bron; I liked her better.

"At this rate of debauchery I'll be as celibate as a monk," I said.

Her eyes, her whole being, begged of me. "Just for a bit longer, darling — wait for me?" Glancing furtively about her, she gripped my hand. "Look, I live in Ben's house, but it isn't mine. The agent only let me stay because I teach at the Board School. The Board of Guardians . . ."

"Do you think the Board of Guardians might let us marry in a couple of months?"

"Now you're being impossible!" She was chin up, angry.

I sighed. "All right. When do we meet again?"

It turned her, instantly warm. "Come to tea, eh? As I said? I'll make a cake after I've had dinner. You always did like a caraway cake."

"Caraway cake?"

"You know — a seedy cake."

I shook my head. "No, not seedy cake." I was thinking of Ma Bron.

"But why not? You used to love them. Can't I do anything to please you?"

I was being churlish and inept; I wanted to put my arms around her, and here I was teetering on the edge of a quarrel.

She said, "Toby, I really must go if I'm to be on time for Sunday School — and I've got loads of books to mark. But promise you'll come for tea?"

"Yes, of course."

I stood properly for her, taking off my cap.

"And if we're in luck, Ceinie might come home — I'll make a fire and we'll have it on trays — just the three of us!"

In the confrontation, I had almost forgotten Ceinie.

I bowed to her, watching as she made her way with a marvellous grace, inclining her head this way and that to neighbours.

Vaguely, I wondered how I'd have handled it with Bron.

375

37

THE ABER VALLEY, about nine miles from Tonypandy as the hawk goes, was as different from it as stout is to cider. The Rhondda towns were black-faced, the terraced houses stained. And even the mountains framing them had to rub coal dust out of their eyes before waking every morning, for coal dust was in the air, the mouth, the throat.

But the Aber Valley was green-gold; the twin pits of Senghenydd and Windsor being but small, mutilated fingers in a fair land of mountains and tiny tenant farms.

Here the little rivers and brooks, sparkling and bright, were filled to the banks with speckled trout. But the sad fish of the Rhondda, fighting their way up to the spawning grounds, were thin, poisoned by old furnace washings; and the great salmon of the Fach and Fawr had long since gasped out their lives on beaches of coal.

In this valley, the Windsor pit, being lower down the mountain, was comparatively free of gas; it spewed its fumes up the subterranean crevices and these filled the higher, bigger Universal chock-a-block with gas. As late as three years back she'd had a gas flow that closed her down for nearly a week. Nine years before that she'd closed down eighty men's lives in one gigantic flash, instantaneously igniting down her miles of galleries.

But colliers never learn, said Mattie — they still poured in from nearby Cardiff and Ponty to work the giant Universal: and managements never bloody learn, neither, said Heinie — least of all coal owners like Lord Merthyr, who owned the gassy bitch: few of the safety precautions recommended by the Mines Commission had been implemented since the 1901 explosion. The profits were good, the seams were full, the shareholders happy, so Lord Merthyr let it lie.

I'd been down the Universal for the two months since coming to Mrs. Best's in Woodland Terrace, Senghenydd: now, on this hot, early July day, I was downing tools off shift with Heinie and Mattie.

The cage of the upcast clanged back, and we filed out, Snookey Boxer leading.

"Where did you spring from?" demanded Mattie. "I thought you was down the Windsor — Christ, we got rough stuff comin' in again."

"Signed me on yesterday," said Snookey. "To hell with the Rhondda, and to the devil with the Windsor pit, says me Effie, ye'll be happier back with the lads. Ay ay, Tobe!" Marriage to Effie had improved Snookey; he was actually coherent.

I gave him a nod.

Mattie said, "He was with Duck down the Scotch when Lark, Duck's mare, was killed. Duck reckoned Snookey did all right — mind, losing Lark has broke up old Duck something cruel — he ain't the same fella."

We tramped on in silence, steaming coal dust; red-lipped, red-eyed, grieving for Lark.

"One day I'm getting out of blutty coal," said Heinie, at my elbow, "before everything's killed. I'm goin' to sit me on a South Sea island beach with six buxom beauties and to hell with you black-faced sambos."

"You be content with Sarah and Dozey, ye maniac," said Mattie.

We shoved and elbowed our way towards the lamp room and the pit wheels of the York Upshaft whirred in sunlight, bringing up the shift: the new shift were waiting at the Lancaster downcast as the cage went back; dour-faced men of wan features, the pale cosmetic of the collier: and they were free of their classical humour, coal's birth-right, for they were going down on shift, not coming up, like us.

"Right, lads, make a start," cried old Dai Parcel, coming on shift.

377

"Dig deep for Baron Senghenydd, my sons — Gwilym, Owen and me'll be with you directly," and he said to me as I came along with Heinie and Mattie, "How's your hair doing, Tobe? That twopenny cut ain't quite the same as lovely, flowin' locks."

"The mice 'ave been at him," commented Gwilym, joining us.

"What stall you lot in, then?" demanded Dai.

"Forty." I looked round the tap; new men were coming in every day.

"We're the same road as you, ye blind old bat," called Heinie, "Bottanic. We see you going past every other shift, but you're too stuck up for a wave."

"Perhaps, but I'll drink with anyone, if they pay."

"You old faggot," cried Mattie. "All three of you — you're supposed to be going on shift — now come on, get going!"

"A pint going down is worth two comin' up," said Dai. "You drinking, my lovelies? And where's little Heinie?"

"He'll buy the second," I said. "They weren't all born in Jerusalem, and I've heard his money rattling."

"Then I'm away to tickle trout — you fancy coming, Mattie?" asked Heinie.

"He fancies Mrs. Best, if I know him," said Dai.

"I do not, it's all platonic," protested Mattie as we handed in our lamps and pushed into the Universal tap room. "Right now I'm shovelling in a ton of compassionate coal for me landlady, then I'm getting my head down."

"Who with?" asked Heinie, and Dai called for the pints.

"With Bestie," said Dai. "I heard all about it. Between now and Easter she's buying him silk pyjamas."

"You're a blutty rotten lot, all of you," said Mattie.

The banter went on as the old shift flooded into the room, and I gave a thought to the day, over two years back, when I had left that tap for Cardiff Assizes; it seemed like another age, but I saw Bron's face in the amber slant of the ale, and closed my eyes, Mattie was still getting some stick; the lads were still pumping me for news of the happy event; sharing lodgings with Mattie in Number Ten Woodland was landing me with responsibility, but I never let on, even though I could see a pretty romance flourishing.

Very billing and cooing, it was between them, bless them, and if ever Bestie broke an egg in the pan, it always landed on me.

"But ye'll have to make your mind up between Mrs. Best and your pigeons, won't you, son?"

Sweet it is, when older people fall in love. And the suitor as usual, was getting the thin edge of it. "Ignoramuses, all of you," said Mattie.

"Mind, he could do worse," said Heinie once. "I'd like to see him settled — before I depart this mortal life."

"Very clever," said Mattie. "Meanwhile, mind your own blutty business. Proper gentlemen wouldn't mention a lady's name, they wouldn't."

"No offence intended."

"None taken," said Mattie. "Now lay off. All right, ain't she, Tobe?"

"One of the best is Mrs. Best," I said.

"So when are you two taking the plunge?" asked Heinie. "It's your souls I'm bothered about — feel responsible, I do."

"Listen to who's talking!" cried Mattie. "And him in the middle of Sarah Bosom and Dozey."

"When's your happy event, Tobe?" asked Owen, and Mattie said:

"He wants to know when you're marryin'. And that Nan O'Hara blooming like a Welsh rose — come on!"

"She'll keep. She's healthy enough."

It was going on a long time: usually, they'd forget your business when once they smelled the ale.

"Time you wed the lady, talking serious," said Heinie.

I didn't reply. You let folks in slow when it comes to deep intentions. It was something I had learned from Grandpa.

The shift swarmed in after us, kicking up the sawdust. Ed Masumbala, the big Texas negro came in; most respected was Ed, living with Beli, his wife, and baby son up in Fifteen Woodland, just above us. Kept to himself, mostly, but every man in the village accepted him. This was the joy of the Welsh valleys. You could be a Chinese compradore or a Sioux Indian as long as you behaved yourself, and Ed and Beli did just that: he worked the next stall to ours down Bottanic; and always read a verse or two of his bible during snap. Now his white teeth appeared magically in his black face as he lowered his glass and grinned at me.

Stange how I knew in that moment a faint affinity with him, for we rarely exchanged more than a glance.

Heinie called, "Six pints, landlord — never let it be said I don't pay me whack with you ungrateful buggers," and the landlord jugged them out while Heinie fished in his pockets.

"*Diawch!*" exclaimed he. "Me wallet's dropped out!"

Hoots and jeers at this, with Mattie shouting, "Here we go — the chosen race is at it again!"

"Damn me," whispered Heinie, searching himself. "I got important things in that wallet . . ."

"You've really lost it?" I asked, beside him.

"Aye," he answered, his little face worried.

"Caught again," cried Mattie, and slapped down the cost, and Dai Parcel cried:

"You're lucky to have the money for pints — poor old beggars like Gwilym, Owen and me are licking halves, eh, mates?"

"God knows why we rioted in the Rhondda," added Owen.

"And God knows why we're down here at all," said Gwilym, his battered old face turned up. "Ought to be pensioned off and living retirement while you young 'uns here buy the drinks. Me chest's bad, ye know," and he coughed, thumping it. "The gas do get me. This blutty pit wants reporting to the Mines Commission."

"So does God," said Dai Parcel, "but he'd still get away with it."

"Can't think what's happened to that wallet," said Heinie, still searching.

"*Ach*, forget it — mention it to the shift foreman and the lads'll keep an eye out — you're not going down again, for God's sake?"

"You can get your legs chopped off too, mind — you don't need a chest full of gas — remember Ben O'Hara?"

The name stilled me. I drained my glass and pushed my way out through the door followed by Heinie and Mattie; the clear July sunlight nearly blinded us; the air of the mountains was like wine after the fug of the Universal bar.

"Ay ay, then — be seeing you," said Heinie.

"Reckon I'll just slip back for another to settle me stomach," said Mattie. "Tell little old Bestie that I won't be long, Tobe?"

"I'll tell her she's got no future with you," I replied. "I'll do more — I'll tell her you're a drunken old bugger."

"I'll 'ave your blutty head off," said Mattie.

"One thing's sure," said Heinie, "I ain't beholden to anybody, and I don't explain to nobody. Being virgo intacta, as the sayin' goes, I just go fishing. The pair I live with 'ave got ears like Navy mops."

"You poor little scratch," I said. "I'm right sorry for you," and was off, giving a wave to Dai Parcel, Gwilym and Owen as they went down on shift.

Leaving Heinie to his poaching and Mattie to his debauchery, I whistled me along in the sunshine up the pitch to Woodland. Just the same as down the Sinkers, the old folks were sitting out of doors in the sun; cranked old grandpas like the one I buried up in Coetmor: wizened old crones, who once were lithe and gay in beauty, greeted me with their lovely gummy smiles. But Jaundice Evans, so named for his pallor, was there, too; off sick from the Universal for backing the milkman's cart over his size thirteens, and I didn't go a lot on Jaundice, he being the local gas-bag. Being human, though, I still commiserated on his toes.

"Well, I never did!" cried a voice from the upstairs window of Number Four, "Just look who's arriving!" and Mrs. Menna Price (the part-time midwife known locally as Mrs. Menna Pause) put her bosom on the window sill and beamed down at me. "What you doing down there, Toby Davies?"

Very romantic by nature, she was the mother of Woodland, and she was good for the place. Brass shining knocker had she, snow-white doorstep. I shouted up to her, "Looking at Jaundy's toes — I've never seen toes done better."

All down the street the colliers, off shift, were going into doors, greeting children, shouting to neighbours: white-aproned wives with anxious faces were awaiting those delayed in the publics.

"And I've never seen Mattie done better — dished up, done

brown and basted — you reckon they're marrying — him and Mrs. Best?"

"You rotten old faggot," I cried up. "There's always someone getting it in the neck!" and out of next door came Gladys Bad Fairy, her neighbour, as thin as a shin-bone, crying:

"Mind, she got him through the stomach, didn't she? I'll give her that — old Bestie do turn up a very fair dinner. I saw her hand him one last Sunday — kangaroos couldn't 'ave jumped it. How does she do for you, Tobe?"

"She slides 'em under the door," I said.

Menna now, "You hungry then, Toby lad?"

"Blutty starved," I said. "I've lost two stone — look at me."

"Then you slip in with me, son, and I'll feed you tripe and onions — ye can have me old man's."

"If I slip up there, missus, I'll want more than tripe and onions," I shouted, and this put them into stitches, of course.

"Mind, I'll tell you one thing interesting . . ." began Menna, and Jaundy Evans interjected with a smirk:

"I thought you was only hungry for that barmaid over in Pandy — I could go for her myself . . ."

I got him by the shirt and his toes left the ground. "Mouth almighty," I whispered, "you get your blutty toes straight!"

"Put Jaundy down," commanded Menna. "He isn't very fit, you know."

Gladys Bad Fairy and others around me now; women smoothing and patting me and Jaundy didn't mean it, did you, Jaundy?

Ten years younger and I'd have had the rest of his bloody toes.

My temper diminished as I went up Woodland, for there was Aunty Mari forking hay over the road, saving an old spragman in Number Twelve the agony of the wheels — concussion, two months back: some folks said he'd never make it. I knocked up my cap to her and went into Number Ten, and there was Mrs. Best as plump and mirthful as ever, bustling about the kitchen, red in the face from the fire, and she looked around for Mattie.

I stood in the doorway and watched her. In her presence, as always, I knew the old nostalgia: she was of my beloved Tonypandy; she had cooked my first meals when coming to the Rhondda; she had sent me washed and clean and fed, with my old clothes brushed and pressed, to Bron.

Now she said, "Where's Mattie?"

"Caught late by the Overman — just coming," I answered, and she stood back, hands on her hips, her face cherubic. "My, ain't you some man, Toby Davies! Bend your head under the door, lovely boy. *Ach*, even under the coal dust you're a fine handsome fella." She linked her hands across her apron and examined me benignly. "If me old man was still livin' I'd turn meself into a widow for ye!"

"If your old man was alive, girl, you'd be lying in the middle. Come on here, you gorgeous old thing, you're handier than Menna," and I tried to kiss her, but she smacked me away, shrieking.

"Where's my dinner, then?"

"Oh, go on with you, you've got to wait for Mattie!" She gasped and fanned herself, one of her flushes. I asked:

"And d'you know where Mattie is? — sinking his wages down the pub!"

"You've no cause to criticise — now then!" She wagged a spoon. "A collier's entitled to a pint off shift, remember."

"A pint? The fella's shifting quarts!"

"A very fine man is that Mattie Kelly, I'll have you know, so let's have no more of it." She hit me sideways. "Anyway, you said he was with the Overman."

"Can't put a foot wrong, can he? But you marry Mattie Kelly, missus, and you'll have to put up with his pigeons — ticky old things." I pinched her under her stays and they heard her halfway up Graig.

Later, I bathed in the tin bath by the fire while she laid the table, and, when Mattie arrived with a bunch of flowers and half a pound of stilton as a bribe, I was poshed up, buttonholed, and away with me down to Windsor Place to Nanwen and Ceinie.

One thing was becoming clear to me: after that first loving welcome on the night I came home, there would always be Ceinie...

But the house was empty when I got there, and a neighbour told me that Nan and Ceinie had taken their dinner to school, so I got

Kilvert's Diaries out of the library and then wandered aimlessly around the town, mingling with the shoppers.

Schoolboys were playing rugby on the Recreation Ground. There was a young prop forward there I'd have given ten years to and ten yards, in splints. I watched them from a distance, listening to their shrill cries. It was a morning of sun and warm winds, and the old Waun Deiliad, where Heinie had gone fishing, was doing its best to paint up the day with its rolling vales and plaintive bleating of sheep. I should really have been in bed, for the shift had been hard, but I didn't feel like bed; I wanted places and people.

On a corner of Commercial Street I bumped into Ginty, of all folks, and his little scrag of a missus, and I don't know who was more surprised.

"Well!" exclaimed he, " 'tis big Toby Davies, the collier chap, I'll be buggered! I was sayin' to my missus here, let's take a train ride to Senghenydd — we've a niece in Brook Street, ye know." Ginty slapped his thigh, delighted, while his wife, as grey as a churchyard ghost, ate him with haggard eyes. "I'm back to the tools, did ye hear? — timberman."

"Aye, Heinie told me. He and Mattie are with me down the Universal."

"We're still living in Tonypandy, of course — I'm down the Ely — not the Bute, mind — I'm too old for the face." He grimaced. "*Ach*, they were good days, indeed, and I miss me customers."

His wife said in her lovely, Connemara brogue, "He's off the groceries, d'ye understand, but still in the trade — even asleep, he's still slicing bacon. 'Pass me the butter, me darlin',' he says, and I hand it over the sheets in the dark. 'I'll see to the York ham now, Pet,' says he, and I give him one of the pillows." She peered at him from a stricken face. "You'll always be in groceries, even in the Upper Palace, won't ye, Ginty?"

The midday shoppers barged between us. Uncertainly, Ginty said:

"Have you had a sight of your Bron since comin' out, Toby?"

"*Heisht*, Ginty," whispered his wife, elbowing.

I shook my head. "Two years now."

"Did ye hear she was back with her husband, then?"

384

"More or less."

"They lived for a bit in Porth; recent, I heard tell they were in Tredegar."

"Sam always got around," I said.

"Holy Mother, she was a rare beauty, that one!"

"You was both a handsome pair, if I might say," said Mrs. Ginty, weakly.

"Talk had it that they were not getting on, though," said her husband. "Not that you'd be interested?"

Ginty was all right, but there was always more tongue-pie in his shop than sides of bacon. His wife said quietly, "Enough now, not our business, is it?"

We moved uncertainly; I didn't want to hear more of it.

"Is it true you're marrying, son?"

"Could be."

"You could do worse, be God. I've seen the O'Hara widow a couple of times, and she's a feast o' the mind — *Arrah!* May I always be young enough to worship at the shrine of a lovely woman."

I did not reply.

"Ginty, we got to go," said his wife, worried at the silence.

An urchin with a lollipop in his gob was staring up into my face and I wished him to the devil, I wished them all to the devil, Ginty especially — single fare.

And there was a strange, new emptiness in me as I wandered up to Bryn-hyfryd where Heinie lodged with Sarah and Dozey, recently removed. And then I recalled that he wasn't in; having gone poaching up the Bryn, so I came back down to the Square, thinking of Bron and where she had got to; wondering, as always, why I had never heard from her. In the crush of the people along High Street I saw a bright head and knew a momentary, ridiculous excitement. Tredegar, did Ginty say? Mattie and Heinie, I reflected, had been forgetful on that particular point, even if it were true.

With an hour or so to spare before going back to Mrs. Best for dinner and a sleep, I left the road and took a track up the hillside, making for Glan Nant, and Heinie. After climbing the mountain for

385

a bit, I sat down where Nan and I used to sit on Sundays, and looked down on to the Universal Pit.

The mist of the fields, shimmering in the midday heat, brought weird shapes to the giant structures of the pit-head; forming, before my shielded eyes, a tormented edifice of trestles and wires crowned by the refracted light of whirring wheels. And the more I stared at the phenomena in the valley, the greater the illusion of instability, so that the towers and smoke-shot chimneys of the Universal, rearing skywards, rocked and swayed, as in a dance of death.

Lying back, I closed my eyes to the red-set brilliance of the sun; feeling against my shoulders the very earth trembling as a leaf wind-trembles, to the shot-firing of the galleries two thousand feet below.

When I looked again the whole imagery of the pit industry made shape; the snaking railway-lines, clanking wagons, shunting locomotives with their belching funnels, all combining into an orchestral roar of metallic hammering.

With such, I thought, men forge the sacrifice for coal; sink their hopes within dark galleries. Eyes are put out here, sleeves tied with string; entombed, men die in fire-damp gas and flood-water. And yet, in the tally of the cost, there lived, within the boundaries of coal's Black Kingdom, a knowledge of achievement that accompanied no other industry.

Below the bright fields of Nature's decoration lay the rich seams of prehistoric forests: here was the stored sunlight of ancient centuries, a source of energy more valuable than gold. We were the first country to mine coal; we were now its biggest producer — seven million tons of it exported from Barry alone this year so far — mainly from the rich seams of the Rhondda, Aberdare and Aber Valleys. And I knew a strange sense of pride that I was having a hand in it.

What lure lies in coal, I wondered, that brings such pride to the heart?

Despite its hazards, the labour, the blood of it, coal fashioned in its stalls a comradeship of men and a kinship with beasts. Down the clanging galleries, under the roof-creaks, there existed a weird, perverted love; it was an affinity of hatred and devotion that

386

erected, beyond the bloody stretchers, a monumental satisfaction that no other trade designed — ship-building, slate, the iron trades, wool — I have talked to men in these; you name it, said Mattie, and the answer was the same — the call was strongest from Old King Coal.

I got to my feet, looking down into the valley, seeing the huddled houses, the strings of coloured washing blowing on the lines. The voices of street-criers drifted up to me — rag-and-bone man, a knife-grinder; cat's-meat man and muffin man, cries of children — all combined to build within me an elation, because I was a part of this industry, and its people. And I think I knew, at that moment, that I could never leave them.

And even as I stood there, I heard, in quick flushes of the wind, the thin, wailing siren — an accident. It commanded me as it commanded every collier in Aber. It was persistent, calling, *calling*.

I ran down into the valley.

There was a lot of men around the Lancaster downcast by the time I got there, but I heard the agent shout:

"Bottanic men — I only want people who know the district."

I yelled from the back, "I'm working Bottanic, mister."

"Face men, mind."

"I'm a face man."

The overman called, "Is that Davies of Woodland?"

"Ay ay."

"Bring him."

I shoved my way to the front. "What's happened?"

"It's a fall down the Lewis Morgan road, and I want six reliefs. When did you come off?"

"Eight o'clock, but I've slept."

"Good man, get your things," so I ran to the lamp room; another five men were crowding into the Lancaster downcast cage when I got back. The York upcast shaft was bringing up the first rescue shift. Hustling into the cage, I asked:

"If it's the Lewis Morgan area, why do you want Bottanic people?"

He was sour-faced and grimy, this agent, having just come up from the fall. "Because there's a fresh air shaft in Ladysmith, in between, and perhaps we can use it."

I looked at the men about me; a couple I knew — the rest I'd never seen before: full shift working, there could be a thousand colliers down the Universal at any one time. Alby Churchill was there (they say he never got over it) who was Dai Parcel's mate, also Taliesin Roberts, whose mother was Irish, and I knew him through Heinie.

The downcast cage was dropping like a bolt; the winder was giving us a hell of a ride. I shouted to Alby, through his snow-white whiskers, "Dai Parcel, Gwilym and Owen, are down the Bottanic, I think — you heard?"

"Ay ay! — day-shift clerks."

"Are they in this?"

"So says the overman — them and three others we're relieving, I suppose."

"With Dai Parcel in this, it'll be a bloody pantomime," said Taliesin, in Welsh, being his father's tongue.

At the bottom of the shaft a horse and dram were awaiting us, and we made good time on a clear run, to back up the first rescue shift. An overman said:

"I checked the fall between Bottanic and Ladysmith — looks like six yards — but it'll take some moving because it's right across the width inside."

"Gas?" I asked, as the horse stopped at the turnout.

"There's always gas."

"Casualties?"

"Four, they tell — it must have caught all Forty Stall."

"Forty Stall?" We were clanking down the road beside him now. "That's mine. I work Forty Stall."

"That's why you're here, butty — must be old Dai Parcel and two of his mates."

"Christ," I whispered. "And the fourth?"

"The fourth we can't trace — he don't belong."

"Could be anyone," said Taliesin.

"A journeyman between here and Ladysmith?" asked Alby, and the overman said:

"Just get 'em out, Winston Churchill, and quick. It don't matter who they are." He made a strange, lamenting sound, as one speaking with his soul.

But Dai Parcel wasn't buried; neither was Gwilym; this was the way of it — rumour. "They'd box you in cedar and brass handles if you went for a slash round the corner down here," said Dai, when we reached the fall.

"Owen's caught it?"

"Owen at least," said Gwilym, near to tears.

"It don't mean he's dead," said Dai shovelling. "It'll take more than a roof fall to kill that old bugger. Are you the relief?"

"Yes," I said, coming up with the others.

"Then get stuck into it — where's the canary?"

"You don't need a canary, mate, you've got your Davy lamp."

"Sod the Davy — I want a canary." He wheezed; a man with Death's trumpet.

"You've got me instead, you miserable thing," I said, "shift over."

"I'll leave you to it, I'm going back to the telephone," said the overman.

Stripped to the belts, we picked and shovelled into the fall; it was a high one, but the stuff was big — easy to get out. Alby worked one side of me, Taliesin on the other, singing in Welsh, a fine, pure tenor. It was dry, thank God, and the floor was firm; Gwilym, supposed to be resting, went away for the horse; backed up by the others — three working, three resting — we were four yards into it after an hour and a half, propping as we went. There was a plug above my head; this is what brings the falls.

"Watch that bugger," said Dai, poking up at the roof.

Plugs were the trouble. Usually of ironstone, they were heavier than the surrounding coal; through endless centuries they'd work themselves through the strata on gravity, cutting vertical shafts. Once in the apex of the roof, it needed but a touch to bring them down.

"Come on, move over," commanded Dai.

"I'm all right," I said, "fetch old Alby out of it."

"Now you'll have to work, me son," said Dai, " 'cause I'm coming in."

Stripped to the waist, sweating and gasping, we hacked and shovelled in silence in the glow of the Davys: listening, at times, for knocking from the entombed, but didn't hear a sound.

"*Diawch*," gasped Dai, "I'm gettin' too old for this bloody caper — does any of you young ones really need me here?"

"Lay out," said a man, pushing Dai aside, "ye can't stand the pace now, can you — ought to be pensioned off."

"He's a poor old sod, really, ain't you, Dai?" said another.

"Trouble was he walked his tabs off for the blutty G.P.O. — as a collier, my flower, I wouldn't pay you in washers."

"Thank God for that," said Dai, easing out on his belly. "The aged and infirm — nobody wants us, do they, Gwilym?"

"His daughter-in-law don't, that's certain," gasped Gwilym, trying to forget about Owen, his butty. "Owen told me this morning — his daughter-in-law got one on him — ain't she, Dai?"

"Now now, you wicked old bugger," said Dai, sitting by the gob and fanning.

"Started wetting the bed, mate — 'aven't you?"

Gwilym looked as if he was crying for Owen, but perhaps it was sweat.

They were a caution, these two old colliers, Gwilym and Owen, Dai's two mates. People used to say that they were the pugilists and Dai the referee.

Head bumps and collier's tattoes had cut their design on Owen, who was knocking sixty-three in private: a good pug in his time, he was walking on his heels now, his speech slurred through head punches, and Gwilym cared for him like a mother.

Years back, according to Dai Parcel, they'd box their way up one valley and down another for a couple of sovereigns, taking on the best — the best trial horses who ever trod canvas. And these days, if you saw them in Town, they might be walking arm in arm, like sisters.

Often in the pits there was talk of queer chaps and fancy trews, but this didn't apply to Gwilym and Owen. A love existed between these two old fighting colliers that was undefiled. They ate together, slept together; in their prime, they'd shared the same woman. Sometimes, just for the fun of it, they hit hell out of each other.

Now Gwilym cried falsetto, baiting Dai Parcel:

"She's chucking you out, ain't she, Dai?"

"Just for bed-wetting?" I asked. "That ain't fair, we're all at it."

"She's never been fair, that daughter-in-law of mine," said Dai, moodily. "Don't know what my lad sees in 'er — she wouldn't give ye a nod if she were on a blutty rocking horse."

"It's a sign of age that, though," said someone. "What's come over you, Dai Parcel — back to your childhood, is it?"

"Probably wet working," interjected Taliesin, grinning into my face in the tunnel. "The sound of water do have a bladder effect, some say — the nurse turned a tap on once, to make me do a sample."

We stopped working, listening for knocking. Silence. Then Dai said, "Mind, I don't make a habit of it — bed-wetting ain't my particular, really — I'm a paid up member of the Miners' Library."

"Perhaps you ain't permanently deformed, though, you poor old soak," said Gwilym. "Me and my mate Owen worked a stall wi' a farrier chap once, I recall . . ." He gasped, and swung, burying his pick in the fall. "Peg Pride was his name, and he claimed wet working. But the Overman cut him fifty per cent because he had a wooden leg."

"That were the Stone Age, though," commented Alby Churchill. "Now we've got the Miners' Federation."

"And me daughter-in-law don't approve of that, neither," called Dai from the gob. "Are you lot through there yet? What's taking you so long?"

"Damned near it," I said, shovelling out, for the fall was getting light. "Watch it, lads, she's going down . . ."

And she went as I said it; the coal cascaded, there was a rush of air. I put an arm through the hole, waving at nothing. Gwilym sat on his hunkers beside me and peered over the wall.

"Oh, Jesus," he whispered, "poor little Owen."

Owen was dead when they brought him out. I crawled in, with Gwilym and Dai Parcel following.

"Just the one, is it?" called the overman.

"No," I shouted back, "there's another in here."

He was lying where the fall had thrown him, heaped in a corner with his chin on his chest. I knew him instantly, and held the lamp higher.

"Jesus," whispered Dai, "it's poor little Heinie."

Instantly, I was beside Heinie, but I knew it was too late; I straightened him out, and pulled the boulders off his legs: not a heart-beat, not a sigh. And there wasn't a mark on him.

"*Duw*, I remember!" whispered Dai, now kneeling beside me. "He came down an hour after we started shift. He came looking for that wallet."

"He came looking for this," I said, and took from Heinie's cold hand the photograph of his wife.

"His missus?" asked Dai.

"Who's this one, then?" asked the overman, crawling in.

He peered from me to Heinie.

I couldn't see him for tears.

My whole being was numb as I walked from the pit, in all the grime of the working, down to Windsor Place, and Nanwen. As in a dream, I remembered that I was due there for tea; now it was nearer eight in the evening.

We had brought Heinie's body out after Owen's, and there was a great hush among the groups of waiting people. Somebody had told Mattie, and he was there, with others of Heinie's mates. He still had the photo of Hannah in his hand when they took him away, but nobody mentioned it.

Although the evening sun was warm, the world was colder than a landlord's heart as I walked down to Windsor Place, and knocked. Nanwen opened it.

"Heinie Goldberg? Oh, Toby, I'm so sorry!"

I nodded.

"Come in, come in," she whispered, looking around at the watching neighbours.

"No, not in this state. I'll take back home first, and wash."

The panic was in her face; she was probably remembering how Ben had died.

"Look, please come in, darling — don't stand there on the doorstep — Ceinie isn't here . . ."

"Best not. I . . . I only wanted to tell you . . ."

In the silence of lost words, she said, desperately, "Oh, Toby, please — let's get away from this dreadful place. . . !"

38

THE SUMMER OF warm, pattering rain shone through that July. August came, the brown-haired matron of sprinkled gold. With the Strike behind them, the people of the Rhondda, their larders no longer empty, began to lay in stores of wood and concessionary coal for the old hag Winter, for the valleys — Fach, Fawr, and Aber were just about the coldest place on earth.

Come late September, with the trees beginning to creak rheumatic, I was kiss-courting Nan O'Hara strong, but not averse to a wilder romance on the side (wives and lovers being happiest apart). Annie Gay, once of The Golden Age, now serving in the Pandy Inn since Bron departed there, had pretty legs, I discovered, mainly above the knee. After a pint or two in the Pandy tap (with Red Rubbler safe on shift and Nan reluctant) they came prettier every minute.

Sometimes, when I was over in the old beloved haunts, I'd wander around the doors of the Sinkers, trying for a peep into Number Six. There was a distinct danger in doing this, of course: being captured by either Primrose or Rachel, who seemed always on the prowl, meant spending the evening listening to the moanings of Moses and Bill about trying to get a living out of the Bute, down the Ely; a frugal supper, and the kids crawling all over you.

There were a lot of people on the street, but I didn't see anyone I knew as I wandered aimlessly along Court. I could have called in to see old Richard Jones and his missus and scrounged a cup of tea — there were dozens of families who would have welcomed me — but I wanted to be alone. Passing the neat little doors, the whitened steps, I stole glances at the rooms within. Streets like these — Thomas Street, Charles, Jones, Maddox and Railway Terrace — were the beating heart of Tonypandy, yet they clustered about me now as strangers: I had never really known them. Now they seemed to reach out welcoming arms: sunshine gleaming on brass, the samplers on the walls, the china dogs and little Horns of Plenty; some front doors were open and I knocked up my cap to women sweeping out: children, huddled together on the pavements or swinging on front garden gates, regarded me with toffee-stuck mouths and curious stares; cats arched their backs on pillars, expecting attention, dogs sniffed at my heels. It was the very normality that riveted me; in my race for love and reading, the pull of Union matters (the call of the ale at the Pandy and elsewhere) I had lost sight, I reflected, of the town's *respectability* — the every-day lives of the everyday people. It came as a shock to me that, within the rank on rank of terraced streets lived an army of ordinary folk who didn't agitate for reform, who did not riot, who went to church or chapel on Sundays; there were countless women who were home-makers and men who did not drink. It was a different Tonypandy to the one I had accepted as the norm.

Possibly, it was sheer habit that took me back to the Square. And then I recalled Heinie saying how he used to wander around the streets of a Sunday evening, listening outside the chapels and churches to the services in English and Welsh. Great choirs were here, as he said: the soaring tenors and mud-caked basses, their tonsils liquid with Allsops, all joining in massive shouts of praise. Sometimes Heinie used to sing at the face, I remembered — aye, Jew-boy, he used to say, but a Welsh Jew-boy, with songs in my belly.

Especially, he used to love the breathy, adenoidal singing of the children.

Where is he now, I wondered — he who faced the might of the great Shoni Engineer?

On this occasion, to my joy and astonishment, Number Six, the Sinkers, where I had lived with Bron, was actually empty.

The door, ajar to the next tenants about to move in, opened to my touch.

The room, by some strange trick of imagination, though bare of furniture, appeared exactly as we had left it. I saw the table and chairs, the bright grate and its red-toothed fire: the bed with the knitted counterpane, the bosh in the corner. And there even pervaded the smell of Bron's cooking; the stews, fried bread, the flapjacks and bakestones. Standing there in the middle of it all the memory of her filled me with increasing intensity, so that, when I closed my eyes, I even heard her voice. Here was where she hung her clothes; here she put her shoes — two pairs (one patent leather) and her high-buttoned boots — very, very particular about her shoes was Bron. Here, on the line above the grate, hung the long, black stockings. The place breathed of her, coming to life, by some strange phenomenon, with astonishing clarity so that, had she appeared in the doorway at that moment in time, I would merely have accepted her as part of the day. I wandered to the mantel, touching its iron coldness; here it was, in jam jars, that she kept her flowers: flowers to Bron were as books to me; she could not live without them.

"Bron," I said, unaccountably.

The very sound I had made accentuated my need of her. Turning in the empty room, I called again:

"*Bron!*"

The room echoed its coldness; the open door creaked in the wind. I regretted, bitterly, that I was always promising to oil it, but never did . . .

After a bit I thought it was bloody silly to be in there looking for things that were passed: peering carefully for a sight of the Odds's and Culpeppers, I went out into the summer sunshine.

Heinie, without a doubt, would have approved of Ceinwen's voice, especially when she sang in Welsh.

Sunlight streamed into the little front room in Windsor Place, Senghenydd, when first I heard her sing:

> *'Nant y mynydd groyw loyw*
> *Yn ymdroelli tua'r pant*
> *Rhwng y brwyn yn sisial ganu*
> *O na bawn i fel y nant . . .'*

Her eyes, while she sang to Nan's playing, never moved from my face.

"There now, what do you think of that, Uncle Toby?" Nanwen closed the piano — another of her accomplishments, and I didn't know the difference between Beethoven and Handel. "Aunty Etta will be here any minute," she added.

"Etta McCarthy?" I asked.

"Aye, she's taking Ceinie up to the cemetery. She visits one Sunday in the month — fond of Aunty Etta, aren't you, darling?" she said to Ceinie.

No reply. Only Ceinwen's eyes, a copy of Nan's, moving like lights in her pale, oval face.

"Taking flowers to your dad's grave?" I asked.

No answer; Nan interjected:

"Ben's buried in the next grave to one of Etta's — she lost her first, you know — a girl. She and Dano were married in Senghenydd then moved to Pandy."

"And had six lads afterwards — that was bitter."

"It's life," said she, and sprang up from the piano as Mrs. McCarthy knocked.

The young and the old, I thought, bearing flowers; in their black dresses, black bonnets and boots, it was a rendezvous with death.

Now they stood hand in hand, Etta and Ceinwen, two black crows, in search of buried love.

I often wondered if Mrs. McCarthy approved of me: she was a deeply religious woman in her rough, Irish way: Dano and his six sons had pestered her in the breast and womb; males, to Etta, were like life's necessities — there to be tolerated.

" 'Afternoon, Mr. Davies," she said, looking past me.

I bowed to her. It was reasonable; I wasn't an angel, and not a lot missed Etta McCarthy.

Tall, angular was she; waisted and bustled, like a spectre from an Irish famine. Nan said, dying to please:

"You've heard about us marrying at the end of the year, Etta?"

"Not official, if ye get me, but rumour has it. And not down here, either, they say?"

I'd rarely heard Etta speak so much.

"Well, Toby wants to stay down here, but I'm longing to go north."

"Ye could do worse in the south, mind — it's been my hearth and home these years."

"And mine, in many ways," I added.

"So I know," said Etta, archly, and I knew she was referring to my life with Bron. "*Ach*, what does it matter, eh? North or South, the young should be together. Ye can't grieve a life-time, Mrs. O'Hara, and ye've a fine set-up fella here, so ye have, though a bit of Church or Chapel might improve him."

I gave her a grin.

The sun was striking shafts of gold into the room; dust-motes danced within a holy silence. Nan said, with an effort, "Ah well, away with you! Will you be back for tea?"

"Wonderful words," cried Etta, leading Ceinwen out. "Time was, at her age, I used to go home to see if there was any tea. But don't ye worry about us, missus, we'll be having tea — and likely supper, too, with Shaun."

Hand in hand (to give something to the neighbours) Nan and I watched them walk to the end of the road; curtains were fluttering around captive aspidistras as we closed the front door.

"Nan," I said, and took her into my arms.

The old, stifling need of her swept over me.

"Oh, not now!" She pushed me away.

"Come on, girl — they won't be back till dark!"

I cajoled her, whispering things into her ear enough to drive a woman demented.

"*Toby!*" She was outraged.

"I love you," I said. "Why not?"

"Darling, it's Sunday." She hauled out her new dress to change the subject. "You like it?"

398

"Great. I like the colour."

"Blue, you see — it'll help you to know your women apart." She laughed impishly. "Define them, might be better?"

I gave her a sigh.

"Anyway, blue suits me," she added.

"Anything suits you. Did you get it in Ponty market?"

"And cheap — but I usually make my own." She put the dress away. "Remember I used to sew in Caerberllan, when Grandad was alive?"

She settled in a chair on the other side of the fire; it was cold in the room, despite the sunny day; as if a chill wind was already putting his fingers on the soul of the town.

Every day, in one way or another, Senghenydd took its toll; a death here, a maiming there. Only the night before last the Universal siren had gone for a fall — a man up in Parc Terrace — a father of three: his back was broken when they got him out. Ironically, for all the heart-ache the old Rhondda Ely had caused us, she was comparatively free of accidents; but Nan had lost Ben and I'd lost Heinie in Senghenydd.

I began to wonder at the wisdom of making a run for it, before the Universal got me.

Nan said, stitching at her sampler, "Face it, darling — it isn't as if there's much to keep you here now — Heinie's gone, Mattie's got Mrs. Best, and all your other friends are married." She raised her face to mine. "You've worked with slate before — wouldn't they take you on as a rockman?"

"The slate trade's dead, Nan."

"How many times have I heard that!"

"But it is now. Fourteen hundred people left Bethesda after the Big Strike, and over three hundred cottages were left empty."

"Where did you hear that?"

"Through the Union pamphlets — Penrhyn killed the industry."

"Really? I thought the quarrymen had a hand in it."

It surprised me, and she knew it. I said, "Ben wouldn't have been happy to hear that. He fought against the injustice of Penrhyn."

She looked about her casually. I said, in the silence, "Anyway,

399

whoever was to blame, there's an old, old adage — never go back."

Nanwen was engaged in thought; I knew the signs — a silent contemplation; a communion that forbade entry.

Now she smiled at me over her needle, and rising, made the tea; there was suddenly a sweet sense of home and belonging; the kettle sang on the hob, the teapot was under its cosy; firelight played on the cups.

"You realise, of course, that we've got Ceinie to consider?"

"Later, Nan . . ."

"I mean, well . . . she . . . she doesn't belong here, does she? These aren't her people."

"Southerners? Down here, you mean?" I lit my pipe, watching her through the flame. "All Welsh, aren't they? — but we've been through all this before."

She emptied her hands. "You just don't try to understand, do you?"

I answered drearily, "Now we're getting back to Ben and his theories about nationalism. The older I get the more I agree with him."

"But it isn't our *home* here. I'll still be a Johnny North if I lived here a life-time." She stitched vigorously at a sampler. I replied:

"That's because you are making differences where none exist. You can be a Chinese Turk in this place for all the locals care."

"But half of them don't even speak Welsh!"

"Oh, God! — is that important?"

She sought another tack.

"You don't care about Ceinie, do you?"

"That's childish, Nan — of course I care."

"She'd get a better education back up north, and you know it."

"All the scholars aren't up north."

She was tight-lipped, almost peevish.

"If . . . if we returned to Bethesda, I might even get her into Llandegai."

"Penrhyn's Girls' School? You'd even change her religion?"

"That's an old, old story!"

"And to think you invited me to Congregational Sunday School!"

Her face went up. "Listen, I'm only trying to do what's best for

400

my child — God knows it's hard enough, what with one thing and another." She stared about her. "I hate this black-faced place — I hated the valleys from the moment I arrived here. It's . . . it's where I lost Ben . . ." She got up from the fire and wandered about. "Slate was bad enough up north, but this place. . . ! Rows and rows of terraces, every one waiting for the next roof fall or explosion."

"Slate wasn't much better — Bethesda was a slaughter-house."

"Perhaps, but it was clean. I've . . . lost one man to the pits and I'm not losing another. If you love me, we'll marry up north."

I sighed. There wasn't much point in arguing about it. For my part, now I had lost Heinie, there was a vacuum that nothing down here could fill. Nan was speaking again, but I wasn't very attentive. She said, "Darling, I'm talking to you."

"Sorry."

"Look, I've already asked for a week off school — starting the middle of next month — October the twelfth, actually . . ."

"What for?"

"To go up north and look around — visit all the old places, the old haunts. There's empty cottages for the asking, you say?"

"A week off? I'd get the push."

"And suppose you did? I'm sure you'd get another job up there."

She was excited, wholly expectant; I hesitated.

"What about Ceinie?"

"Oh, she'd come, too." She took my hands. "Look, I know you'd love it again, once you were there — we could even stay at Caerberllan — I bet we'd find a host of old friends."

"It'd cost money."

"I've got the money." She yearned at the ceiling. "Oh, God — I'd give so much just to see the sea again — somewhere clean, away from this land-locked place."

I shrugged. "All right, if you're so set on it."

"And then. . .?" Her expression teased.

"Then what?"

"A December bride?" She added, hastily, "I mean, if we could find a place to live, and you got a job . . ."

Heinie used to say that women had only got one brain between the lot of them, but I was rapidly finding that Heinie was wrong

She was better than Bron for dangling a man, this one.

In the tiny kitchen, pervaded with memories of Ben (though she had at last put away his slippers and pipe), we were washing up when I turned Nan into my arms.

Time had done much to dispel her grief, yet its mark had touched her features with a new, enticing beauty. What is there in grief that beautifies? I wonder. Still as a cat, her hands paused in the bosh; she was looking through the window at the world, and I watched.

Her brow was high and pale, the shadows deep around her eyes, which were large and bright in the high-boned dark texture of her face. And her hair, once so black, was painting itself silver at the temples, the hallmark of widowhood.

The loss of Ben had brought her to a new and delightful fragility: it seemed impossible that she was mine. And there came to me then all the love I had borne her through the years: her eyes grew wide with surprise when I kissed her.

Perhaps, I thought, this was the end of the coldness: we fought in a small hunger of kisses that momentarily obliterated the pair of us. Moments only, those kisses, till I felt the touch of a warning finger, and turned.

Ceinie was standing in the kitchen doorway, watching.

So still she stood that I wondered if she was alive; in a frigid indifference, she watched, motionless. Nan was instantly aware, patting her hair, smoothing her dress. Slowly, I moved away.

"Why *cariad*, you're back early," said Nan.

Ceinwen raised her hands and clapped them to her face. Crying tunelessly, she turned and raced upstairs. A door slammed.

"Oh, God," whispered Nan in panic, and followed her.

With my back to the front door, I pulled up my coat collar against the wind and looked at the pale stars. Faintly, from the bedroom window above me, I could hear Ceinie crying, and Nan's consoling replies.

High in the sky a glow was burning: it wasn't far enough away for Pontypridd or Aberdare, I reflected, so like as not, it was my old, beloved Rhondda.

I watched it for a bit, listening to Ceinie crying, then, hands deep in my pockets, I strode through the gate and along the empty street.

The Universal was simmering like a witch's cauldron as I walked aimlessly up to Woodland. Despite the knowledge that Nan was soon to be my wife, I knew an emptiness that nothing could fill.

39

A VERY IMPORTANT day it was, come early October, when Tonypandy played Pontypridd in the Challenge Cup.

People were up and doing at dawn, children yanked out of bed, faces skinned with the rag for the sixpenny newspaper round; grandmas and grandpas were allowed to sleep on, to be out of the way while doorsteps were scrubbed and brass thresholds polished. Best suits were brought out of moth balls, best shirts ironed for creases; boots polished, bowlers brushed, and every man in the valleys shaving extra close; tea caddies were peeped into for savings, wives actually kissed.

Those off duty were thankful, those on duty heartbroken, and the agent down the Universal had a heart attack: half the colliers of the Aber Valley were sick, lame or halt.

The valleys were like a set of fighting bulls every time there was a game in the championship; it only needed a cock-snoot from a Pontypridd fly half to send a Tonypandy Welshman raving mad; rival wives turned up their noses at each other in the market; rival urchins fought in the streets. So very hostile looked Mattie that cold, crisp Saturday when Ponty played Pandy; his stock arched proudly, his wing collar up to his ears; whiskers waxed and his sideburns brilliantined. And Mrs. Best, stayed and bulging in her new astrakan, was beaming, expectant.

"Christ, mate," I whispered to Mattie, "you're not taking Bestie."

"Ay ay — dearly beloved, and all that. Getting married, remember?" said he.

"So am I, come December, but I'm not going berserk. This is rugby, mate — you can't bring blutty women."

And Mrs. Best cried, "And he anna leavin' me behind, neither — with my old man the best prop forward in the business?"

"He never was!" Confounded, I stared with a new and vital respect.

"Up in Lancashire, mate. Compared with the North, this lot don't know rugby from postman's knock."

So I danced her in a circle and her hat fell off and she cursed flashes as Mattie and I high-stepped her in the middle of us down Woodland, with all the neighbours cheering. Snookey Boxer had arrived with Dai Parcel and Gwilym and a crate of Old and Mild, Ed Masumbala and his Beli were dressed posh for the charabanc; even Jaundy Evans's toes were better for the rugby excursion to see Ponty play Pandy.

Dear me, how I remember the days when I first came to the Rhondda! — courting Bron spare time and getting fit for it in shorts and jersey on a bitter winter's day, sleet sweeping over the ground and the wind with knives in him.

What woman can understand the joy of it? The gasps and heaves of sweating bodies in the scrum; and the *chang chang chang* of a rugby ball on grass? We used to hit hell out of each other in the ruck on the blind side of the ref; elbows coming up, fists driving in. And I used to love the talk about the big games at Arms Park; the inquests, the pints, the bloody noses and the thick ears. And they can spout all they like about their pansy kick and rush. Give me an up and under and trying to make a mark with a couple of tons of rugby flesh roaring out of the sun; or some bastard in the boiler house handing you a thumping.

Ay ay — Heinie and me used to love the Challenge Cup.

These days, knocking thirty, I used to watch the kids at it down at the Rec, but it wasn't the same as the old boots and pints: or a charabanc bumping along the valley roads, a little barrel of ale, rugby fanatics, and bawdy rugby songs.

Tonypandy, host to the Pontypridd fifteen, was packed to the walls that sunlit morning before the big match. Everybody sporting favours, everybody talking thirteen to the dozen, with the publics open and drinking on the pavements. Down at the station the excursions were streaming in, broughams and traps swaying in from the mountains, and black streams of colliers already thronging into the Mid-Rhondda Athletic.

Mattie handed out Mrs. Best when our charabanc arrived on the Square by the fountain, and damn me, there outside the Pandy Inn, where Bron used to serve, were a dozen or so of my old mates from down the Ely. The commotion that went up then nearly lifted the slates.

"Ay ay, Tobe!"

"What the hell you doing here? Aren't you Aber these days?"

"Pandy now," I shouted. "Come to see Ponty crucified."

The charabanc contingent piled in and Annie Gay was going demented with her jugs; Scotch farriers and ostlers off midday shift clumped up in their coal-dust; top workers from Clydach and engine-men from the Navals. Dano and his five sons were there (Etta kept Shaun at home, still in disgrace) Ed Masumbala the black man, also Albert Arse, and I was just getting my teeth into a quart when Ben Block came in with Bill Odd and Moses, also Red Rubbler, eyeing me for good behaviour with Annie. It was like the old days, except that I hadn't got Heinie and Bron, with people bawling unanswered questions and backs being thumped in joyous greeting. And yet, withal, there was growing within me a nagging wish for a solitary walk, somewhere away from all these happy, noisy people: it was singular and unaccountable, in the midst of such companionship.

It was as if some distant voice was calling me.

"Hell, Tobe — where are you off to?"

Annie Gay, vivacious and dark, flashed me a petticoat look from the bar.

"I'll be back," I said.

"You'd best not," said Red Rubbler, barring the way as I shouldered to the door, and I shoved him aside.

"Go and fly your kite, son — this time I'm sober."

"*Toby*, where're ye off?"

406

It was Mattie in the middle of them, slopping his pint.

"It's a call of nature," I said, and went.

It was a call of nature right enough: a baying of the moon, as the wild moose hears, in rut.

I never explained it, but I went commanded.

Halfway along Dunraven, I met her, and wasn't the least surprised. *Bron!*

"Good God!" said she, flushed, "if it ain't old six foot three!" She had a couple of laughing buck navvies on her arms, both two sheets in the wind, and I don't know who was more astonished of the four of us. She waved them off, gently pushing them away.

"*Why, Tobe!* Would you believe it!" Head on one side, she eyed me like Delilah before the roof came down. "My! Ain't you growed!"

"That's what you always say!"

The people barged us, knocking us together, but she stood back again in mock awe. "Can you get under a door, mate? What's she feedin' you on? And d' you know somethin? Your hair's gone lighter'n the old days."

Aye, I thought, perhaps my heart was lighter then.

But now I looked at her, smiling.

Life might have short-counted me on times, but never on beautiful women; passing wives perked up their noses, hurrying their chaps along. Bron had a big black straw hat on with an apple-pie affair and grapes on top, tied under her chin with black crepe, like you see in the London magazines: her blouse was snow-white, wrinkled in agony over the fine stretch of her breasts, the buttons gleaming pridefully. She looked taller, somehow, and willowy, sure in her beauty, her eyes switching with the old sly wickedness. I'd possessed other women since I left her in the Sinkers, but no woman I'd come across made so scarlet in my being.

"You finished?" Eyes slanting at me now, an admonishing regard.

"Just about," I said.

"Can I put me clothes back on?"

I gave her a grin.

It was the way of her that got you, I thought; you never knew the pain of her: Sam Jones was a sod; he'd hooked her young and played her like a fish. But, on that sunny October day, she looked cast in a mould for nobody but me.

Seeing my black arm-band, she said, "Sorry in my heart, I am, about your Heinie."

I nodded.

"Made me cry, it did — *nice* little fella." She sighed. "All the good people die — that's why I'm flourishin'."

"You're all right, mun."

She went on tiptoe, vividly alive with pleasure. "You always used to say that, didn't ye? Just all right, am I? Hey — what's this about old Mattie and Mrs. Best!"

"Aye, it's true — next month some time, I believe."

"Everyone's splicing — it's a disease — how about you?"

I shuffled my boots at her, grinning sheepish. "Wedding come December, God willing."

"Gawd help you, son! — being wed down here?"

"No — up north — Bethesda, more than likely." I added, into her waiting, expectant face, "We're . . . Nan and me, I mean — we're going up there Wednesday week — to have a look around."

The people pushed us about on the pavement; we stood unsurely, eyes rising and lowering. Bron said, "I'm glad, Tobe — she's right for you, really speakin', that Nanwen . . ."

"O, aye," I said with sureness.

"I mean, ye'll always be, well . . . sort of safe, if you know what I mean."

She smiled, but not with her eyes.

The people hit between us again, glum-faced with us, because we'd blocked the pavement, and Bron said, brightly, "My old beggar's off again, you know."

"Sam?"

"Who else? We was settled fine in Tredegar — he'd lifted most of the young skirt up there, I thought — now to settle down to an ever-loving family — kids?" Her eyes searched my face. "I'm very fond of children you know. Now I'm up there and he's down here."

"In Tonypandy, you mean? He's here?"

"No Senghenydd — he was at the Windsor pit first, but he's

transferring to the Universal, they say, I wonder you ain't seen him."

"Not a sign."

She raised her face and smiled. "He's a bugger, ain't he? They tell me he's living there with Rosie Arse-Jenkins now. Always fancied her, he did. But if it weren't little Rosie it'd be someone else. What's wrong with him, Tobe?"

"He's a polygamist."

"Christ, I wouldn't call a dog that — what's it mean?"

"Half a dozen women still wouldn't be enough."

She stroked me warmly with her mind, saying, "My, you're wonderful with words, ain't you? I just never met a fella in all my life like you for words — where d'you get them all from?"

"Books."

"What you reading now, then?" She was trifling with me.

"Now? — *The Ancient Mariner* — Taylor Coleridge."

"A love story is it?"

"No."

My mind was fumbling at her, becoming merged into her being, while she, self-possessed, regarded me with a sort of warm, maternal pride. Flicking dust off me, she said:

"I had a letter from my little Bibbs-Two yesterday."

Passing men were staring into her face. She continued, "She's ten now — don't time fly? She . . . she writes a better letter'n me."

"Is she still with the aunt?"

"Ay ay — Tyddyn Llewelyn up in Waen Wen — you remember?" She paused, thinking. "That Nanwen's girl's about three years older, ain't she?" She smiled brilliantly. "You . . . you'll have a daughter ready made, so to speak."

I thought it was ridiculous that we should be standing here talking in the midst of people. A sudden, urgent necessity gripped me — that I should seize her hand and run with her away from all the complications of new and lost loves. She shrugged.

"Ah, well, I suppose I'd best go and look for the bugger — more'n likely he's come over for the rugby, see? But talk has it that he's got little Rosie in Hendre Road. Where's that in Senghy?"

"Opposite end to Woodland, where I lodge."

"I'm sorry for Rosie, really, 'cause she's only a kid. But if I catch her with him she'll bloody evaporate."

I made a mental note to have a word with Annie and Albert, Rosie's parents, over in the Sinkers.

We were walking back slowly along Dunraven now. Sarah Bosom and Dozey Dinah went past on the other side of the road, still in weeds for Heinie. Earlier, while talking, I'd seen the Livingstones — Guto carrying a travel poster about Bavaria. Mrs. Ledoux was stroking a little marmalade cat at the end of Gilfach Road: the Salvation Army band was playing *Nearer My God to Thee*.

Bron stopped us along De Winton. "Where you bound for now then, you old soak?"

"The Pandy — fancy a port wine?"

She said, "What I got to tell you, Tobe, can't be said in a pub . . ." She added, "I . . . I got somethin' to show you, really speaking . . ."

I retorted, coldly:

"You could have said a lot to me once, mun, but you didn't even try."

She lowered her face. "It . . . it were for the best."

"It wasn't, and you know it. Two years I waited." I glared at her, steering her across the road, and we nearly got run over.

"Aye — two years!" I said. "And you didn't care if I lived or died."

Her eyes moved over mine, in frowns; it was a pity for I preferred her smiling. She said, "Tobe, it were best, truly — see it my way? She's good for you that Nanwen — she's educated — a teacher, ain't she? Gawd, if I'd got what she's got we might 'ave made a go of it."

I said, bitterly, "While I was in gaol you never even sent a word with Heinie or Mattie."

"And you were perfect, weren't ye?" she returned. "When are ye going to walk on water? That Nanwen was a bother to us, you know."

We looked at each other, then smiled. Chuckling together, first, then laughing aloud so that people looked, apprehensive.

I said, "What did ye want to show me just now, then?"

She was pulling on her gloves. "Don't matter now, do it?"

"Aw, come on, don't start that!"

She looked at me. "No — another time, perhaps."

"It can't be that important."

"I got to go," she said.

I wanted her to stay. She was fussing with her fingers. "Lawful wedded husband, and all that. And if he's got Rosie Arse with him, rugby tackles won't come into it. Goodbye, Uncle Tobe."

A flower-seller was sitting on the corner of Post Office Row so I bought her a bunch of Christmas roses: she swallowed hard and I thought she was going to cry.

Duck and Dai Parcel arrived, halloing, from the crowd then, slapping our backs and waltzing Bron in circles, and her hat fell off and she shrieked, and passing colliers fought for her gloves, sparring up in fun.

"And what might you be up to, woman?" demanded Duck. "Don't you know this man's spoken for?"

"She's lost her chance," I said.

And Dai smiled into Bron's face, saying, "*Duw*, you're a rare beauty indeed, missus. Never have I seen the like, and I've courted some. I'd give a finger from each hand for a minute of joy in ye."

"She's a rose of a woman," said Duck. Bron glanced nervously about her. I thought, *please stay. . . ?*

"I got to go," she said, and I took off my cap to her. We all looked awkward at each other, as people do before parting.

"Don't . . . don't let 'em get you down," I said.

There grew about her a new and spirited coquettishness. "Don't you worry, mun, they're very small pop."

"Goodbye."

"Remember me, Tobe?" Head on one side, she regarded me.

I nodded.

The three of us stood watching her as she went along De Winton. The flower-seller said to me, in Welsh:

"Where did you grow her, mister? I've got nothing like it in this old basket."

40

SOME SAY, WHO were awake early on Tuesday the thirteenth of October in the Aber Valley, that an angel appeared in the sky above the Bryn: the same chap, said Tommy Arse, that he saw later standing in the sky above Mons, when he was fighting for the King of England, and not King Coal. But little exceptional happened so far as I was concerned, for my thoughts were full of what was happening next day — Nan, Ceinie and I catching the night train up north to Bethesda to scout around for a job and a cottage to go with it.

"We'll not miss ye," said Mattie. "Be nice to 'ave a bit of peace, won't it, Bestie?"

"Aye, but he'll be back, mark me," she replied, and looked up and down Woodland in her curlers. "Once the South always the South they say. Mind, I'll be at the station tomorrow to see you off — very romantic it is. I'll do meself up posh for you."

She needn't have bothered.

The whistle went for the change of shift.

Mattie drained his cup. "Get your skates on," said he.

We had face colliers like Mattie and me, we had top men; spragmen and banksmen — hauliers, ostlers, farriers and timbermen — and a score of others — all getting through their breakfasts, leaving their wives with kisses or scowls (as they went upstairs to make the beds) — or chucking them under the chin, as I did Mrs.

Best, but Mattie, strangely, kissed her goodbye; the first time he'd done it.

"Oh, go on with you," said she, very pretty with her, despite her curlers.

"Goodbye, Petal," said Mattie.

And we all went to the pit in a thundering of boots along Woodland.

The day shift was going down, the night shift was coming up. Nine hundred and thirty-five men were down the Universal pit at ten-past-eight that morning.

Some of my mates from down the Ely were there, too — people like Mattie, of course, old Dai Parcel and Gwilym who worked with the ghost of Owen. Snookey Boxer was in the next stall to Forty, as was big Ed Masumbala, the negro who lived a few doors up from me in Woodland. Then there were a couple of butties I'd made — Bert Jebb, Welsh speaking, who was married with six kids in Number Eight, Cenydd Terrace, and Softy Jones who was lodging up in Brook Street, near the school where he was once a master, teaching English: very educated was Softy, though he could get out coal as good as the rest of them; in the event he'd have done better, I reckon, to stick to teaching English.

"Plus another Jones you'll be interested in," mentioned Mattie as we all clanked along for the morning shift, "and this one ain't a softy."

I turned to him; he had adopted an air of studious indifference.

"Who?" I asked, but I reckon I knew before I asked.

"Sam Jones," said Mattie, "but don't look now."

I wasn't too surprised. Bron had told me at the rugby outing that Sam was being transferred from the Windsor to the Universal: meeting him on or off a shift was only a question of time.

I wiped my mouth with the back of my hand, and Mattie said, elbowing me, "Now, come on, Tobe, it ain't the end of the world."

I was glaring at Sam on the other side of the road; he hadn't yet seen me, and Mattie added, "And don't start that, neither — there's room down the Universal for the pair of you."

I doubted it.

And hand in hand with Sam was Rosie Arse-Jenkins — come to see him off, apparently, and she's a caution, said Mattie, marching with the colliers.

Bright and early was she, up with the colliers — off scrubbing at an agent's house farther down the valley, I learned later, and her hair was tossing in the wind and her eyes were alive: waist for a dog-collar, hips on the sway, and her young breasts cavorting and gallivanting in her blouse like a pair of cooking apples. I reckon she stopped more than one leak in the Mineworkers' Federation that morning, and she stopped me up the slope in the press of the men, for I was remembering Bron.

As for Sam Jones beside her, it fascinated me to see him in boots. For years, to me, he'd been the ghost in Bron's face. Mattie said now, as the pair of them approached, "He's a swine, isn't he, doin' that to Ma Bron."

"He's never been any good," I replied.

The men drifted either side of us, but Sam and Rosie paused.

"Ay ay," said he. Hands deep in his trews, he looked me over.

The years had savoured his dark, handsome looks, and broadened him; he was a hunk of a man, wider than me, if shorter, and I'd have liked to try him for size, for Bron. Rosie, as spry as a virgin maid, raised her cheeky little face to mine, and said, coyly:

"Well, well, Toby Davies, just fancy seeing you! What you want?"

"A word in your ear before you get a flea in it."

"Tell him to bugger off," said Sam, bored.

"Don't you two love-birds talk direct to each other, then?" asked Mattie, innocent.

"Not to a *bradwr*," said I.

"A what?"

I was weighing Sam for size, and he said, droll:

"You'd best make off, Toby Davies, before I tan your backside." This he said in Welsh, his dark eyes smiling. In English, he added, "Ay ay, *cariad* — you first, and your little hoppo after."

"After when?" asked Mattie. "Is he threatening violence?"

"After shift?" I said to Sam.

414

"After shift; or now, down the Bottanic — when you like."

"God help you," said Mattie.

Because of Bron there was burning in me a sullen anger now Sam was there in the flesh. He made bonfires of people's hopes and warmed his behind on them. I said:

"You're a dirty bugger, aren't you, doing this to Bron."

"I've told you before and I'll tell you again, son — she's yours, on a plate."

I indicated Rosie. "This bit of crumpet for a woman like her? You must be toop."

"You'd best go, boyo, lest I have you now," he said, and took his hands out of his pockets.

"Not here," said Mattie, and towed me along.

Being late queue for the cage, we got to the Lancaster downcast shaft nearer eight o'clock than six, the time the shift started. The cage slammed shut. Mattie, Bert Jebb, Softy and me were first in; Sam was last, and we glared at each other over the heads of the others.

"There's high rise gas this mornin'," said somebody as the cage rattled down in flashing lights. Strangely, I remembered that Nan was taking Ceinie to Caerphilly market that evening, on the train, and mentioned it. I was trying desperately to canalise my thoughts away from Sam.

"There's no market in 'Philly today," said Mattie.

"*Diawch*, this winder's giving us a ride again."

"Aye, I can smell gas, too," I said. "But not enough to kill a 'flu canary."

"A fox can always smell his own hole," said Sam.

"I can't smell it," said somebody, "but then, I get gas day and night from my missus."

"I'd put this engine-winder on a merry-go-round," said Ed Masumbala, and I realised he was with us.

"He ain't in the Union, ye know?"

"Likely a peer in the House of Lords — he must hate colliers."

The cage dropped faster. Eight hundred feet, a thousand feet, fifteen hundred, two thousand feet, then it slowed. Lights began to flood the cage, flashing slower on the brattice. The floor of the Lancaster level made shape. As the cage door clanged back and we all trooped out, I said to Sam, in Welsh:

"You grow a tail on Rosie, mate, and Tommy, her brother'll have you for dinner."

"I'll grow a tail on you, when we hit Forty Stall — never mind Tommy."

"Must you two talk Chinese? — can't you speak English?" asked Mattie as we shouldered down the underground road.

"He won't know English from Chinese five minutes from now," answered Sam. "Nobody — least of all him — is telling me what to do with my missus." He scowled at me. "Didn't miss a trick, did you? — bedded her first opportunity."

"It wasn't like that."

"So now you can keep her."

"God," I said, "you're not fit to clean her Monday boots."

Somewhere, far away, I heard a faint alarm bell ringing.

Mattie cried, breaking it up, "Here we comes, lads — work hard for the Consolidated Collieries — Lord Merthyr's giving me a wedding present, you heard? Is anyone here giving me a wedding present?" He was leaking the news at last.

"Sod Lord Merthyr and the Consolidated Collieries, butty, you included."

"Don't be like that," said Mattie.

As we passed the engine house the dynamos were sparking and the belts slapping good enough for Pandy merry-go-round.

I looked at my watch as we got to the lamp room; to this day I don't know why. It was six minutes past eight. The lamp man checked us and we drew tools.

A journey of coal drams was coming, towed by Nellie, an old mare Heinie had loved — he usually had a bit of something for her, so I gave her the apple out of my bait tin.

"You won't be needing it, anyway," said Sam, clanking along beside me.

"Dear God," said Bert Jebb, glancing over his shoulder. "I don't know who you are son, or what's up, but you're just begging for an outing."

"And he'll get it," said Ed Masumbala. "If you ain't Forty Stall, stranger, why're you coming?"

"I'm thirty-two stall, black man," replied Sam. "But I've got a big appointment eight stalls up."

"The overman'll suspend the pair of you, if you are found fighting," said Mattie, apprehensively.

"And I'll have the overman — you, as well," said Sam.

"He don't give a monkey's bum for anybody, do he, Tobe, includin' the monkey," said Snookey.

"Certainly there's a hint of carelessness in his manner," said Softy.

"It do make the imagination lurch," commented Dai Parcel, joining us along the road. "But he's got the whole county to sleep under after, so he'll rest snug."

"Don't be too sure," I said, "this isn't Red Rubbler."

I looked at my watch again. It was ten-past-eight.

As I put it back into my pocket the Universal blew up.

According to talk later, the Lancaster downcast exploded with a roar that brought down ceilings, sending a shaft of flame a hundred feet into the air, and billowing smoke: it blew the top of the pit shaft to pieces, it blew off the head of Joe Moggridge, a banksman.

Two thousand feet lower, where the night shift was coming off and the day shift going on, it did rather more.

Snookey Boxer, one of the first of the four hundred and thirty-nine men to die, died in Welsh, his mother tongue.

The roof came down at the intersection of Lancaster and Number One North — all of us but Snookey had got round the corner: it pinned him from buttocks to shoulders, and the press, slowly subsiding, made him one with coal.

The blast blew me flat, with Ed Masumbala on top of me, and we scrambled up and attacked the fall, heaving on Snookey's feet, which were projecting from the burning mass; shock waves of fire were blasting up and down the Lancaster, knocking us over.

We could hear the flames roaring behind the fall as we hauled and sweated, but all we got was Snookey's boots — boxing boots — they came off in my hands as I fell backwards.

"Jesus, man, get out!" shouted Ed, for flames were now spurting at us through the rubbish of the fall. Later, we heard that the heat vacuum following the explosion had sucked back, rushing from the engine house down the level like cordite through a gun, incinerating most of the day shift, men and horses. And, even as we fled I heard Snookey's voice crying above the flames:

"*Does ond y chwi a mi y byd. Effie — chwi a mi. . . !*"

"Run for it!" yelled Masumbala, and the roof started to go down like dropping sticks behind us; the walls about us bulged, the floor caved and bucked. Heat fanned about us as new explosions rocked the pit, blowing up individual stalls and headings. Boulders were dropping out of the roof; I ducked some but ran into one that knocked me flat. Everything seemed to be flashing light and sound as Masumbala dragged me upright.

"Run! *Run!*" Towing me after him, he staggered through the debris, scrambling over falls. And suddenly Mattie's face appeared before me in the gloom of the road, a lamp waving beside it. The face gasped and spluttered, an astral countenance lacking a body, crying:

"You all right, Tobe?"

"Aye." I fell against Masumbala again, and he held me.

"Then come on! The Bottanic, the *Bottanic!*"

With Mattie one side and the black man on the other, I floundered on, half-conscious to the stunning blow on the back of my head: reaching the Bottanic corner, we leaped into it, and dived flat, seconds before the roof went down in Number One North.

"You all right?" Mattie gripped me, turning my face to his in the shine of his lamp.

I rubbed my head. My fingers were red with blood.

There were several men sheltering in the Bottanic roadway, including Ed Masumbala, Mattie, Bert Jebb and Softy.

"Where's Dai Parcel and Gwilym?" I got up, raising my Davy.

"No sign of 'em."

"Sam Jones?" I asked, steadying myself; distantly came the reverberation of deeper explosions; the confining walls of the chamber trembled.

"He went ahead of us," said someone.

Strangers were in the chamber; men I had not seen before. There was young Ben Davies of Commercial Street, crying aloud to the pain of a burned hand, his right; and he held up his left hand, which was untouched, waving it in agony: bending above him was little Billy Eldridge, and he was weeping, a mere child. Tom Lewis I knew an old collier who used to work the Windsor, and I said to him:

"Which way did you lot come in?"

"Same way as you." He rose to his feet and pushed his grizzled face near to mine. "All lamps out except mine, lads — we'll need the oil."

"What are the chances?" I asked him, soft.

"Practically none," replied Mattie, who had ears like mice.

Someone said from the dark. "The bloody place has gone up, that's what. Sounds to me like the Lancaster Level, from Kimberley to the Downcast."

"You're likely right," said the old collier. "But it won't do no good thinking about it — we've got to get out."

"Take it slow for a bit, eh? Till I get me breath back," said Bert Jebb, and lay down by the gob beside Softy.

"What we done to deserve this — buried alive?" asked a man.

"Because we're bad buggers, that's what," said Mattie. "And my Bestie'll play hell if I'm late home for dinner."

We sat in silence, saving breath, looking at the old collier's lamp in the middle of the floor, and I thought of the rolling hills of the county above us in sunlight, and the ash, the willows and the young spruce garlanding themselves with the tints of winter. Vaguely, I wondered if I would see them again.

"Mind," said Softy, stretching out his skinny little legs, "we can't be entirely alone — there'll be lots of people on top by now — Mr. Hutchinson, for instance, the new agent — now, they say he's a genius on safety in the mines."

"And Mr. Shaw, the manager?" asked Masumbala, his white eyes rolling in the dark.

"Ay ay," answered Mattie, "he's bound to be there, like old Evan Owen of the Miners' Provident."

"But Baron Senghenydd, who owns this hell, won't be out of bed yet."

They groused and grumbled; they hawked, spat and coughed; Old Tom Lewis had a chest that sounded like Miner's Asthma.

"Save your breath," I said, leaning back on the gob.

A man said, bass, like a voice from a crypt, "I'd like to get my shovel up that fuggin' Inspector of Mines, though."

"Me first," said Mattie.

Most of this I heard in a vague, red dream; my balance was unsteady, my head still spinning: the shape of old Tom Lewis's face made strange gyrations in the dusty light from the middle of the floor.

We rested in silence, save for roof trickles and faint subterranean hammerings: and with such a languid ease that I suspected gas. But the Davy was still burning brightly after an hour of it. The old collier said:

"Anyone got a watch?"

"Half-past-nine."

I was thinking of Bron, wondering, amid the coughing and spluttering if they'd heard about the explosion in Tredegar and what she'd do if Sam had been killed. Then I remembered Nanwen, and, with a little shock, wondered what would happen about our week up north. I watched, a man detached, as Tom, the old collier, examined the fall that blocked us to Mafeking.

"Mind, there's some fresh air coming in somewhere," he called.

"Perhaps there's an air shaft," suggested Mattie.

"Crawl through that, mun, and we're all set for the walk home. My woman's got Irish stew for me tonight, she promised," said Ed, bassly.

Tom Lewis, the old one, as inscrutable as a Chinese god, sat against the fall; beside him was Billy Eldridge, the lad, seemingly half asleep.

I looked at the other men around us.

Two were impossibly young for this kind of death — Billy Eldridge, for instance — probably fifteen. I wondered how they'd behave when things got worse. You could never know. I'd had some narrow squeaks underground and still couldn't judge what a man

420

might do. I've seen boxers crying like children and urchins playing Dolly Stones.

So far, however, the new men with us were adopting the usual listless attitude of colliers trapped underground; it was a convenient pose. Only time would tell how any of us would handle it.

"You think we'll get out?" asked Billy Eldridge, suddenly.

"Any time now, son," replied Tom Lewis.

"Then why aren't we moving?"

"Just resting — slow, steady, easy does it . . ."

"Those are burying words — I want to go up."

"All in good time."

Boots in a circle, we sat listlessly, sweating cobs, for the air was coming in hotter still, so we stripped to our belts.

"I'm done this side," said Softy, "will someone turn me over?"

More smoke was drifting through the broken-faced slope of the fall; people began to cough again.

"Best make up," I said, and rose. "It's cooler farther down."

"It's firing behind there, isn't it?" said Mattie, softly, nodding at the roof fall.

"Of course not!"

"Well, somebody's stoking us — must be the Devil."

"Beyond the blockage — in Number One North? Remember the timber was alight when we first come in?"

"Perhaps," I whispered, "but lower your voice."

"It'll be the fire-damp next, that'll cook us for sure."

This was the after-explosion gas; the death was reasonable.

"Look," said the old collier, wheezing. "Keep your death to yourself. We're goin' to be all right, aren't we, Billy Eldridge?" and he patted the boy's knee. "I got a lad up there same age as you."

"God 'elp him," said a voice.

I was sweating badly. The Davy on the floor was lower. *Gas.* The other men undoubtedly noticed it, but nobody said anything because of the boy . . .

Later, they found eighty bodies in the Mafeking area, and the heading was choked with fire-damp. Everything east of the engine house at the shaft bottom was alight. No wonder it was hot.

"Well," said Tom Lewis, getting a pick. "We'd best start digging."

"Which end — Number One North, or Mafeking?" asked Ben Davies. I admired his guts. His hand was dreadfully burned; there was nothing we could do for it.

"Take your choice."

Men rose lethargically, raising their tools; the flickering light of the solitary Davy cast weird shadows on their sweating, dust-stained bodies. Tom said to Billy Eldridge. "You stay here with Ben Davies, son. . . . The rest of us make shifts. We'll poke a hole in this blutty lot. God helps those who help themselves."

Nobody spoke for a time. Ed and Bert Jebb, great in the shoulders, began picking at the fall that blocked the road to Mafeking. The confined space began to swirl with dust again. I said to Tom Lewis:

"You stopped to think, that Ladysmith runs across Bottanic? If her roof's down as well we'll be digging for years."

"But the air's cleaner, mun. It's the chance we take."

After four hours of digging, with exhaustion claiming us, we lay back, sweating against the cavern walls.

"Likely we're wasting our time," said Ed Masumbala.

I looked at my watch, carefully winding it. It was one o'clock. The air was filthy and it was difficult to breathe.

Somebody said there was a band of iron around his chest and that he thought he was going to die, but nobody answered.

"Right," said the old collier, with command, "we'll dig the other way."

"Make up your bloody mind," said Mattie.

Deeply in the bowels of the county came muted reverberations; the thunder of the old workings (probably lamination faults revived by the major explosion). Smoke and dust trickled down from our roof. There was no sound save Ben Davies groaning.

"Listen!"

Somebody, standing, slipped on stones.

"*Heisht*, for God's sake! *Listen!*"

We heard distant crackling, like things on fire; a sudden explosive air moved in the chamber, bringing waves of heat.

"You feel that?" asked Softy.

"What?"

"Hot air came in from somewhere."

"You're imagining it."

The old collier rose and went to the fall that blocked the road to Number One North, listening.

I looked at the men about me.

After only five hours or so they were listless. In prostrate shapes their half naked bodies made it a charnel house. Their movements were the slow-motion of the drugged entombed. Had the chamber been smaller, we all would have died, but air, amazingly, was somehow getting in through the rubbish of the fall from Number One North.

After an interminable wait, somebody said:

"What's the time, Toby?"

"Don't keep asking the damned time," said Softy.

"Why not?"

"It's a variable element," replied he. "Precisely in accordance with the attention one pays it, it shortens or lengthens."

"Educated bastard!"

"I assure you I am right," said Softy. "It possesses variable factors — I've read about it. God invented Time, it was Man who tried to measure it."

"Half-past two," I put back my watch.

"Is that all?" cried Billy, sitting up. "I've been down here days."

"That's what I mean," said Softy.

I was more worried about Bron.

If Sam Jones was dead, and this seemed likely, she'd be lost, like most women who yearned for such fancy old footers, the bad lads.

I was thinking, too, about the fires beyond the blocked roadways that isolated us; the long galleries of smashed timbers, twisted brattic; a debris of men, animals and steel, all blazing, for I knew the effect of such a thunderous detonation.

As long ago as thirty years back scientists had discovered the source of such explosions — it was the mantling coal dust that needed but a spark. But schemes for neutralising it with stone dust had been abandoned by Owner after Owner on grounds of cost. Nearly three hundred dead down the old Albion nineteen years back; a hundred and seventy-six down Llanerch pit four years before — eight thousand miners killed in the past sixty years.

Contravention of the laws of the Mines Commission and the findings of its inquiries; slip-shod safety precautions, the push for higher profits, all combined to turn the coalfields into a gigantic slaughter-house. And we in Wales, producing but an eighth of the total British output, yet suffered a third of Britain's disasters.

"I hope old Bestie feeds my pigeons, though," said Mattie.

Yes if Sam died, I thought, Bron would probably wander from one place to another, in search of nothing. I'd read about a woman who did that once — just wandered; sitting at the tables where she had sat with her lover, sleeping in the same beds: for nothing, it seemed, could replace Sam Jones in Bron's heart. Softy, sitting near me, said to somebody:

"Aye, well that happened to me, too. I was driving a heading down Windsor, I remember, and there was a little hole in the rock; in the middle was a little bright stone — onyx, I think, with the grain of a leaf in it. Before I could stop myself, I'd picked it up. It must have been the first time that little thing had been moved since God made the world. It quite upset me."

"Dear me," rumbled Bert. "Bloody listen to it."

Nan, on the other hand, would be all right, I thought; she was contained, self-possessed: also, she was armed with kind memories of Ben: Bron would have no such memories of Sam. It was a malignancy without a cure; she would be finished.

"We'll be all right as long as this air's coming in," remarked Tom Lewis, the old collier.

Strangely, I knew no pestering sense of urgency about it.

I imagined the scene on top, the wailing sirens, the stolid, wet-faced relatives.

There were some good men over at Porth Rescue Station, too, excellent engineers.

Bert Jebb said to me:

"*Nid oes bradwr yn y ty hwn*, eh?" and it turned me: it was good Welsh, and I was surprised, saying:

"Where did you get that from?"

"What does it mean?" asked the old collier.

I translated, " 'There is no traitor in this house.' "

"What you on about?"

The lad said, "An old Johnny North I knew told it me — they used to put it in the windows up Bethesda way, during the Big Strike. That right?"

"There'll be a bigger blutty strike down Senghenydd way when I get out of here," said someone.

"If you get out," growled Mattie, and Bert added:

"He reckoned you had forty publics in Bethesda alone, that right? *Iechyd da!*" He drank from his jack.

"You should have seen the barmaids!"

"*Duw*," breathed little Billy Eldridge, "just look what's arrivin'!"

We followed his pointing fingers. In the glow of the Davy lamp black pats were streaming over the floor.

"So what?" asked Masumbala. "Ain't you seen those little fellas before?"

Nobody replied, because they hadn't seen so many. They were beetles of the hard-backed variety that infested most mines: big as the top of a man's thumb, they were entering the chamber in swarms. Old Tom said softly:

"They're escaping from the fire — it must be hot out there."

"It's hot all right," I answered.

"Mind, a pound or two of these'd make a good meal, pushed to it," said Mattie, sweeping beetles up into his palm. "D'ye know they pick the bones of a horse cleaner than a coat o' whitewash?"

"But they don't touch humans," I interjected.

"Oh, no — course not." Ed glanced at Billy Eldridge. "They never been known to touch the likes of folk — but they nip a bit, though." He shook his hand, sucking a finger.

Softy said, cultured, "When I go up I'll take some with me and train them to bite my creditors."

I must have slept. I was grateful for this for I had an appalling headache. Yet it was a hypnotic, almost languid sense of security I experienced in lying there, watching the Davy.

Over in the corner by the fall, Ben Davies was snoring, asleep with the pain. Earlier, we'd tried and failed to bring him round. Suddenly, old Tom said, crawling into the light:

"Listen, lads, we're doin' all right, see?" I saw his face clearly for the first time. Time had ravaged it, but it was still square and strong; the sweat of his chest made livid the raws and burns of his escape from the fire, but he showed no sign of pain. "I know this old pit backwards, and I reckon the bottom of the downcast's blocked — most ways right up the Lancaster Level, too, and this has sealed us off. But the lads'll be at it, you know — O, aye — you can imagine? They'll 'ave even told the King."

"Bugger the King, you stupid old goat," said Bert.

"Ay ay, but ye know what I mean — they'll be lifting Heaven and Earth, like. The Federation . . ."

"And bugger the Federation."

"Look, see sense, boys." Tom Lewis stared about him with red-rimmed eyes. Playing with pieces of coal, they watched him bitterly. "It's only a question of numbers — but they've got to collect the rescue teams, and the equipment, see? This'll take a day." He suddenly wrung his hands like a man hunted, and I wondered if he'd be the first to crack. The young ones were doing all right, I thought, so why the devil all this talk?

"It's you making the fuss about it, old 'un," said Billy Eldridge.

"I bet Baron Senghenydd's playing Hamlet up on top." The old man chuckled. "I mean . . ."

"He'd play Hamlet if I had him down by 'ere."

"They say he's all right, though — sent my missus a bottle o' wine once — first labour."

"Did she survive it? The wine, I mean," said Softy.

"The bastard's too mean to give ye a gumboil."

"Got his purse up his bloomers."

"A couple of hundred spent on mine precautions, mate, and we wouldn't be here." A man swore violently. "What a bloody place to die."

426

"Nobody's going to die," I said. "That right, Softy?"

"I certainly don't intend to." He was cleaning his fingernails.

"And you, Mattie?" I knew this was safe ground.

"I'm dying for a pint of Liverpool Milk, that's all," said he. "Has anyone got a chew?"

"Got some rough cut — Bulwark?"

"Don't chew down here," I said.

"At best, it's a filthy habit," said Softy.

A man was whispering softly from the dark, "*Uffern dan, Uffern dan!*"

It sounded like Heinie, but I remembered that he wasn't with us, and then we heard it . . . slowly, silently, men sat upright, listening.

The chamber was silent save for scurrying beetles.

"Start praying, lads," said somebody. "Nobody ever went to Hell on his knees."

"*Listen!*"

The old collier began to chuckle softly; sitting on his hunkers, he was holding his sides. A man shouted, gripping him:

"Will you shut up, stupid old man?"

Again, we listened. It was no tapping. It was a faint but unmistakable dull thumping of picks and the treble shrieks of a shovel.

"What did I tell ye? Now then!" cried old Tom. "The lads are coming!"

"*They're coming!*" shrieked Billy Eldridge, leaping up.

Frantic, we ran to the fall, hauling away boulders. Warm air was blowing in waves through the fall: we gasped at it, flinging out our arms to it, men revived; it was a wondrous, life-giving nectar. Soon the middle of the fall collapsed and a pick came through, then a hand, yanking away coal.

In the middle of the floor, I raised the Davy. Men were shouting, joyously dancing about.

"Porth Rescue — it's the lads!"

Billy Eldridge was crying with relief. "Will my mam be up top, you think?"

"And all your relatives — you'll be a hero!" I snatched him against me.

427

The hole became wider; somebody was bawling through it an unintelligible greeting, and we yelled replies: now we crowded around the ever-larger hole, expectant, till a head appeared and a cheeky face perked up.

It was Dai Parcel.

"Are you the rescue party?" cried Mattie.

"Christ, no, mun — we're in the next hole down and need the company."

Empty of hope, we watched as Sam Jones, Gwilym and Dai crawled through into our chamber.

"Mind, we aren't entirely alone," said Sam as a rat jumped past him.

"Aye, that's better," said Dai and straightened, peering at the chamber about him. "We had the air, of course, but yours is an improvement — ours was so low you couldn't stand up. How you doing, my lovelies?"

At nine o'clock that night, after thirteen hours of being walled up, Ben Davies, awake again, said, "Can anybody tell me what we're waiting for?"

"The fire to die down," I replied.

"And then we break through?"

"Aye, into the air shaft, if we can."

"It leads to Mafeking?"

"It likely leads to Number One North," said the old collier. "Leastwise, if the gallery's still alight, it'll turn us into hell."

"Now you see why we're waiting," added Softy.

"Meanwhile, tighten your yorks," interjected Bert tightening the straps below his knees. "Our little mates are coming," and he threw a stone at a rat that had suddenly appeared. "Comfort they're after, ye know. They'll be sharp up your shins and sleepin' on your fannies."

One by one they came, scuttling through the fall holes in whiskering inquiry, escaping from the fire, noses sniffing the ventilation air of the cavern, eyes beady bright in the lamplight like people requesting permission.

"Come in, lads," said old Tom Lewis, sweeting with his lips, "You're entitled — hot work up along Lancaster, is it?"

Now they arrived in twos and threes, darting from behind fallen stones, peek-a-booing at humans, who usually gave them boots for welcome, and Billy Eldridge began to cry. A few of them, crawling about, were methodically eating black pats.

"After they're gone they'll start on us," said Billy, brokenly.

"Don't you believe it," said Bert, patting him. "I know a blind woman in Pontmorlais and she fed a rat she thought was a kitten — used to take the bread from her fingers."

"Is that a fact?" asked Billy, hopeful.

"Of course. They're friendly things, really." Softy beckoned the rats to come to him. "Brothers in adversity, aren't we, little people?"

His cavalier attitude was infectious, though there was nothing of him. Sam, however, was shivering badly: everybody is afraid of something.

"You're a madman," he said, "talking to rats like that."

"That's why I'm cooped up with you down here," said Softy.

My headache was getting worse. It was bringing a sickness that reached my throat. I felt the back of my head; the pain was crystallising there in short, vicious stabs. I consoled myself that I was better off than most — young Ben Davies, for instance, with his burned hand.

Dai Parcel put his head through the hole in the fall. "The air's getting cooler," he said. "The lads must have been fire-fighting. Give us an hour and we'll start looking for that air shaft."

"It runs east," said Tom the old collier, "but I can't remember what side." He started chuckling again, and it was the last thing I heard as sleep claimed me. When I awoke Sam Jones was bending over me.

"You all right, then?"

"No better for asking."

"Lucky it was your head," he said. "It could have been vital."

"You're the one weak in the nut, chasing up that Rosie with a real woman back home." I spoke softly, aware of listeners.

"Don't give up, do you?"

"Not where's Bron's concerned."

"You had your share." He spat on the gob.

"And hung on to her, if I could."

"Lawful wedded wife. She always come back to Sam."

I said, bitterly, "She can't be a full pound up top, putting up with you. But you'll move her too far one day, mate, and she'll land you with the likes of Rosie."

Sam sighed like a man after Sunday dinner. "Ach, you take them and leave them, boyo — you always were too serious. A thump or two — they always come back for more."

"So it's Rosie Arse-Jenkins now, is it?"

"Rose Harse, if you please — it's a slander. You Rhondda lot down here never did pronounce your aitches."

"She'll drop some aitches if Bron gets at her."

He grinned wide. "It's worth the risk — sweet sixteen, she's got it going in all the right places."

He had raised his voice and men were looking in our direction. Gossip comes as naturally trapped underground, the old ones say, as swimming the River Jordan in the chapel pews on Sunday. I whispered:

"You're no damned good, Sam. Celtic blood is it? Welsh princes? Bron's got the breeding and you're as common as dirt."

"Mind, I agree with that," said Mattie, leaning towards us. "Most of these randy sods 'ave classical backgrounds — I knew one who reckoned his people was in the ark with Noah."

"This bugger had his own boat," I said.

"Talking about romantic stuff, I had a woman once," said Dai, "though she weren't so special. She used to wash up in me bath water and send me a heliograph message when she was ready for love." He sighed. "Always went to bed with her hat on. She didn't give a lot away — second Sunday after Lent, it were usually."

Gwilym said, "They do come in very strange varieties. Owen, my mate, had one who wore wire wool drawers, he reckoned." He grinned reflectively, thinking of Owen, who died. "He was a regular Casanova, ye know, before we met up. I told him — he ought to be bloody well hung."

"He was, if I remember correctly," said Softy.

"And did I have an idle one!" Gwilym warmed to his memories. "Always 'aving one of her turns, she was. And hang on to it! I said

430

to her once, 'What you saving it for, Minnie, widow's memories?'"

"Aye, but she were a girl, remember," said Mattie. "It didn't do a lot for her."

"Never again," said Gwilym.

"Aw, come off it," said Dai, "I told you before — woman are all right." He shook his head nostalgically. "And mine were all right, too, come to think of it. When she died it were the graveyard of my dreams. I knew her when she wore orange box rope for garters; a tiny little thing she was, and her maiden name was Cule, so I called her Molly."

It was the last thing said before we heard singing. By some strange trick of hot air and echo, we heard the sound of a choir.

"*Heisht!*" commanded the old collier, and stopped his chuckling.

"It's the Treorchy Male Voice," said Bert.

"My crutch, will you shut it?" whispered Dai.

"It's chaps singing — poor buggers entombed, same as us."

Hushed, we listened to faint voices rising and falling in the flushes of warm air.

"There's a fella down there with pernicious anaemia," said Sam.

"Tenor, by the sound of him."

"And all the basses 'ave strangled hernias. Who's the conductor?"

"The poor sods are buried alive, man — what do you expect, the Hallelujah Chorus?" asked Ed Masumbala.

We strained our ears, but the voices died.

Afterwards, I wondered if any of us had really heard it.

"The lamp's gone out," I said.

"The lamp's still alight, son," said Dai Parcel.

"I tell you it's gone out."

Somebody moved in my pitch blackness; Sam said, his face near mine. "The lamp's alight. Can't you see it?"

I shook my head.

He raised it; I felt the heat of it and a redness grew in my eyes. "Can you see that?" he asked.

"No."

"Christ."

Dai Parcel moved over and squatted between my legs, moving his hand in front of my eyes; I felt his fingers touch me.

"That'll make a pension — five bob a week," said somebody.

"You'll be all right, lad," said the old collier.

I gripped my hands.

Later, I heard them working at the fall, tunnelling in, looking for the air shaft. The rescue teams must have got the fans going again, for cooler air was blasting through now, chilling us; all Dai Parcel had to do was follow the fans.

"Likely we're crawling straight into the fire?" asked someone, Ben Davies I think.

"Not at this temperature."

I don't know who led the tunnel dig to get to the shaft — I think it was Sam Jones, being the strongest, and they pushed me in after Mattie.

I worked, too; blindness was no disadvantage, for only the lead men had Davys. The rats were delighted, running over us in their efforts to get to pure air: with the roof no more than six inches from my nose and with just enough room to move my arms, I elbowed and kicked back the muck to the next man down.

Soon I heard voices growing in the air tunnel; next ten minutes I was into the air shaft with the rest of them.

"We've done it, lads," said Billy Eldridge, but nobody else said anything.

Most of those walled up got clear, but the tunnel, temporarily arched, went down with a roar before the last four reached the shaft, and Glamorgan county came down on top of them.

"God Almighty," said Mattie, beside me.

Dust spouted out of the air shaft like smoke from a gun muzzle.

There was no time to grieve, and somebody shouted, "Look, there's lamps coming! There's lamps coming down between the fires."

Coughing, spluttering in the smoke of burning timbers, we picked our way down Number One North, over dead men and horses, under smashed props, over journeys of drams and roof falls, working down the left of the double parting. And the rescue party picked us up as they fought a way through to Bottanic.

As the cage was wound up the York Upcast, I said to the man next to me:

"Who are you?"

"Billy Eldridge," said he.

"There now, didn't I tell you we'd get out?"

"Aye, butty," said he.

"And your mam'll be waiting, too!"

"More'n likely." He was not so forthcoming now, being a man. Cold air kissed our faces: the cage began to slow.

"Tell me when we're in daylight, is it?" I asked him.

The cage was bucking and dancing like a merry-go-round, the ropes clanging in the York Upcast.

"You're in daylight now, mister. Leastwise, it's about two o'clock in the mornin'."

I stared up, looking vainly for the stars.

The music of the pit, the whining of ambulances, fire engines; the wailing of relatives and the barked commands of police and rescuers beat about me.

Bert Jebb (and he had six kids), Ed Masumbala, Gwilym, and poor old Dai Parcel.

Later, they told me . . .

"Come," said Mattie, and took my arm.

41

Is HEINIE GONE to his girl wife? Dai Parcel, Gwilym, Owen and big Ed Masumbala? Somewhere in the darkness, as I sat in a corner with Mattie, I heard a woman's voice. And Bert Jebb's wife, seeing me, came then, clutching at my hands.

"Oh, Gawd — isn't there a chance?"

"Not one, missus," said Mattie. "But it were quick; he didn't take a breath."

Beli came now, Ed Masumbala's girl, with Precious, their son — so black, people said, that you couldn't see them before dawn, but nobody mourned for Dai or Gwilym.

Near me, George Waldron, the banksman who escaped, was telling Echo reporters how his mate Moggridge was blown to pieces: the Salvation Army was handing out food and drinks; nurses from Cardiff were attending to the injured, said Mattie, and men down the East Side were being brought up; so were the dead. Bells were clanging amid the shrill crying of children; they were already making coffins in the carpenter's shop. Dead horses and smashed drams were being hauled up the York Upcast; fire hoses being run down, volunteers organised for pumping.

I turned my face to the sky.

"What's wrong with him?" asked a cultured voice.

"He's blind, Dr. Thomas," said Mattie.

"Toby Davies of Woodland, isn't it?" the doctor asked.

"Aye," I said.

His cool, smooth hands moved over my face and eyes.

In one swipe the Universal had taken my friends, the gassy bitch, and their only crime was to labour in coal.

Where was George Smales? I wondered, whom I used to see out shopping with his son — one of the best prop forwards in the game. And Taliesin Roberts of High Street, Aber, who plagued the Scarrott professionals when short of a guinea, but preferred to dig his patch? And Dai Davies, the haulier who called himself Dai Rhymney, cousin to Georgie Hallet, aged fifteen, who worshipped Joe Choynski?

"Down Number Two South, weren't he?" asked Mattie.

"Aye," I said.

"His mother's pestering me to death," said Dr. Thomas. "You say you haven't been near the fire?"

"No," I answered, and he sighed.

"There's a few who have, God help them." He said to Mattie, "Best get him home — old Best has lost one already, she's a mine expert."

Where was old Bob Roche, I wondered, when the roof came down?

"You seen him, mister?"

Effie came, wife to Snookey; married but unchurched.

I put out my hand to her.

"We got his boots," I said.

Ed Masumbala gave them to Mattie, it turned out. A pair of boxing boots for Effie.

"Mind, he liked to wear his boxing boots," said she, and took them.

I began to wonder where Nan had got to — Bron, too, come to that. It was funny she hadn't come looking for Sam.

It was raining; I hadn't realised it. Mattie said dolefully, "Come on home, Tobe — we're all getting wet, you know."

"Get him under cover while I see to this head," said a nurse, and helped me to my feet.

Her hands were rough but she served me well.

"You've got a bad cut here," she said, and bandaged. "What did the doctor say?"

"Not much."

She brought the bandage over my eyes; it was like the end of the world.

"He won't come home, you know?" said Mattie, hopefully.

"It's the shock," said the nurse. "You'll go home now, won't you Mr. Davies?"

I pushed them aside. Near me, a clergyman — the Rev. Rees, I think it was, was giving last rites. The rain was enhancing the smells of death. Someone said that the bodies were falling apart on the stretchers: relatives fainting at the identifications. All around us people were vomiting, for a blown up horse had been hauled out of the Upcast. I began to wonder, sitting there in the rain, what would happen to the Masumbalas, now Ed had gone; they wouldn't keep blacks on the rates when he ceased to be a dead coal hero.

"Will you go home now, then?" asked the nurse.

"No," I said.

A neighbour whispered, "I reckon he's waiting for someone." She bent to me. "You waiting for somebody, Mr. Davies?"

"Ay ay," said Sam, coming up, jaunty. "Well, I never — how's the old man doin'?"

"He's just about your size now, butty," said Mattie. "You piss off."

"Sorry, Tobe," said Sam.

"Piss off just the same," said Mattie.

I heard the voice of Rosie Arse-Jenkins calling above the clamouring sounds; I heard Sam's reply.

"Ah, well, be seeing you," he said, and went.

Strangely, above the bell-clanging, the grating of wheels on rails, escaping steam, the panic of it all, I could hear Heinie's voice and a woman's soft replies.

A man nearby said, "This'll turn Senghenydd into a town of widows and orphans — Christ, there's nigh five hundred men still down there, and only eighteen got out of Lancaster East Side."

"Owner's compensation . . ."

"From Lord Merthyr? Make me laugh!"

"But Keir Hardie's here, too — give somebody credit."

"*Keir Hardie!* God! Where's my son?"

Mattie said warmly, "You ready to come now, Tobe?"

436

It was raining harder. "No," I replied, "I want to stay here."

"You waiting for Nan O'Hara?" a man asked gently, into my face: I never discovered who he was.

"Blood on coal, you say?" asked a woman. "He's blind, isn't he?"

Mrs. Best arrived and put a shawl around my shoulders. Her softness touched me, as coming warm from a fire. "Come home now, son? Look, I got a bit of lobscows on the hob, and . . ."

I gently pushed her away. I wanted to stay, to listen to Senghenydd; to know its chaos, agony and grief, so that I would never forget it.

It seemed impossible that Nanwen hadn't come. Every woman in the Aber Valley with feet must have been there, waiting for their men; husbands, fathers, brothers, lovers. Bron? Well, Bron, I reasoned, was up in Tredegar; she'd likely take some time to get down to Aber . . .

Softy said, arriving, "Toby, how very good to see you safe and well!"

"He's safe, but he's not so well," said Mattie. Other people came, some I didn't know. Then Mattie, speaking to Softy, said, "Look butty — find that Nan O'Hara, for God's sake — we can't shift the fella, and we want him home."

"Is she about?" whispered Softy portentously.

"I don't care if she's about — just find her — she lives down Windsor — turn her out if needs be."

"Do your poor old eyes pain you, then?" asked Mrs. Best.

"No," I answered.

"That's a good thing, then — be thankful for small mercies. Dear me," she added, "we'll soon build you up. I'll give ye an egg for your breakfast every morning. And after that — carrots — good for the eyes."

I nodded against her.

"Mind, blind or not, you're among friends, ain't you?" She warmed to me, cuddling up. "When my time comes I'd like to have friends put pennies on my lids."

"You'd best move before she has you buried," said Mattie.

"Here comes Widow O'Hara and her girl," said Mattie. "Thanks for fetching 'em. Now, perhaps, we'll get this boyo home."

I could hear Nanwen calling me above the din of rescue, and Ceinwen's higher, plaintive voice. Next moment they were beside me and Nan seized my hands. "Darling, your eyes are bandaged!"

"Aye, well . . ."

"Oh, God — your eyes . . . ?"

Mattie said, calmly, "Look, missus, it may be nothing, but . . ."

"Can't you see?" Nan gripped my arms, calling about her. "What's wrong with him? For God's sake somebody tell me."

Softy said, "Aye, well he's blind, isn't he? But he'll likely see like the rest of us when that bandage comes off."

"The fire? Was it the fire?"

"A bump on the head," I replied.

Nan was shivering. She was alternately enwrapping me in her arms and staring at my bandaged face, said Mattie later: then she began to cry, softly at first.

I imagined Ceinwen standing alone, watching me with her usual half-veiled disregard. Nan put her head against me and began to sob uncontrollably, and I recalled, with a little shock of realisation, her temperamental show of panic and grief years back, when Grandpa died.

"Nan, get hold of yourself," I whispered.

People were watching, those who might one day be neighbours; I was a bit ashamed that folks I knew as friends should see her in this predicament.

A passing nurse said, "You shouldn't distress yourself, Mrs. O'Hara. He's comparatively unhurt compared with others — it's probably only a temporary thing . . ."

It did not avail her. Nan wept on. Vaguely, I wondered how she had reacted when she'd heard that Ben had died. Perhaps, I reflected, this was her trouble. The pit-head scenes, the stretchers, the bandages — all might be serving to revive the spectacle of the casualty, and her loss, and then she said, brokenly:

"Oh, God, I hate this black-faced place and everything it stands for!" She was weeping aloud now. "And to think, in another few hours, we'd have been going north, out of coal."

438

"Easy, missus," said Mattie, touching her, but she shook him off, saying:

"Well, it's true! I've lost one man to the pit, and now this! How much more does coal want?" She held me in a vice. "Oh, Toby!"

"You ready for home now, son?" asked Mrs. Best, softly.

I did not reply, for Mattie said, "Mrs. O'Hara, your girl's gone off, you know?"

"Gone off? What do you mean?" Nanwen swung in my arms.

"She's really upset," said Softy. "After all, she's a bit young for all this . . ."

"Oh, God, I hadn't realised!" Nan rose, calling, "Ceinie!" She waited. "*Ceinie!*"

People took up the name.

"Probably running back home," interjected Mattie.

"You shouldn't have brought her," I said. "This is no place for a child."

"Oh, Toby, what shall I do?" Distraught, she hung on to me again.

"Go after her," I said. "That's all you can do."

In truth, I was hoping she would go. Her panic was foreign in this place where women waited with the stoicism born to coal. Nor had her presence served me, for I was already enduring the dread of permanent blindness, something I had always feared: now it was assailing me with the nausea of a bilious attack and I wanted to be sick; this in itself, in the company of neighbours, would be an appalling degradation.

"Toby . . ." her tone begged of me. "Say you'll be all right!"

"Give me a day or so and I'll see better than you."

"And you don't mind if I go now? I'll come and see you later . . ."

"He's going home, anyway, aren't you, *bach*," said Mattie.

I listened to Nanwen's departing; it was fraught with the same apprehension of her arrival, and her voice was filled with dismay as she called:

"Ceinie, *Ceinie!*"

Yes, I thought, there would always be Ceinie.

"She's got it bad," said Mattie.

Softy said, "Right, me lad, will you go now?"

439

"Not yet," I replied.

I heard Mrs. Best say, "Matt, don't look now . . ."

I didn't hear his reply, but someone said, "He's got a female following, all right — look who's arriving."

Nanwen must have actually run past Bron in her flight after Ceinwen: it was only a matter of seconds before Bron knelt beside me.

"God pity us! What the hell 'ave you been up to now?"

"He can't see," said Mattie. "He got a hit on the head."

"I know." Bron put her arm around me. "They've just told me. Are you swinging it, Tobe? — your head's your strongest point."

She was soaked with rain and there was a smell of smoke and chloroform in her wet, straggling hair.

"The trouble is getting him home," protested Mattie. "Bestie and me'll catch our deaths waiting out by here . . ."

"I've just seen Nan O'Hara going like the wind," said Bron. "Is she coming back?"

"She's gone after Ceinie," I replied.

"Aye, but is she comin' back?"

"I suppose so."

"You seen the doctor?"

"Yes, and he says I'll be all right. So don't you blutty start."

"What's she yellin' about, then?"

"Look, girl," said Mattie. "Whistle up a stretcher and we'll take him home in style — wounded hero, and all that."

"He don't need a stretcher, do ye, son?" She thrust her arm under mine. "Come on — you're making too much of it, as usual. You've collected more from me — heave him up, Mattie."

"Watch it, I'm delicate," I said.

"I'll give ye delicate. I bet you'd see if I lifted me skirt." She got me upright. "Now arm me down Woodland and give the neighbours a treat."

I went.

"Damn me," said Mattie, "he wouldn't shift for me."

Bron left us outside the door of Bestie's house. "One thing's sure," she said, "you ain't catching any night trains to Bethesda."

I gave her a grin. "You remembered?"

"Not much misses me." She elbowed me in the ribs. "You get yourself into bed, and if I've nothing better to do I might slip down later."

Gladys Bad Fairy, who saw her going up Woodland though, reckoned she was crying.

42

THE NURSE CAME again later, replaced the bandage over my eyes, then left. Now I sat propped up on pillows in Mrs. Best's front bedroom facing the window overlooking the street. Earlier, I had slept. Awaking, I listened to the sounds coming down from the pit-head.

It was like lying amid a concourse of the living but unable to communicate, save with the dead. The dawn was breaking, I think, for I heard distant hooters calling men to early shift.

Contained within this coffined isolation, I tuned my ears to every sound, a trick of the blind; the slightest noise being vital to my existence.

Women were chattering in isolated groups down Woodland on this, the next morning after the explosion — the day on which Nanwen, Ceinie and I were due to travel north. Chairs scraped the flags — grandmas and grandpas sat there, I imagined, locked in the sallow grieving of the aged in a town of widows. A kettle was whistling; the methodical tramping of boots — the stretcher-bearers who had been at it all night; the faint crying of children — all this beat upon me as I lay there thinking of Nanwen.

Her reaction to my blindness had been astonishing, even allowing for her dismay for her future. Her fear seemed something more than the horror of injury; this can terrorise some; it was inherent in her demand for Ceinie's well-being.

I wondered how she would behave if I proved to be permanently blind. . . .

Earlier — about an hour back (when the nurse had changed the bandage) I had seen the world in pastel shades of green and grey; the window, framed as it was with the rescue lighting, had burned on my eyes as a dull, phosphorescent glow.

Now I longed for Nan to arrive and share my hope.

I was a little surprised that she had not come to date. It was hard to accept that her plans for Ceinie's future and her own longing to return north could deeply influence her love of me.

Outside in the back Mattie's pigeons were coo-cooing to the dawn; a soft, throbbing note; a weak chorus of birds began their song, while up at the pit-head the tempo of the rescue was increasing. An alarm bell was incessantly ringing: as if signalled by the coming light, sirens and hooters all over the mountains began a quiet staccato chorus. I thought of the rescue underground at the Universal; the timbering, burning in creosote flares, made vivid mental pictures: I heard, as echoes, the machine-gun barking of the props as the roof came down, the glowing of gas-pockets, the crying of chained horses.

I supposed Mattie had gone down again. It would be hell down there, I thought; a mangled web of ropes, men, horses and brattice. I could hear the *hee-haa hee-haa* of the fire-engine pumps and the whining of the York Upcast as the lads were brought up.

After a while, I slept.

Bron came. It was then evening, she told me.

"How you doing?" She sat down, gasping, on the bedside chair.

"Bloody terrible — I need the sympathy."

"I reckon you're putting it on," said she, and rose.

I was prompted to tell her how I had seen the window lights, but did not. It was a position of advantage, I was discovering, to let people make their own assessment.

Her voice came from the window when she said, "Dear God, what will become of the town? There's hardly any men left . . ."

"How many have they got up?"

She came back and sat on the bed. "Most of the night shift. But there's about three hundred and fifty unaccounted for and nigh a hundred more thought dead."

"But Sam got out."

"Sam got out, mun, but that's about all." She sighed.

"What do you mean by that?"

"He's back in his lodgings with Rosie Arse-Jenkins — can you believe it? He's been nowhere near the pit-head? They're bringing in colliers from Cardiff for rescue. Volunteers are marching in from the west — you know colliers. But no Sam Jones."

"God, he's slipped," I said. "What's wrong with him?"

"The bottom's dropped out of him — I think he's disgusting. D'you know, Tobe — this has had more effect on me than anything he's done to date . . ."

"You've been a glutton for punishment."

"I can forgive him chasing skirt, that's the way Sam's made. But I'll never forgive him for dumping his mates."

"Don't worry," I said, "you'll come to it."

"Aye? Then you sit round and damn well see!"

The room was silent save for our breathing. Bron added, limply, "And it's so unlike him — he just loves to impress. A devil in the house and a saint in public."

I began to wonder whether or not she meant it and I cursed myself for not being able to see. Then, gradually, the realisation dawned that she was enduring an inner fury: this matched the fierce loyalty of her nature. It was ironic, I reflected, that at the time Bron had come to her senses, it was too late for me to grasp the opportunity. I said, softly:

"You mean it this time, don't you?"

She said, "I swear to God I'll never have him back. If he came crawling now on his hands and knees . . ."

"Give him time."

"So now, son, I'm on me jack," she said, with finality, and rose again, leaning on the bed-rail facing me. "And, while I'm on the subject, you are, too."

"What do you mean?" I raised myself on the pillows.

"That Nanwen — she's away."

"Away? What're you talking about?"

"She's off — scarpered, vamoosed — you might as well know it now as later."

I sat bolt upright now. "She's *gone*? I don't believe it."

"You'd better, mate — I've just seen her off."

"At the station — on the train?"

"Five ten sharp — you might as well have it on the chin. All the way to Bethesda — her and Ceinie — baggaged and ticketed, single fare."

My voice rose. "Without even saying goodbye?"

"She couldn't say goodbye, could she?"

I said, weakly, "You mean this, don't you? It's true!"

Bron replied, sitting on the bed beside me, "I met Mattie up at the head when I got back from the station, and he said hold it till your eyes improve, if ever. But this is for your ears. Best you learn now, if she can't stand the thought of living with the blind."

"Did she tell you that?"

"Aye!"

"Isn't she jumping to some quick conclusions?"

Bron sighed. "I don't know — one's got to be fair, Tobe. Some folks can't stand the thought of blindness, you know — me, for instance. You'd need one good eye in your head before I'd take ye on. I told her that."

"What the hell were you doing poking in your nose. . . ?"

"God, be reasonable, mun — you've got to be represented! So I took myself along to Windsor Place. I only had your interests at heart."

"I bet!"

"And there they were packing up, the pair of them, and crying. Well, I had to help 'em, didn't I? Mind, she's got the daughter to consider as well, you know."

"So you both had a long, interesting talk!"

"Aye, well, not a lot, really speaking — she cried and I patted — woman to woman, and all that — you know, about you being blind. And like I told her, it may be all right now, but you're a passionate chap — you sow a few more kids in her when you're up and about, and she's got problems, ain't she?"

"Tell me more," I said, faintly.

"Well, that's it, really — I mean, I wouldn't want you to think I

445

interfered, or anything. Up to folks to sort out their own troubles, I always say."

I cried, "She was all set to come here when you put your oar in!"

"But she weren't — that's the point — and she was worried to death about what would happen to you, being blind. Mind, she cheered up no end when I showed her the photograph . . ."

I turned my face to hers. "Photograph? What photograph?"

"One of Bibbs-Two."

"Bibbs-Two — what's she got to do with it?"

"Our daughter — come on, son, wake up. It's news, ain't it?"

"What the hell are you talking about?" I sat upright.

She took a deep breath. "Aye, well I realise it's a bit late in the day, but I tried to tell ye once, you know — remember the Rugby Outing when we met over in Pandy? I'd just got the photo that morning, actual — the aunt sent it . . . here, hold on. I've got it here . . ."

She hesitated, then added softly, "Oh, I forgot, of course — ye can't see it, can you. . . ? Never mind, keep it just the same," and she put the photograph into my hand.

"Bibbs-Two. . . ?" There was growing in me an unknown emotion.

"Ay ay — and she's the blutty spit and image of you, Tobe, just like Nanwen said. I suppose I should have told you earlier, and I was coming round to it, ye know. Can't . . . can't rush these things, can we, until we're sensible sure."

"Good God," I whispered.

Now she added joyfully. "Think of it, Tobe — *you're a father!*"

I said, wearily, after a bit, "So you worked it your way, as usual. You gave them a shove in the right direction."

"Don't put it like that — it sounds terrible!"

"And you'll take on a blind man? I thought you wouldn't — you just said . . ."

She cuddled up to me on the pillow. "Aw, forget it! I just told Nanwen that for comfort. For better or worse, ain't it?" She kissed my cheek. "Besides, you always was mine when Sam weren't about.

Oh, and I nearly forgot. That Nanwen's sending our Bibbs down on the very next train."

"*Dear me*," I whispered.

There was a long pause, and she said, in a voice of tears, "Rotten lot, ain't I, Tobe?"

But I wasn't really listening.

The street was awaking again to a new and vibrant activity. Somewhere among the strident sounds I thought I heard the voice of Heinie. . . .

Lifting the bottom of the bandage, I looked at the window where the sky was flaring. Raising the photograph, I saw it unmistakably against the lightness, and the dim outline of a child made shape.

"Can you see her, Tobe?"

"No," I lied.

"Ah, well," said Bron. "We'll 'ave to make the best of it — you and me, eh?"

"If that's how you want it," I said.

She was so quiet then that I thought she had moved away, so I reached for her and found her hand.

Softly, she said, "Mattie's still down on rescue, ye know — don't expect he'll be up for hours . . ."

I nodded, thinking of Mattie

"And . . . and I asked old Bestie to be a sport, and hop it. Was was that all right?"

"Strikes me the arrangements are best left to you, I replied.

"That's what I thought. Good old Tobe, I always say. Shift you over a bit, so I can come in. . ?"